HANG-UPS

BUD's was an ugly guilt that time couldn't erase . . .

HELEN's was an unfulfilled need for revenge . . .

CAROL's was a 21-year-old trumpet-playing junkie . . .

ANDY's was life—and an expensive habit he knew would destroy him.

AN ELECTRIFYING NOVEL OF ADOLESCENT KICKS AND MATURE PASSIONS

SECOND ENDING

SECOND ENDING

EVAN HUNTER

AVON
PUBLISHERS OF BARD, CAMELOT, DISCUS, EQUINOX AND FLARE BOOKS

ACKNOWLEDGMENTS

Lyrics from the following songs have been used by special permission of the respective copyright owners:

"I'll Get By," copyright, 1928, by Bourne Inc.

"I've Heard That Song Before," copyright, 1942, by Edwin H. Morris & Company, Inc.

"Let's Get Lost," copyright, 1943, by Paramount Music Corporation.

"They're Either Too Young or Too Old," copyright, 1943, by M. Witmark & Sons.

"Tampico," copyright by Criterion Music Corporation.

"Skylark," copyright, 1941, by George Simon, Inc.

The quotation on page 8 is from T. S. Eliot, "The Love Song of J. Alfred Prufrock," which appears in *Collected Poems: 1909–1935* and is copyright, 1936, by Harcourt, Brace & Co., Inc.

AVON BOOKS
A division of
The Hearst Corporation
959 Eighth Avenue
New York, New York 10019

© 1954, 1956 by Evan Hunter.
Published by arrangement with Simon and Schuster, Inc.

ISBN: 0-380-00787-8

First Avon Printing, August, 1976

This is for my eldest son, Ted,
on his fifth birthday

CONTENTS

For I have known them all already, known them all:—
Have known the evenings, mornings, afternoons,
I have measured out my life with coffee spoons;
I know the voices dying with a dying fall
Beneath the music from a farther room.
      So how should I presume?

—T. S. ELIOT

Part 1

1

The room was long and furnished with anonymity, a carbon copy of every other furnished room in New York City. There were two oversize windows at the far end of the room, opening on the brownstone front of the building and West Seventy-fourth Street. A long table which served as a desk rested before the windows. The windows were open now, and a mild spring breeze rustled the sheer curtains as he worked. The room owned a bed, and a sofa, and a chintz-covered butterfly chair, and a mantel and fireplace that had been bricked up many years ago. Opposite the windows, the room angled off sharply to enter into a kitchen and an adjoining toilet. There was nothing distinctive about either the room or its furnishings, except perhaps the two college pennants which hung one beneath the other between the long windows—the orange-and-black one from Princeton (the school he'd wanted to attend) and the lavender-and-white one from City College (the school he *did* attend).

He had trained himself to concentrate with the radio going, and this was a feat he usually accomplished except when he did not feel like concentrating, and he did not feel like concentrating tonight. He listened to the music, and he watched the fluid movement of the curtains, and he sniffed of the mild breeze, and for the fiftieth time that night he yanked his attention back to the notes.

Hell is a state of mind, the notes said—a statement he thoroughly agreed with at the moment. *Milton converts state of mind to a place . . .*

I'm getting groggy, he thought. I can't tell Satan from Beelzebub without a score card. I don't give a damn about either of them, and who cares whether or not Milton described the intimate habits of angels? Dr. Mason cares—that's who, he thought. Dr. Mason cares deeply, and she's searching for fellow *aficionados.*

When was the test, anyway?

It was important to know the date and the time of a test, wasn't it? This could not be called procrastination. This was simply checking the facts. He flipped the spiral notebook closed, studied his own scrawling handwriting across the stiff cardboard-cover front. *May 24, 1949—9:00* A.M. The *1949* was an affectation, an attempt to record the date of the test for posterity. Hell, everybody knew it was 1949. Or was that the way Dr. Mason had read off the date? Probably. Dr. Mason was a meticulous woman. Dr. Mason would brook no confusion concerning the date of a final exam. Dr. Mason would hear no excuses beginning "I thought it was 1950," or "You didn't make the year clear, Doctor." No, no, Dr. Mason was a careful, careful scholar.

What had she said that time about Satan's temptation attempt?

Now that had been a good one, and he couldn't even remember which of the poems it had been in. The business about "Well, Jesus old boy, you've got to eat, you know." And her brilliant reply: "You *don't* have to eat!"

Well, not if you were Dr. Mason. Dr. Mason looked as if she didn't eat much. She and the angels, back to the angels . . .

Where was I? he thought.

You were procrastinating, he further thought.

Ah, yes, procrastination. Did you know I'd written a pamphlet on the subject?

Come on, now, come on, let's get back to the notes. Let's not . . .

The phone rang.

He rose from the table and consulted the notes briefly, trying to commit a sentence to memory, thinking all he wanted for the course was a "C." He was overcut, and a "D" would mean a flunk, and a flunk would mean a repeat next semester, and a repeat would throw his carefully planned three-and-a-half-year graduation schedule all out of whack. If Mason came up with a true-or-false or multiple-choice, he was saved. But knowing Mason, he was sure she'd drop some essay questions on their skulls, and good-by Milton, good-by graduation next semester—all right, all right, I'm coming.

He lifted the receiver. "Hello?" he said.

"Bud?"

"Yes. Who's this?"

"Carol."

"Oh, hello, Carol. How are you?" He dropped into the butterfly chair and made himself comfortable.

"I'm fine, thanks. Were you busy?"

"No, no, just . . . no, I wasn't busy. What is it?" He was sure they would be essay questions. In *Areopagitica*, discuss Milton's views on the censorship of ideas, telling why you agree or disagree with those views. 80 per cent.

"Andy's with me," she said.

For the remaining 20 per cent, compare *Samson Agonistes* with *Paradise Regained*, using . . . "What did you say?" he asked.

"I said Andy's with me."

"Andy?" he said. "I don't understand."

"He's here with me. Now."

"Oh." He was surprised, and he was unable for a moment to grasp the importance of what she'd just said. His head was full of notes for the impending examination, notes he had read and reread and still not understood. He had a long way to go before the notes would become a working part of his mind and . . .

"Is anything wrong?" he asked.

"No. No, everything's fine. Bud, he's been off the stuff for a week now. And he's got a job audition coming up. He . . . he looks fine."

He wet his lips. "Is that right? Well, gee, that's swell. Swell."

"That's why I'm calling you," Carol said.

"I still don't understand," he told her.

"Well, he needs help, Bud."

"Again?" he said sourly.

"No, he's really sincere this time, Bud. He's come a long way, believe me, and he doesn't want to fall back now. He's been with his folks for the past week, but he says they're driving him crazy, and you know what happened last time."

"Yes," Bud said. He had begun tapping his foot impatiently, anticipating what was coming, and already figuring on a way of wiggling out of it.

"He doesn't want to take a place near any of his old friends, either, for fear . . . well, they'll find him wherever he is, Bud. You know that. It's happened before. And if they . . . well, the point is, I was wondering . . . I know it's a terrible imposition . . . but you do live alone, Bud—I mean you haven't a roommate or anything—and he does need help, Bud, he really does, and this time he's sincere about it all."

"Is he under a doctor's care?" Bud asked.

"No. You know how he feels about that. He—"

"A doctor is the only person who can help him," Bud said, stalling for time. "When's he going to realize that?"

"I think he can do it alone this time, Bud. Really, you should see him. The point is, I thought . . . This wasn't his idea, Bud. In fact he opposed it all the way . . . but I thought you could put him up for a while. The audition is next week, and he thinks he can be in shape by then. It's a good band, Bud—Laddy Fredericks, the one who—"

"You want an honest answer?"

"Yes, of course."

"No."

"He said you would say no, and I don't blame you, Bud, if that's the way you feel. But after he's come so far, it seems a shame—"

"He's come this far before, hasn't he? You should know that better than I. He's come this far, and then he's slipped back again. What makes you think it'll be any different this time?"

"I just know it will," she said.

"Oh, hell, I'm in the middle of finals. How could I—"

"It's not that you'd have to do anything, Bud—nothing like that. You see, he doesn't need watching or anything like that. That's why he wants to get out of his parents'—"

"Answer me one question, will you, Carol?"

"What's that?"

"Why? Why the hell are you bothering?"

"I'll tell you later," she said.

"Is he near the phone?"

"Yes."

"I see. Where are you now?"

"At his house. His parents went to a movie. They . . . they left him in my care. That's the whole thing, Bud. They don't trust him at all. He feels like a prisoner, and this time he's really determined to break it, so he shouldn't have two strikes against him to start. Do you see?"

"Sure, I see. But I've got exams coming up next week. Jesus, Carol, did he have to pick—"

"Well, if you don't want to . . ."

"It's not that I want to or I don't want to. It's just that I can't believe him, and I happen to be goddamn busy. What would you do in my position?"

"He's your closest friend," Carol said.

"Don't make me laugh," Bud answered.

"Well, it's up to you," she said, sighing.

"You're really putting me on a spot. I've got a lot of studying to do, Carol. I'm graduating next semester, I hope. How can I . . . You said he has an audition coming up. Does that mean he'll be practicing?"

"Yes, but he won't bother you. He just wants to get his lip back in shape. He can use a mute."

"Oh, hell, I don't know." He was silent for a moment, chewing his lip thoughtfully. "He's right there with you?"

"Yes."

"You could have called from outside, you know. Now I'll look like a Grade-A louse if I say no."

"It's up to you," Carol said. "Maybe I shouldn't have asked."

"Now *you're* getting offended."

"No, no, it's completely up to you. Honestly. What do you say, Bud? If it's no, we've got to think of something else."

"What'll you do if I say no?"

"I'll worry about that after you say it."

"I must be crazy," he mumbled.

"Bud?"

"Bring him over, bring him over. Damnit, I must be crazy."

"I appreciate this, Bud. I really do."

"You'd better be ready to explain it all to me, because I certainly can't see why—"

"You're on Seventy-fourth, aren't you?"

"Yes."

"Give us about forty minutes."

"All right, I'll be looking for you. But I still can't—"

"I'll explain when I see you."

"It better be good."

"Forty minutes, Bud."

"All right. So long, Carol."

"Good-by, Bud," she said, and then she hung up.

He replaced the receiver and stood staring at the phone for a long time. Idiotically, he tried to tell himself that the call had never happened, that he had dreamed the entire thing, that it was a combination of Dr. Mason and eyestrain. He had not seen Andy in two—no, almost two and a half—years. That was a long time—too long a time. And now he'd picked the worst possible moment to come back from the dead. Any other time but . . .

He remembered when he was twelve and had gone to confession the week before Easter. He had been full of religious spirit and had wanted to set things straight in the house of his soul. He had said, "Bless me, Father, for I have sinned. This is one year since my last confession." He had heard the sullen grumble through the screen, and then the priest asked, "It's one *year* since your last confession?" He had answered, "Yes, Father," and the priest exploded with "And you pick the busiest time of the year to come again!" The experience had shaken him deeply, a major link in the chain of events which had brought him to his current religious feelings or lack of feelings. But reflecting back on the incident in the light of what had just happened, he could understand a little of the priest's feelings on the matter. It was all right to make a stab at self-redemption, but even salvation can wait a week or two. All right, Andy was trying to pick himself up, but couldn't he have waited until finals were over? Life was all a matter of timing, by God, and Andy had certainly picked the wrong time this time.

Nor did he honestly believe that this time would be any different than all the other times he'd been told about. They all started with the same fervor, and then Andy always wound up right back where he'd started. The amazing part was that Carol had been taken in again. How had he possibly talked her into that? Why was she bothering? Hadn't she tried to help him often enough over the past two years, God only knew why? And hadn't she always been left holding the empty sack? So why was she bothering? Why . . .

For that matter, he thought, why am *I* bothering? How

on earth did I get suckered into this deal, right smack in the middle of finals, aren't finals important, too, isn't my three-and-a-half-year plan important, isn't it all relative, and isn't my own damn salvation every bit as important as Andy's? How, how did I get suckered into it, why couldn't I have stuck to *No,* why did I let her talk me into it, why can she talk me into things like that? Friendship, sure friendship, throw the trigger word at me, ring the trigger bell and watch me begin to salivate, friendship, friendship, just a perfect blendship, but there's nothing as dead as last year's friends. But it had been a good friendship, don't belittle that, don't shake the foundations of the universe, because you *know* it was good, you know it was something you've never found again, but who is this new Andy, is this the Andy who was your friend? Was he your friend two years ago for that matter, or had it all died before then? What can we talk about? What's our common ground now? A dead friendship, is that what we'll talk about? Can we discuss Milton's angels? Shall we talk about metathesis? Or how about deferring to the guest and discussing the ratio of sugar to pure heroin in an average injection?

It would be murder. He should have said no. He should have said no and stuck to it, and that was that. But he hadn't said no, he'd said yes, all right, all right, reluctantly, but yes, and they'd be here in forty minutes and the place looked like a filthy pigsty and Satan was leering between the covers of that spiral notebook, and oh hell, oh goddamnit to hell, anyway.

He began straightening the apartment.

He was immersed in Milton when the doorbell rang. He pulled himself away from the notes, resenting the intrusion because he'd finally achieved a high level of concentration for the first time that night. But the doorbell reminded him of what was ahead, and his concentration shattered like a piece of fragile crystal, and he cursed himself again and then shoved himself away from the table and went to the door, giving a last look around the tidied place.

"Who is it?" he asked.

"Carol," she answered.

"Second," he said. He unlocked the door, fumbling with it a little because he didn't know how to greet a dead friend. What do you say? Hello, boy, how have you been? What the hell do you say? He got the door open, and he threw it wide, and his eyes went to Carol first, the way they always did whenever she was with another person. There was something compelling about her beauty, he realized, something that forced attention to her face. But this time his eyes did not linger. This time they touched her features lightly and then fled to the face alongside hers.

The face was smiling. The smile was a fixed one, and he studied the smile, and then he found the miniature white ring of muscle on the upper lip of the smile, and he grasped at the circle as a means of recognition, and then his eyes traveled upward on the face, using the muscle-ring as a nucleus. His eyes met Andy's eyes. They were sunken and hollow, two deep pits of despair on either side of a straight, slightly flaring nose.

"Hello, Andy," he said warmly. "How are you?" He hoped he had not sounded solicitous. He had tried to generate a warmth he no longer felt, and he hoped his voice did not betray the pity or the rich-cousin attitude he really felt.

"Come in, come in," he said, and when they were inside the door, he extended his hand, and Andy took it in a firm grip, covering the clasp with his other hand so that both his hands were closed in embrace over Bud's hand. He stepped close to Bud, and those fathomless eyes stared penetratingly at Bud's face—liquid brown eyes with amber flecks swimming in them, large and round, circled with dark, sick-looking skin, receding dark-brown tunnels punched in the flesh of the face.

"Bud," he said softly, "how are you? You look great, great."

He did not release Bud's hand. He kept holding it between his own hands, and he kept smiling the fixed, pasty smile and staring, staring so hard and so long that the eyes began to frighten Bud a little, like looking into the soul of a maniac, staring, staring as if he were trying to pick Bud's face with his eyes. "Man, you look great," he said, still holding the hand, still staring, staring until the stare became a probing, searching, relentless spotlight. And then he began nodding, the nod accompanying the stare like two burlesque performers in a soft-shoe routine, soundlessly nodding, while the pasty smile changed imperceptibly, changed to become a smile with meaning behind it, changed to become a derisive smile of self-mockery.

"And me, man?" he said softly, some of the mockery tingeing his voice. "I look great, too, don't I?"

"You look fine," Bud said, trying to sound sincere. He freed his hand and took Andy by the elbow. "Come on in."

"Sure, great," Andy said. "Carol, he thinks I look fine. Say, this is a nice place you've got here, Bud. You don't know how much I appreciate this." He stepped deeper into the apartment and looked around. "I was ready to flip with my parents. Well, you remember how it was. I don't have to tell you. I really appreciate this, man. You've got no idea. Gee, it's good to see you again. What've you been doing with yourself?"

Bud closed the door. "Oh, you know. Work, work, work."

"You're still going to school, Carol tells me. That's a smart move, all right. I should have gone to school, Bud. I wouldn't have fouled up if I'd gone to school. It's all environment, you know, and influence that . . ." He stopped, as if he were unsure of what he wanted to say. A perplexed frown crossed his wide brow, and then he gave a tiny shrug and said, "Well, that's the way it goes."

"Can I get you something to drink, Andy? Carol? Anything? Why don't you take off your coat?"

"Well, I can't stay long," Carol said.

"Here, I'll hang it up."

She took off her coat, and he asked her eyes a question, but she did not answer. She handed him the light duster, and he took it to the closet. He slipped it onto a hanger and then sneaked a look at Andy. He had changed a lot—not in a way that you could exactly put your finger on, except for the eyes, those eyes, but he had definitely changed. He had not expected so great a physical change. He had expected to see the Andy he had known as a boy.

"So how about that drink?" he asked, turning away from the closet.

"Nothing for me," Andy said.

"Carol?"

"No, Bud. Thanks."

He hoped this would not get difficult. It exhibited all the

beginnings of a nice session in a funeral parlor. He hoped it would not turn into that.

"This is really a nice place," Andy said again. "I certainly appreciate this. I'll try not to get in your way, Bud. I mean it. It'll just be for a week, anyway. Just until I take that audition. I'm almost okay now, you know. Did you know I was an addict?"

"Yes," Bud said, thinking, *Of course I knew. Are you kidding?*

"Yeah, well I was. Pretty good, huh? Some end, huh? Did you ever think Andy Silvera would become an addict?"

"Well, no," Bud said, embarrassed to hear him talk of it so freely.

"Me neither. Well, that's the way it is. I look bad, don't I? Tell the truth."

"No, you look all right."

"No, I look bad. You don't have to lie, Bud. No, I mean it, it's okay. I can still see myself in a mirror. Jesus, it's good to see you again. Carol, isn't it great seeing Bud again? Jesus, you don't know what this means to me."

"Sit down," Bud said. "Take a load off your feet." There was something very unreal about the whole thing. He tried to find out what was wrong with the picture, and he couldn't pin-point it. But something was all wrong, the feel of it, the . . . the *feel*. . . .

"No, I'd rather stand," Andy said. "It's better if I walk around. I mean, you don't mind, do you? It's better if I walk. I've almost got the thing beat, but I can't sit still for too long. You know? I've got to pace every now and then. Like a tiger, eh, Carol? Well, gee, this is really a fine setup you've got here. Say, were you studying or something? I don't want to bust in like—"

"No, that's all right," Bud said, his mind momentarily yanked back to Milton. "It can wait." He hoped his voice had carried the conviction he definitely did not feel.

"Did Carol tell you about my audition?" Andy asked.

"Yes," Bud said, "but not all the deta—"

"Oh, it's a good deal," Andy said. "Laddy Fredericks. Do you know him? He's been at the Edison forever. Man, that band never leaves New York. That's what killed me in the first place, you know—that road business. When I was on the Jerralds band. That's when I met Rog Kiner, bless him. You remember that, don't you? You were out of the service then, weren't you?"

"Yes."

"Well, that road stuff is nowhere, man. Hey, you sure you weren't studying? Carol says you've got finals coming up."

"I can study later," Bud said, resigned to his fate. "What about the audition?"

"Oh, yeah, yeah. Well, Mike Daley—you remember Mike? Oh, sure you do. When we had the old band, when we were kids, you remember, don't you? Man, that was kicks all right, wasn't it?"

"Yes, it was . . ."

"No gold, but a lot of kicks. That was a real happy time, wasn't it? Well, Mike, I dug him on Forty-second a month, two months ago—sure, it must've been at least two months. I'm always all screwed up when it comes to time. Well, I ran into him and I could see like he was a little embarrassed, you know. The word gets around when you're hooked, and people can't understand what it's like unless they're hooked themselves. Like when I was down at Lexington—I went down there for the cure, you know. Did you know that? . . . Well, I did. Well, those guys knew the score, dad, said we were all sick—but, Jesus, I couldn't make that place. Sick, that's what we are, all right, but people can't always understand that. That's because the newspapers run articles on dope fiends—*fiends,* that's a laugh—and the people get the wrong idea. Man, those articles are for the birds, believe me. If you ever want the real truth about drugs, just get me talking sometime. I'll tell you stories about it, but not what the papers said. That was for the birds. Like what they said about marijuana, hell, Buddy, mootah never hurt a fly, I mean it. I know guys who bust a joint before each meal, like taking a cocktail, you know? Are cocktails harmful, do you mind if I pace?"

"No, go right ahead," Bud said. He leaned forward in his chair and listened to Andy, his brow knotted.

"Sure, that was for the sparrows. Well, anyway, I ran into Mike, and he shifted around and hemmed and hawed and *How are you, Andy?* and *Fine, how are you, Mike?* all the time avoiding what was on his mind and in his eyes—

that I was a hophead, you understand. In fact, I think I was turned on when I ran into him, but that didn't affect my thinking any, it doesn't really make you dopey, you know, like the papers and magazines say, as a matter of fact it makes you kind of sharp, real sharp. Well, he's been with Fredericks for many moons now, and he told me they're getting ready to bounce this cat they got blowing second. He asked me if I was still playing and if I'd be interested, and I could see by his eyes that he was just making talk, that he figured I couldn't blow any more, being a hophead and all, I can read eyes like that, all that goddamn pity in them, you know. His eyes got me sore. I told him sure I was still playing and could he fix an audition, and he hemmed and hawed a little more, which he had no right to do, hell I could always blow rings around Mike, you know that, but he said he'd talk to Fredericks and see what he could swing.

"I gave him the number at my pad, I was living in some crumby dump on Forty-eighth at the time—I think it was Forty-eighth—yeah sure, sure, and Mike gave me a buzz that night. He sounded surprised as hell, but he said Fredericks was interested, that he'd heard some of the sides I'd cut when I was on the Jerralds band. He said he wouldn't be ready to audition until June first, but he'd give me first crack at the chair then.

"I felt pretty damn good, you know, as if I'd shown Mike. I went to a party that night. I didn't buzz Helen to come with me because she had kicked the habit already, and this was a real hophead affair, a pass-the-needle ball. We used to go to a lot of them together, you know. I'd give her a ring and then she'd meet me. Well, this place was one big shooting party, and by the time I got there, things were really swinging. Somebody was shooting up, and I walked over, and the guy finished with the spike and he handed it to me, and I loaded it and blew my brains out, and then I passed the spike to somebody else, it was one of those affairs, a community joy ride, you know what I mean? I was up in the clouds, and when I came down, I began to think about Mike and that look in his eyes, and I made up my mind right then and there to kick the junk.

"This must have been about two months ago when I first got the idea. I kept throwing the idea around, but it didn't do any good, and it's not an easy thing to make up your mind about the break, you know. But that audition kept getting closer and closer, and I kept remembering that comedown look on Mike's face, and I kept thinking about what I'd decided that night, when everybody was passing around the same needle, and last week I really made up my mind. No more for me, I told myself, no more of that.

"May I drop dead in the gutter, I told myself, *if I ever touch another drop of it."* He knocked the table top and then said, "So far, I've got it going. It's been rough, but I'm on the way. And this Laddy Fredericks is big time, Bud—you know that, don't you? And I'm sure I'll be ready for him by the first. He's got a shmaltzy society outfit, Bud, so I won't have to blow any tricky stuff for him when I audition, no screech work, nothing like that, hell, he doesn't even know what a screech trumpet is. I can limber up my lip easily in the next week, the hardest part is over now, you know, even though I heave every now and then, but I'm keeping down a lot more than I used to.

"So that's the story. Once I land this gig, I've really got it made. This is the first break I've had in a long time. I was real bad, you know, a real addict."

"He was taking heroin," Carol said.

"Yes, I know," Bud answered, listening to the conversation and knowing he was a part of it, but sensing this something that was wrong with the picture and not knowing what it was.

"It's poison, man, believe me. Say, you want to hear something interesting? Here's a fact for you, Buddy. When I was down at Lex—I only stayed two days, man, I couldn't take that joint. I mean, they do wonderful things down there, all right, but you don't think of that when you're there, all you think of is getting a fix—well, anyway, some of the guys there were doctors, how's that for a fact? I don't mean the ones who were treating us, I mean the patients. The patients were guys who used to be doctors and who got hooked. Oh, we had all kinds down there, all right, even guys who'd been on the junk for ten, twenty years. Boy, what a place that was. Like they really want you to kick it, you know? I mean, these guys are what you call dedicated, I guess. Except for one shlmozzle, man, I'll never forget him. All of them are sympathetic, you know? They realize what you're going through because they see it every day, but they don't look down on you, they try to help, and they make you feel like you're not alone. All except this one jerk. I was being examined, and he came over to me and said, 'You're new here, aren't you?' I said yes, and he just nodded like a wise old owl and said, 'You'll be back.' How's that for giving a person confidence. *'You'll be back!'* Of course, a lot of the guys there were on their fourth and fifth trips, and some of them practically live in the place. They kick it, and they get out and hop aboard again, and *wham!* right back to Lex. Like a big game. You know they had a bunch of guys in an experimental group down there, the way they have people volunteer to get bitten by mosquitoes, that kind of thing. These guys were the guinea pigs for drug experiments, because those doctors are trying all the time to find out more about it, so they can help, you know? So with these guys, like, they'd raise the fix and keep raising it and raising it, all the way up, so they could study how strong a habit gets. And they'd give it to them right on the dot, like say the first fix was at nine in the morning, then the next fix would be at noon, but *right* at noon, not a minute before or a minute after.

"And then sometimes they'd hold out on them, to see the effects, things like that so they could help the other guys who are hooked. But these cats in the group, man, they loved it. They were getting all the jive they wanted free, what the hell did they care? And it was certainly a hell of a lot better than that substitute junk they taper you off on, that methadone. Well, I'm glad I cut out of there, that's for sure. I couldn't make it, that's all. I needed a fix. I was bangin' my head against the wall for a fix. So I took off. They can't hold you there, you know, even though the full cure is four months. You're there under voluntary commitment, you know. But I'm telling you, man . . ."

Bud listened to him rattling on and tried to find something in the man who stood before him that was even remotely related to the boy and adolescent he had known. The features had changed, lengthening into maturity, except for the mouth, which still remained boyish somehow. The eyes had changed most of all, of course, but he knew that was caused by the drugs, or at least he suspected as much. The body, too, was leaner, not as padded as it had been, but he knew none of these things added up to the whole change, the sum of the parts *not* being equal to the whole in this case. And yet he could not describe the change because it was something he could feel rather than see, and suddenly realizing he was incapable of *seeing* any real change, he wondered if he too had invisibly changed, if he too sounded as alien as Andy did, and his gaze shifted to Carol as though to reassure himself that some things remain ever and always the same.

Her beauty did not shriek at you, but it demanded attention in a quietly unassuming way. You looked at Carol and your eyes lingered, and you found yourself staring at her incredible beauty, and then wondering why you stared, and then realizing that you couldn't help staring. You turned away, but your eyes roamed back again of their own volition until you began to feel guilty and a little embarrassed, until you were certain she too was uncomfortable. Only later did you realize that Carol was almost totally unaware of her compelling good looks, that she had learned to live with them the way someone learns to live with the Mona Lisa in his living room.

Her hair was an ash blond, clipped close to her head, casually falling onto her forehead in the front, hugging the nape of her neck in the back. She had wide brown eyes fringed with lashes a shade darker than her hair. Her nose was not a perfect nose, perhaps a little too long for her face, but it blended with the rest of her features so that it seemed an integral part of the whole, a part without which the beauty would have been marred, perfect as it was, though not classically perfect. Her mouth was wide, with full lips that rarely smiled any more.

That's how Carol has changed, he thought. *She doesn't smile any more.* He could remember the brilliance of her smile, and he blamed Andy for taking away the smile and for replacing it with the wrinkles at the corners of her eyes.

He wondered why she had tried to help him over the years, wondered why she was indeed trying to help him now, and he realized abruptly that he didn't know half of Andy's full story, that probably no one but Andy would ever know that story. And then, simultaneously, he remembered that he would be living with Andy for the next week

—no, actually longer than a week, until June first he had said—hell, that was almost two weeks. How had they talked him into this, how in God's holy name had he got talked into this crazy deal?

". . . guys who had used up the tread marks on their legs already, their *legs,* mind you, and were starting a retread on their arms. Did you ever see an addict's arm, Bud?"

"What?"

"An addict's arm. Man, here take a look." He took off his jacket and threw it onto the sofa, and for the first time Bud noticed what he was wearing. A good jacket, blue flannel, with a DePinna label showing on the inside pocket. He'd always dressed well, but it seemed strange that he'd cling to an expensive jacket. Didn't drug addicts hock everything they owned? The sports shirt was a cheap one, but it was in good taste, patterned with a simple motif. Andy was rolling up the sleeve now, patiently creasing the folds. He seemed to lose patience with the task almost immediately, and he shoved the wadded material up to his biceps and said, "Here, Buddy, look at this."

There was something of pride in his voice, or awe, Bud couldn't tell which. The arm was a tangled stretch of brownish-red puncture marks, blurred together until they resembled a healed burn, the scar tissue of broken and repeatedly rebroken skin.

"How do you like that?" Andy said, and Bud again felt this unwarranted pride, or awe, or boastfulness, or perhaps bravado—perhaps that's what it was. "That's an addict's arm, man. Pretty, huh?"

Bud could only nod dumbly.

"Don't ever get started on this stuff, man," Andy said. "I'm telling you, it's murder."

"Why'd *you* start?" Bud asked, the words sounding more accusing than he'd intended them to be.

"You tell me," Andy answered. "That's the sixty-four-dollar one, all right. Well, I'm off it now, that's for sure. I've kicked the habit, and it's going to stay kicked."

"He means it this time," Carol said.

"Oh, I mean it, all right. I wouldn't be barging in like this if I didn't, Bud. Hell, I know what you must be thinking. Guy pops up after—how long has it been? No, I wouldn't barge in if I wasn't serious this time. That's why this means so much to me. If I'd kept my old place, well, I'd always be running into the old crowd. Not Helen, no, because she's already kicked it and, man, it's poison to her. I used to see a lot of her, you know, but not since she kicked it. But all the others, you know. 'Come on, Andy, let's scout up the Man' or, 'Hey, Andy, how about a fix, man?'—you know, like that. Hell, there's always somebody with some of the junk on him, and how can you resist it when it's right there under your nose?

"This way, I'm cut off from it, not that I even get the yen now, man, I've been heaving my guts out for the past week, but even if I *did* want some, I couldn't get it, now could I? You don't keep any, do you, Bud—no, I didn't think you did. Living with my folks would have been safe, too, but I just can't make that, Buddy, well you know what a drag that always was. My mother always fussing around me with her waving little hands, and my dad just ignoring me. Hell, I mean it's not his fault. He was forty-two when I was born, and when a first kid comes unexpected like that, you can't expect the father to go rolling around on the floor in glee. But that doesn't make it any less a drag, now does it? So I appreciate what you're doing, I really do. Once I've kicked it for good, once I get on this band, well things are going to be much better."

There was an uncomfortable silence, during which Bud weighed his earlier reluctance against the sudden title of benefactor which had been thrust upon him.

"Helen kicked it, you know," Andy said. "She kicked that monkey clear off her back. A good kid, Helen. Say, did you know I was the one got her hooked, did you? Say, look, if you want to get back to your studying . . ."

"No, that's all right."

"I hate like hell to impose on you this way, but I thought . . ."

"It's no imposition at all, believe me," Bud lied.

"Well, I appreciate it, you can bet on that."

"Would you like some coffee?" Bud asked.

"None for me," Andy said. "I'm lucky I've kept my supper down. I don't want to tempt the gods."

"Carol, how about you?"

"If we can have a fast cup. I've got to be running."

"I use instant," Bud said. "It'll be ready in an instant." Andy chuckled a bit, and Carol attempted a smile which didn't quite come off. Bud rose and walked into the kitchen, filling the pot with water and setting it on the stove. He took down the cups and was spooning coffee into them when Andy started talking again.

"You mustn't misunderstand about my dad, Bud," he said. "I mean, he's all right, that's for sure, but he doesn't understand about me. I mean, like he never did, you know, even when I was a kid. Never had much time for me, never played ball with me, or cared about what kind of clothes I wore—stuff like that. Funny, I guess. He worries more about me now than he did when I really needed his worry —well, hell, he's an accountant, how many accountants have addict sons? He sicced a private detective on me once, would you believe it? That was after I went off with my mother's watch—well, I shouldn't have done that, I know it, but the watch was just laying there, and, man, did I need a fix, this was the last time I tried to kick the habit, did Carol tell you about it? The dick was a good one, and he stuck with me for four days. I finally shook him at a session up in Harlem. I used to blow at a lot of sessions before I hocked my horn."

Bud came back into the living room. "You . . . hocked your horn?" he asked incredulously.

"Yeah, isn't that the end, though. I haven't played in— how long has it been, Carol? You remember, I told you before."

"Six months," Carol said.

"Yeah. Man, I should cut a disk now. I'd be the greatest since Seven-Up. I'm lucky I can blow a C scale." He shook his head. "Well, what're you gonna do? That's life."

"What's life?" Bud asked automatically.

"Huh?" Andy said, surprised. He smiled then and said, "Oh, yeah, sure. Why, *Life*'s a magazine."

"How much does it cost?" Bud asked, falling into the old routine, remembering the hundreds of times they'd used it in the old days.

"Twenty cents," Andy said.

"I've only got a dime."

Andy shrugged. "Well, that's life."

"What's life?" Bud said, and Andy burst out laughing.

"How do you like that? Man, I haven't heard that bit in ages. Say, how are all the boys? Do you see any of them any more? Frank? Or Reen? Or what about Tony Banner? Old Ahmed Ben Banner? Is he still blowing that ruptured horn of his? Man, he never could play, you know."

"He's in Texas with the symphony orchestra there," Bud said.

"Symphony? No joke? Man, I'm dead! Tony in symphony!"

"He picked up the oboe at Julliard."

"And Frank?"

"I still see him at school. There's nothing there any more, though."

"Yeah, well, friends drift. What about Reen?"

Bud looked at Andy curiously. "Reen was——"

"Tony blowing the oboe, huh? Damn, if that doesn't cut it all. Who'd have dreamt he was serious about being a musician?"

"Is the coffee about ready?" Carol asked.

"Yes, it should be. Want to give me a hand?"

"Ah-ah," Andy said, wagging his finger jokingly. "I don't trust you two alone together."

Bud smiled, and Carol tried to smile again, but the smile materialized as a painful parody. They went into the kitchen for the coffee, and Bud whispered, "Now, tell me what this is all——"

"Later," she whispered back.

They brought out the coffee, sitting and drinking in silence. When they'd finished, Carol said, "Time to climb into the old shebang."

"I keep forgetting you drive now."

"She's a regular cowboy," Andy said. "You should see her."

Bud brought Carol her duster and helped her into it. She went to Andy and said, "Be careful now. I'll bring your horn and your music tomorrow." She patted his hand and started for the door. "Will you walk me down, Bud? I'm afraid of dark streets."

"Sure," Bud said. "Make yourself comfortable, Andy. I'll be right back."

When they were in the hallway, he asked, "Now what——"

"He'll hear you. Wait until we're downstairs."

He waited patiently. They walked out onto the sidewalk and then over to where her old Pontiac was parked. She climbed in and rolled down the window on his side.

"All right, what's it all about?" he asked. "Why are you helping him?"

"I love him," Carol said flatly.

"Oh, for Christ's sake," Bud said.

"I love him now, and I've always loved him, and I guess I always will. That's why—Bud, do you remember when we first found out? I was hurt then, and shocked, and all I could do was condemn. And then I tried to help later—the other times he tried to break it—but I didn't give him enough. This time I'm going all the way. He's got to break it, Bud! And I'm going to help him all I can. Bud, they . . . they say you never break the habit. They say it's always with you, till the day you die. But I won't believe that. I know he has to break it. Maybe he can't do it alone, though, maybe . . . Bud, I want to help him. I want to see him the . . . way he used to be."

"We all do, Carol, but how can we—"

"He's wasting his life this way, Bud. And he's wasting his talent. He has such a big talent, so big. I can't see him waste that. And I can't see him waste his life, either. Andy's life is very important to me. He really intends to break the habit this time, and I'm going to help him do it."

"*If* he really intends," Bud said.

"He does. I can feel he does. And I *want* him to. I want him to so much that I . . . Maybe I shouldn't have dragged you into it, but you were the only person I could think of. Do you understand?"

"He's come this far before, Carol. But he always—"

"Yes, but this time he means it. He's determined to lick it this time, Bud. You'll see."

"I hope so," he said dubiously.

"I do, too. Oh, God, how I hope so."

"You'll be bringing his horn tomorrow?"

"Yes. He gave me the pawn ticket. It was one of the few tickets he didn't sell."

"All right, I'll see you then."

"Good night, Bud. Try to understand." She leaned out of the car and kissed him on the cheek, and then she slid over behind the wheel. He waited until she started the car and pulled out into the street. He waved then, not at all sure she saw him.

Reluctantly, he turned back to the stoop of his building and started up the steps. He did not want to be alone with Andy Silvera.

2

Andy was standing by the windows when Bud came back into the room. He wondered if Andy'd been watching the conversation at the car, and he suddenly felt curiously uneasy.

Andy turned and smiled. His eyes did not smile with the rest of his face. His eyes remained fixed and staring, so that the smile seemed grotesque. "You're bleeding," he said.

"Huh?"

"Your cheek."

"Oh. Yes." Bud fumbled for a handkerchief. "Thanks." He wiped Carol's lipstick from his cheek, feeling strangely guilty, knowing he should not feel guilty over so innocent a thing as a good-night peck between friends, and yet feeling this enormous guilt, as if he were cheating with another man's wife. He knew that Andy should have no doubts on that score, that Carol was simply a good friend and nothing more, and yet this good-night gesture of friendship had nonetheless brought on an embarrassed feeling of having been caught at something forbidden. If only Andy weren't such a stranger, if only . . .

"She's a wonderful girl," Andy said.

"Carol?"

"Yes."

"I always said so."

They stood staring at each other awkwardly.

"Say, I certainly hope I'm not putting you out."

"No, not at all," Bud said.

The atmosphere was strained with Carol gone. Carol had been an oasis in a vast dry desert. Both men had

approached the oasis with a common desire in mind. They
both wanted water to irrigate their dusty, dead friendship.
They had approached the oasis from opposite sides of the
desert, and their common desire had negated the fact that
they did not know each other. The oasis was gone now.
They had tracked across a hot, wide expanse of sand and
had come face to face with each other and had suddenly
realized that they did not know each other, and their thirst
had only intensified their plight. The silence was deafening.
Even the room seemed strange to Bud, as if he did not
really belong in it. He searched in his mind for some means
of crashing through the silence. The effort only seemed to
intensify the silence. He wet his lips and reached for
something to say, but nothing came to his tongue.

"This is a nice place you've got here," Andy said, the attempt as obvious as the sheepish look with which it was delivered.

"Yes," Bud said, hating himself for saying only *Yes*, hating anyone and everyone who stifled conversation by giving yes or no answers and cutting short any opportunity
for embellishment.

"Are you on the GI Bill?" Andy asked.

"Yes," Bud said again, thinking, *Give him something to
work with, for Christ's sake. Can't you see he's trying?*

"Listen, if you've got studying to do, go right ahead. Just
pretend I'm not here."

"Well, I do have some studying, but . . ."

"No, go ahead. I know finals are important."

He could not tell whether or not Andy's tongue was in
his cheek. There was a time when he could almost tell
what Andy was thinking by looking at his face, but he
found himself incapable of doing that now, and his sudden
sterility reminded him again of how alien Andy was to
him. He realized quite abruptly that finals were probably
very unimportant so far as Andy was concerned. Finals
were kid stuff, college-boy-swiping-panties stuff. Andy was,
in a sense, undergoing an examination, too, a test that
might very well change his entire future. Milton was
somehow remote and ridiculous in comparison to Andy's
own struggle. But he had not asked to be included in
Andy's life. And maybe finals were relatively unimportant,
maybe finals were downright silly by comparison, but if he

did not pass his finals—and, by God, the outlook seemed gloomy at this point—he would have to repeat, and repetition would mean another semester at school, and he didn't want that, not after all the careful, tight planning he'd done.

In self-defense, he said, "Well, they are pretty important. I'm trying to get through in three and a half."

"Sure," Andy said. "Go ahead, Bud, go back to your studying."

Andy's calm acceptance made the entire thing seem even sillier. He tried desperately to justify finals in his own mind, and finally said, "I guess this seems like kid stuff to you."

"Kid stuff? No, no. This is all the foundation, isn't it? If you're going to build, you've got to have a foundation."

"Well, I hadn't thought of it in just that way." He couldn't stop feeling inferior. His problem seemed infinitesimal when compared to Andy's. He told himself he should not blame himself for not having experienced Andy's misfortune. Hell, that was plain silly—but he could not convince himself. And looking for a stronger weapon of self-defense, seeking to justify the finals which had suddenly become silly and insignificant, he turned to self-belittlement. "Hell, college is all a lot of nonsense, anyway. What I mean to say . . . well, you must think I'm a big jerk, worrying about a few tests."

"No, I don't think that at all."

"Any other time I'd say screw the tests. But I'm pushing through in three and a half, and so it's a little important, if you know what I mean."

"I know exactly what you mean. Man, you don't have to apologize to me."

"Well, I wasn't exactly apologizing," he said, suddenly miffed by the turn in the conversation, the turn he himself had engineered. What the hell was he doing, anyway? Apologizing to a dope addict for being a college student? What kind of sense did that make?

"I know I'm a forced guest," Andy said, "so go right ahead and do whatever you've got to do. Just show me where I'm supposed to sack in, and show me where the john is, and that's it." Andy smiled. "Really, Bud, I know the tests are important."

"Yes, they are important," he said somewhat coldly. "I didn't want you to think I was making a mountain out of a molehill." He paused, still unreasonably angry. "You can sleep on the sofa, if that's all right with you."

"Oh, that'll be fine," Andy said.

"I'll get you some sheets. I . . . Do you sleep with a pillow?"

"Yes."

"Well, you can have mine. I've only got one."

"No, that's okay. I don't need a—"

"I usually throw it on the floor, anyway. It doesn't matter to—"

"No, I wouldn't think of taking your pillow. I haven't been sleeping well anyway, Bud. There's no sense in both of us having a bad night."

"Well . . ."

"Really. I'm up half the night. You take it, Bud."

"Well, okay, if you say so. I'll get the sheets."

"I'll get them. Just show me where they are."

"By the time I show you, I can get them myself."

He crossed the room to the closet, pulled open the door, and then yanked out a leather suitcase.

"That's a nice valise," Andy said.

"Yes," he answered, knowing it was a good piece of luggage but not feeling like discussing its merits at the moment. He stood on the suitcase, reaching up to the top shelf of the closet. "Want to catch these?" he said.

"Sure." Andy came over, and he threw the sheets down to him. He got off the suitcase, shoved it back into the closet, and said, "I'll help you make up the sofa."

"I can do it alone," Andy said.

"No, I'll help you."

They went to the sofa, a starkly modern slab of wood with a foam-rubber one-piece mattress on it, strongly out of place against the chintz-covered butterfly chair. They shoved it out from the wall so that one of them could tuck the sheets in on that side, and then they began covering it.

"Do you know what this reminds me of?" Andy asked.

"No, what?"

"That time on First Avenue."

"First Avenue?" He remembered immediately, but he did not feel like getting embroiled in a lengthy discussion.

He had studying to do. He could not waste any time reminiscing.

"With those two girls," Andy said. "What were their names?"

"I don't remember," Bud lied.

Their glances met over the sofa. Andy seemed to be going to say more, and then his face took on a pained look, and he continued working on the sofa, not looking at Bud again. And then, as if he could not control himself any longer, he said softly, "Those were the times, all right."

Bud did not comment. He had finals to worry about. The time on First Avenue had been a long while ago. It had been a hell of a lot of fun, and it was certainly something to remember, but it was dead and gone. He turned down the blanket and said, "Well, there's your bed." His voice carried an undercurrent of pressing reality, he hoped. He wanted Andy to know that he could waste no time shooting the bull, not tonight anyway.

"Yeah," Andy said, staring at the sofa. "I don't feel like turning in just yet, if you don't mind."

"Any time you want to."

"You go ahead with your studying."

"All right. I hate to do this, but you know—"

"I understand." Andy paused. "Say, I could use a cigarette. Have you got one?"

"Sure." Bud took the package from his pocket and extended it to Andy.

"Funny how I never really got the habit, isn't it? Andy said. "I picked up all the *really* bad habits, but never this one." He took a cigarette and then the match folder, lighting the cigarette quickly. "I've been smoking a lot this past week. It relaxes me, you know. Times when I can't sit still, I light a cigarette, and everything's all right. Funny."

Bud nodded.

"Well, go ahead, do your studying. Don't worry about me, just forget I'm here."

"Okay," Bud said. "You talked me into it." He walked to the table, thought briefly of the time on First Avenue, and then shoved it rudely out of his mind, only to find it shoving back again just as rudely. He had really enjoyed that night. It had worked remarkably smoothly, and Marcia had really been good. He wondered what had ever become of her. Well, no matter. Back to Milton.

Milton, Milton, he told himself, leave us by all means get back to dear old Miltie. Where was I? What good does it do to know where I was? I'll have to start from scratch. My memory works that way, from beginning to end, from start to finish, from inception to conclusion. When I get through with these notes, they'll be photographed on my mind, but to get to any one part of them, I'll have to start from the beginning and leaf through the photographs until I get to the section I want. Is that total recall? If so, let's total recall away.

III. *Beelzebub's answer*
    A. *Addresses him not as equal*
    B. *Admits that S was glorious leader, etc.*
    C. *But—after all—we are defeated, and—*

"Do you think the pastrami could have given me that stomach-ache?"

"What?" Bud asked.

"The pastrami we bought. Remember we got up in the middle of the night and made sandwiches?"

"Oh. Oh, yes."

"Just thinking of it, I feel sick again. I'm sure it was a novena, though. My mother probably used up three sets of prayer beads that night. I'll bet she prayed her fingers to the bone."

"Yeah, I'll bet."

"Look, I don't want to bother you. Go ahead, study."

    B. *Admits that S. was glorious leader, etc.*
    C. *But—after all—we are defeated, and that's a fact we've got to face.*

IV. *Satan's characteristics*
    A. *Courageous*
    B. *Skillful leader and orator*

"You know, I can still remember the color of her pajamas."

"Yeah?" Bud said absently.

"Pink. Connie's, I mean. Hey, that was her name, Connie. And yours was Marcia. Pink silk with that little blue flower design on the pocket, right where her left—say, she had a remarkable set, you know?"

"Uhm," Bud said.

"And smooth, just like all the rest of her. She had the

smoothest skin in all the world, smoother even than—Oh, say, I'm interrupting you. I'm sorry."

"S'all right," Bud said.

A. *Courageous*
B. *Skillful leader and orator*
C. *Good psychologist*

"What always amazes me is how fast we set that thing up. I mean, we'd only met the chicks that afternoon. Fatal charm, I guess it was."

D. *Heart, enthusi—*
C. *Good psychologist*
D. *Heart, enthusiasm*
E. *Persistence*

"I'll never forget that night, all right. That was really something to—"

"Say, Andy, I hate to—"

"Oh, I'm sorry. Really, I'm sorry. I won't say another word. Go ahead. You don't mind if I pace a little, though, do you? It sounds stupid as hell, but I get restless, you know, and I have to pace. Is that all right?"

"Yes, fine. Sure, pace."

"Okay, thanks. And I won't say another word. I mean, this is getting like the comic bit where one guy's trying to figure out the atomic bomb, and the other guy keeps busting his nuts, isn't it?"

Bud sighed: "A little."

"Well, not another word out of me. That's a promise."

"Fine," Bud said.

A. *Courageous*
B. *Skillful leader and orator*

Satan's characteristics, A courageous B skillful leader and orator good psychologist heart enthusiasm persistence Andy pacing pacing behind me courageous skillful leader and orator good psychologist good god! is he going to pace all goddamn night?

Satan's characteristics, now let's get them pat this time and then shove off, we're spending the whole damn night on Satan's characteristics, *Satan's characteristics: Courage,* all right, courage, courage, *skillful leader and orator,* orator, orator, *good psychologist,* good pacer, pacer, pacing, pacing, back and forth, back and forth, imagine remembering the color of Connie's pajamas, could he remember the color of Marcia's? Marcia was wearing, wearing, pacing, pacing, white background with floral design in red and blue, no, not flowers, something, a small design, bells, were they bells, in red and blue, the small rip in her pajama pants, imagine Andy's remembering a thing like the color, a tiny tear, still it did show her flesh underneath, and, oh, she had been so good *psychologist, good psychologist,* psychologist, *heart, enthusiasm,* heartburn it was it probably was, Andy's stomach-ache, heartburn from the pastrami, but the pastrami had been good, and the coffee perking on the small electric grill, the deep aroma of it in the small room, and the girls in their pajamas, and Marcia bringing him the sandwich, and then sitting next to him, the curve of her backside tight against his leg, as if they were all married and at some lodge in the mountains and not in a friend's borrowed cold-water flat on First Avenue where . . .

Satan's goddamn characteristics are, my friend, courage, oh, yes, a courageous son-of-a-bitch Satan, a courageous clever little devil, why doesn't Dr. Mason drop dead some cold and eerie night? Skillful leader and orator, which Dr. Mason is not, I'll never memorize these, not with him pacing that way, courageous, skillful leader and orator, damn Satan, let's go to something else, no let's stick with Satan because she's just liable to pull that one out of the hat, the bitch—*in P.L., using the entire text as a basis for your discussion, evaluate the character of Satan, 60 per cent.*

Satan, Satan, satin it was, not silk Connie was wearing, pink satin, Andy should have remembered that, hell, he was the one who undressed her, smooth flesh he said, like satin, Satan . . .

Pacing, pacing, Satan, Satan, back and forth, pacing, oh, Christ, I'll never get this done, never in a million years, why did I take him in, why, why, *why?*

"Can I turn off this light on the end table, Bud? I think I'd like to lie down for a while."

"Yes, certainly. Go right ahead."

He heard the click of the light behind him. There was only the circle of light on the table then, and the open notebook before him.

Thank God, he thought.

You haven't got me yet, Dr. Mason, you old prostitute!

3

The circle of light on the table circumscribed a world of Good and Evil, a world of Heaven and Hell, a world of naked Eves and slithering serpents. On either side of the table, the window curtains fluttered with the early morning breeze, and through the windows the city slept, or tossed restlessly, carried on the lullaby of hushed automobile tires and silently blinking neons. There was nothing beyond the circle of light as far as Bud was concerned. The circle of light was a harsh core of concentration. His own handwriting stared up at him from the lined pages of the spiral notebook, the indelible blue of the ball-point penmanship recording itself on his knotted brain. There were two levels to his concentration. One was a completely automatic level, upon which the major part of his effort descended. This level concerned itself with the purely robotlike task of memorization. The second level was a conscious needle that stabbed at him spasmodically, a needle the prick of which reminded him of the importance of these final examinations.

The first test, the Milton examination, was on Tuesday morning, May twenty-fourth. He had glossed over the notes for every subject he'd studied that semester. He had done that last week, as a part of his habitual study pattern. The notes lay on his unconscious like a group of light sleepers. He was now applying the insistent ring of an alarm clock to these uneasy slumberers. This was Sunday night—no, really Monday morning already. He would thoroughly digest the Milton notes by the end of the day. He would then purify his mind by forgetting the examination and the preparation for it. He would do that by reading a detective story or by going out to see a picture about the Foreign Legion. On Tuesday morning at nine o'clock he would enter the examination room without any notebooks, without even thinking about the exam. He would wait until the proctor passed out the booklets, and he would then fill his fountain pen from the small bottle of ink he would carry to the test, and he would not even begin thinking about the exam until the question sheet was placed face down on his desk by the proctor. When the proctor gave the signal to begin, he would turn over the sheet, and the notes he'd memorized would leap into his consciousness, ready for use. That was the way his system worked, and it had worked well for him thus far. He had no reason to believe it would not work again. He would pass Milton. He would pass all his subjects. He would graduate next semester, a college man who'd made it in three and a half years instead of the more usual four.

After the Milton exam, he had a test Wednesday afternoon, another on Friday morning, and two more on the following Monday. That meant study on Tuesday after the Milton exam, and rest on Tuesday night in preparation for the Wednesday afternoon test. He was not worried. For now there was only Milton to worry about, only Milton to shake out of slumber.

The circle of light aided his concentration. It provided a glaring, merciless ring within which his mind and his body were entrapped. He studied with relish, proud of his memorizing abilities, pleased with the way the notes fell into place. He stopped occasionally, going back to the beginning, silently reeling off everything he'd already memorized. It was going well. He would have it down pat in a few hours, and then he'd hit the sack and relax, putting it all out of his conscious mind.

The scream intruded stridently on his concentration. It was a scream from another planet in another universe, and it took him several moments to realize that the scream had phonetic body and shape. It was a hollow scream, an empty scream, but the scream was a word, and the word was "Helen!"

And then, like an echoed moan in a subterranean torture chamber, the scream came again, and again.

"Helen! Helen! *Helen!*"

He shoved back his chair, his hackles rising. He whirled abruptly, as if to face an intruder with a shotgun. Andy was sitting up in bed staring into the blackness beyond the circle of light on the table. No sound came from his mouth now. He sat tensed, his knees forming a tent of the sheet, his arms straight behind him, elbows locked, staring into the darkness.

"What is it?" Bud asked. He did not move from the table. He seemed incapable of movement. He looked at Andy, and he wet his lips, and Andy continued staring into the blackness, saying nothing, shaking his head.

"Are you all right?"

"Yes," Andy said. The word was a parched whisper.

"Can I . . . can I get you something?"

"No, it's all right."

He went to the sofa and flicked on the end-table light. Andy blinked his eyes and then shook his head again.

"I was dreaming," he said. He wiped the palm of one hand across his eyes. "I'm sorry I disturbed you."

"Can I get you a glass of water or something?"

"No, no, nothing." He wiped his eyes again. "I've . . . I've got to get up. I don't feel so hot."

"What is it?"

"Nothing. Where's . . . where's the john?"

"Around there, near the kitchen. Come on, I'll help you."

"No, go back to your studying. Jesus, I'm sorry about this, Bud. You've no idea how—"

"Forget it. Come on."

He helped Andy out of bed and then brought him to the bathroom.

"You'd better go," Andy said.

"I'll stay."

"No, please go. I'm . . . I'm not proud when I do this. Please go."

"All right."

He went back into the other room, hearing the silence of the apartment, and then hearing Andy in the bathroom, the sound grating on his nerves. He tried to shut out the sound until finally it was all over, and he heard the sound of the water tap replacing the other sick ugly sound. When Andy came out of the bathroom, he was pale and weak-looking. He smiled wanly and said, "I'm sorry."

"That's all right." Bud paused. "How do you feel?"

"Better," Andy said.

"Would you like a cigarette?"

"No, I'd better not. I'm all right now. Go ahead, Bud, do your work. Jesus, I didn't mean to be a pest."

"The work can wait. Are you sure you're all right?"

"Yes, I'm fine." He squeezed his eyes shut and opened his mouth, sucking in a deep breath of air. "If you only knew how much I wanted—" He cut himself short.

"What, Andy?"

"A fix," he said. "Oh, God, how I want a fix!"

"Well . . ."

"No, don't worry. I haven't got any. Besides, I'm going to shake it this time. You don't have to worry. But, Jesus, how I want it, oh, sweet suffering Jesus, how I want it! I'd cut off my arm for it right now, do you know that? I'd cut off my arm and sell the bleeding stump for it, can you believe that?"

"Is it that bad?" Bud asked.

"It's bad, all right. Not my body, you understand. I think I've shaken that. I mean, my body doesn't scream for it any more. When your body is screaming for it, you'll do anything. You can't imagine half the things I did to get the stuff. Filthy things, Bud, things I'm ashamed of now, but they didn't seem filthy then, they seemed all right then when every goddamn muscle was yelling for the junk. Oh, Jesus, how'd I ever get started, how the hell did I ever get started?"

"Well, that's all gone now," Bud said weakly.

"From my body, yes. It's still up here, though, right up here." He tapped his temple with his forefinger. "It'll *always* be up here. And that's where it hurts most. You begin thinking, What the hell am I going through this hell for? Why am I putting up with the yawning and the sneezing and the aches and pains and the throwing up my guts? Isn't it easier just to take a shot? What's so bad about it, anyway? It's a habit, all right, so it's a habit. Smoking is a habit, too, isn't it? So this habit costs a little more, but I'm healthy, ain't I? It hasn't made my hair fall out, and it hasn't discolored my teeth—opium discolors your teeth, did you know that?—so why should I knock myself out? That's what my mind keeps saying. And I keep remembering, too. I keep remembering what it's like when you're turned on. Euphoria and excitation, the medics call it, Bud. There's nothing like it. You're away from everything, everything, oh, Jesus, there are no problems, can you visualize that? You're just up there someplace and everybody below is just nothing, nothing at all. You feel so wise, Buddy, oh, so wise, you feel the wisest in the world, and there's nothing to bother you, nothing to touch you. You've got a nice warm cocoon around you, and the cocoon has a metal shell, and there's nobody who can bust into that cocoon, nobody in the world. It's all your own, and it's the wildest because there's music there, too, Bud, music you never hear anywhere else, high, crazy music, discord sometimes, and harmony that's a little off, but you don't know where it's off, better than a bop chorus, because you can follow the chords in a bop chorus and you know the progression, but there's no progression here, just this harmony that's not harmony, and these colors that swim around.

"It's lazy, and it's clean, and it's unpolluted, and that's all there is, nothing else, just you alone in this world where there's not a thing to worry about, where you don't have to think about clothes, or cars, or where your next gig is coming from, or who's going to tell you not to do this or that, or who's going to chase you, or who's going to not chase you, none of these goddamn worries. Bud, none of them at all. You can't imagine what it's like, Bud, unless you've been on it—didn't I give you a stick of M once? Sure I did, don't you remember what it was like?"

"I didn't feel anything at all," Bud said.

"No, not from M, maybe, and besides it was the first time, the first time you always have ideas it's going to blow the top of your skull off. M doesn't do that, the big stuff does, though, in the beginning. I took an opium ride once, Bud, and, man, it was the end, but opium is a trip to the graveyard, I know guys who are on opium and, Jesus, even their skin looks yellow, as if they have jaundice or something. But it was really the end, that time with opium. I only took it once and this was when I was on the Jerralds band, when I was first beginning to piddle with the big stuff, you know. Oh, man, I felt like I was on the back of a great big swan, an enormous swan, do you know, and that old swan was away up there in the sky, and I could feel the clouds against my face, wispy like, and cottony, and a little damp and moist but warm-moist, like a woman, and I could see the houses down below, like little toy houses in a toy village, like you could squash them in your hand, and I was way up there far away from it all, with the people just crawling around like tiny ants, and these warm-moist clouds licking my face, and the sound of the swan's wings, a *whir, whir, whir,* up and down, just flapping those big wings, *whir, whir,* lazy, lazy without a care in the world. That was the time on opium, I'll never forget that time, but I never went back to that stuff, it's funny how you get channeled onto one thing, isn't it, like the way I got channeled onto heroin and then stayed with it, even though I've had them all—cocaine, opium, even morphine once or twice, that's another mean habit to kick, Barney Ross was on morph, do you know that?"

"Yes," Bud said.

"He kicked it, though, look at the comeback he made. And don't think it's easy. And heroin is worse, you know. Heroin is four to eight times as potent as morphine—that's a fact. Oh, sure. Most of the hopheads you run across are on H. When I was down Lexington, they told me about sixty per cent of all the addicts use heroin, how's that for news? It gets you, the goddamn stuff. The habit is right in your guts, right down there hooked into your guts. I don't get the pains any more, but last week I thought I'd die from them. Worse than labor pains, I swear it, I'll bet no goddamn woman ever had labor pains like the pains I had last week. They start in your stomach and they twist and they roil until you think you've got appendicitis. And they hit you in the back and the arms and the neck, and at the same time you're sweating like a son-of-a-bitch, and then when the sweating stops, you're freezing to death, and you got goose flesh all over you, and you look like a plucked turkey. That's where the expression comes from, you know. Cold turkey. The goose flesh when you drop the junk without a substitute drug. Cold turkey. And all the while that rotten pain is knifing up your insides and you're heaving and twitching and sweating and freezing and yawning, oh Jesus, you yawn like a bastard, it's like you can never stop yawning, and that's when you wonder most if it's worth it all, because you know there's no one in the wide world who gives a damn but you yourself. Sure, everybody says kick it, kick it, like taking off a dirty pair of undershorts. But they don't know what it's like, trying to kick it. Only you know, because it's right there inside your own goddamn stomach, and inside your blood, and inside your head. It's *still* inside my head. You think I'll ever kick it from my head? Do you think Helen kicked it from her head? It'll always be there, always, the way it's there now, the memory of it, the memory of what it does. It's like a disease, Bud, I swear to God. Right now, just talking to you, just talking about the junk, I can feel that itch start inside my skull. I feel like rushing out of here and finding the Man and saying, 'Daddy, lay it on me, I'm sick.' That's just how I feel. I can almost taste the stuff, just sitting here and talking to you."

"Well, then let's talk about something else," Bud suggested.

"No, what good will that do? I've got to live with it, don't I? Am I supposed to pretend there's no such thing as drugs in the world? What'll that get me? I've got to live with the idea, and I've just got to stick to what I'm trying to do, that's the only way. I've got to say the hell with it, I've got to. Otherwise, well, Jesus, there's no end in sight, is there? You see, after a while you need it to feel *normal*, do you know what I mean? You forget about that when the itch starts. You remember only how great it was in the beginning, when the high was the end, when you got a big charge on a small dose, and when your skull hit the ceiling every time you popped off. But after a while, after you've been on the stuff, you need more, and then more, and then you need it to feel normal. Oh, there's still a boot, I mean you still get a boot, but not like in the beginning. You wake up in the morning, and you're subnormal, I guess. Then you take the fix, and you're normal again. You get your small charge, and you're normal. Just normal. If you don't get the fix, you begin to claw the damn walls down, but once you get it, once you get that quick boot, and once you begin to nod, you're just normal, until it's time for the next fix. You forget that. You remember only the good part, and the good part is the best thing in the world, Bud, better than a woman, you don't even think of women when you're on drugs, do you know that? Ah, the good part. That's what you remember. Not the things you had to do, not those, no, not those, and not that deadline all the time, where's the next fix coming from, where, where, where? Always scrounging for the buck, not giving a good goddamn about anything but hoss any more, not caring about the horn or Carol, or anything. The way you start with a world of your own, the world you're in when you're high, well that world spreads out until it's the only world there is. Everybody vanishes. Everybody walking the streets, their problems are nothing. *I am great, you are gornischt,* you know. Who said that, a friend of yours, wasn't it, I don't even remember any more, a guy on the band, Reen? I am great, you are *gornischt,* my problems are everything, and my problem is the monkey on my back, weighing twenty-five pounds and scratching the hell out of me, and where will I get the loot for my next fix, or do I have enough, or will I score, or, Jesus, suppose the Man isn't on the scene, or can I grub from Tom, Dick, or Harry, or who has some of the jive, and what can I do to get a fix, what can I sell, what can I hock, what can I steal? That's your world. It's all wrapped up in H, a pretty white package, pure H cut with sugar, and it's wrapped up in a tablespoon, and a match under the bowl of the spoon, that little flame, and a glistening goddamn syringe with a sharp needle, I'm beginning to feel the itch talking about it, would you believe it, I can almost feel that goddamn spike going into my vein. I was mainlining it, you know, even though I started with simple skin pops, mainlining it is the only way, the drug goes straight into your blood stream. There's a way to build the high, you know, after a while when you've built a tolerance. You shoot it into the vein, and then you draw it back into the syringe, mixed with blood, that's called kicking it, not like kicking the habit, it's funny both terms should apply to two different things, isn't it? You kick the stuff, and the more you kick it, the bigger the pop, oh, I can tell you things about drugs, all right, Helen too, Helen knows the score all right, Helen was hooked through the bag and back again. A hell of a wonderful girl, Helen, you could always depend on her. Call Helen, and Helen came. If you needed her, she came. Whenever you needed her. I shouldn't have got her hooked on the junk, I guess, but I suppose she wanted to, a strange girl, Helen, in a lot of ways. But you could always depend on her, Jesus, what a girl. And she kicked it, by Christ, and if she could do it, I can do it!

"It's all behind me now, no more of it for me, no more

of that, Bud, I swear to God. I've got to move around. Jesus, I've got to walk around or the goddamn ceiling will close down on me."

He began pacing the floor. He was wearing striped shorts and a tee shirt, blond hair curling on his legs and arms. The intimacy of the room, of Andy's costume, of Andy pacing the floor in his underwear, was somehow all out of kilter. Bud had accepted him, expecting a stranger, not feeling any sympathy for the stranger, but doing what he did out of a sense of auld lang syne. The stranger was here now, in his underwear, a stranger who retched in Bud's bathroom, a stranger who spoke of an alien world, and yet the stranger was Andy, he could see that the stranger *was* Andy, and seeing this, he felt a little bit sorry, in spite of all Andy had done, in spite of what he'd known Andy had done. He wanted to get back to his notes, but the empathy was strong inside him, and he couldn't leave Andy alone now, not now, not when Andy's struggle seemed so intensely magnified.

"Remember how we used to talk about Cadillacs?" Andy asked, abruptly turning from his talk of drugs. "Remember sitting in that sun porch of yours, with your father's stamps on the bridge table, and all that junk cluttering up the room. Jesus, your father collects everything in the world, doesn't he? Does he still collect?"

"Yes," Bud said.

"He always gave me a kick, your old man, a nice guy in his own way, I guess all fathers are all right, if only they could understand, huh? You know, my mother used to bring me my lunch at school whenever it rained, have I already told you this?"

"I think so," Bud said.

"She used to bring my lunch in one of those metal lunch pails, and my rubbers, every time it rained. She used to embarrass the hell out of me, coming through the rain with that goddamn lunch pail and the rubbers, that's one of the things I mean, you don't have that kind of baloney when you're turned on, none of these little petty things that rankle you, Jesus, I know guys who've gone psycho from little things that rankled them, did you ever read *The Naked and the Dead?* There's a part there, one of the characters, I forget who, I can only remember Croft, now he was a son-of-a-bitch, wasn't he, one of the characters who's married to this broad, and mashed potatoes stick to her upper lip, and that just about drives him nuts, those mashed potatoes clinging to her lip whenever they eat. Well, Jesus, it's understandable, isn't it? Mashed potatoes on a woman's lip, you don't think of a woman that way, you think of a clean line of lipstick, don't you? Well, those little things can drive you nuts. Like stockings hanging from the shower curtain, was that Mailer, too? He's a damn good writer, you know, did you read the book?"

"Yes," Bud said.

"Well, he is. Well, that lunch pail just about drove me nuts, too, whenever it rained, here comes the pony express with lunch pail and rubbers. *To the round house, men! They can't corner us there!* That sun porch of yours was something like a fortress, too, do you realize that? If the Japs had ever invaded this country, all we'd have had to do was bring the militia to your sun porch and have them fire down from those long windows. Those windows are the eeriest. But do you remember how we talked about Cadillacs, and all the things we wanted out of life? I still want a Cadillac, you know. I still can see myself driving a Caddy, with those goddamn fins sticking out in back, well, who knows, maybe someday."

"I can take them or leave them alone," Bud said.

"Well, you were always that way. Even back then. But I had a taste of it, and you didn't. You've got to remember that. I know what it was like to have gold in my pockets. I was pulling down good loot on the Jerralds band, Bud, you musn't forget that. Once you've tasted loot you get to hate all the poor slobs around you, all the ants with their ant jobs."

"Ants," Bud said. "I remember."

"Oh, sure, all ants, all goddamned ants. There's nothing poorer than a man who's poor. He gets poor all over, in his heart, in his spirit."

"Poor men . . ."

"I used to wonder what it would be like to line up all the ants and give them a heroin fix, and then lead them to a hamburger machine and chop them all up to meat. Give them one big heroin fix, one moment of living, and then cut them dead with the memory of that moment fresh in their minds. That's a crazy idea, isn't it? You must think I'm nuts."

Bud was thinking exactly that. "No," he said. "No, of course not."

"Well, you get ideas like that sometimes. The biggest men get ideas like that, I understand. Rape, murder, things like that. So with me, it's grinding up a bunch of ants. Is that so bad?"

"Well . . ."

"Oh, who gives a damn, anyway? I was just saying, all those talks we used to have, you know, where we used to tell each other how goddamn great we were, how above the herd we were, and here I am a drug addict. That's a big comedown, all right. Andy Silvera, addict. Ta-rah! Put it in lights on a marquee someplace. Addict! When I think of how I used to blow that horn, boy, what a comedown. What a goddamn comedown."

There was self-pity in Andy's voice, and the self-pity suddenly dissolved any sympathy Bud was feeling. He remembered Milton again, remembered it wearily, and he glanced at his wrist watch. Holy Jesus, it was three-thirty.

"I'm keeping you from your studying," Andy said.

"Well, yes, you are," Bud said honestly. In his own mind the two struggles had suddenly become parallel ones. It was certainly easy to sit here and listen to Andy talk, as easy as it would have been for Andy to go out and get himself a shot. Milton was painful, but the examination loomed on the horizon like a hairy monster. The examination had to be faced. He wasn't going to pass it if he kept appeasing Andy with wishy-washy, "Well, that's all right" answers. He had to make his position clear right now, and he had to stick to it. There'd be no more interruptions. Milton had to be taken by the horns. "I've got to get back to it, Andy. Half the night is shot already."

"Go ahead," Andy said.

"Are you going back to bed?"

"No, I thought I'd sit around a little. I don't feel very sleepy."

"You can put on the radio if you like."

"Won't it bother you?"

"No, I can study with it on. Just keep it soft."

"Remember that time in Tony's car when we closed all the windows and turned up the radio full blast, with 'Sing, Sing, Sing' pounding at our ears?"

"Yes, I remember," Bud said, "but I've got to get to work."

"Oh, sure, I was just saying. I've always held that's the only way to listen to music, the volume up full. It makes you feel as if you're a part of the band, right in the middle of it. That's what you're supposed to feel when music is playing. If you don't feel that, who needs it?"

"Andy, really, I've got to—"

"Kenton is delicious that way. I know guys who keep a stack of Kenton records by the bedside, dropping on the turntable whenever they're turned on. It's the greatest—or don't you dig distortion?" He laughed suddenly, as if enjoying a joke Bud did not understand, and the private laughter annoyed Bud immensely. He suddenly recalled his release from the navy, and that night on Fifty-second Street when Andy introduced him to the bop craze, when Andy kept referring to Bud as "my boy" when a friend of his had come over to the table. Bud had picked up the tab that night, flushed with his discharge money, but the "my boy" had held a sour connotation for him, and he'd been annoyed by it then as much as the private laughter annoyed him now.

"We'd better knock it off," he said a little harshly. "I've got work to do. I'm serious, Andy."

Andy seemed suddenly embarrassed. "Oh, sure. I'm sorry, Bud."

"That's all right," Bud said, still miffed.

He walked back to the table, seeing Andy moving to the radio from the corner of his eye. Andy twisted the dial and then turned it up a little, and when the radio came on, it nearly blasted the walls loose from the ceiling.

"Jes-us Christ!" Bud exploded, and Andy turned down the volume instantly.

"It just—"

"All right, keep it soft."

"Would you rather I didn't—"

"Just keep the damn thing soft, that's all."

He sat down and tried to get back to the notes again. Behind him he could hear the radio softly insinuating itself

on his ears and his mind. *I'll get by, as long as I, have you
. . . why* did disk jockeys rob graves for their early morning shows? . . . *may be rain, and darkness, too . . .* how
could he ever get back to Milton? . . . *I won't complain,
I'll see it through . . .*

"Is this disturbing you?"

"No," he said.

"If it is, I'll—"

"I said no."

"Maybe I should go down and take a walk or something?"

"At this time of the night? It's almost four o'clock, for
Christ's sake!"

"Is it? Well, that's all right. I think I'll go take a walk. I
think I need a walk."

"Where will you go?"

"Oh, just around," Andy said. He turned his head, and
his eyes avoided Bud's, and it was suddenly very clear to
Bud.

"You're not going to try to get a shot, are you?"

"Me?" Andy said.

"Yes. Maybe you'd better stay here."

"What for? I'm only going for a little walk."

"I think you'd better stay here. You'll be better off."

"Man, you sound just like my mother. I'll expect a lunch
pail and rubbers any minute. I told you, I'm just going for
a walk. Jesus."

"You'd better stay here, Andy," Bud said tightly.

"Doesn't anybody trust me? I told you I was off the
stuff, didn't I?"

"Then why do you want to leave the apartment?"

"To take a walk. Besides, the radio is bothering you."

"It's not bothering me. I was going to knock off anyway.
I'll pick it up again after I get some sleep." He paused.
"We can both use some sleep."

"I'm not sleepy," Andy said. "I feel like taking a walk."

"You can walk here, if you like."

"I want some fresh air."

"Stand near the windows then. Look, Andy, you're not
leaving this damned apartment. I didn't ask for you here,
but now that you're here I'm going to see that you stay."

"Dig the warden," Andy said, smiling. "Okay, I'll stay.

But I wasn't going to try for a cop, believe me."

"I believe you."

"Okay."

"Come on, let's get to bed."

"You go to bed. I want to walk around a little."

"All right. You can leave the radio on if you like. But don't leave the apartment."

"I said I wouldn't, didn't I?"

"Yes," Bud said. He unbuttoned his shirt and then threw it over the back of the butterfly chair. He slipped out of his trousers and then kicked off his loafers and pulled off his socks. "If you need me—if you have to go to the john again—well, you can wake me."

"I won't need you," Andy said.

"Well, if you should. Can I turn out the lights? You won't mind, will you?"

"No, go ahead."

He walked to the front door and locked it, and then he turned out the light on the end table and walked to his bed on the wall opposite the sofa and pulled back the covers. He went to the table then and turned out the light there, looking once at the open notebook before he did. He found his way back to the bed in the dark, climbed in, and pulled the sheet and cover to his throat. "Good night," he said.

"Good night, Buddy."

"You'll be all right, won't you?"

"Yes."

He felt compelled to say something more. "Stick with it, Andy. You've almost got it beat."

"I know."

"Just stick with it."

He made his head comfortable on the pillow, and then he stretched out his legs. God, he was tired, more tired than he thought. Well, he'd accomplished something at least. Tomorrow—well, it was *today* already—today, when he got up, he'd knock off the rest of the notes. Did Carol say she was coming again? Yes, with Andy's horn and music. Maybe it wouldn't be so bad, after all. He'd laid down the law, and Andy and he now knew where they stood. He didn't quite know why he'd given a damn about Andy's leaving the apartment, but he had. He'd been appointed jailer, much to his regret, and even if the job had been unasked for, it was his, and he couldn't very well let Andy walk out and get right aboard the merry-go-round again. No, he couldn't allow that.

The things Andy remembered—that time in the car with the windows rolled up, how had a thing like that stuck in his mind. And his references to Reen, now that was strange all right.

He lay back and stared up at the ceiling, the darkness closing in on him, and he could hear Andy pacing in the darkness, the barefoot, hushed *slap-slap* of his feet on the wooden floor, back and forth, like a tiger, like a tiger in a cage, probably wanting, wanting, that itch inside his skull, wanting to get out and find a fix, back and forth, back and forth. He listened to the *slap-slap*, and all desire for sleep suddenly fled.

The ceiling was a black vortex, and he found himself thinking of that time in the car—"Sing, Sing, Sing," Goodman, Krupa, James, Goodman, Krupa, James, how long ago, how very long ago, with the ceiling a black vortex, a long, black tunnel, and the barefoot *slap-slap*, pacing, pacing down that long tunnel of blackness, until the room dissolved and there was only the blackness and somewhere far off the sound of music, distant and indistinct, music from a faraway phonograph, distorted, *don't you dig distortion*, chorus after chorus of blurred, half-heard music, indistinct, far off down the long black tunnel

first chorus, i

FEBRUARY, 1944

4

From where Bud Donato sat at the piano he could see all of Club Stardust, and through the rosily distorted cones and rods of his seventeen-year-old vision the place assumed a certain glamour. He wasn't sure whether it was actually the place itself or just the idea of having a rehearsal hall all their own, but through Bud's eyes the sign outside Club Stardust did not hang from a rusted bar on rusted hinges. The five-and-dime gilt dust which had been sprinkled onto the letters when the paint was still wet was not that but shavings of pure silver.

The club was not, to Bud, a big square room with a toilet tacked on the wall opposite the entrance doorway. The streamers left over from the Christmas party did not seem limp or faded to his eyes. The naked light bulb hanging over the piano near the windows might very well have been a blazing sun. The subtle aroma of commingled stale beer and fresh urine was an exotic smell, a worldly smell, the smell you might find in a Chinese whore house. All the color and intrigue of an Oriental bazaar were here in Club Stardust. The magically marked and scarred piano ("Meg loves Bill" carved in a heart on the music rack, directly above middle C), the musty smell coming from deep inside the piano, the pennies dropped between the treble keys making several notes unattainable, the empty beer keg squatting stoutly in the far corner of the room, the "Loose Lips Sink Ships" poster tacked near the bathroom door, the crossed American flags with the large photograph of Franklin D. Roosevelt under them, the broken window behind Bud with the shirt cardboard tacked against it, the banked snow in the back yard outside the window, and the clothes stiff with winter clinging to taut clotheslines, the cat meowing to be let in, the sound of the wind and the gentle lap of snowflakes against the windows—all these overlapped, overran Bud's mind and stirred his body. He was aware of being a part of something, aware in a way that only the seventeen-year-old can know.

The club was set between a butcher shop and a delicatessen on St. John's Place, and it was a "social" club, consisting mostly of married couples who wanted a place for drinking beer and holding parties. Mike's uncle belonged to the club, and Mike had talked him into letting the newly formed band play at the Christmas party the club was giving for all the children of the members. The band didn't get paid for the party, but the agreement with Mike's uncle was that they could use the club for rehearsals from then on, and the band doggedly kept him to that agreement.

This present rehearsal, even though it was still in its slipshod organizational stages, was as exciting to Bud as all the other rehearsals had been.

Frank was in the john, the door open. Tony was pacing the open stretch of floor between the "bandstand" and the tables on the other side of the room, his sax to his mouth, incessantly puffing up and down scales, pacing and puffing, his eyes closed as if the ecstasy of having a mouthpiece between his lips was altogether too much to bear. Vic was sitting at one of the tables, running a chamois cloth over his trumpet, devoting all his attention to the horn, and not noticing anyone else in the club.

Ox, the tenor man, was standing near another of the tables discussing music with Reen, who was not a musician. Reen nodded impatiently and then said, "Yes, but you're wrong."

Ox, a small boy with small hands and small feet and a small body, asked, "How can I be wrong and right at the same time?" His narrow, angular face was plainly confused. He always looked confused. He had pale blue eyes and a thin nose which drew his face downward toward his mouth. At the same time his hair was wavy and long, rising from his high forehead in a series of shelflike combings which stretched his face out in the other direction, giving it a perpetually surprised expression.

Reen looked down from his six-foot-two advantage. "You're right because Barnett did 'Cherokee' and 'Redskin Rumba' both," he said, his eyes intense, leaning forward the way he always did when he was pounding a point home. "But they're not on separate disks. 'Redskin Rumba' is on the back of 'Cherokee.' Hell, it's even a continuation of 'Cherokee.'"

Ox did not seem convinced. He continued shaking his head, but apparently he could think of no suitable argument to give voice to.

"Look," Reen said, assuming the patient attitude of a father-to-child relationship, "use your common sense. Even the title is a giveaway: 'Redskin Rumba.' What the hell are Cherokees if not redskins? Don't you get the connection?"

Frank came out of the toilet zipping up his fly. "Reen's right," he said.

"Oh, what the hell do you know?" Ox asked, turning, thankful for the intrusion.

"I know Reen's right," Frank said. "And you should be

ashamed of yourself! A tenor man who doesn't know 'Cherokee' from a pole in the totem." Frank grinned expansively, obviously having devoted his time in the toilet to concocting this delightful pun. As a matter of fact, he'd lingered longer than usual, desperately trying to find a better word than "totem" to complete the parallel. When his witty attempt went unappreciated by both Reen and Ox, he retreated into a sullen silence and walked over to the drums set up near the piano.

"When the hell do we start?" he asked Bud.

"Soon as Mike gets here, I suppose."

"And when the hell does Mike get here?"

Tony Banner took the sax from his mouth long enough to say, "He'll be a little late. He has to wait for his brother to come home with the key."

"For Christ's sake, let's chip in and have another goddamn key made for him," Frank said. "We hold up more rehearsals because his snotnose brother has the only key to his—"

"He'll be here," Tony said, and then he immediately put the saxophone to his mouth again, puffing and pacing like an expectant father with a curved, metallic cigar between his lips. Frank listened to the elementary monotony of the scales, absorbed momentarily, absorbed with a drummer's absorption, listening to the even spacing of the notes as the scales fell from the bell of Tony's horn. His interest died as suddenly as it had found life. He searched the closet of his mind for a means of interrupting the monotony, and then he asked, "What arrangements did you get, Tony?"

Tony completed a scale before taking the mouthpiece from his lips. "Some nice ones," he answered.

"Like what?" Frank asked pointedly. A look of muted understanding passed between him and Bud. The band usually went down to Hub Music en masse. They invaded the shop like a horde of locusts, crawling over every arrangement in the place, pawing through the music to make sure it didn't feature trombone solos or glockenspiel duets. They also made sure they didn't pick stuff too difficult for them, or stuff that would make a small band sound sick. Actually, they were only exercising a stockholder's prerogative. For whereas Tony Banner was legally the

duly appointed leader of the band, his leadership was
was nothing more than a mock post. He had been chosen
because he had the nicest-sounding name, the name that
would look best on a stand. His duties did not extend
beyond calling off the tempo for a tune and generally
supervising rehearsals. Any important decision was made
by band vote. The band also chipped in for all the arrangements and were now saving for cardboard stands to re-
place the unsightly metal music racks they were using.
(The advertisement in *Down Beat* showed four musicians
with their trousers pulled almost to their knees, their socks
falling, their garters loose, sitting behind the metal racks.
Beneath that was a picture of the same musicians behind
the sleek, folding cardboard stands, a smooth, music-
making machine. The pictorial metamorphosis was most
convincing.)

So whereas the stockholder's prerogative was generally
exercised, it had not been taken advantage of that morning. The members of the band had all made previous en-
gagements or appointments (some of which had been skillfully spawned by duty-minded parents) and Tony had been
reluctantly sent downtown alone. He'd been sent with much
misgiving, not because the boys didn't like him, but only
because they'd suspected he'd return with a pile of numbers featuring solos for the alto sax, which, of course,
he played. Frank's anxiety was reflected on Bud's face as
they waited for Tony's answer.

"Well," he said. "I got some real nice ones." The club
suddenly seemed very silent. Reen and Ox abruptly ended
their discussion and walked over to the piano. Tony, as if
realizing his judgment was about to be put on trial, busied
himself with the leather strap around his neck, toying with
the hook where it joined the saxophone.

"What'd you get?" Frank asked again, suspiciously this
time.

" 'I Dreamt I Dwelt in Harlem,' " Tony answered. Be-
latedly, he added, "A nice number."

"I never heard of it," Frank said. He turned from
Tony and began tightening the nuts on his cymbals. Vic,
apparently drawn by the talk of the new arrangements,
put down his chamois and walked over to the piano, his
trumpet hooked over his arm like a shotgun.

"You'll recognize it when you hear it," Tony said uneasily. He paused and wiped his hand across his mouth, more unsure of himself now. "I also picked up 'Stardust.' I figured we should start buying some standards. We got almost all pops and—"

"That's good," Bud said, nodding in agreement.

"What else?" Frank asked.

" 'Trumpet Blues.' "

"Harry James's?" Reen asked.

"Yeah."

"We'll never play that," Frank said sourly. Maybe he didn't know that Vic had silently walked over to the piano and was standing there now, thin-lipped, solemn-eyed. Maybe he didn't know, but Bud suspected he just didn't give a damn. But looked up and caught the quick spark in Vic's eyes almost the instant it was kindled.

"Why not?" Vic asked quietly. "Why won't we play it?"

Frank looked up from his cymbals, and he didn't seem surprised to see Vic there at all. "We've only got one trumpet," he said. "James has six."

Vic wouldn't let it go. "So what?" he said.

Frank shrugged. "So that."

"One trumpet can carry the melody," Vic said doggedly. "The first trumpet sheet—"

"Are you comparing yourself to James?" Frank said suddenly. Bud felt the shocked silence that greeted Frank's outburst. He glanced to Vic uneasily, saw Vic bite his lip for a moment.

"No," Vic said, "I know I'm not James, but—"

"Then what the hell are you talking about?" Frank said, flaring into anger. "You think 'Trumpet Blues' is one of your damn C scales?"

"Oh, knock it off, Frank," Reen said.

"I can play it," Vic said to no one in particular.

"Play with this a while," Frank said nastily.

"If you can play the drum part, I can play the trumpet part."

"I can play the drum part, all right," Frank said, straightening up from his cymbals. "Don't worry about that, boy. I can play the drum part fine. There hasn't been a drum part yet I couldn't play."

"Well, I can play the trumpet part," Vic persisted.

"We'll see," Frank said, unwilling to continue with what seemed a pointless argument to him.

Tony Banner, a boy who hated awkward situations of any sort, a boy who'd walk a mile to avoid a scene, listented to the completeness of the silence all around him. He wiped his hand over his mouth again, glanced toward the door hurriedly, and almost thanked the Virgin Mary when he saw Mike entering the room.

"Here's Mike now," he said, sighing thankfully. "We can start as soon as you tune us up, Bud."

"Sure," Bud said. He watched Vic slouch over to his metal stand and sit in the chair behind it. Vic had thin lips, and he blew from the side of his mouth, and all the boys in the band knew he wasn't so hot, which was why they were looking for an additional trumpet player. But Bud's sense of right and wrong could not eliminate the fact that the idea for a band had originated with Vic, and that he'd done the initial legwork, getting hold of Ox and Mike, and later Bud and Frank. It was funny they'd chosen Tony as leader, because he'd actually been the last one to join the band. It was funny to everyone but Vic, Bud knew, and he couldn't help feeling sorry for the trumpet player. Vic, despite his show of bravado, sensed he was not a very good musician, and Frank shouldn't have hopped on him like that, especially for no apparent good reason.

Mike Daley came over, his red face even redder from the cold outside, and stamped around and got everyone wet when he shook off his coat. He kept rubbing his hands together while Bud gave Tony and Ox the A. Vic came over to the piano and tuned up, taking longer than the other fellows because his ear wasn't as good and he was unable to tell whether he was flat or sharp unless Bud prompted him. Frank sat behind his drums, up high on the special box he'd built with the cushion on it. He played a few rolls with his brushes, and Vic put in a cup mute and blew a few scales softly, while Ox and Tony ran up some chromatics together. When Mike came over to the piano with his alto sax, Bud yelled for everyone to shut up and then gave him the A. Mike blew a note, pulled his mouthpiece out a little, and then hit it again, right on the button this time. He warmed up a little, joining Tony and Ox in the chromatics. Reen walked to one of the tables on the other side of the room, sat down, and then as an afterthought propped his legs up on the table.

"Let's take 'Elk's Parade,' " Tony said, and Bud smiled a little. He'd known what was coming because Tony always chose that number for the warm-up. The band played it better than any of their other arrangements, and it also gave each of the boys an opportunity to solo. It was a jump tune, too, and jumps were always better for warm-ups than something slow and draggy.

Tony called off the beat, standing up to do it, the way he'd seen bigtimers do it, Bud surmised. He sat down as soon as the band started playing, and they ran through the number without a hitch, playing it competently if without any particular distinction. When they were finished, Reen applauded, and Tony hammed it up the way he always did, standing up and bowing and smiling and saying, "Thank you, thank you," as if he were addressing an adulating audience at the Paramount. Frank said, "Come on, let's get this damn rehearsal over with," and Tony turned all business, going over to the piano and taking the new arrangements from its top where he'd left them.

He gave out all the parts, saving the trombone sheets, and the guitar sheet, and the second and third trumpet sheets, and the fourth tenor sheet, and the bass sheet for when the band was bigger and needed them. Bud glanced through the stuff Tony handed him, and he had to admit it looked pretty good, with some nice chords in the "Harlem" number. Frank looked over his simple drum parts and then said, "Let's try 'Trumpet Blues' first, Tony."

A worried look came onto Tony's face—the look that always arrived whenever he had a decision to make. "I thought we'd try some of the simpler stuff first," he said.

"Hell, this is simple enough," Frank answered. "Vic can play it. You heard him say so, didn't you?"

"Yeah, but . . ."

"Then why not? Come on, let's try it."

"I'm game," Vic said, perhaps a little too loudly. He was sitting alongside Frank, with the three saxes in front of him and with Bud on his left, facing the piano.

"There," Frank said. "Harry James is game. Let's try it."

"Well, all right," Tony said reluctantly. "I want to number the sheets first, though." He said this apologetically, keenly aware of his puppet status, knowing he'd been chosen for leadership simply because of his name. Oddly enough—oddly because Tony was Italian—his real name was Tony Banner. Reen had often voiced the opinion that the immigration authorities on Ellis Island had undoubtedly wrangled with a great-grandfather's Bannalinza or Bannicossoni before resignedly recording it as Banner, but Tony remained noncommittal on the possibility. He made no attempt to reconcile the Anglo-Saxon handle with the obvious Italianness of his features. For even though he had blond hair, the blond was a muddied color which combined with his deep brown eyes and his swarthy complexion to cancel itself out in an over-all impression of darkness. His brows, as if in perpetual disagreement with the accidental light coloring of his hair, were jet black—a combination any young lady in the United States would have envied deeply. There was nothing unmasculine about Tony Banner, though. He was five feet ten inches tall, and he was solidly packed with bulging muscles, of which he was uncommonly proud.

"What's the number?" Bud asked.

"Twenty-seven," Tony answered.

"I can remember when we had only three," Mike said, proudly awed.

"Well, we've got twenty-seven now," Frank informed him. "Come on, let's number the damn thing and play it."

Tony passed a pencil stub around and they all scribbled a "27" on the fronts of their sheets. Bud propped his on the rack, spreading it out, testing a few chords with his fingers, but not striking them. Vic was staring at his sheet solemnly, his eyes squinted as if he were reading a Hebrew newspaper.

"We'll take it slow," Tony said, "very slow. Ah-one, ah-two, ah-three, ah-four, like that. One, two, three, four. You got that, Frank?"

"I got it," Frank said.

"And don't speed it up. This is the first time we're playing it. We don't have to sound like stars."

"The trumpet is the star of this one," Frank said, de-

riving a perverse pleasure from giving Vic the needle.
Vic looked at him briefly and then turned back to his
music.

"Okay," Tony said, "let's take it." He arranged his own
sheet on the stand, adjusted the strap around his neck,
and then called, "Ah-one, ah-two, ah-three, ah-four; *one*,
two, three, four . . .'

Frank and Bud started with the rhythm, a four-bar introduction with a boogie beat. Vic missed the pickup at
the end of the fourth measure, and Tony called a stop
and said, "Okay, let's try it again. Watch that pickup,
Vic."

Vic nodded, ignoring Frank's grin of superiority, and
then Tony counted off again. Bud and Frank took the
intro once more, and this time Vic caught his pickup and
went sailing into the fifth bar with it. He wasn't Harry
James, and no member of the band doubted that fact.
He had a thin, feeble tone, and he gave the trumpet part
all the power of a ruptured flea. On the sustained notes his
tone cracked and wobbled, and when the business began
to get a little tricky, he went completely berserk, playing
in a little vacuum all by himself, not listening to the
rhythm and not paying any attention at all to the background the saxes were giving him.

"Okay," Tony yelled, "hold it, hold it."

They all stopped, and Vic came to a reluctant, preoccupied halt about four beats after the rest of the band.
Frank sat at his drums with a big smile on his face.

"Uh, I think we ought to try that again," Tony said
diplomatically. "From [A] this time. You all got that?"

The boys nodded, and Tony said, "Set the beat, Frank.
You know what it is."

Frank gave the boys four beats on the bass drum, using
the foot pedal, and then he gave them another four, and
they all came in from [A]. If anything, it was worse this
time. They started out together, but Vic got lost somewhere in the shuffle, and pretty soon he was back in his
little vacuum again, playing for his own private audience,
forgetting all about the band, studying his sheet with those
solemn eyes of his, blowing his feeble music from the side
of his mouth. Bud looked at Frank, and Frank looked back
at him, and they kept the rhythm going, both wondering

just where Vic was on the sheet. Bud read ahead a little, but he still couldn't find just where Vic was, and he didn't know where the saxes were any more, either. Tony and Mike, on first and third altos, were blowing together, but Ox was somewhere up on a cloud, blowing his own carefree way, and Vic had already left the land of the living and was running completely amok.

Bud lost his own place then, what with trying to read ahead and all, and the resultant cacophony was really a marvel to hear. Everyone kept pounding away or blasting away, apparently blaming the guy sitting next to him for playing either ahead or behind. Tony was so absorbed in following his own sheet that he didn't hear a sound around him. He was probably the best sight-reader in the group, and when he sight-read, he threw all of his muscular five feet ten into it. He finally was blasted out of his unconsciousness, and he stood up suddenly, as if he'd been goosed, and shouted, "All right, all right, *hold it!*"

If the band hadn't been playing exactly together, they certainly stopped together. One minute there was this godawful sound that pounded at the walls, and the next there was complete silence. And then, through the silence, even before their ears had grown accustomed to the welcome peace, the voice from the door said, "Buddy?"

Bud swung around on the piano bench, and every pair of eyes in the band swung toward the door at the same time.

A kid with a trumpet case was standing there. He wore a boxlike raincoat and a battered rain hat, and his green trousers were rolled up over his ankles, showing orange-and-black striped socks. His shoes were caked with snow, and he stood there with a trumpet case in one hand and a man's black umbrella in the other. He searched the faces of the seated musicians, apparently wondering which one of them was Bud's. He rubbed one finger across the bridge of his nose, cleared his throat, and repeated, "Buddy?"

"I'm Bud," Bud said, puzzled.

The kid did not move from the door. He seemed afraid to enter, as if he'd stumbled into the Ladies' Room by error.

"I'm Andy Silvera," he said.

"Who?" Bud asked.

The kid gulped down something in his throat, grunted after it was gone, and then repeated, "Andy Silvera."

Bud couldn't think of anyone he knew by the name of Andy Silvera. He kept staring at the kid and waiting for him to say something else, but Andy Silvera had apparently said all he was going to say. He stood by the door silently, the snow melting under his shoes and spreading in a small blackish puddle. Tony looked at Bud wonderingly, and Bud shrugged slightly and turned back to the kid.

"Well," he said, "what can I do for you, Andy?"

"My father sent me down," Andy said, his voice cracking.

"Oh," Bud said, still not understanding.

"He works in your father's office. Your father told him you needed a trumpet player."

"Oh, yes," Bud said, abruptly remembering. He'd told his father about needing a trumpet player one night at supper. His father had mentioned the kid to him a few days ago, telling him the kid had been playing trumpet for close to eight years. Bud had given his father the address of the club and told him to send the kid down. He looked at Andy Silvera now, figuring him for no more than sixteen and wondering about the truth of that "eight years" business. He got off the bench, walked to him, and extended his hand. Andy shifted the umbrella from his right hand and then reached out abruptly, awkwardly, like someone who is not used to the convention of handshaking. From the corner of his eye Bud could see Reen regarding them with wry amusement. Reen was the one who'd called Tony "Bundler Banner" the first time he'd seen Tony in his mackinaw. As far as Reen was concerned, you either wore mackinaws when you were twelve years old or when you were up in the North Woods. He'd explained this to Tony, whose mother had bought him the bulky red-and-blue plaid job, but Tony—for some obscure reason—couldn't see any humor in it. Reen observed the orange-and-black socks on Andy Silvera's feet now, and then his eyes took in the rolled green trousers, and Bud saw his heavy eyebrows quirk upward like individual shaggy grinning mouths.

"Come on in," Bud said to the kid. "Come meet the boys."

Andy nodded self-consciously, then smiled self-consciously, and then followed Bud like an uncertain ghost, the black umbrella in one hand dripping a watery trail onto the floor, the trumpet case in the other. Bud led him over to Tony and said, "This is Tony Banner, the leader of the band."

Tony stuck out his hand, and the kid fumbled awkwardly with the umbrella, shifting it to the hand that held the trumpet case and then taking Tony's hand. Tony smiled and gave him his special weight-lifter, bear-crusher, bone-cracker, knuckle-gnarler handshake, and the kid just nodded with a pained, shocked look on his smooth, peach-fuzz face. When Tony released his hand, the kid shifted the umbrella back again, looked quickly at the hand that had suffered Tony's treatment, and then raised his eyes just as quickly, a little guiltily. He had a nice-enough-looking face, Bud thought, with high cheekbones and a good wide mouth, weak still, the way a mouth will be when it hasn't matured yet. He had ears that hugged his head, and his eyebrows and sideburns were a sandy brown, and his eyes were deep brown, almost black, flecked with chips of amber. His eyes looked intelligent, but they were stabbed with this fear now, and the fear made it impossible to tell anything about them or from them. He had a good nose, cleanly sweeping down from the arch of his brows, unbroken, with wide flaring nostrils that somehow intensified the frightened-animal look about him. His hands looked surprisingly mature for a kid's hands—wide, with square fingers and well-pared nails, the backs of the fingers curling with blond-bronze hair.

Bud introduced him to all the boys, and the umbrella shift occurred just before each handshake, like a football team going into action after the signal for the snapback has been given. Frank sat at his drums with a curious smirk on his face, and he looked down at the kid from his superior perch, and Bud hoped he wouldn't hop on him the way he'd hopped on Vic just a little while ago.

Frank acknowledged the introduction without reaching down to shake hands, and then he said, "You play trumpet, huh?"

"Yes," Andy said. "Yes, I do." He looked up at Frank as though he were having trouble focusing him properly. He wet his lips, and Bud noticed for the first time the pink, almost white ring of muscle smack in the center of his upper lip, the coat of arms of the trumpet player. It looked like a miniature smoke ring that had slipped out of his mouth and somehow got glued to his lip, hanging there in the bow of his mouth.

Frank, enjoying his elevated position on the cushioned box, enjoying the superiority of advanced age, enjoying just being a bastard, asked, "How long you been playing, kid?"

"Seven years. Well, almost eight years."

"Yeah?"

"Yes," Andy said.

"How old are you, kid?" Frank asked, the smirk still on his mouth.

"Fifteen," Andy said. He didn't say it with embarrassment, the way a fifteen-year-old will when he wants to be sixteen or seventeen. He said it matter-of-factly, the direct answer to a direct question, and Bud realized he was not yet conscious of the vast difference between fifteen and sixteen.

"And you've been playing eight years?" Frank asked, his eyebrows raised in skepticism.

"Yes, almost," Andy said.

"You ever play with a band before?"

"At . . . in school," Andy said.

"Which school?"

"Boys' High."

"You go to Boys' High?"

"Yes."

"You know a guy named Goldstein? Allan Goldstein?"

"No," Andy said.

"What term are you in?"

"Fourth."

"Goldstein plays trumpet. You sure you don't know him?"

"No," Andy said. "No, I . . . I never heard of him. Is he . . . does he play in the band there?"

"Sure," Frank said.

"Well, I don't know him," Andy answered. "I'm sorry."

Tony was listening to all this, slightly bored by the conversation. Frank shrugged and retightened the nut on one of his cymbals, dismissing the kid, and Tony said, "You want to warm up over there in the corner, Andy? We'll run through a number and then you can sit in after that, okay?"

"All right," Andy said. He looked around, seemingly confused, and then walked over to where Reen was sitting.

"Take off your coat and hat, kid," Reen said. "You'll catch pee-numonia."

"Thanks," Andy said, unsmiling. He made a big production of putting down first the umbrella, then the trumpet case, then taking off the hat, then the raincoat. Reen winced when he saw the kid was wearing a faded red sweater with the green trousers. Andy hung his coat on the rack, unsnapped his trumpet case, and tenderly lifted his horn from its velvet bed. From one of the pockets in the case, he took out a chamois cloth and wiped the horn slowly and gently, passing the cloth over the gleaming surface. He reached into his pocket then and pulled out a mouthpiece in a leather holster. He unsnapped the holster and fitted the mouthpiece to the horn instantly. He put the horn to his mouth, *prbb-prbb*-ing his lips against the mouthpiece, and then opened the spit valve on the bend of the brass and blew effortlessly, a dribbling of moisture hitting the floor. He closed the spit valve and then worked his fingers over the valves for a few minutes, shaking the cold out of them, and then he began to blow some prolonged warm-up notes, nothing fancy, just long low notes, very softly, to take the stiffness out of his lip. He didn't sound like much. To Bud's ears, Vic sounded better when he warmed up. He turned his attention away from the kid and back to Tony.

"Let's take 'Elk's Parade,'" Tony said. He said it offhandedly, nonchalantly, preoccupied with hooking his sax to the strap around his neck. He said it innocently, as if he didn't know it was the band's best number, and as if the band didn't know he was showing off for the benefit of the kid who was warming up on the other side of the room. The boys fished out their music, Tony counted off, and then they went into the number, playing it as well as they always did, maybe giving it a little more get-up-and-go for the benefit of the newcomer.

The kid didn't seem to pay much attention, though. He just stood back there near the table, his horn pointed at the floor, those long low notes oozing out of the bell. When they finished the number Tony looked at him expectantly, but the kid went right on warming up, not paying any attention to what was going on near the piano. Tony stared at him for a second, and when he called the kid over he used his Angry Voice, the voice he used whenever the sax section was blowing particularly sour.

"You want to come over now?" he said. "Bring a chair, will you?" He worded both sentences as questions, but there was no mistaking they were delivered as orders.

Andy stopped blowing and then picked up a chair from one of the tables where it was stacked upside down. He brought the chair over to where Vic was sitting, and Vic looked up at him from his big solemn eyes, studying first the ring of muscle on his lip and then looking down to the well-kept horn and the fingers holding it. Andy put down the chair, and it was plain to see he was annoying the hell out of Tony, though Bud couldn't understand quite why. Maybe Tony had expected some hearty applause after "Elk's Parade," instead of the indifference Andy had exhibited. Or maybe Tony was annoyed because the kid automatically sat down beside Vic, without waiting to be told where to sit. It seemed to Bud, though, that a trumpet player would automatically sit next to another trumpet player, and he couldn't see any reason for Tony's getting angry about that. He was certainly angry, no question about it, and he began sniffing through his nostrils, the way he always did when he got angry.

"Give him the first-trumpet sheet, Vic," he said, and he sniffed and then dug into the extra sheets he had near his stand, handing Vic the second-trumpet part. He looked at the kid and asked in his Angry Voice, "You ever play lead trumpet?"

"In school," Andy said.

"Well, you may find this a little different from school," Tony snapped, and Frank was smirking all over again.

"We want to find out how you read, and I'll be listening to your tone, too, so play the best you can."

"All right," Andy said. He looked at the sheet and said, "Oh, 'Trumpet Blues.' "

"You ever play it before?" Tony asked, sniffing.

"No, but I heard the James record."

Vic moved over a little, placing his music on the stand so that Andy could share a part of the metal rack. Andy spread his music, reading it as he put it down. Bud gave the kid his A, and Tony looked at him hostilely for a moment and then said, "Take it slow, Frank. We don't want to confuse the kid."

"Okay," Frank said, smile-smirking.

"One, two, three, four," Tony said, *"one,* two, three, four . . ."

Bud and Frank went into the intro, a nice stepladder boogie. They played it slowly, expecting the kid to miss the pickup, the way Vic had done. But he didn't miss it. He came in right when he was supposed to, and Vic surprisingly came in with him, and Bud heard the sound of the two trumpets and turned momentarily to look at them. Vic was hunched in his chair, studying the sheet intently, painfully, the way he always did—like a Swiss watchmaker with an intricate clock to repair. He had the bell of his horn turned toward Andy's, and he blew with the mouthpiece on the left side of his lip, off-center.

Andy seemed completely relaxed. He leaned back in the chair, and his feet were spread wide, like Charlie Chaplin's, a stance which, coupled with the orange-and-black socks, made Bud want to laugh. He seemed to blow effortlessly, playing slowly because the beat was very slow, the way Tony had wanted it. He hit the notes hard and solid, and he got a big round tone from his horn, and Bud got the feeling that he was holding back, so he nodded to Frank, and Frank began speeding up the tempo a little.

The kid picked up the quicker beat right away, and Vic followed him, and the saxes followed the trumpet. Andy just kept following his music, but he began to play a little louder now, as if the increased tempo was what he'd been waiting for. Bud listened to the big notes flowing from the bell of his horn, and he unconsciously began hitting the piano a little harder, and he heard Frank's footbeat on the bass drum get a little stronger, with more of a drive behind it.

The kid put a solid rock behind that horn of his, and he began riding that rock, tipping the horn up toward the ceiling. The tune began to jump a little because he was like a man behind a pneumatic drill, pushing on those valves, his cheeks only puffed a little, but the pressure flowing from his mouth and through the horn, the notes blasting up at the ceiling, but not blasting with a hard flat trumpet sound. There was a brassy sound, but it was clean brass, brass you could almost taste in your mouth, brass you could almost see glistening. Brass that was almost like gold.

The music was a part of him, and it started with the jiggle of his toes inside those ludicrous orange-and-black socks, and it spread up the length of his leg and into the pit of his diaphragm, and up through his lungs, and out through his lips, and down through the horn, around the brass bend, channeled by the valves, and then floating out of that bell, blooming out of that bell like a big spring flower, bursting into the room big and round, always with that solid rocking beat behind it, always with that full big brass tone. He cut through the tricky business like a scythe in a hayfield, and Vic threw in the towel, the going too rough for him now. His solemn eyes watched the kid's fingering and the kid's lipwork, and Bud could feel him listening to the sound that came from that horn, and his eyes got even more solemn than they usually were. The saxes hung on, blowing together, catching some of the spirit that the horn created. Andy pointed his bell up at the ceiling, and the Christmas decorations in the hall began to sway a little when he really cut loose.

It was something like a fever. The band heard him blowing back there, and the fire spread to them. Bud felt chords coming to life under his fingers, and he felt warm all at once, a strange warmth that spread through his body, that flamed up around him until there was only the sound they were making, the sound of the band, and being a part of the band, beating the piano like the heart pump of the band, and then listening to that horn take the blood away roaring through the veins. There was no

Club Stardust any more, no four walls hemming them
in, no world outside anywhere, no universe, no anything
but the music they were making. It was like being with a
girl, Bud felt, only better somehow because there was a
bigger sense of fulfillment, but the same reaching quality,
the same straining for something that was always just out
of reach.

They rode into the sock chorus like a storm cloud of
marauders on strong black horses, riding high up in the
sky there, following that Gabriel horn, letting it become
a part of them. They heard the blasting back there, and
the blasting was a wild kind of unleashed thing that lapped
nervously at their roots, a restless kind of music that
reached up and kept reaching, and always reached for
more, but never quite got there until they wanted to reach
up with it, wanted to give it a boost, wanted to play harder,
and better, and get up there with that horn, away up there
where the horn was, where it was clean and clear and pure
and sweet and where their lungs were washed with dry
ice and fire. They were in the same kind of vacuum Vic
had been in earlier that day, but this was a different
vacuum, this was a vacuum they all created, this was their
baby, like a real baby squeezed from a woman's loins, only
the woman was a horn, and the baby was a big golden
bubble that burst from the bell of that horn, and rose
swiftly, and touched the ceiling, and then shattered there
into a million golden bubbles that knocked each other
around and sped around the room in a dizzying swirl,
gleaming hotly, gleaming with the taste of gold-brass,
slapping the walls, and then bursting again into millions
and millions of bubbles that enveloped them, and floated
and rose and descended and rose again, carrying the boys,
all around them, inside them. Bud wanted to keep listening to that trumpet, wanted to keep feeling the music as a
part of him, feeling it vibrate around the room, showering golden bubbles on him, showering all that restless
brassy searching feeling on him, that high shrill climbing,
that straining yearning reaching.

But the bubble burst for the last time, and then it was
all over, like it's all over with a girl, and there was a
curious emptiness inside Bud, of something that had been
almost touched but not quite, something that had been a

part of him for just a very little while, and was no more. There were only the echoes around him now, and then even the echoes disappeared, dissipated on the air, leaving only a vast, empty silence, a speechless, wondrous silence.

Reen's applause came from the back of the room: not the shallow, mocking applause he reserved for Tony Banner's clowning. Not that at all. It burst from those big hands of his, filling the empty stillness the music had left.

Bud felt tired and weak. He sat at the piano and he looked at Frank, and the wise-guy smirk was gone from Frank's face. He was staring at Andy, and Andy sat in his chair with the horn in his lap, out of breath, looking down at the horn and not looking at any of the boys. And Vic sat beside him, the solemn eyes sad now because he was reading the big writing on the wall.

There was another long silence after Reen stopped clapping. Bud could hear his own breathing at the piano, and then Tony stood up and unhooked his sax from the strap, and then he put the sax down across the seat of his chair, and he lifted one leg, resting his foot alongside the sax, leaning over and elbowing his weight onto his knee. He looked at Andy, and he wet his lips, and he asked, "How would you ... how would you like to play with us, Andy?"

He said it softly and nervously, his anger all gone now, that harried look on his face, as if he had touched greatness, as if he wanted this kid to play with them very badly, and as if he were afraid the kid would say no.

Andy looked at him, and there was no smile on his face, no apparent knowledge there of what he'd just done. He nodded slowly, and then he said, "All right, I think so."

first chorus ii

FEBRUARY, 1944

5

The rehearsal had been called for seven o'clock sharp on that February eighteenth.

There was a dance every Friday night at Our Merciful Father on Brooklyn Avenue, and Bud and Frank had got into the habit of attending it, along with Reen and the other boys in the clique before those boys were drafted. Tony hadn't liked the idea of a too-early rehearsal, but Bud and Frank pounded at his ear, telling him they were going to rehearse tomorrow anyway, weren't they, so what difference would it make if they started a little earlier, and knocked off in time to make the dance?

Tony reluctantly conceded—reluctantly, because he didn't like to dance himself, even though they'd dragged him along several times. Actually, he wasn't a very good dancer, having learned from his mother, who'd taught him all the old-fashioned curlicues and none of the basic rhythm.

Bud and Frank went to rehearsal in suits that night, figuring they'd go directly to the dance afterward, saving the time of a trip home for changing clothes. Reen, who'd rather have been shot than appear at any public function alone, went to the rehearsal with them, also wearing a suit. They arrived at Club Stardust at about a quarter to seven, figuring they'd set up the drums and be ready to go at seven on the dot. Vic and Tony were already there, and Ox drifted in at five to seven. Mike came in at about a minute after seven, and by the time everyone warmed up and tuned up the band was ready to start playing at seven-ten. But Andy hadn't arrived yet.

Bud sat at the piano in his blue suit, feeling strangely resplendent. Frank was on his left, looking very dressed up, looking as strange as Bud felt. They usually rehearsed in sports shirts or collars-unbuttoned, sleeves-rolled-up dress shirts, and Bud felt very stiff and formal sitting at the piano with pressed pants, and tie, and jacket.

Tony was wearing a suit, too. Bud did a little fast calculation and gathered Tony was going to the dance with them—either that or a funeral or wedding. They hung around making small talk, almost afraid to move because they were dressed to the teeth and they'd never dressed for Club Stardust before, except at the Christmas party, and even then they'd only worn sports jackets.

Frank glanced at his watch, and then Reen glanced at his watch, and then everyone who owned a watch glanced at it, the movement having become as contagious as a yawn. Ox asked, "What are we waiting for?" and Tony said, "We're waiting for Andy," and then Tony looked at his watch.

Bud turned on the bench, and his elbow accidentally struck the keyboard, and everyone in the band turned to look at him, as if he'd burped.

"You know, they still haven't cleared the snow on my street," Ox said.

"Take that up with the D.S.C.," Frank said.

"I think my father already has," Ox said, the surprised expression on his face.

"He's an upstanding citizen," Reen said from the back of the room.

Normally, Reen's comment would have presented an opening for some banter at Ox's expense. Tonight it was greeted with silence. The silence mushroomed in on itself. In the bathroom the toilet tank gurgled in unusually loud voice.

"It's hot as hell in here," Frank said.

"Take off your jacket."

"And get my shirt dirty? Not a chance."

"What time is it?" Mike, who did not own a watch, asked.

"Seven-fifteen," Bud answered. "No, seven-sixteen."

"Well, we've got time yet," Frank said.

"Yeah."

Vic began playing some scales, a cup mute in his horn. He dropped the scales abruptly and began slaughtering "Carnival in Venice." Behind him, in the silence of the room, the toilet tank played a Shep Fields accompaniment, bubbling, bubbling, bubbling. Frank listened to him, fidgeting, running his finger under his tight collar, hounding his watch:

Daaah-dah, daah-dah, daaah-da-da went Vic's horn.

Urb-ulluh, urb-ulluh went the toilet tank.

Daaah-dah-dah, dah-dah, urb-ulluh, daah-dabbuluh, ulluh, daaa . . .

"Where the hell is that kid?" Frank exploded.

"He'll be here soon," Bud said. "Give him time."

Vic took his horn from his lips. "We can rehearse without him," he said.

"Yeah," Frank said sourly.

"We did it before he came along," Vic persisted.

"That was before we knew any better," Frank said.

"What do you mean by that?" Vic asked.

"Well, what the hell does it sound like I mean?"

"It sounds like you're saying, I don't know what it sounds like, but I know I don't like it."

"Then shove it," Frank said.

"Now, listen—"

"What the hell do you want me to do, hold your hand for you?"

"You can get off my back, that's all," Vic said. "Nobody asked you to stick your nose into this anyway."

"I only commented on your suggestion. You said we could rehearse without him, and I don't think we can."

"Why not?" Vic asked.

"Look," Tony said, trying to smile, "we'll be kicked out of here if you guys make so much—"

"Why not?" Vic asked again.

"Why not?" Frank leaned forward over his drums. "You really want to know why not, Vic? You really want to know?"

"Leave him alone, Frank," Bud said.

"No, he wants to know. He wants to know why we can't rehearse without the kid. All right, I'll tell him."

"Come on, Frank," Tony said. "Cut it out."

"What's the matter?" Frank said, his voice rising. "Can't I tell him if he wants to know? A guy asks a question, he deserves an answer."

"Let it go, Frank," Tony said. "Why do you want to start—"

"I'll tell you, Vic," Frank said sweetly. "If you really want to know, why I'll tell you, Vic." He sucked in a deep breath. "It's because you stink in spades, Vic. Not only—"

"Listen—"

"Not only," Frank shouted, gaining momentum, "can't you carry the first-trumpet sheet, I don't think you could carry a two-ounce bag of marshmallows around the block, that's what I think. Now do you know why we can't start rehearsal without the kid? Do you—"

"Frank, for Christ's sake—" Tony started.

"No, let him talk," Vic said tightly.

"I'm finished talking. I said all I've got to say. You stink. Period. You play trumpet like a man with a stomach-ache."

"You're God Almighty, I suppose," Vic said, plainly embarrassed, but still not losing his temper.

"No," Frank answered, "but at least I can play my instrument. That's more than you can do."

"I was taking trumpet lessons before you even heard of the drums," Vic said ineffectively.

"Then you didn't learn a hell of a lot. You ought to change teachers."

"Who the hell died and left you boss, anyway?" Vic asked, his voice a little louder, but the cliché still sounding weak on his lips.

"You don't have to be boss to know a lousy trumpet player when you see one."

Vic blinked his eyes for a moment, realizing he was on the losing end of the argument. He rose suddenly, yanking the mouthpiece from his horn. "Maybe you won't have to see much more of me," he said angrily.

"What? Are you threatening us?" Frank asked, smirking.

"No, I'm not threatening. I'm quitting. You can shove your band. There are plenty of other bands around."

"None that'll have you," Frank said, still riding him, enjoying his offensive advantage now.

"What the hell do you care who'll have me or not?" Vic said. He hesitated for a moment, as if he would keep the real cause of the argument hidden. But the real cause burned in his lungs and his throat, and it bubbled out of his mouth like molten lava. "You've got your little Golden Boy, haven't you? What the hell do you care about me? He's all that counts. Go kiss his ass a little. Go ahead." He whirled and lifted his trumpet case from the floor beside his chair.

"Look," Tony said, "there's no need to quit, Vic. Frank was just—"

"Don't try to kid me, boy," Vic said heatedly. "Don't shovel it at me, boy. You *all* feel the way he does. You think I'm going to hang around when you feel like that?"

"Vic, we don't—"

"The hell you don't! Listen, you think I'm cockeyed? You think I can't see what's been going on? First you give him all the hot rides, and then you give him all the sweet solos. What does that leave for me? *Harmony?* Well, look, don't worry about me. Don't worry your head about me. No, just worry about your Golden Boy, he's the one to worry about. Why don't you give him sheets for the whole damn trumpet section and let him play six trumpet parts at once? That ought to suit Frank fine. That ought to make you all happy. You should all wet your pants over that one."

"Vic, we didn't—"

"Agh, what the hell are you trying to tell me? I should have seen this right from the beginning. From the minute they made you leader."

"Now wait a minute," Tony said. "Let's not start—"

"Who started this goddamn band, anyway? You? Did you buy the first three arrangements? Did you go shagging all over Brooklyn looking for musicians? What the hell did *you* do except come in when everybody was here already? What right do you have to be leader?"

"The boys chose me," Tony said. "You know that."

"Sure, because your name is Banner. So what kind of bull is that? What's the matter with Vic Andrada on a stand? What's the matter with that name? Is it any worse than Charlie Ventura ... or Vido Musso? Or ... or ... What the hell difference does a name make?"

"The boys felt—"

"Yeah, the boys felt, the boys felt. Well, I know what the boys feel. The boys feel Andy is better than me, and so do you, so what the hell am I hanging around for? To give him harmony so he'll sound better? What fun is there in that? I can play harmony with anybody. I don't have to play it for a snotnosed kid."

"Especially when he plays rings around you," Frank said.

"Shut up, you!" Vic snarled, turning and snapping his trumpet case shut. "I don't have to take anything from you any more."

"If you're going, why the hell don't you go?" Frank said. "You're stinking up the joint."

"I'm going, all right. I'm—" He started to walk around Ox, who was sitting at the end of the sax section, and then he stopped when the door opened and Andy walked in. He looked at Andy coldly for a second and then said,

"Here's your goddamn star now. You can start your rehearsal."

"What's the matter?" Andy asked innocently, walking
over toward the piano.

"Ask your pals what's the matter," Vic shouted. "Ask
them what it's all about. Go ahead, ask them."

Andy looked at the boys, bewildered, and Frank said,
"Blowhard is quitting the band."

"Yeah?" Andy asked. "Gee, what's the matter, Vi—"

"Damn right I'm quitting," Vic yelled. "And don't look
so damn surprised, wise guy. Don't think you're kidding
me any. You can have the limelight all to yourself now.
You can play all the solos, all the parts. You can do it all
by yourself."

"What—"

"What are you kicking about?" Frank asked. "You know
Andy's better than you are."

"Sure I know it," Vic said, on the verge of wild tears
now. "So what? So what am I supposed to do? Are all the
trumpet players in the world supposed to drop dead because
Andy Silvera picks up his horn? Is that what's supposed
to happen?"

"Oh, knock it off," Bud said suddenly. "If you're going,
get the hell out." His eyes held Vic's steadily, coldly.

"You don't like to hear it, do you?" Vic said, woman-
ishly. "Why not? Does the truth hurt? So what if he's good?
So what? Answer me that—so what?"

"You don't know what you're talking about, Vic," Bud
said. "You're out of your head."

"Am I? Why don't you answer me then? If I'm so out of
my head, why can't you give me an answer? So what if he's
good? Is it worth breaking up a band over? Is it worth—"

"Nobody's breaking up any band," Bud said.

"No? I'm leaving, ain't I? Who's gonna be next? You
think you'll get a trumpet man to sit alongside him? So
he can make a fool out of him? You think you'll get a
trumpet man who'll be happy to blow background while
this bastard shines? You think you'll get one?"

"Andy never—"

"No, he never, huh? Wait until he finds out how you
guys sounded before he came along. Wait until then, and

then you'll see how much of a bargain you've got. Boy,
I'm glad I'm getting out now, while the getting's—"

"All right, so get out," Bud said menacingly, "before I
kick you out!"

"Sure," Vic said tersely, his face white. "Sure." He
picked up his case and started for the door, passing
Andy, who still stood bewildered. He stopped about three
paces beyond Andy, turned, and looked at him squarely,
contempt unveiled in his eyes as he put on his coat.

"Good luck, Golden Boy," he said, and he made it
sound like a curse. He walked to the door, fumbled angrily
with the knob, and then slammed out of the room, leaving a deep silence behind him.

Andy stared at the closed door, his back to the band.
The band sat at the nucleus of the silence, like a group
of people who'd just seen a baseball crashing through a
plate-glass window. The shopkeeper may have been concerned solely with his window, and the policeman may
have been concerned with examining the baseball, but
the psychology of the group turned toward the cause
of the broken window, the one who'd hit the ball. Andy
had hit this ball, all right. Andy had hit it the day he'd
sat in for a tryout. It had taken the ball a long time to
smash into the store front, but the window was shattered
now, and the boys turned their attention to the batter,
wondering what his reaction would be.

There was nothing on Andy Silvera's face when he
turned toward the band. His mouth was expressionless,
and his eyes were hooded. Bud tried to read those eyes, but
they weren't telling any secrets. Maybe he was proud of
the ball he'd hit, or maybe he was sorry he'd broken
the window, or maybe he just didn't give a damn one
way or the other. His face wasn't telling, and no one in
the band was asking.

The silence persisted. It was a thoughtful silence, a
silence in which every member of the band relived Vic's
recent explosion. They'd been too involved in experiencing
it while it was happening to pay any real attention to it, but
they reflected upon it now, and they came to the unan-
imous, unspoken conclusion that Vic had behaved like a
Grade-A bastard. Even if he'd had a legitimate beef, he

shouldn't have attacked it in just that way. He deserved everything he'd gotten, the stupid jerk, and it's a wonder Andy hadn't hit him in the mouth.

So went their reasoning, separately calculated in separate minds, separately following separate logical channels to reach a united, sympathetic conclusion: Andy had been wronged. They turned the full power of their collective sympathy on Andy as he walked toward the band, his face still unreadable.

"I'm sorry I'm late," he said. "I missed the bus."

"That's okay, kid," Tony said consolingly.

"About Vic. Gee, I'm sorry—"

"Good riddance," Frank said.

"Don't worry about him, kid," Mike said.

"I feel like some kind of heel," Andy completed. He turned from the band again, looking over at the closed door, over near where Reen was sitting. Reen, his eyes squinched up tight, a frown on his forehead, watched Andy's face. He kept watching him until Andy finally turned and went back to the band again.

"Forget about Vic," Tony said. "Tune up, will you? We're late as it is."

"Sure," Andy said, nodding solemnly. He began warming up, and when he went to the piano for his A, Bud said, "Look, don't let Vic bother you. He was hysterical."

Andy nodded, and Bud hit the A and kept hitting it while Andy adjusted the slide until he was in tune. He went to sit beside Frank then, at the stand Vic had deserted.

Tony made a big show of looking through the arrangements. Then he cleared his throat and offhandedly said, "All right, 'Elk's Parade.' "

first chorus iii

FEBRUARY, 1944

6

They rehearsed for close to two hours, knocking off at about nine-thirty. They didn't stop for a break all that time, and when Tony finally called a halt they all lighted up

cigarettes and just relaxed. It had been a good rehearsal.
Vic's desertion had somehow knitted them together more
solidly, as if they'd had to play better to show they really
didn't need him at all. And the sad truth was they didn't
need him at all. Andy was a trumpet section all by himself. It had been a damned fine rehearsal.

They finished their cigarettes and began packing Frank's
drums. Bud unscrewed the cow bell and cymbals and then
put the snare drum into its case and fitted the circular
piece of linoleum over the skin. He put the cymbals down
on top of the linoleum and then began dropping the spare
parts into the compartments on either side of the drum
space. Reen handed him the high-hat cymbals and then
folded the pedaled mechanism itself. Frank had already
cleared the bass drum of the foot pedal and wooden
block, and he was pulling on its cover.

"What about the kid?" Bud asked. He glanced to the
other side of the room where Andy stood, carefully cleaning his horn.

"What about him?" Frank said.

"Should we ask him to come along to the dance?"

"He's a *kid*," Frank said, outraged by the suggestion.
"What is he, fifteen?"

"You'd better hang onto that kid," Reen said. "He's the
best damn thing that ever happened to you."

"I know it," Bud said.

"I'll tell you something else," Reen said. *"He* knows it,
too."

Bud looked at Reen steadily. "What do you mean?
That business with Vic?"

"That business with Vic," Reen said. "It won't be a bad
idea at all to ask him to come with us."

"Yeah," Bud said thoughtfully. He lighted a fresh cigarette, took a few drags, and then walked over to Andy.

"Hi," he said.

Andy looked up, surprised. "Oh, hello, Bud."

"You sounded good tonight," Bud said.

"Thanks," Andy said.

But had expected more, but perhaps he hadn't delivered
his speech just right. He tried again. "You sounded real
good."

"Well, thanks." Andy said.

Bud nodded and smiled and watched Andy cleaning his trumpet until he began to feel a little foolish just standing there and smiling like an idiot. *Didn't the kid know how to keep a conversation alive?* He toyed with several fresh approaches in his mind, gave them all up, and finally said conversationally, "Say, would you like to come along to the dance at Merciful Father?"

Andy looked up briefly. "I don't know how to dance," he said.

"Oh."

He dropped his eyes again. The chamois cloth ran over the bright brass of the horn. The lights in the wall of the club reflected from the curling hairs on the backs of Andy's hands. Bud digested the information and tried to think of something further to say.

"Well, you don't know how to dance, you don't know how," he said lamely. "Hell, no crime in that."

"No," Andy said.

The silence closed in again like a mailed fist. Why was the kid so goddamn hard to talk to? Jesus, didn't he ever crack a smile?

"You feel like coming along anyway, you can do that," Bud said. "I mean, you can hang around, you know, and watch the chicks, or whatever. Lots of guys just ... uh ... hang around. If you want to come along, I mean."

Andy did not look up from his trumpet. "I'm not dressed up," he said. His response surprised Bud because Bud hadn't thought the kid was aware of clothes. But the response inspired him into continuing with his persuasion. He had a wedge now.

"Well, that's nothing," he said. "Frank'll drop you off, if you want to come, and you can throw on a sports jacket quick."

Still not looking up, Andy tucked his horn into the case. "I haven't got a sports jacket," he said, and then matter-of-factly, "My father says sports jackets are very expensive."

"Oh."

"Thanks, anyway."

"Sure." Bud paused. He had tried, and he'd lost, and he should have let it go at that. But there had been something exceedingly exasperating about the run of conversation thus far, and it rankled him. He wanted to convince

Andy now, dammit. Doggedly, he pressed on.

"How about a suit?"

"I've only got my confirmation suit."

"Oh." Bud scratched his eyebrow. "One of those blue serge things, you mean?"

"Yes. My father says that's all a boy my age needs."

"Oh."

"I'm not even wearing a tie," Andy said.

"Yeah. Yeah, I see that."

"But thanks, anyway. Maybe next time."

They lifted their eyes simultaneously, as if to end the conversation with a final direct meeting of glances. Bud started to say, "Well, sure, there's always next ti—" and then the sentence died on his lips because he was seeing Andy's face for the first time during the conversation, and embarrassment and sadness were mingled on that face. He hadn't realized until then that the kid might actually *want* to go to the dance, and that all the talk about sports jackets and suits he didn't own was probably painful to him. The realization struck home, and he felt like apologizing, but he felt that an apology would be inadequate, and he suddenly became embarrassed himself. And in his own embarrassment he wanted to ... to *help* the kid now because of something in those sad brown eyes, and because of something inside him which suddenly assumed responsibility for the kids sadness and embarrassment. He balked for a moment, unwilling to accept the responsibility. Wavering he thought, *What the hell am I about to do? Take a kid under my wing, be a mother hen, what the hell am I letting myself in for?*

No, he thought. *No, the hell with it.*

And then he heard himself saying, "If you just need a jacket and tie ... I mean, that's no problem. Hell, why that's no problem at all. I can lend you those, if you like. I mean, if you want to come along with us."

Andy's face brightened imperceptibly. Cautiously he said, "Well, that's awfully nice of you."

"I've got a jacket that's a little small for me, and you'd probably get into it. What do you say? Do you want to come?"

"If it's all right with you, I guess ..."

"Yeah, it's fine," Bud said, sighing, relieved. "Come on."

He had never been to a dance before.

He stood on the side of the large room now, in a group with the other boys, but not feeling exactly a part of them, listening to them and hearing their voices, and hearing the muted hum of conversation in the high echoing room, and hearing the music that came from the record player, and seeing the girls in their sweaters and in their dresses, seeing lip-sticked lips and pointed breasts, seeing the priest on the other side of the room standing near where they were selling beer, smelling the heated warmth of the room, and the perfumed air of the room, and the wet-tweed smell of the room, and the resined-floor smell of the room, hearing, and seeing, and smelling, and trying to record it all on his brain, trigger-fast.

"When a band plays soft, that's pianissimo," Frank said.

"Yeah?" Reen said.

"And when a band plays loud, that's fortissimo."

"So?"

"But when a band doesn't play at all, that's Petrillo," Frank said, smiling and waiting for his laugh.

"That son-of-a-bitch," Tony said. "I'm getting sick of hearing Sinatra sing with a voice background."

"*It seems*," the record player sang,

> "*to me I've heard that song bee-*
>   *fore.*
>
>   *It's from an old . . .*"

"Look at the one in the blue sweater," Frank said.

"Where?" Tony asked.

"There. With Bud. The one with the string of pearls."

Tony looked at the girl's pointed breasts. "Some string of pearls," he commented. He looked around and then said, "I see something better," and he left them and headed for a girl in a black silk dress.

> "*It's funn-ee how*
>   *a theme*
>   *ree-calls a*
>
>   *fav-or-ritt dream . . .*"

"Look what I found," Bud said, coming over. The girl with him smiled and began toying with her pearls. "Patty, like you to meet Frank, Reen, and Andy." Patty opened her eyes wide and batted her lashes. "Patty is here with some friends. I told her why doesn't she bring them over."

"I bet you'd like that," Patty said shyly, her hands casually toying with the pearls, drawing attention to the large breasts beneath them.

"We would," Reen said. "We would indeed like that."

"Where'd you pick up this character?" Patty said pleasantly.

"We won him on a chance," Frank said.

"You should have given him back."

"Go get your friends," Frank said.

"I've only got two friends," Patty said, glancing quickly at Andy.

Andy felt suddenly uncomfortable. He waited for one of the boys to say something, but they had apparently tossed the ball into his lap. Awkwardly, he said, "That's all right. I've got to get home, anyway."

"Come on," Bud said to Patty. "I'll help you get your friends."

Frank and Reen watched them walk away. "What do you think?" Reen asked.

"She's got big teeth," Frank said.

"I didn't know you lisped, boy."

"And she's bowlegged also."

"Pleasure-bent, you mean. Listen, if you're not interested, we'll get Tony. I mean, if you're going to foul us up—"

"Who said I was?"

"Let's get lost," Vaughn Monroe sang,

> *"lost in each others . . .*

Bud was coming back now, three girls in tow. "Boys," he said, "I'd like you to meet Frances and Sue. Reen, Frank, and Andy."

"Reen, that's a funny name," Frances said. She had her hair combed into the same high pompadour the other girls sported, but her hair wasn't as dark, nor were her eyes as brown.

"It's René Pierre Dumar, to be exact," Reen said. "When I was in kindergarten, there was a girl named Rena in the class. The kids assumed René was the masculine counterpart. *Voilà*. Reen."

Patty blinked. "This one is the character in the click," she said.

"Clique," Reen corrected automatically.

"Cleek, shmleek," the girl named Sue said.

"He's really all right," Frank said, smiling.

"Sure," Bud said. "He reminds me of the man."

"What man?" Frank asked, going into the routine.

"The man with the power," Bud said.

"What power?"

"The power of voodoo."

"Voodoo?"

"Voodoo."

"Who do?"

"He do what?"

"He reminds me of the man."

"What man?"

"Aren't they crazy?" Patty said.

"Come on, let's dance," Frank said, taking Sue's arm.

Andy watched all the boys move onto the floor, wondering what had become of Tony. He wondered, too, if he should leave. He wasn't very far from home, and the boys certainly wouldn't miss him.

The room was jumping now. Bodies hopped up and down, arms were hurled skyward, legs flashed, thighs showed occasionally, silk stockings threw back their sheen, bobby-socks glittered white. The floor seemed to rock with the frantic, frenetic movement of the dance. The tiled walls seemed to shake. Hair bobbed, breasts bobbed, pearls bobbed, faces bobbed, bobbed, faces turning, and smiling, and laughing, and bobbing.

"They're either too young or too old

"They're either too gray or too gras-eee

green . . ."

He stood there with the sounds and smells and sights unfolding before him, rising before him like a great cloud of strangeness, black in its depth, black with spastic bursts of color, and he felt peculiar. He felt peculiar in a strange way, alone, not the loneliness he felt when walking with his mother and father, when no one spoke, not that, but a peculiar aloneness. He felt peculiar *all* over now. He felt peculiar in the sports jacket Bud had loaned him, and he felt peculiar in the tie Bud had taken from the rack in his closet—*awfully nice of Bud; even his own father never loaned a tie to him.* And he even felt peculiar about the knot, which wasn't like the knot he usually tied—*What had Bud called it?* A Windsor knot, yes. Bud had said something about a spread collar, but he hadn't understood that too well, and the knot felt very big now, and if he cast his eyes downward just a little bit, not even enough so that anyone could see him looking, he could see the knot standing out like a big wart on his throat—*Windsor knot. Had the Duke of Windsor invented it?*

He tried to understand why he was feeling so peculiar because he knew he couldn't blame it all on the jacket and tie, but he couldn't find an answer. It was just that everything was so strange, not like his mother's and father's solemn grownup world at all, and not like his own quietly regular world, either. It was a sort of in-between thing where kids talked like grownups and acted like grownups and drank beer like grownups, but who didn't seem like grownups while they were doing all these things. Now that was very peculiar, something like seeing a midget smoking a cigar and thinking, *Gee, look at the little kid smoking a cigar,* only he's not a little kid, he's a man. This was just like that, except in reverse, because these weren't grownups doing the grownup things. They were kids. Well, that wasn't quite true either because they weren't exactly kids. Oh, nuts, he felt peculiar.

"He may be a good dancer," a girl somewhere on Andy's right said, "but he dances too close."

"That's why he's a good dancer," her girlfriend answered.

"Well, I'm just not that kind of a girl."

"So the wife goes to the closet," a boy said to a group of three girls standing close to Andy, "and the husband is sitting in the living room, and he hears the paper on the package making a rustling sound, you know?"

"I heard this joke," one of the girls said.

"Did you all hear it?" the boy asked.

"No, go ahead, tell it."

"Well, I don't like the one I got," a boy in a brown suit said.

"What's wrong with her?" his friend asked. "Tell me that."

"She's a dog."

"So what? So I never done you a favor? Listen, I really like this girl, I mean it."

"You say that every week."

"This week I mean it."

From the corner of his eye, Andy saw the priest approaching, and for a panicky moment he thought the priest was coming toward him. The panic outlived the moment when he saw the priest actually was heading his way. He tried to shrug closer to the wall, tried to become a part of the coats hanging there, but the priest wasn't being fooled. He walked swiftly and purposefully, his black robe swirling about his black trousered legs.

Bless me, Father, for I have sinned ...

"Hello there," the priest said. "I'm Father Dominick."

"Hello, Father Dominick," Andy said cautiously, softly. He had never spoken to a priest before, not close up like this. He had listened to priests delivering the Mass on Sundays, and he had talked to Father Ignatius in his own parish, but then only through the screened opening of the confession box, where he could hardly even see the priest's face. He felt strange talking to this priest, and he told himself it was all part of the peculiarity he was feeling, but that didn't stop him from feeling strange. The priest was a short man with a wide round face and a long nose. He had thick black eyebrows that matched the hair curling close to his scalp. His eyes were small and brown, the eyes of a ferret. He was not a good-looking man at all, not the handsome kind of priest who warrants a bewildered headshake and a wondrous "Why would *he* become a priest?"

"I've been watching you," Father Dominick said.

"H ... have you?" Andy asked.

"You haven't been dancing," the priest said, smiling benignly.

"No, I haven't," Andy said.

"I haven't seen you around before," Father Dominick said. "I was wondering if you liked our little gathering."

"Oh, yes," Andy said. "It's fine. Fine."

"We get a nice crowd here," Father Dominick said, nodding his head. He was obviously trying to put Andy at ease, and Andy appreciated his efforts, but he still wished the priest would leave him alone instead of contributing to his feeling of peculiarity, God forgive him.

"Yes, it seems like a ... nice crowd," he said, wondering if Father Dominick had seen the three girls Bud had picked up.

"A very nice crowd. Don't you like to dance?"

"I don't know how," Andy said wearily.

"*Don't* you?" said Father Dominick. "Well now. Well now."

"No, I don't," Andy said, feeling suddenly stubborn.

"Well, that's no problem at all, Father Dominick said. "You just come along with me, son." He took Andy's elbow. "What did you say your name was?"

"Andy."

"Andrew, ah yes, a good name. Andrew. One of the Twelve Apostles."

"Father, I—"

Father Dominick's grip tightened on Andy's elbow. "Now, just come along," he said kindly, beginning to walk, steering Andy along the wall. "There's no need for anyone not to know how to dance," the priest went on. "Not when we have so many nice girls here. And a nice boy like you should know how to dance, don't you think?"

"Yes," Andy said, "but . . ."

The priest's pressure on his elbow was very strong, like the steel jaws of a trap. *A trap,* he thought, *a trap,* and the thought strengthened his original panic. He wanted to pull away from the priest's grip, but he was afraid of offending God, so he allowed himself to be led, thinking, *A trap, a trap,* all the while.

The priest led him skillfully around the edge of the dance floor, nodding to the boys and girls seated or standing near the wall. They walked together, the priest's fingers firm on his elbow. *I shall walk in the shadow of the valley of death . . .*

"Ah now," Father Dominick said. "Ah now, here we are." They stopped walking suddenly, but the priest did not release his arm. "Hello, Rose," Father Dominick said. "How are you tonight?"

"Hello, Father," the girl answered. "Fine." Andy did not look up. The desire to run leaped into his throat, but the priest kept holding his elbow. The priest swung him around now, and he was face to face with the girl, a thin girl in a cotton dress, a thin girl with no breasts, no string of pearls, a boy-girl, not at all like the girl Bud had. The girl was smiling shyly, anticipation on her narrow face and in the forward lean of her body.

"Rose," said Father Dominick, "I'd like you to meet a very nice young man named Andrew. Andy, this is Rose."

"How do you do?" Rose said.

"How do you do?" Andy answered stiffly.

"Seems as if Andy doesn't know how to dance, Rose. Now I told him that was certainly no problem, and I'm sure you'll agree it isn't. Am I right, Rose?"

"Oh, that's no problem," Rose assured Father Dominick.

"I didn't think it was," Father Dominick said, smiling roguishly. "Now don't you think it would be a good idea for you to teach Andy a few of the elementary steps? He's a bright young man, Andy is, and I'm sure he'll learn quickly. What do you say, Rose?"

"I'd love to, Father," Rose said.

"Good, good." The priest released his elbow. "She'll teach you, Andy," he said. "She's a very fine dancer, Rose is."

"Thank you, Father," Andy mumbled.

"Come on now," Father Dominick said jokingly, "don't be bashful. She's not going to bite you, are you, Rose?"

Rose giggled, and Father Dominick backed off a few paces, leaning against the wall, smiling, his arms crossed over his chest. A new record dropped to the turntable, a slow, moody fox trot.

"Haven't you ever danced before, Andy?" Rose asked.

"No," he said viciously, taking his anger out on her, having been unwilling to vent any spleen on a representative of God.

Rose remained happily unaware, like an idiot child with a toy balloon. "It's really very easy," she said, smiling.

She has bad teeth, Andy thought. *She's not at all like the girl Bud has.* He swiveled his head over his shoulder suddenly, desperately wishing that Bud were not being a witness to all this. God, if Bud saw—

"Just put your arm around my waist," Rose said.

"Look, Rose, couldn't—"

"Oh, come on now," she said, playfully. "You heard Father Dominick. I'm not going to bite you."

"Rose—"

"Oh, come on, Andy. It's really very easy. I mean it."

He looked over his shoulder again, not seeing Bud, thankful for that at least. Rose reached out and took his wrist, and he felt her bony fingers close on his flesh. He heard someone giggle, and he whirled abruptly, sure the giggle had been directed at him.

"This way," Rose said, pulling his arm around her. "That's it, just put your arm around me. There, now was that hard?"

"No," he said, the word choking in his throat, so embarrassed he wanted to cry. He could hear separate gusts of laughter all around him now. He felt his cheeks flame into color, and he would have turned and bolted, pulled away from this trap and run for all he was worth if he hadn't seen Father Dominick leaning against the wall a few feet away, smiling and nodding his head.

"Now just listen to the music," Rose said, "and you'll get the rhythm. This is called a fox trot."

"I know," he said.

"Oh, do you? Well, that's good. Fine. A fox trot has four beats. Do you know what a beat is?"

"Yes, I know what a beat is," he said tightly. His collar felt rough and stiff. He could feel the too-large Windsor knot on his throat, choking the breath out of him.

"You go forward with your right foot, then forward with your left foot, then over with your right foot, then close with your left foot. One, two, three, four. Just like that. Four beats."

"Rose," he pleaded desperately, "can't we just—"

"Come on, try it. Forward, one, forward, two, over— no, no, that's wrong, try it again. You're doing fine, Andy, really."

They're laughing at me, he thought. *They're laughing at me.*

His ears plucked laughter from the room. Dilligently they plucked laughter, dropped laughter into a quaking hilarious subconscious self-conscious basket.

Ha ha ha ha ha ha

"All right, now let's try it again."

Ho ho ho ho ho ho ho

"That's the way. Now you're getting it."

Hee hee hee hee hee hee hee hee

HaHaHa HoHoHoHo HeeHeeHeeHeeHeeHeeHee

"Forward, one, forward, two, that's it, three, and cross, four. Forward, one, forwaHaHa, two, ovOHoHO, three HeeHee . . ."

"Rose, please, please . . ."

"Cross, foHoHohohohohohohohohoho . . ."

The laughter crowded in on his flaming face, thundered at his ears, gripped his throat. He felt all the eyes on him, eyes, eyes everywhere, all watching him and laughing, laughing.

"Mind if I cut in?" the voice asked.

He thought he dreamed the voice, and then he felt a strong hand on his shoulder, and the pressure of the hand increased, forcing him back and away from Rose. He looked up at the face.

"Can't keep all the good-looking ones to yourself," Bud said. He winked at Andy and then smoothly led the astonished girl onto the floor.

Andy stared after them, shame and relief mingled within him. He ran to the side of the room, shouldering his way through the dancing crowd, running, running past Father Dominick with his small surprised eyes and unsmiling mouth, running past the tiled walls, running to the other end of the room, snatching his coat from the rack, running past the hawk-faced boy at the ticket table, and then outside into the corridor, and to the windowed doors fogged with steam, and then pushing the doors open and running up the long ramp to Brooklyn Avenue, and through the gate in the cyclone fence, pulling on his coat at the same time, reaching the sidewalk and still running, hearing the laughter behind him, and thinking of Bud, and knowing that Bud was the only one who had not laughed, the only one, the one who had saved him.

He ran all the way to Eastern Parkway, and then he stopped running, and the neon glitter of the shops was a kaleidoscopic blur because there were tears in his eyes.

7

The boys were in a joviál "full-name" mood that afternoon. It was bitter cold outside, and they could hear the February gusts rattling the windowpanes, moaning under the eaves of Frank's house. They had never enjoyed inclement weather on Saturdays, and they insulated themselves from the cold by wrapping themselves in a warm cocoon of banter. The radio was tuned to WNEW, and they listened to the music that came from the speaker, but even the music could not drown out the sound of the angry wind.

"It's your play, René Pierre," Bud said.

"Thank you, Charles Robert," Reen said. "I know it."

The two boys were seated at a small wooden table near one of the windows in the finished basement. The wind seeped through the gap where sash met window, but the heat from the coal furnace in the adjoining segment of basement compensated for the cold blast. The radio rested on a shelf of the cupboard against the opposite wall of the room. Frank stood before the cupboard, his drumsticks in his hands, beating on a rubber practice pad in time to the radio music.

"Are you holding all the queens?" Reen asked.

"No, sir," Bud said.

"Well, someone's holding them."

"It must be Francis Joseph," Bud said.

"Quiet," Frank said. "I'm trying to hear the music."

"You make a lot of noise with that pad, Francis," Bud said. "Don't they sell noiseless pads?"

"No," Frank said, beating harder. "They don't sell noiseless pads."

"There's a fat deuce for you, Charles," Reen said.

"Thanks," Bud said sourly. He ignored the discarded deuce and took a card from the pack. "Here's one for you," he said, covering the first deuce with the one he'd drawn.

"There must be six deuces in this deck," Reen said.

"Do you want to hear a paradiddle?" Frank asked.

"What the hell's a paradiddle?" Bud asked.

"Some kind of bird," Reen said.

"It's a drum . . ."

"I heard it already," Bud said.

"You heard a ruff. This is a paradiddle. They're entirely different."

"All right, Francis," Reen said, "let's hear your paradiddle."

Frank turned down the volume on the radio. "Listen," he said. He began beating his sticks on the pad, chanting as he played. "Pa-ra-did-dle, par-ra-did-dle, pa-ra-did-dle." His chant began speeding up, and his stick beats followed the increased tempo. He stopped abruptly and then turned up the radio again.

"It sounded like a roll," Reen said.

"You can use it in a roll," Frank said.

"I prefer ham on roll," Bud said.

"Yok," Frank said.

Reen fished another card from the pack. He studied it and then discarded it. "Tell me, Charles," he said, "what did you think of last night?"

"You want to hear a double paradiddle?" Frank asked.

"I asked Charles a question, Francis," Reen said.

"Last night was a beaut," Bud said emphatically.

"It's different from a single paradiddle," Frank said.

"A beaut, indeed," Reen said.

"I think we can thank our friend Francis Joseph for that."

"Thank you, Francis Joseph."

"What the hell did I do?" Frank asked.

"Nothing."

"Nothing at all," Reen said. "You only fouled up the works."

"Well next time you can drive," Frank said righteously.

"I don't know how to drive," Reen said.

"Then don't look a gift hearse in the mouth."

"Francis is in a fine fettle," Reen said. "Did you catch that last pun, Charles?"

"Oh, I caught it," Bud said. "It resembled a hearse last night, too."

"No," Reen said. "Only the driver was dead."

"The girl with the driver was dead, too," Frank said angrily.

"Play your paradiddles, boy," Reen said.

"You'd have done the same thing if you were driving," Frank continued.

"I doubt it."

"What was I supposed to do, making conversation all night? And I thought you were supposed to chip in for gas? What happened to that idea?"

"Your play," Bud said.

"That's right, change the subject."

"How much did you put in?" Reen asked. "A lousy two gallons?" He drew and discarded. "Are you sure you're not holding the queens?"

"I put in five gallons," Frank said. "And it was black market, so it cost more."

"You shouldn't buy black-market gas, Francis."

"No? Why not?"

"It's unpatriotic."

"Bull. You heard what Four Eyes said when he was in on leave."

"What did Four Eyes say?"

"He said they use five-gallon drums of gas to start fires with when they're on maneuvers. If they can't use ordinary matches, then I'll get all the gas I want without coupons."

"Would you deprive our boys of a little heat?"

"No, but why should they deprive me of a little gas?"

"He's changing the subject, René," Bud said. "Gin."

"Gin?" Reen watched Bud as he laid down his hand. "You were saving queens, you bastard."

"Your deal," Bud said. "That's another dime you owe me." He marked the debt on a sheet of paper. Reen gathered up the cards and began shuffling.

"Who tacked the horseshoe on your behind?" he wanted to know.

"I was born with it," Bud said.

"It's chilly in here," Reen said. "Francis, how about shoveling a little coal on the fire?"

"You crippled or something?"

"I'm not up on the latest furnace designs," Reen said.

"Get up on this a while," Frank answered.

"He's got a filthy mind, you know, Charles?"

"The filthiest," Bud said.

"You'd think he'd be a little penitent after last night." Reen shook his head forlornly. "Some people just have no conscience at all."

"You got in your licks," Frank said. "What the hell are you kicking about?"

"Oh, it was a big night, all right," Reen said grandly. "I was home and asleep by twelve-thirty."

"We don't get to town often," Bud said, "but when we do, row-dee-dow!"

"Next time you can do without the car," Frank said. "I don't have to be a chauffeur. You guys think—"

"Did you know Tony was sore last night, Francis?"

"Anthony, you mean," Bud corrected.

"Anthony, of course. Did you know that?"

"What's that got to do with the price of fish? He wasn't sore at me."

"He was sore at *all* of us for taking off without him. But you hit him for a buck before we left, didn't you?"

"So what?"

"That's adding insult to injury," Reen said.

"Do you get anything extra for gin without picking up a card?" Bud asked.

"You're kidding," Reen said, appalled.

"I'm kidding," Bud confirmed.

"Next time just leave me out of it," Frank said. "Just pick up whoever you like, and do whatever you like, and forget all about me. *And* the car."

"He's holding the car over our heads, Charles."

"So long as he doesn't drop it," Bud said.

"Why don't you admit you were a bastard, Francis?"

"I was no more bastardish than usual," Frank said, and then—realizing what he'd admitted—he began laughing. The laughter cleared the air, and Frank was thankful he'd been left off the hook. There was always one goat whenever the boys gathered, and he didn't relish the idea of being the goat on a cold Saturday afternoon.

"Listen to that wind," Reen said.

They listened in silence for a moment, the wind magnifying the cold outside. Through the basement window they could see a man struggling to keep on his hat, the skirts of

his coat flapping wildly around his knees. The radio
pierced the silence with "I Had the Craziest Dream."

"It's gonna be a cold winter, McGee," Bud said.

"Did I ever tell you about the winter of eighty-eight?"
Reen asked.

"I was born in that year," Bud offered.

"Then you remember the snow."

"Up to our eyeballs in snow that winter," Bud said.

"Even the horses went berserk."

"You can't blame them."

"Hell, no. 'Twasn't a fit winter for man *nor* beast."

"Speaking of beasts," Frank said, hazardously reopening
the subject, "you've got to admit that Sue wasn't exactly
a prize package."

"She was born in the winter of eighty-eight, too," Bud
said. "You can't blame her."

"She kept telling me about the time she went to the
Astor Roof. Now who the hell cares about the time she
went to the Astor Roof?"

"Woody Herman is on the Astor Roof, isn't he?"

"He'd better come inside," Reen said. "He'll get blown
off with all this wind."

"What a dizzy chick, I swear," Frank said, shaking his
head. "I wanted to tell her just what she could do with
the Astor Roof."

"She couldn't," Bud said. "Not in a million years."

"Real dizzy," Frank said, appreciating the boy's sympathy.

When the knock sounded on the back door, Bud looked
up, turning his attention from the cards.

"Somebody at the door," he said.

"That's the wind," Frank said.

"The knocking came again, unmistakable this time.

"Mighty talented wind," Bud said.

Frank put down his sticks. "I'll get it," he said, even
though neither of the other boys had made a move to
rise. He walked past the card table and then through the
door into the room with the furnace, glancing briefly at the
big metal monster and then moving past the coalbin to the
door.

"I'll take this game," Reen said, discarding.

"We'll see."

They heard the door opening and then the sullen rush of the wind. The debt sheet on the table flapped wildly as Bud clutched for it, pinning it to the table. They heard Frank say something which the wind carried away.

"That's the FBI," Reen said. "My draft board sent 'em."

"I'll mail you cigarettes," Bud said.

The sound of the door closing reached them. Bud released his grip on the debt sheet, and then Frank's voice said, "Come on in. We were just hanging around."

Bud turned, interested, as Frank entered the room again. Andy Silvera was behind him.

"Look who's here," Frank said. His back was to Andy, and he raised his eyebrows in a shrug that only Reen and Bud could see.

"I came to—"

"Hello, Andrew," Reen said. "Pull up a Ouija board. The séance starts in ten minutes."

Andy smiled weakly, wetting his lips, his tongue touching the tiny white ring of muscle and then retreating quickly into his mouth. "I came to return your jacket and tie, Bud," he said. It sounded weak and thin coming from his mouth. "I . . . I didn't get a chance to return it last night, I . . ." He let the sentence trail. He had mulled over the excuse all morning, and now that he was delivering it he was sure they could see clear through it, sure they would understand his motivation. He shouldn't have tried to outsmart them. He should have known better than that. "I went to your house first," he said, "and your mother told me you were here." *Then why didn't you just leave the stuff with my mother?* he thought he could read in Bud's eyes. "I . . . well . . ." He smiled weakly, feeling utterly miserable, knowing he shouldn't have tried to crash in this way. "Well, here it is!" he blurted.

"Oh," Bud said, rising from the table. "Thanks."

Andy held out the sports jacket, holding his flimsy excuse gingerly. Bud lifted it from his hands and tossed it onto one of the chairs, as if recognizing the flimsiness of the excuse and treating it as summarily as it warranted.

"The tie is in the pocket," Andy said. "The right-hand pocket."

Bud nodded. "Where'd you disappear to last night?" he

asked. "Take off your coat, why don't you?"

He'd been afraid they wouldn't ask him to stay, and his relief must have shown on his face. Casually he said, "All right," and then he hastily shrugged out of his coat, hoping they wouldn't change their minds before he'd finished. The boys regarded him silently. He felt the silence of the room, and something told him he should try to break it.

"It's very cold outside," he said. He looked around for someplace to put his coat.

"There's a rack in the corner," Frank said.

Andy walked to the rack and hung the coat on a peg. He turned and began rubbing his hands together, feeling like a discovered stowaway. "Very cold," he said.

"Where'd you disappear to last night?" Bud repeated, sitting and picking up his cards.

"Well, I went home," Andy said.

Bud raised his eyes. "I guess it's not much fun if you can't dance," he said softly.

"No. No, it isn't. I . . . I went home."

"We went home, too," Reen said sourly. Frank glanced at him hastily, expecting more, glad when more did not come.

"How'd you like the dance otherwise?" Frank said.

"It was all right."

The boys were silent for a moment. Reen and Bud played seriously. Frank leaned against the cupboard, staring out the window across the room. Andy shifted his weight uneasily.

"Listen to that wind," Frank said.

"It's very cold outside," Andy said, feeling foolish as soon as he'd said it. Of course they knew it was cold outside.

"This begins to sound like the Weather Bureau," Reen said, making Andy feel even more foolish. He picked a card from the discard pile. "Suppose I knock with four, Bud?"

"Try it and see," Bud said.

"Is that gin rummy?" Andy asked, again feeling foolish, wondering why he'd come here in the first place, wondering whatever gave him the idea he could fit, wondering if anyone would ever welcome him anywhere.

"It ain't bridge," Reen said. "You want to play?"

"No. Oh, no, I just wondered."

"We're playing for very high stakes, anyway," Bud said.

"How much do I owe you now, Gaylord?"

"Fifty thousand," Bud said.

Of course they're kidding, Andy thought. *Are they kidding?*

"Merciful Father isn't much," Frank said. "We run down to the Dance Palace every now and then. They've got a good setup there."

"Yeah," Bud said. "A live band. And an older crowd."

"I prefer records," Reen said. "Give me canned Barnet to these half-assed local outfits any day."

"Watch your language," Bud said. "We're a half-assed local outfit."

"You don't count," Reen said. "How about knocking with three?"

"Go ahead."

"You're probably sitting there with two."

"Go ahead," Bud taunted. "Knock."

"No thanks."

"If you'd known how to dance," Bud said carefully, "you'd probably have had a better time."

"Yes, I guess so," Andy said. It wasn't going too badly now. If he just shut up and listened, everything was all right. It was when he opened his mouth that things began getting hard.

"You didn't dance at all, huh?" Reen asked.

"No," Andy lied, wanting to forget Rose completely, and then looking toward Bud, hoping he would not be contradicted. Bud said nothing, letting the lie pass, and Andy felt a sudden exultance from knowing he had an ally in the room.

"Yeah, well that's why you didn't care for it," Reen said. "It's really not so bad. It's not the Dance Palace, but it's not so bad."

"Oh, it wasn't bad at all," Andy said agreeably, not wanting them to get the wrong idea. He had, after all, been their guest—sort of.

"You want to take my hand, Frank?" Bud asked suddenly.

"Whose money?" Frank asked.

"Play with mine. I'm ahead, anyway."

Frank shrugged. "Why?"

"I'm gonna teach Andy to dance," Bud said matter-of-factly. "You want to learn, Andy?"

Andy felt his heart quicken. He *did* want to learn. More than anything else in the world, he wanted to learn. But the suddenness of the suggestion took him completely by surprise. Not in his wildest imaginings had he figured they'd offer to—

"Of course he wants to learn," Reen said. He leaned back in his chair. "This is the best dancer in Brooklyn, Andrew."

"Sure," Bud said deprecatingly.

"Go on, teach him," Reen said.

"What do you say?" Bud asked.

Andy touched the ring of muscle with his tongue. "Well, I . . . I don't know," he said. He tried a smile that froze horribly on his face. "Do you . . . you want to teach?"

"He taught Gene Kelly how," Reen said.

"Oh, sure," Bud answered.

"You taught Alonsobrigazzo," Frank said, unwilling to accept Bud's self-belittlement. "Go on, Bud, teach him. I'll take your hand."

"Okay?" Bud asked. He raised his eyebrows questioningly and then stood up, putting his cards face down. Frank took his chair quickly.

"All right," Andy said, hoping he hadn't said it too eagerly. Their casual complacency amazed him—as if learning to dance were a common occurrence, a thing they did every day of the week. Oh, this was going wonderfully, this was marvelous!

"Show him the fox trot," Reen said, discarding. "That's easiest."

Frank picked up the card. "Once he's got the fox trot, he can handle anything," he said. "Gin."

"What?" Reen said.

"Gin," Frank repeated, laying down the cards.

"Son-of-a-bitch! I should have knocked."

"You should have. I just won you a dime, Bud."

"You deal," Reen said sourly. "It must be that goddamn seat. You want to change seats, Frank?"

"No changing seats," Bud said. He turned to Andy. "Do you know anything at all about the fox trot?"

"A little."

"What do you know?" He went to the radio and fiddled. with the dial until he got a slow tune.

"Right, left, over, cross," Andy said, trying to be off-handed. "Right, left . . ."

"Bull," Bud said. "Come on, I'll show you." He stepped up to Andy, completely unself-consciously, listening to the music. "I'm the girl," he said.

Andy expected one of the boys to whistle or wolfcall. He was surprised when they didn't. He realized then that they took their dancing seriously, and that they'd probably played the girl's part often in learning new steps. His respect for them increased immeasurably. He gave Bud his undivided attention, not wanting to miss a word he said.

"Your right hand in the small of my back," Bud said. "Your left hand out here, holding mine."

"All right," Andy said nervously.

"Now listen to the music. That shouldn't give you any trouble at all."

"Not the way you blow that horn," Reen said in admiration.

"Now," Bud said, "instead of starting from a dead stop with both feet glued to the floor, you do this. The minute the girl is in your arms, you dip. That means you pull the girl toward you while you move your right foot back. Try it."

Andy tried it, his feet tangling up miserably. "I . . . I'm sorry. I didn't—"

"You're worrying too much about your goddamn feet," Bud said. "Forget you got feet. Look, just move your right foot back, that's all. And a little pressure on the small of my back. Remember that the chick doesn't know what the hell you're going to do unless you tell her. You can't tell her with your mouth. You can't say, 'Honey, I'm going to dip now,' so you tell her with your hand. You just increase the pressure a little, toward you, and at the same time you move your right foot back, and if the chick isn't a Mongolian idiot, she does the natural thing —she moves forward. Now try it again. Just move your right foot back, arch your body a little, and remember the pressure. That's it, that's it. All right, let's try it again."

Andy nodded, remembering his ordeal with Rose, thinking how different this was, feeling he was really learning something, the happiness inside him ready to burst out the the top of his skull.

"This accomplishes two things at the same time," Bud said, as they went through the step again and again. "First, it leaves your left foot in the starting position automatically. You don't feel like a wooden Indian when you get on the floor. And, second, you know just where you stand with the chick, right from go. You start with a dip, and if she gives you her headlights—"

"What the hell are you teaching the kid?" Reen asked, looking up from his cards.

"Only what he has to know," Bud said professorially.

"You'd better pay some attention here," Frank said, "or I'll run away with this one, too."

"In other words," Bud said to Andy, "you both know the score right from that first dip. Now you're still in the dip, with your right foot back, you see? All right, you just slide your left foot forward a little, just a very little because its forward already, you see? That's the first beat. That's it, that's the way. And for the second beat, you slide your right foot forward, as if you're walking, just as if you're walking, except your feet are flat on the floor, and you're sliding them. Come on, do it, that's the only way to learn."

Andy nodded, unable to keep the smile off his face. He looked at his feet while Bud moved back, actually leading him while playing the follower's role.

"What are you doing?" Bud asked.

"Huh?"

"Don't look at your feet."

"I was just—"

"Don't look at them. And don't count in your head. You're going to have to talk with the chick while you're dancing, and you can't talk and count at the same time."

"I wasn't counting," Andy said innocently.

"Good. Don't start now. Now look, never mind this baloney about going to the side with your left foot and then closing with your right. That's strictly for the birds. You just keep going straight forward. You got that—in a straight line? Just as if you're walking, except you happen to have a girl in your arms."

"Dancing is just walking set to music," Frank said.

"It is," Bud said, ready to take offense.

"Dancing is vertical petting," Reen corrected.

"The hell with you," Bud said. "Look, Andy, a straight line, remember. Your right foot forward is the second beat. You take a full left step for the third beat, and then you just bring your right foot up parallel to your left foot for the fourth beat, closing off the figure. That's it, pal. You're back where you started from. The rest is all repetition—like a second chorus."

"Gin, you bastards!" Reen bellowed.

Frank looked at the cards he put down. "You still owe Bud half a buck," he said calmly.

"I'll cut you for the half, Bud," Reen said. "Double or nothing."

Bud released Andy. "All right," he said, walking over. He tapped Frank on the shoulder. "Take over the dance lesson, Francis." He turned to Reen. "High card wins."

"You ever hear of low card winning?"

"Yes, I have. And with you, I want to make sure beforehand."

"Come on, Andy," Frank said, rising. "You're about to learn from a master." He went to Andy, and together they worked their way up the length of the small room, Andy looking conscientiously ahead, not daring to look down at his feet, not daring to count.

"Cut," Reen said.

"Ladies first," Bud answered.

Reen cut the deck, and Bud began laughing.

"A son-of-a-bitchin' four!" Reen shouted. "Jesus, have you got this deck trained or something?"

Bud cut a king, and Reen swore again, shaking his head violently. On their left, Frank and Andy kept moving across the room.

"That makes a buck even," Bud said.

"I can add," Reen answered.

"When?" Bud asked pointedly.

"Listen to this bastard, will you? He wins a few hands and right away he's J.P. Morgan."

"When?" Bud repeated.

"Wednesday. How's that?"

"That's fine, if it's Wednesday. Not Thursday or Friday or—"

"You want to chain my mother in the cellar for security?"

"No, but I'll take your sister," Bud said, grinning lewdly.

"Seconds," Frank chimed over his shoulders.

Reen ignored them. He knew he possessed an older, pretty sister, and he didn't relish a discussion of her obvious assets.

"Did you teach him to turn yet?" Bud asked Frank.

"No."

"Show him how, Reen," Bud said casually. "You're a whiz at turns."

"First he takes all my money, then he turns me into a dance instructor," Reen complained.

"Go ahead," Bud said lightly.

"He's about got this down pat," Frank said. Reen shrugged and walked over to the pair. "Never dance with a girl taller than you are," he said to Andy. "You know what happens, don't you?"

"No," Andy said, smiling, feeling very much a part of the boys even though he knew he was not as yet a part of them.

"You get a bust in the mouth," Reen said.

"That one has a beard," Frank said.

The criticism left Reen unfazed. He looked down at Andy and said, "Come, Little One. Let's see what you know so far."

A rumba came from the radio speaker, and Frank thoughtfully crossed the room and tuned in another station. Andy exhibited his newly found skill to Reen, and Reen nodded appreciatively.

"Why do we always get lousy weather on Saturdays?" Bud asked.

"It's a conspiracy," Frank said.

"You got a date tonight?"

"No."

"You feel like bowling?"

"I don't know. Maybe."

Bud put his foot up on the window sill and stared through

the pane of glass. Behind him, Reen was showing Andy how to reverse his direction on the dance floor, explaining he had to know this or else he'd crash right into the wall.

"That tree's gonna snap right in two," Bud said.

Frank walked to the window and looked out. "It'll hold," he said. He squinted and leaned forward, suddenly attentive. "Hey, who's that with her skirts blowing up?"

"She's married," Bud said disinterestedly.

Frank continued watching the girl. "Give me a young mother any day of the week," he said.

"Give you anything any day of the week," Bud corrected. He turned and added, "Don't ever get like this guy, Andy. He lives for it."

Andy smiled briefly, absorbed in Reen's lesson.

"I got a letter from Freddie today," Frank said when the girl had passed out of his line of vision.

"Yeah? What'd he have to say?"

"The usual junk. He writes like a Chink, you know?"

"They still working his butt off?"

"Oh, sure. I don't think he likes the army very much."

"Who does?" Reen said from the other side of the room.

"You'll like it," Bud said. "You've got the makings of a good army man, Reen."

"Up yours," Reen said. "You want to try that again, Andy?"

"Why'd Tony call off the rehearsal today?" Bud asked suddenly.

"Who knows?" Frank said. "You know that crazy bastard."

"I'll bet it's 'cause he was sore last night."

"Naw," Frank said, secretly and guiltily believing that to be the reason.

"I'll bet all the tea in China."

"This would've been a good day for rehearsal, too."

"Yeah," Bud said. He watched Andy silently for several moments.

Then he said, "You're gonna be a good dancer. You've got good rhythm. Next time you come along with us you'll know what to do, believe me."

Next time you come along with us.

Andy digested Bud's sentence, and a smile formed on his mouth. He felt quite guilty, but guilty in a sneaking, proud way, like an OSS man who had sneaked into Berchtesgaden. And then, suddenly, he realized he hadn't done any of the sneaking at all. It was Bud who'd suggested the dance lesson, Bud who'd subtly and skillfully led the other boys into participating, deftly led them in the first tentative steps toward the acceptance of a newcomer.

Next time you come along with us.

"Liss-en to that goddamn wind," Frank said, staring through the window.

Part 2

8

It was morning somehow.

Somehow it was morning, and somehow Bud's thoughts had found voice, and they had talked the night away, and now the traffic sounds of a new day beginning were crowding the open windows, and the sunlight streamed through and patched the wooden floor with long golden rectangles.

"Morning already," Bud said.

"It's amazing the way time goes," Andy said. "You sleep and then you get up, and then you sleep again, and your whole life is being rushed away." He paused and shook his head. "I have measured out my life with coffee spoons—do you know that one? Carol is a bug for poetry, you know. Before our show closed she used to read a lot of poetry to me aloud. Only with me it's tablespoons, not coffee spoons like the poem says. Tablespoons piled high with heroin. You cook it in a spoon, Bud, the hoss. I have measured out my life with tablespoons." He was silent for a moment, the self-pity that had crowded his voice now spreading to his eyes and his mouth. "You know, this may sound crazy, but sometimes I feel the drug part of my life never really happened. It's almost as if I crawled into somebody else's skin, and that guy happened to be a junkie. Does that sound crazy?"

"No," Bud said.

"Well, I know it does," Andy said, "but that's the way I feel." He shrugged. "It's real peculiar, too. Like . . . like I keep remembering things from when we were kids, as if that were the only really important part of my life, as if this other part never happened at all. It's probably my unconscious at work—a guilt complex or something."

"Maybe," Bud said.

"Sure, I guess that's it. Or maybe my memory is just crazy. But . . . well, like I wonder about it sometimes, about the way you get on channels, like me with heroin. Do you believe in fate, Bud?"

"No," he said.

"I think I do, sometimes. You know, what makes some-body go down a certain path? We all start the same way, don't we? So what's the answer? For example, Bud, I gave you marijuana once. Once, was it? Twice, that's right. You had it twice, and look at you now. You're not an addict, are you? So why am I an addict? I had marijuana, and you had marijuana—I hate that word, don't you? It makes you think of something lurid, a goddamn Oriental den or some-thing, with everybody laying around in a cloud of smoke, and naked girls with those sheer pantaloons on, doesn't it? Hell, you can bust a joint right on the street now without the cops tipping, I mean you don't need a smoke-filled den or anything like that, that's for the comic books. Why, the first time I gave you a joint, it was right on the street, wasn't it? Sure, near the church. Oh, no, you don't need a shooting gallery for a stick of M. Was that after you got out of the service? It's hard to remember time exactly. Sometimes I think time is in one big conspiracy against me."

"It was after I got out," Bud said.

"Sure. You didn't want the stuff, I remember, but I forced it on you. That's an occupational disease, you know, with addicts I mean. Christ knows how many times I tried to get Helen on the stuff before she tumbled. A stick of M, and then a sniff of C, and then on to the White God. You see? That's what I mean. Helen tumbled, but you didn't. Hey, remember when I used to buy those Benzedrine inhal-ers and crack them open and then swallow the Benzedrine-soaked paper? That was after you got out of the service too. No, no, it was while you were gone. What the hell made me do that? Kicks? Hell, it wasn't so great. Oh, it hopped me up and gave me the jumps, but it wasn't a grand kick, not like the big stuff is. So what made me do that? And even after all the guys kept saying it was poison. You know, you can't get a Benzedrine inhaler any more. They got this substitute called Benzedrex. Benzedrex, methadone—nothing's like the real stuff." He shrugged again. "But that's what I mean. I was swallowing Benze-drine-soaked paper, and you were—"

"Everybody takes bennies now and then," Bud said. "I

know lots of kids at school who take it to keep awake when they're studying for exams."

He remembered Milton abruptly. Milton shoved itself into his mind and he sighed involuntarily. He had not studied, and he had not slept either. And the test was tomorrow morning. Tomorrow morning at nine.

"Sure, sure, but they've got reasons. I did it—what for? Do I know? Do you know? Hell, I just did it, that's all. Like M. Somebody gave me a stick, just the way I gave you a stick. I dug it; I went back to it. You didn't dig it at all. Now I'm an addict, and you're a college boy. Fate. Channels."

"I might have gone back to it," Bud said thoughtfully. "You never can tell. But it just didn't affect me one way or the other."

"Oh, it affected you," Andy said. "The first time, anyway. I know it affected you because I was watching you, man. Don't try to snow *me*."

"It didn't affect me," Bud insisted.

"You said the street got longer, didn't you?"

"Only because you suggested it. You kept saying, 'Look back over your shoulder. Doesn't it seem like we've come miles?' After a while I began to believe you."

"So? So there you are, man. All it does is increase your . . . your . . . oh, what the hell would you call it? When somebody suggests something and you're receptive to it. That. It increases that. You also said the buildings seemed to be tilting. I remember, man, believe me. My memory is the longest. So don't bring the stuff down. Admit it was crazy, will you?"

The pride had crept into Andy's voice again. Whenever he spoke of the power of drugs, the pride sneaked in like an assassin in a black robe. And yet, the self-pity was always there, too, behind the pride, like a white-clothed Lady Macbeth steering the hand with the knife. It was a peculiar combination, and it rankled Bud.

"Well," he said reluctantly, "maybe I did say the buildings seemed to be tilting."

"Oh, no question about it! And you also giggled like a bastard at everything we said."

"That was a release of nervous energy," Bud said. "I was

actually afraid. I had this feeling of doing something that was dangerous."

"Nervous energy, my foot. That was Mother M, daddy, good old Mother M. All right, I'll grant you it didn't knock you out. It never does the first time. But it sure as hell affected you, now don't tell me it didn't."

Bud felt as if he were being backed against the wall. The memory of the incident was hazy in his mind, anyway, and he had no reason to doubt the accuracy of Andy's recollection. In self-defense he tried to channel the course of conversation elsewhere. "The second time," he said, "nothing at all happened."

"Well, that's 'cause you shared the joint with that friend of yours from school—what was his name?"

"He was your friend, too," Bud said. "He went to Boys' High with you."

"Davidoff," Andy said. "David Davidoff—what a hell of a name. Like Newton Hooton. Played oboe, didn't he? It was funny your running into him at college, wasn't it? Sure, David Davidoff. He had a great sense of humor, you know? Oh, not that I was real buddy-buddy with him or anything. Hell he was a senior when I was just a soph, I think. But it was funny I knew him at all, and then your running into him at college."

"I still know him," Bud said.

"Yeah, well, that's what I mean. Channels, fate. He was scared that night, though. He was really scared. I think the only reason he lit up was because he was afraid we'd call him chicken."

"No, I don't think so," Bud said. "He was just curious, the way I was. You hear so much about it you want to know what all the shooting's about."

"But he was scared. Man, I've seen them when they're scared. Maybe he was curious, too, but he was mostly scared. That's because we were in the men's room, and maybe that wasn't the best place in the world to light up. Man, I was stoned! But you shared the joint with him, so it didn't affect you at all. It didn't affect him, either. He kept shrugging, as if it were a big disappointment, but man I think he was relieved he could still think straight. There're lots of guys like that, you know, guys who're afraid they won't be able to think straight, and who're afraid of what

they'll do when their minds aren't their own. Do you remember the movie we saw that night? Something with
'night' in the title—*Dead of Night?* Yes, a British film.
About this guy who keeps thinking he's lived through all this
before, and the ventriloquist, and the room in the mirror,
don't you remember? A real crazy picture, and it was even
crazier because I was stoned. But what I'm driving at is
that you had a taste of it. Hell, even Davidoff had a taste,
and here you are, and here I am, and never the twain shall
meet. You know what I mean?"

"Yes, I think so," Bud said.

"Just talking about it makes me itchy," Andy said. "I
shouldn't have tried to fool you last night, Bud. Man, I
really wanted to cut out of here and scare up something,
though—anything—just to take that itch out of my skull."

"Well, don't start getting the itch now."

"No, no, I was just saying. Oh, I feel a little of the itch. I
guess I'll always feel that. I mean, like I could bust a joint
now if I wanted to, but nothing serious. I guess I'll always
take a reefer or two, now and then, even when I'm off the
big stuff for good."

"That doesn't sound very smart," Bud said. "If you're
going to get off it, you should get off it completely."

"Oh, sure, sure, I will. But a sip of tea never hurt anybody. Hell, I could blast right now, and would you believe
it, it wouldn't affect me at all? Except maybe to soothe my
nerves a little, that's all. Man, when I was just taking
marijuana, I had it completely under control, what I mean,
completely. I could have stopped any time I wanted to."

"Then why didn't you?"

Andy shrugged. "Search me. I just didn't. I got on the
bigger stuff."

"Why?" Bud asked.

"If I knew that, man, I'd be oh so wise."

"Well, let's not talk about it. The more you talk about it,
the more you'll want it. Let's get some breakfast, okay?"

"Fine," Andy said.

They both got out of bed and dressed quickly. Bud went
into the kitchen and Andy followed him there. They were
looking into the refrigerator when the phone rang.

"I'll get it," Bud said. He glanced at his watch. "Kind of
early for anyone . . ." He let the sentence die, shook his

head, and walked to the phone, lifting the receiver.

"Hello?" he said.

"Hello, Andy?"

"No, this is Bud."

"Oh. Oh, hello, Bud. How are you?"

He did not recognize the voice. "Who is this?" he asked.

"Helen. Helen Cantor."

He felt suddenly warm. He tried to think of something to say, but nothing came to his mind. The line was silent for several moments, and then he said softly, "How are you, Helen?"

"Oh, I'm fine, thanks, Bud. May I speak to Andy, please? He *is* with you, isn't he?"

"Yes, he is," Bud said. "How did you—"

"He called me yesterday, before he went over there. It's awfully good of you to do what you're doing, Bud."

"I . . . yes," he said.

"May I speak to him now, please? He's all right, isn't he?"

"Yes, yes, he's fine. Just a moment." He cupped the receiver. "Andy, it's for you."

Andy came out of the kitchen. "Who is it?"

"Helen."

"Oh." He nodded abstractedly and went to the phone, taking the receiver from Bud. "Hello," he said. "Yes, I know, Bud— What? . . . No, I'm fine, Helen . . . Well, it's been bad, but you know how . . . Yes, yes, I am . . . No, this time it's for good, Helen . . . I know I've said that before . . . Look . . . Look, Helen . . . Yes, I will. . . ." He sighed heavily. "I haven't got any of the stuff. . . . I haven't even got the works. . . . I'm telling you. Helen? Helen? Oh, I thought you'd . . . No, go ahead. . . . All right, all right, I promise. . . . Helen, it's for good this time, I promise you that. . . . Yes, yes, have you been all right? . . . Good . . . What? . . . Oh . . . Well, I don't know. . . . I mean, it's not my place, Helen."

"What does she want?" Bud asked.

"Just a minute, Helen." He cupped the mouthpiece. "She wants to know if she can come over."

"Now?"

"Did you mean *now*, Helen?" Andy asked. "Oh, well

just a minute." He turned to Bud again. "Tonight, she said. After work."

Bud hesitated. He did not know if he wanted to see Helen again, and especially under these circumstances. "I've got a test tomorrow," he said lamely.

"Helen, he's got a test tomorrow," Andy said into the phone. "What? . . . Well, gee, Helen . . . all right, just a minute." He did not bother cupping the mouthpiece this time. "She wants to know *when* she can come, Bud. Look, if you don't want—"

"After my test," Bud said. "Tomorrow night."

"Helen? Can you come tomorrow night? . . . Look, I don't even see why . . . Yes, tomorrow . . . all right . . . about six? . . . Just a minute, Helen . . . Well, for Christ's sake, I have to check it, don't I? . . . Now just a second." He turned to Bud again. "Six all right?"

"All right," Bud said.

"All right," Andy said. "Do you know where it is? Oh, okay. I'll see you tomorrow then. Take care. . . . I'll be all right, don't worry. . . . Fine. . . . Yes, tomorrow at six. . . . Okay, Helen, so long." He hung up and then wet his lips. "She knows where you live," he said.

"Yes, I know," Bud answered.

"How . . . I mean . . ."

"She's been here before."

"Oh." Andy hesitated. "Nice kid, Helen. Still checking up on me, even though . . . well, like I hardly see her any more, you know."

"You called her yesterday, didn't you? You just said—"

"Yeah, sure. Well, I mean, like you owe it to people, don't you? Like if . . . if they're interested, you know, you shouldn't just sort of drop dead on them. I thought she'd like to know I was making the break, see, and I guess she does. Like her calling just now. Wants to make sure I stick to it this time, I guess. Nice kid."

"Yes."

"You don't mind her coming over, do you? Look, if you've got any objections, I can call her back."

"No, I don't mind."

"I mean, I never did get it straight between Helen and you so I don't know what the story is. I know she didn't talk about it, and whenever I brought it up—"

"She's welcome here," Bud interrupted.

"Just like that," Andy said. "Whenever I brought the subject up, she interrupted with something. What was it with you two, anyway?"

"Nothing," Bud said.

"It wasn't that first time, was it? You know, when I—"

"No," Bud said.

"Something when I was on the road then?"

"Well," Bud said. "Look, I've no objection to Helen's coming here, believe me."

"I always got the feeling . . . well, never mind. We'll let it ride."

"Let's let it ride," Bud agreed. "Come on, we still haven't had breakfast."

They went into the kitchen together and back to the refrigerator to pick up where they'd left off when the phone rang.

"No eggs," Bud said.

"I never eat eggs in the morning, anyway," Andy said.

"I do. I'd better run down for a dozen. Is there anything else we need? I wasn't exactly expecting company."

"Cup of coffee and a slice of toast is good enough for me," Andy said.

"You should eat more than that."

"Yeah, but I don't want to give it back again."

"Well, I'll get some eggs. I think a few quarts of milk, too. Do you still drink a lot of milk?"

"Not so much any more. Look, if you're going on my account—"

"No, I want the eggs. I usually get breakfast near the school, but exams—"

"Oh, sure."

"You'll be all right while I'm gone?"

"Yes," Andy said.

Bud looked at him for a moment. "Maybe you ought to come with me."

"No, I'll be all right."

"You won't—"

"No, don't worry. I'll be here when you come back."

Bud nodded. "There's a record player in the living room, and I've got some good Kenton. You like Kenton, don't you?"

"Man, are you kidding? I love the lad."

"Well, good, make yourself at home. I'll be right back. I'm just going over to Columbus Avenue."

"Fine. Take your time."

Andy walked him to the door, and before he left Bud said, "Maybe you can get the coffee water going. I won't be long at all."

"All right, I will," Andy said.

He left the apartment, and it took him three minutes to get to Columbus Avenue and another two minutes to get to the grocery store he usually bought at. There was one woman ahead of him in the store, and she took seven minutes to complete her purchase. It took him exactly four and a half minutes to get the eggs, the milk, and a loaf of rye bread. The walk back to the apartment took another five minutes. He could hear the record player as he started up the steps, and he thought it was a little too loud, and he told himself he'd have to remind Andy about playing it so loudly. "Artistry in Rhythm" was on the turntable, and he found himself whistling to it as he walked down the hall to his apartment. He threw open the door and went directly into the kitchen, not stopping to look into the living room, dropping the groceries on the kitchen table.

"Hey, Andy," he called, "you'd better lower that."

When there was no answer, he poked his head into the living room. "Andy?"

The record player was spinning at 78 r.p.m.'s, but no one was sitting in the living room listening to it.

He looked around the room quickly, panic starting inside him. He rushed to the bathroom and threw open the door. "Andy?"

He went in quickly and pulled back the shower curtain. Andy was not in the tub. Andy was not in the apartment.

9

He was out.

He was out, and he could feel a feverish excitement within him. The fever had started with the Kenton records, the wildness of them stirring memories somewhere deep within him. The four walls had moved in on him, ready to crush him, and he had stood suddenly, unreasonably frightened, wanting to get out. He had felt small and insignificant, caught in the slashing power of the music, trapped within the four walls which were closing in on him, moving closer, and closer and closer until he had to run, run or be crushed. He had to be big again. He had to stop being so small the walls could crush him.

And now he was out, and he had the bag in his hands, and it was a good bag, and it would bring bread. And when he had the bread, he could cop. No, he mustn't think of that. He was off the stuff, off it for good. Then why had he taken the bag from the closet? Why had he rushed to the closet and taken the bag when he knew he was off the stuff for good?

I'm going on a trip, he lied to himself.

I'm going on a trip to the moon. I'm growing as I walk. I'm getting taller and taller and taller, and I won't need a rocket ship because pretty soon my head will be in the clouds, and then my nose will touch the moon, and I'll nibble green cheese, and I'll climb up there, dragging my long, long legs up through the atmosphere and the stratosphere and the any-sphere, and I'll lay down in my bigness on the moon and just nibble green cheese and look down at the ants far below on earth and spit a big glob of spit at them.

They won't be able to touch me up there until they build a rocket ship to catch me, or a space station or something, and then I'll fool the bastards by going on to Mars. Will I gas those Martians. I'll tell them earthside jokes, and they'll give me a loincloth and the Martian equivalent of an opium derivative, and I shall blast my brains out every hour on the hour while the Martians come around me with their feelers. I'll be the God who came from earth, and they'll build me a shrine, and they'll send Martian dancing girls whose skins are green to dance for me with their feelers.

But first I have to hock the bag.

Don't argue with me, because I have to hock this mother-loving bag. What the hell use does Buddy-boy have for a leather bag like this one, anyway? Sitting in his closet, doing nothing. No good at all. *It t'aint no good, it t'aint no good, a purse ain't good if it's got a hole in it.* No hole in this goddamn bag, and no sense its sitting in the closet not going anywhere. Bags were made for trips, and this bag is now going on a trip.

Straight to the hock shop.

It has to go to the hock shop. It has to go, so shut your mother-loving tater trap and make your feet move. This bag is going to market, and then I will . . .

Will what?

Will whatever. And that's enough for you, for now. I will whatever I want to, and nobody can stop me. I'll climb Mt. Everest or I'll go down to the bottom of the sea. Or I'll head for the Union Floor, and maybe I'll see somebody I know, and maybe he'll ask me how would you like to blow with Harry James, or Stan Kenton, or T.D., and I will say what's the salary, Sam? And then I will tell him to go to hell.

And in the meantime I'll look for somebody else, because once I hock this bag, I'll have loot, lots of loot, how much will the bag bring, five, ten, fifteen? No, not fifteen. Well, maybe fifteen, what the hell are you, a goddamn pessimist?

Say fifteen.

Okay, fifteen. Now what can we buy with fifteen crisp hot little bills?

Fifteen bills will buy a fairly decent alligator belt, you know, if you're in the market for alligator belts. As it so happens, I am a most humane cat who could not stomach the idea of some poor horny alligator losing his skin to hold up my pants.

So I guess we won't be able to buy an alligator belt, eh George? Well now, that's a goddamn shame, and my heart bleeds for the alligator merchants, every last son of them. But what're you gonna do, Jack, when a man belongs to the A.S.P.C.A., eh?

We'll look for something else to buy. Must be dozens of things a man can buy with fifteen crisp juicy lettuce leaves.

Especially now that the man has kicked the habit.

It's a grand wonderful feeling, all right, not having to worry about spending that fifteen bucks on anything illicit, provided it amounts to fifteen bucks, which it might not, you know. But no matter what it amounts to, it sure is a wonderful free feeling to know that no one and nothing is forcing me into spending that pile on H. Now there's no better feeling in the world than that, all right, and there sure as hell must be a lot of worth-while things you can buy with fifteen bucks, and I'm sure I can think of some—given time—but in the meanwhile the important thing is to find the three balls and get rid of this bag. Once we get rid of it, we'll have the dough, and then we can decide on how to spend it.

With no one forcing us to the Union Floor to see if we can spot anyone we know there who might be holding.

No one forcing us to do that at all, especially now that the habit is kicked. Well, it wasn't even a really bad habit when you get right down to it, not if you can kick it clean away in a week. How bad can a habit be if you can shake it so easy? It might not even be called a habit at all, if you can just drop it like that. Why, right now—would you believe it—I don't feel any need for the stuff, just a need to hock this bag, so how bad could the habit have been?

Hell, there are people who can't even break the *smoking* habit in a week!

Of course, this is an entirely different kind of habit, naturally. If you could call it a habit at all.

Well, it doesn't matter what you call it because I am no longer an addict, anyway. All I have to do is hock this bag of Bud's, a fellow shouldn't leave an expensive bag laying around in his closet, this is a damn fine-looking bag, maybe it'll bring twenty, Christ, what twenty couldn't buy, enough stuff to last me a few days—if, of course, I was interested in buying stuff, which I'm definitely not. I'm only interested in hocking this bag.

Why?

Why, to have a few bills in my pocket, that's why. What's a man without a few bills in his pocket? Nothing.

So let's find Honest John and get rid of this bag, it's getting heavier as I go along, this goddamn bag is burning a hole in my pocket—how's that for a mixed metaphor, Buddy-boy?

Aren't there any hock shops at all in this crumby neighborhood? Don't people hock things around here? Do I have to go all the way downtown? Well, it doesn't matter because I've got to go to the Union Floor, anyway, after I hock the bag, but it seems as if a man should be able to hock something in his own neighborhood if he wanted to, not that it's my neighborhood, I wouldn't have it if you handed it to me with a golden key and a lifetime pass to the RKO Palace.

He walked up Seventy-second Street, and he passed the Provident Loan Society, and he wondered if he should try hocking the bag there, but he decided against it in favor of the shops with which he was familiar. He caught a train on Broadway, and he sat in the car and watched the faces around him, and he thought, *They know I'm going on a trip.*

I'm wearing a good jacket, and I look pretty good, in fact I look pretty damn good, and they see this expensive bag at my feet and they're thinking. Look at the lucky bastard, heading down for Penn Station, probably going on a short vacation somewheres, or maybe a fifty-million-dollar business trip, picking up a few oil wells here or there, or a brassière factory, or something. Envying me like crazy because their ant jobs pay thirty-two-fifty per, and they couldn't afford a vacation right now—even if they had the money.

He got off the train, and he walked down toward Sixth Avenue, wondering why anyone would want to mutilate such a sweet-sounding street to "Avenue of the Americas," and wondering if anyone except the mayor ever called it that. The pawnshops were lined up in a row, eeny-meeny-miney-mo.

He put on his best Rich-Man-Needing-Some-Pin-Money look and walked into the closest shop. The shop was small. He felt at home in it immediately. This was where he belonged, a big businessman making a deal for an expensive piece of luggage he'd picked up in Venezuela. God, there were so many things in a pawnshop! The jetsam of a vast army in retreat, the Army of Humanity, fleeing from the enemy, Life. Guitars and trumpets and accordions and cameras and projectors and fishing rods and knives and guns and watches and rings and bracelets and coffeepots and chamber pots and chafing dishes and fish dishes and fifty-dollar German gold pieces and feelthy pictures, Mac? Sorry, wrong pew.

The proprietor was a small, lean man with a cast in one eye. He walked sluggishly to where Andy stood, and his good eye studied Andy, and then he said, "Yes?"

Andy swung the bag up onto the counter. The proprietor studied it.

"Yours?" he asked.

"Of course," Andy said.

The proprietor ran his small hands over the leather. His mouth kept working as his hands moved, as if he were grumbling silently to himself, as if this were the worst piece of luggage he'd seen in his entire lifetime, as if he would throw Andy out of the shop at any moment. He clicked open the snaps and then looked inside the bag. His nostrils twitched, his mouth worked. He was very upset, this man. This man needed Carter's Little Liver Pills, Andy thought, in huge quantities.

"How much do you want?" the little man asked.

"How much will you give?" Andy said.

"Five dollars."

Andy took the bag from the counter without saying a word. He was starting for the door when the little man called, "Hey, wait a minute."

Andy walked back to the counter.

"Where you going?" the little man said, his head tilted, the cast in his eye giving him a gnomish look.

"You said five dollars," Andy said. "The bag cost a hundred new."

"You're a liar," the man said, "but I'm used to liars."

"And you're a crook," Andy said, "but I'm used to crooks."

"Listen, you want five?"

"Do I look crazy?"

"How much do you want?"

"Twenty," Andy said, figuring the little man would come down to fifteen.

"You have heat stroke," the man said. "I'll call an ambulance."

"When I want tired jokes, I'll try television," Andy said, pleased with the way the bargaining was going, enjoying the bargaining as much as he'd enjoyed anything in the past week.

"Six dollars," the man said, "and I'm not making a cent."

"Good-by," Andy said.

"Just a minute, just a minute. You look like a nice young feller, need a few dollars to take in the city. Okay, I'm a man who'll help you out. I was new in town once myself, had to hock *my* luggage, too."

"Mister, I was born and raised in Brooklyn," Andy said.

"Why didn't you say so?" the man answered. "For a native New Yorker, I'll go to seven-fifty and lose a few bucks on the deal."

"You'll go it alone, friend," Andy said.

"I can't do better than seven-fifty," the man said, shrugging.

"Well, it's been nice," Andy said, and he started out of the shop. He waited for the man to call him back, but there was no further offer. He opened the door, and the bell tinkled, and he stepped onto the sidewalk and into the moving stream of pedestrians.

That cheap cockeyed bastard, he thought. Seven-fifty. Took me for a hick from Squaresville at first, and then jacked his price a big two and a half bucks when he figured I knew the score. Seven-fifty! I can get more for the bag if I sell it to a necktie salesman.

Disgustedly, he walked into the next shop. He had been happy with the bargaining, but only while he thought he would get his price. Fifteen dollars would set him up fine. Fifteen dollars would be the ticket, all right, and the more he thought of that ticket the more anxious he was to conclude the deal, get this goddamn bag off his back. What does a guy have to do to get a little gold, anyway? Hock his mother? He was angry even before the new owner came out of his cage. A small plaque on the cage read "M. Daniels." Andy digested the name and then digested Daniels as the man walked past the array of junk behind his counter. He was a tall man with loose bones, a man who seemed somehow unhinged as he ambled toward Andy, a bright smile on his face.

"Morning, young man," he boomed cheerily. "What can I do you for, eh?"

Andy swung the bag up. "Good morning. I need a little ready cash," he said.

"That's what I'm here for, eh? Nice bag you've got there."

"I know." He did not want to bargain any more. He

wanted to hock the damn bag and get the hell out of here
and over to the Union Floor. There was an overwhelming
and sudden desire within him, a desire which had been
there all along but which he could no longer deny, a desire
which urged him to get some money and get out, get over
to the Union Floor, get what he needed, and get it fast.

"Good leather," Daniels said. "Must have cost you a bit,
young man."

"It cost me plenty," Andy said harshly. "How much?"

"Ten," Daniels said.

"This street is lined with stick-up artists," Andy said,
more irritated now. "I want fifteen."

"You won't get it here, son."

"How much will I get?"

"Ten," Daniels said. "I give a price, and I stick to it. I
don't underquote and then wait to be jacked up."

"You said ten?"

"That's what I said."

Andy hesitated. "This is a good bag," he said weakly.
His feet were beginning to tap. He wanted to get out of
here very badly, he wanted to get out of here and over to
the Union Floor, where he might contact Rog or somebody
—somebody who could help him get what he wanted and
what he needed.

"Assuredly, it's a good bag. I'm thinking of resale if you
don't claim it. People don't like to buy second-hand luggage. They like their luggage new."

"Who you trying to kid?" Andy said. "I know guys who
wear second-hand suits."

"Yes, but these are not the people who need luggage. A
man who needs luggage is a man who travels. And a man
who travels is a man who can afford a new bag. How do I
know what you kept in this bag?"

"Ten dollars is your price?" Andy said.

"My only and final price."

"For ten dollars I can tell you what I kept in this bag."

"And what was that?" Daniels asked.

"Horseshit," Andy said. He yanked the bag from the
counter and started for the door. Daniels did not call him
back. He banged out of the shop, walking blindly into the
crowd, really angry now, and desperately wanting to get rid
of the bag. Why should a guy have so much trouble? Why

were they all against him? For Christ's sake, what was a guy supposed to do, penned up in a rattrap apartment, watched all the time, everybody watching as if he were a prisoner or something, and now these lousy bastards trying to con him out of the bag, taking him for some damn idiot.

He opened the door of the next shop, and he heard the bell tinkle, and the tinkle irritated him. A fat man in a worn overcoat was trying to hock a bellows camera, shaking his head at each new price the proprietor quoted. Finally, the fat man said, "No, I'm sorry, Mr. Taller. I am very sorry, but you are not doing my intelligence justice. I'm sorry, Mr. Taller, but after all these years, I think I must take my business elsewhere."

Taller, a man who was almost as fat as his potential customer, cocked his head philosophically. "Mr. Peters, I am sorry, too, believe me."

Peters picked up his bellows camera and the remnants of his dignity and walked proudly out of the shop, his head high. Taller waddled over to where Andy was standing.

"Yes, sir?" he said.

"I want to hock this bag," Andy said. "I want fifteen bucks for it, and I know it's worth that much, so don't give me a song and dance."

Taller looked at Andy carefully, an expression of mild surprise on his face.

"You get right down to business, don't you?" he said.

"I do. What do you say?"

"Slow down," Taller said. "That's what I say. You've been in here before, haven't you?"

"I don't remember."

"You've been in so many hock shops, you can't remember which you've been in?" Taller asked.

"Look, will you give me fifteen? Yes or no?"

"Maybe," Taller said, shrugging. "I got to look at the bag first, don't I? You won't deny me this privilege?"

"Go ahead, look at it."

"You're in a hurry?" Taller asked.

"Yes, I'm in a hurry."

"Then maybe you should take your business someplace else. I'm a fat man. I don't like to move fast. Of course, the bag may be worth fifteen dollars. I'll have to examine it. Carefully." He eyed Andy expectantly.

For a moment Andy wanted to grab the bag and get the hell out of the shop, show this fat slob he didn't have to take any guff from him. But the possibility of getting fifteen bucks outweighed the necessity for proving himself superior to this tub of lard.

"I'll wait," he said. "Look the bag over. Take all the time you want. Get out your magnifying glass if you want to. Only, let's get on with it."

"Younger generation," Taller said, shaking his massive head. "Always in a rush. Going to burn out your engine before you're thirty, you know that, don't you?"

"I'll worry about that when I'm thirty," Andy said. "Do you think it's worth fifteen?"

"I haven't looked at it yet."

"I was hinting subtly," Andy answered, trying a smile, but knowing he was incapable of a smile. Suppose he missed Rog? Suppose Rog was there, and he missed him? What the hell would he do then? Come on, Fatso, get off your dead rump. Move!

Taller took the bag between his beefy fingers. Carefully, cautiously, he began turning the bag, his eyes scrutinizing every square inch of it.

"You need this money bad?" Taller asked, turning the bag.

"What difference does it make?"

"I look at my customers like humans. The necessity sometimes determines the loan."

"I need it bad."

"What for?"

"That's none of your . . ." Andy hesitated. He did not like Taller's playing with him this way, did not like the careful, methodical, minute attention Taller was giving the bag. But Taller might have fifteen dollars to give him, and once he got that he could get some of the stuff, and if Rog were around he could borrow a spike. "That's my business," he amended.

"And loaning money is mine," Taller said lazily. He pushed the bag across the counter with one pudgy forefinger. Andy panicked.

"What's the matter?" he asked.

"You're not very friendly," Taller said. "I like customers to be friends."

"What the hell do you want?" Andy said. "My life history? I only came in here to hock a bag."

"Who cares about your life?" Taller said. "I ask decent questions. I expect decent answers. What am I—a pariah?"

"I don't know what the hell you are," Andy said. "I thought you were a loan shark, but I think you're Mr. Anthony instead."

Taller smiled. "Okay, keep your business to yourself. I'm just curious."

"I just need the money, that's all. What difference does it make what I need it for?"

"Okay, okay," Taller said. He shrugged and began turning the bag again, looking at it. Andy felt immense relief, and he cursed Taller again for his teasing game, and he wiped his hand across his mouth and watched the fat loan shark.

"A nice bag. I'm surprised you'd want to get rid of it." Taller looked up suddenly, his eyes tightening. "It isn't stolen, is it?"

"No," Andy said.

"I can check against my stolen goods list, you know."

"Go ahead, check," he said confidently. Even if Bud had already discovered the theft, which was unlikely, he probably would not report it. And even if he reported it, it was much too early for it to be showing on any police pawnshop list.

"Well, you don't look like the type of fellow who would steal a bag," Taller said. "Except from necessity, huh?"

"Nobody hocks anything except from necessity," Andy said.

"I didn't say 'hock,' I said 'steal,' " Taller said.

"I didn't steal the bag, so get off that kick," Andy said.

"Are you a musician?"

"Yes."

"What do you play?"

"What difference does it make?"

"Trumpet or trombone?"

"Trumpet. How—"

"You have a muscle on your lip," Taller said shrewdly.

"You win the gold star," Andy answered. "Do I get fifteen?"

"Maybe."

"Do you think you'll know in time for Christmas?"
Taller smiled. "I might."

"I can't wait that long. Decide now."

"What's your hurry?"

"Oh, the hell with this," Andy said. He reached across
the counter for the bag, and Taller pulled it back farther,
and as Andy stretched his arm, his jacket pulled back
slightly, and there was a sudden spark in Taller's eyes, and
then Taller reached out quickly, unbelievably fast for a fat
man, his fat fingers clamping on Andy's wrist. He brought
his other hand around, clasping the material of Andy's jacket, and then he shoved the jacket and the shirt, and Andy
felt the button at his wrist snap, and then the shirt and the
jacket together were moving up the length of his arm, his
hand imprisoned in Taller's firm, fleshy grip.

"What the hell . . ." he started, and then he glanced
down at his arm, and he felt sick inside all at once because
Taller was looking at the exposed arm, too, and the exposed arm was the arm of a drug addict, unmistakably so,
irrevocably so.

"I figured," Taller said.

"Let go of my arm," Andy warned.

"You're a hophead. What's the matter, kid, you got an
itch? You got an itch for a couple of caps of the crap? Is
that why you want the fifteen so bad? Is that why?"

"Listen—"

"You figure you come in here and con an old fat man
into giving you fifteen bucks for a bag you probably stole,
huh? Con an old fat man who can hardly get around he's
so fat into giving you fifteen bucks so you can go out and
shoot yourself full of poison, huh? Well, son, you picked
on the wrong fat man this time. I get your kind of vermin
all the time. I get your kind of filthy animals all the time.
And do you know what I do with them? I take whatever
they bring and throw it down at their feet."

He viciously swept one hamlike hand across the counter,
knocking the bag to the floor. Andy scrambled for it, picking it up, frightened by the intensity in the fat man's eyes.

"I throw it down on the ground, down to their level,"
Taller said vehemently. Andy was standing up now, backing away from the counter.

"And then do you know what I do?" Taller shouted, his

fist clenched, his breath coming hard. "Do you know what I do to these rotten, grubby parasites?"

Andy stared at him, incapable of movement, paralyzed by the trembling, furious hulk before him. Taller drew back his head and then brought it down in a sudden movement that took Andy completely by surprise. In a second he understood, but in that second it was too late. He saw Taller's pursed lips, and he flinched when he realized what was going to happen. When it happened, he stood there stunned for several seconds, and then he reached for a handkerchief and wiped Taller's vile spit from his face.

"I spit at them!" Taller screamed. "I spit right into their faces, and I tell them to take their filthy trade someplace else. I spit at them!" he screamed. *"I spit at them!"*

He fled from the shop and out onto the sidewalk, stopping outside Daniels' shop to catch his breath. He went in to see Daniels again then, fully expecting the price to have dropped, surprised when it was still ten dollars.

He pocketed the bills and went out onto the sidewalk. He had to get to the Union Floor now.

He began walking quickly.

10

The musicians were congregated in the street outside Local 802, even though a sign inside the building warned them that such assembly was a violation. They stood close to the curb, their backs to the street, and they talked. The people passing by paid them scant attention. The musicians wore suits, or sports jackets, or dress shirts, or sports shirts, or tee shirts. They seemed to enjoy each other's company. They talked a lot and they laughed a lot. Some of them carried their instruments with them. Most of them carried nothing but a small engagement book in which they recorded future job dates. They looked like men in the garment district discussing whether they should cut Shantung or corduroy. They looked like men on the television circuit standing outside casting studios and discussing bit parts on

Montgomery or Kraft. They looked like any group of men discussing the intimate aspects of their business. Music was their business, and though they sometimes asked, "How's your wife?" they mostly asked, "Are you booked for this Saturday?"

He scanned them quickly, looking for Rog, not seeing him, and then starting up the long flight of steps that led to the Exchange Floor. He passed someone he knew on the way down, and the musician nodded and said, "Hi, Andy," and he nodded back and said, "Hi," not remembering the man. He stepped onto the Floor, and he was immediately engulfed in a huge wave of sound. The Floor was enormous and bare. The Floor was thronged with men and women, and every man and woman was talking, and the sound of their voices joined to form a crashing crescendo that reached up for the ceiling and bounced down again in a smothering storm of mumbles.

"I went away for Passover. I got matzos coming out of my ears. You know those nice little seeded rolls? The only reason I go away. What? Is the loot so good? I go away for the seeded rolls, and all I get is matzos. But look at that waistline. I must've lost twelve pounds. This hardtack is wonderful. They should put it on the market."

"The only way to reduce, Sam. You try a starvation diet, you wind up with functional disorders of the liver, the heart, and the intestinal tract. Are you booked this Saturday?"

He shoved his way through the crowd, listening to the babel of sound, and above the disjointed, mingled mumbles the harsh boom of the microphone paging people to the desk.

"Johnny Fillera. Johnny Fillera. Michael Storey. Michael Storey. Amos Dale. Amos Dale."

Somewhere in the blurred faces around him there might be Rog. He was interested in none of the faces but Rog's. Rog might be here, and if he were . . .

"I told him, 'What the hell, you want a trumpet player or a slave coolie?' I picked up my ax and almost brained the son-of-a-bitch. But that horn cost me two bills, so I just told him I was gonna report him, that's all, and then I walked out."

"David Bergen. David Bergen. Skippy Fried. Skippy Fried."

"He was getting forty-three as leader, and he was trying to get sidemen for fifteen. I told him to shove his goddamn piccolo."

"Flip Callabia. Flip Callabia."

"You should have let me know sooner. I'm booked solid for the next three week ends. Jesus, Harry, you know I like your outfit."

"Well, I didn't see you. Where you been hiding?"

"Anybody has checks due from Stan Bowles, come and get 'em. Anybody has checks due from Stan Bowles, come and get 'em."

He saw a face he knew, and then the face was beside him, a round cherubic face, and a hand was extended toward him, and he took the hand unconsciously, the sound around him smothering him until he wanted to shout for air, and then a hole opened in the face, and the hole was framed with teeth, and the face said, "Hey, Andy, long time no see."

"Hey, boy, how are you?" he mumbled.

"So-so, can't kick. You still blowing?"

"Oh, sure, dad."

"I'm supposed to meet some creep who's got a gig at White Roe for the summer. So I've been paging the bastard for the past hour, and he still ain't showed. You know him, maybe?"

"What's his name?"

A card appeared in pudgy fingers. The hole in the face opened again. "George Mackler. You know him?"

"Piano?"

"Yeah."

"I know him. He'll be around. He likes to be late. It makes him like a leader."

"Leaders should be hung. And I mean by the—"

"You see Rog Kiner around anywhere?"

"Who's he?"

"Tenor man. Used to be on the Jerralds band with me. You see him?"

"No, I don't even know what he looks like. Hey, was you on the Jerralds band when he had that shakedown in Sioux City?"

"What shakedown?" Andy asked, avoiding the curious eyes.

"You know, man. When a couple of the guys was—"

"Listen, I got to cut out. You see Rog, you tell him Andy's looking for him."

"Yeah, sure, but I don't know him."

He shoved away, colliding with a man holding a box of ties, bow ties in blacks, maroons, blues.

"Need a tie, cousin?" the man asked.

"No."

"Good ties. Cheap. Come on, cousin, you need a tie."

"Get the hell out of my way."

"Sensitive artist," the salesman snarled.

He pushed through, almost knocking the salesman down. Where the hell was Rog? What time was it? He had ten dollars in his pocket now, ten hot, itchy dollars, and he wanted to spend them, and he knew what he wanted with that ten, and he had to find Rog—or somebody else, somebody he knew, but preferably Rog because he had to borrow a spike, too, why the hell had he thrown away his spike, what had ever possessed him to do such a goddamn foolish thing?

You did it because you're off it, he reminded himself. Yes, I know, I'm off it, and I realize I'm off it, and this doesn't mean I'm going back on it, this is just something to calm me down a little, maybe Rog'll be holding some mootah, the mootah won't harm me, or maybe even just a sniff of the bigger stuff, that doesn't mean I'm going back aboard, it doesn't mean that at all, if only I could find Rog, he ought to be here somewhere, Jesus Christ, where is he?

He had to get out of the sound.

The sound was deafening, and he remembered back to a time when the sound had been an exciting thing to him, just stepping onto the Floor had been an exciting thing, seeing the people you knew, feeling a part of the music business, a real part of it, telling jokes, and booking jobs, with the mike booming in the background, and the murmur of voices like a big swelling wave of warm water. But it wasn't that now, it was only noise now, and he had to get away from the noise or he'd bust. He pushed his way through the crowd again, ants, ants, and a girl vocalist he'd seen around raised one shapely leg and said to the man standing with her, "Do you like my new shoes?" and then she took off one of the shoes and handed it to him, and he studied it like the mastermind of the leather industry.

He reached the steps and he climbed upstairs rapidly, walking past the sign which said, "These doors will close at 3:00 P.M.," and then into the office itself, and past the booking and contract windows, and then over to the bulletin board, looking for Rog at the same time, never stopping his search for Rog. A few musicians were standing near the board, and he looked at them and then glanced at some of the notices not really reading them, just wanting the printed words to blot out the memory of the noise below, wanting the well-ordered typewritten notices to obliterate the disorderly chaos he had just left.

Place on Unfair List of Local 802

Pursuant to instructions received from the National Secretary, the following name has been placed on the National Defaulter's List for failure to make payment of balance of $47.75 due on claim of member . . .

And below that:

NOTICE

All talk-over rehearsals must be paid for at regular rehearsal rates. This above ruling of the Executive Board will be strictly enforced.

He scanned the unfair notices, and then he turned away from the bulletin board and walked toward the dues windows, searching the faces of the members waiting in line. A huge white sign stood to the right of the windows, the black letters on it blaring:

IF YOU OWE TAXES PLEASE PAY THEM BEFORE ENTERING DUES PAYMENT LINE AND AVOID INCONVENIENCE TO YOURSELF OR YOUR FELLOW MEMBER.

My fellow member is Rog, he thought, and where the hell is my fellow member? Jesus Christ, do I have to go

down into the arena again? He shook his head disconsolately
and then started for the stairs. The sound rushed up the
stair well, distant now and almost pleasant. It grew in
volume as he got closer to it, and then he was in the center
of it again, and the voices were all around him, and he
squeezed his eyes shut tightly, trying to blot out the sound
that way, knowing he was being foolish, you see with your
eyes, you *see* with your eyes.

"You stupid son-of-a-bitch! What did he give you?
Three Saturdays in a row, right? I warned you about this.
I warned you about that bastard! He's got you tied up for
three Saturdays, and what else did he give you?"

"Well . . . nothing so far. He just . . ."

"Nothing! *Gornischt!* And that's all you're going to get.
And you'll be lucky if the son-of-a-bitch doesn't farm you
out someplace. You think he's giving you those Saturdays
because he loves you? You're a bass man who can sing,
so he's saving on a vocalist. I can get you all the Saturdays
you want, you dumb jerk. What about the Fridays and the
Sundays? None of those, huh? And do you know who's
gonna get dropped first if the job gets cut? You! Goddammit, this burns my ass. Because I warned you, I
warned you!"

"Well, how was I supposed to know . . ."

"Because I told you, that's how. Try to get out of those
jobs. Go ahead, just try. See how easy that'll be. You're
a sucker! A plain, damn-fool sucker."

He spotted Rog.

He spotted him, and his heart leaped up into his face,
and he called, "Rog! Hey, Rog!" but the sound drowned
out his voice, and he cursed the sound, and he cursed the
crowd and he began shoving his way through to where
Rog was standing.

"Tie clasp, cuff links, Mac?"

"No," he said. He glanced at the array of jewelry on the
cardboard box, copper tie clasps and cuff links, each
decorated with a G clef.

"Buck for the clasp, buck and a half for the links, two
bucks for the set, Mac."

"No," he said again, and he pushed past and shouted,
"Rog! For Christ's sake, Rog!"

"*Meyer Koenig. Meyer Koenig. Alfred Bunn. Alfred*

Bunn. Shirley Carp. Shirley Carp. Paul Sidio. Paul Sidio."

He pushed through, feeling as if he were swimming on a sea of crawling flesh and sound, swimming toward land. He felt as if he would cry, and then Rog was standing beside him, and he reached out and touched Rog's shoulder, and Rog spun around.

He was a dark boy with dark hair and dark eyes and a sallow complexion. His face broke into a smile when he saw Andy, his lips skinning back over even white teeth.

"Hey, dad," he said. "How are you?"

"Great." Andy smiled, relieved. "I've been looking for you."

"Oh?" Rog said. His voice was high and reedy. He studied Andy for a moment and then turned to the girl he'd been talking to. "Monica, meet Andy Silvera. She blows piano."

"Hi," Andy said. "Can I talk to you a minute, Rog?"

"Why sure, dad. Talk."

"I meant . . . you know."

"Cool it, dad," Rog said, and he turned again to Monica. "It's not often you get a pretty chick at the piano," he said.

Monica smiled. She was a tall girl with a full bust and glowing brown eyes. She wore her hair long and flowing past her shoulders. Her fingers were narrow, tipped with crimson teardrops. "Why, thanks. That doesn't help next Sunday, though. Are you booking or just looking?"

"Well, I'll tell you, honey," Rog said, "I've been using a pickup band and the results are pretty good, you know? But this piano man I've got, he's a bit corny, do you know? He hits it, but he's not with it. I use him because he doubles on accordion. You blow accordion?"

"Nope."

"Well, that don't matter actually. I mean, so long as the piano stuff is good, and I've heard a lot about your playing, you dig?"

"Mmm-huh," Monica said.

"So let me have the number, and I'll buzz you sometime next week, and we'll see."

"I'm here to book next Sunday," Monica said. "I can't wait until sometime next week."

End it, Andy thought. *End it. Goddamn it, end it!*

"Well, look, if you get something today, you get it. Otherwise I'll give you a buzz, okay? No harm in giving you a buzz, is there?"

"If I get a booking, no. No harm at all."

"Okay, so what's the Ameche?"

She gave him the number and then whirled as an old friend embraced her. She returned the embrace, and they walked over together to where a group of men were chatting.

"Why the snow job?" Andy asked. "You know you don't have a pickup band."

"I like to keep my finger in the pie. What's with you, dad? Long time no see."

"I been . . . well . . . you know . . ."

"No, I don't know."

"Whoever left a guitar case up at the desk, pick it up. Whoever left a guitar case at the desk, pick it up."

"If that son-of-a-bitch doesn't close his mouth," Andy said viciously.

"This is Doublesville," Rog said, smiling. "He says everything twice. He goes home to his wife, he says 'I love you, I love you. What's for supper, what's for supper?' " Rog began chuckling. "Hey, you dig that?"

Andy did not smile. "He's driving me nuts. Can't we get out of here?"

"What's the rush?" Rog said airily. "I like it here. So where you been?"

"With a . . . a friend of mine. I been . . . you know."

"You been what?"

"You holding?" Andy asked suddenly.

"What the hell's the matter with you, you stupid jerk?" Rog answered vehemently.

"I'm askin' a question. I'm—"

"You see the guy in the pink shirt? He's a bull. He's lookin' for some damn stupid fool like you, so just cool it."

"I'm sorry, I . . . I didn't realize . . . I . . . can't we get out of here?"

"Damn jackass," Rog said, smoldering. "What's the matter, 'you sick?"

"Not bad. I just want a calmer. I been—"

"Don't say it. Come on downstairs."

They walked to the fringe of the crowd and then worked their way toward the steps.

"Frank Cippio. Frank Cippio," the mike blasted.

"Bastard," Andy muttered.

They walked down the long, cool, dim flight of steps, the sound retreating behind them. It was suddenly quiet, and he could think again, and when they stepped into the street he sucked in a deep draught of air.

"You want some coffee?"

"Okay," Andy said.

"You got loot?"

"Ten."

"I'll buy the coffee. Why haven't you been around, stranger?"

"I'm kicking it."

"Hah!" Rog snorted.

"I am."

"Sure. Like I'm kicking it. What do you want to know if I'm holding for?"

"I need a calmer. I've been going it cold turkey, and it's murder."

"Sure." Rog smiled. "Why the sudden reform?"

"I got an audition coming up."

"No bull? Who with?"

"Laddy Fredericks."

"Yeah? Good deal. And he don't go for junkies, huh?"

"That ain't it. I can't . . . well, I got to brush up, you know?"

"Sure, kid, I know. So you're going it cold turkey, and now you just want a little pick-me-up, huh? Sure, I understand. You sure you want that coffee?"

"I . . . if you want some."

"Yeah, I can use a cup."

They crossed the street together. Andy felt a lot better now, even though Rog had not said he was holding. But even if he wasn't holding, Rog would know where to get some, and that's what counted. He felt a strange pang of guilt when he'd mentioned the Laddy Fredericks audition, but the guilt had passed quickly. This was not really going back to it. This was just something to steady his nerves, just something to tide him over the next few days. His body was not screaming for the stuff. Back in Bud's apartment, with the records going full blast, he had felt this sudden desire for a fix, but the desire was not as strong now, not as strong at all. He only wanted a pick-me-up now, just a little of the stuff to tide him over, that was all.

They went into the cafeteria, and Rog went for the coffee, and when he returned to the table, he said, "What's Helen doing with herself these days?"

"She kicked it," Andy said simply.

"You *never* kick it, dad," Rog replied. "You only think you do. When the chips are down, you rush right back into its ever-loving arms."

"That's not true," Andy said. "Helen kicked it."

"Sure. Until she needs it again."

"She won't need it again."

Rog raised one eyebrow. "No?"

"No," Andy said firmly.

"Sure," Rog said. "How about you, son? How long you been off?"

"About a week."

"Nice progress. It was rough, huh?"

"Very."

"So then why do you want more?"

"Just a little," Andy said. "You know."

"Sure, I know," Rog said.

"I need a spike, too. I got rid of mine. When I decided to kick it."

"You need a spike, too, huh?" Rog said, whispering now.

"Yes."

"I haven't said I was holding yet."

"Aren't you?"

"Maybe."

"Don't play games with me, Rog."

"Who's playing games? It's just I don't know if I should corrupt an upstanding citizen. Not after he's made so much progress."

"You bastard, you're the one who first started me on—"

"Nobody starts unless they want to start!" Rog said, raising his voice. "Just remember that, Junior."

"Okay, I'm remembering."

"Okay."

"*Are* you holding?"

"Maybe."

Andy sipped at his coffee. He was possessed of a sudden desire to reach across the table and strangle Rog. He knew that Rog might have some junk on him, though, and so he restrained the impulse. Rog had the right idea, all right. Rog had a habit like John Silver, but Rog fed that habit by peddling the stuff, and the peddling gave him enough jive with plenty left over for the little luxuries of life. A smart cookie, Rog. A bastard, Rog.

"So how about it?" he asked.

"How about what?"

"Come on, Rog."

"You're on H, huh? I keep forgetting."

"You know what I'm on," Andy said tightly.

"Sure, but that was before. I mean, you're not *on* any more, are you? You've kicked it, haven't you?"

"Yes."

"Sure. So what was it you wanted?"

"What'll I get for ten?"

"A sixteenth," Rog said softly.

"What!" Andy said, outraged. "Are you kidding?"

"This is good stuff. I've been getting from the Coast. Very good stuff. By China way. Cuts this Italian and Lebanese stuff all to hell. You know something, Andy? In Frisco they're pushing it eighty-five per cent pure. And we've been getting it watered to fifteen per cent. You buying or not?"

"Come down to eight bucks."

"Can't do it. What do you say?" Andy hesitated, wetting his lips. Then, reluctantly, he nodded. "Come on back to the piss-wah," Rog said.

He stood and began walking toward the back of the cafeteria and then down the flight of steps to the men's room. Andy followed close behind him.

"You been blowing?"

"A little."

"Laddy Fredericks, huh? Good deal," Rog said. He shoved open the door to the men's room. Two men were at the urinals, and he waited for them to clear the room. When they were gone, he whispered, "Where's the ten?"

Andy reached into his pocket and handed him the wad

of bills. Rog counted them slowly. He reached into his jacket pocket then and palmed something into Andy's hand. "There's your stuff. A sixteenth. Cheap at half the price." He reached into his inside pocket. "Here's the spike. I want it back, pal." He handed Andy the syringe.

"I'll return it."

"You'd damn well better."

"Sure."

"It's a real pleasure dealing with you," Rog said, smiling. "It ain't often I sell to somebody who ain't an addict."

Andy stared at him for a moment. "I'll see you," he said, and then he walked out of the lavatory.

He hated Rog. He hated Rog because it had been he who first introduced Andy to the drug, and he hated him because they no longer shared the fraternal spirit of the addicted. Sure, Rog still had a habit, but Rog was now the Man, and so Rog was a person to be respected and feared and loved and hated. Rog was the man with the key, *the* Man, and without that key, there was nothing. And so Rog was loved, but he was also despised because he knew the ways of the addict, and sometimes the addict crawled to Rog, and Rog enjoyed the crawling immensely.

Andy walked to the silverware trays, took a tablespoon from one of them, glanced around him briefly, and then put the spoon into his jacket pocket.

He had copped.

He had the junk in his pocket, and all he had to do now was shoot up, and then he'd be all right, then everything would be much easier. And the Fredericks gig, well, hell, this wasn't going to hurt that any, was it? Even if Rog was a bastard, he'd come through, he'd even lent a spike, hell what other pusher would do that? Still, he was a bastard, pulling a tease like that, taking all his sweet—

"Andy?"

He heard Rog's voice behind him, and he whirled. Did he want the stuff back? Had he changed his mind about the syringe?

"What is it?"

"You got any change?"

"What?"

"Pin money. Here." He crushed two folded bills into Andy's palm. "I'll see you when you return the outfit," he said, and then he walked out of the cafeteria. Andy stared at the money in his palm. Two dollars. Well, now how the hell do you like that? Rog parting with money! Will wonders never cease? I'll be goddamned!

He pocketed the money and stepped onto the sidewalk. He walked to the curb, wondering where he could go, and then he had a sudden idea.

He raised his arm. "Taxi!" he called.

11

For a moment Bud didn't know quite what to do.

He stood looking into the tub, then it registered on his mind that Andy had left the apartment, and he felt a curious mixture of relief and responsibility. The relief was short-lived. It fled almost instantly under an enormous guilt feeling, and he rushed back into the living room and picked up the phone, dialing Carol's number quickly. He waited impatiently, drumming his fingers on the arm of the butterfly chair. The phone rang five times and then someone said, "Hello?"

"Carol? This—"

"No, this is Louise. Who's calling, please?"

"Hello, Louise. How are you? This is Bud. May I speak to Carol, please?"

"She's already left for work," Louise said.

He glanced at his watch quickly. So late already. Goddammit, why hadn't he thought of that?

"Louise, do you have the number at her office? This is pretty important."

"Is it about Andy?" Louise asked.

"Yes," Bud said.

"Why can't you leave her alone? Haven't you caused my family enough grief with that bum?" Louise asked. "My mother—"

"Look, Louise—"

"Hold on, I'll get the number," Louise said coldly. She was gone for several moments. When she came back on the line, she said, "Columbus 5-1098. I don't see why—"

"Thanks, Louise," he said, and he hung up quickly. Columbus 5-10 . . . He lifted the phone and dialed rapidly, waiting for the rings on the other end.

"Benson and Parke, good morning," a sweetly innocent voice said.

"May I speak to Miss Ciardi, please?" he asked.

"What extension is that, sir?"

"I don't know."

"One moment, plee-yaz."

He waited again, his feet jiggling, his fingers dancing nervously.

"That's extension fifty-one, sir," the voice came back. "Will you make a note of it for future—"

"Yes, would you ring it, please?"

"One moment, plee-yaz." He heard the hum of the switchboard on the other end of the line, and then another phone was lifted.

"Bookkeeping," a voice said.

"Miss Ciardi, please."

"Second." He listened and he could almost feel a hand coming down over the mouthpiece on the other end. And then, filtered through the fingers of that hand, the muted voice shouting, "Hey, is Carol around? Hey, Carol, telephone." The hand was removed from the mouthpiece, and the voice came through clearly again. "She's on her way. Hold on, will you?"

He waited, and when her voice came onto the line, he almost leaped at it.

"Carol?"

"Yes, who—"

"Carol, he's gone. I went down for some eggs and stuff, and when I got back—"

"Is anything missing?" she asked quickly.

"What do you mean, missing?"

"Your watch, your typewriter, your toaster, anything he might hock. Take a look, Bud, quickly."

His watch was on his wrist. He'd looked at it a few moments before, so he knew Andy had not taken that. The typewriter—that was on the top shelf of the closet, but Andy could hardly know it was there. Still, he may have searched the apartment and possibly—goddammit, he was awfully fond of that typewriter—why . . . He put down the phone and went to the closet, opening the door.

He reached in automatically for the suitcase that rested on the floor, and when his hand grasped empty air, he stepped back and looked curiously at the floor of the closet. He checked again, looking where it should have been, and then looking to the left and right, and then running his hands over the dusty closet floor.

The suitcase was gone.

It had cost him sixty bucks less than three months ago, the time he'd gone up to see . . . well, it was gone now. How much would a hock shop give for a sixty-dollar bag? He went back to the phone.

"My suitcase is gone."

"All right," she said, "all right, now let me see. Oh, God, he could have gone anyplace. You're on Seventy-fourth . . . let me see, let me see. He'll probably try the Union Floor first. Do you know where that is, Bud?"

"Yes."

"He'll probably stop to hock the bag, but he can do that any place. And then he'll head for the Union—that's closest to where you are—and he's bound to meet someone there who's holding. How much of a head start does he have?"

"About a half hour."

"Oh, then you'd better leave right away, Bud. Take a cab, will you? And when you find him, stop him—if it's not too late. Stop him even if you have to hit him."

"Hit . . . ?"

"Go, Bud, please. I'll be waiting to hear from you. Call me, won't you? Either . . . either way."

"All right," he said. "Good-by."

He hung up, checked his wallet to see if he had enough money for a cab, and then locked the apartment and left. He ran all the way up to Columbus Avenue and finally hailed a cab on Seventy-second Street. "Fiftieth and Sixth," he told the cabbie, and then he sat back and tried to relax, telling himself there was nothing he could do until he found Andy. And even then, even after he found him, there might be nothing he could do. The streets were not very crowded, and he was grateful for that at least. He looked through the cab windows, watching the late-arriving executives in their gray pin stripes and black Homburgs.

What had Andy been wearing? Had he taken the sports
jacket with him? He hadn't even thought to look. Did Andy
have a hypodermic? No, no, he didn't. He'd have to get
that, and unauthorized possession of a hypodermic was illegal, so where . . . one of his friends, maybe, or maybe
even his contact—what had he called him—the Man . . .
There was a title for the son-of-a-bitch, all right. The Man,
in capital letters . . . like God. Hell, he could get a hypodermic, no question about it. If he could get the heroin, he
could get the hypo to go with it. Jesus, was it as easy as all
that? Did you just go up to someone and hand him some
money, and there you were? Was that all there was to it?
Did he already have the stuff? Was he crouched in an alley
someplace, right this minute, now, with the needle poised
over his vein, the drug ready to enter his blood stream? Or
would he go to an alley, no not an alley, someone's house,
maybe, or someplace where he wouldn't look furtive or
suspicious, oh, Jesus, why the hell was this all like some
Grade-B melodrama, what was there about the entire subject of drugs that made it sound like purple passages from a
cheap paperback? The illegality of it? In a country like
America, where crime was synonymous with adventure
and suspense, was that what made drug addiction sound so
exotic? What the hell exotic was there about Andy? What
the hell was Andy but a little man, like all the other little
men who plodded to their offices every morning, the ant
complex, oh, Christ, I'm getting the ant complex, but *how*
was he any different, except that he took drugs, and did
even that set him apart? If he chewed licorice or betel nut,
would anyone give a good goddamn? If he—

"This it?" the cabbie asked.

"What?" He looked through the window, recognizing the
drugstore on the corner. "Yes, yes right here'll be fine," he
said.

He stepped onto the sidewalk, taking out his wallet,
thinking Andy can be shooting his arm full of heroin in the
time it takes me to pay off a goddamn cab driver. He paid
the cabbie, and then he looked up and started down Fiftieth Street, and then he stopped cold in his tracks and did a
classic double take, staring across the street.

Andy!

He saw him, and the name registered on his mind, and he opened his mouth to yell, and then he saw what Andy was doing. Andy was getting into a cab. He shook his head for a moment, as if to clear it, and then the name bubbled onto his lips, "Andy!" but the cab door slammed shut on his outburst, and he saw the cab pull away from the curb and head for Seventh Avenue. His own cab pulled away at the same instant, and he made an abortive stab at the door handle, swore, and then immediately, involuntarily, shouted, "Taxi!"

This is a goddamn Marx Brothers movie, he thought. Twelve midgets are going to climb out of the next cab that stops. Twelve midgets, each carrying hypodermic syringes. Oh, Jesus, this can't be real.

"Taxi!" he yelled again, and a cab pulled up in front of him, and he climbed in hastily. "Follow that cab," he said, and he almost laughed aloud at the absurdly urgent tone of his voice.

This is ridiculous, he told himself, but this is real. Either I'm crazy, or this is real. I am in reality sitting in a cab which is following another cab, and there is a drug addict in that other cab, and that addict's name is Andy Silvera, and my name is Bud Donato, and this is all real. It's all crazy, too, as crazy as a son-of-a-bitch, but it's real, I'm going nuts, I must be going nuts.

He leaned forward, looking through the windshield, watching the retreating rear of Andy's cab.

"Can't you hurry?" he said.

"Relax," the cabbie answered. The cabbie was used to these jerks who piled into his load like a house on fire.

"For God's sake, don't lose him," Bud said.

"You going to pay the fine if I—"

"Hurry," Bud said. "Please hurry!"

"Always rushing around, everybody always in a goddamn rush," the cabbie said, but he sighed and pressed his foot tighter against the accelerator. There seemed to be more traffic in the streets now. Where the hell did all the traffic come from all of a sudden? All we need now is a truck coming across our path, Bud thought, just like in the movies, and we'll squeeze past, or maybe carom up onto the sidewalk and crash through a plate-glass window and then come out with the steering wheel disconnected and in our hands, didn't Abbott and Costello pull that routine once?

He could see Andy's cab up ahead, and then the cab suddenly stopped, and he thought, *Good, a red light,* until he saw the door open and Andy stepping out. He looked past the cab and past Andy, trying to ascertain his whereabouts, and then he suddenly realized where they were. Central Park. Andy was heading for the park. He was—

"Anyplace here," Bud said. "Pull over, can't you?"

"With this traffic? Jesus, Mac—"

"Just let me out then. Here." He handed the cabbie a dollar bill and shoved open the door.

"Thanks, Ma—" the cabbie said, surprised, and Bud slammed the door shut on his voice and then backed up against the metal side of the cab when another car shot past him. He gingerly danced his way to the sidewalk and then rushed to the corner, crossing Central Park South. He could see Andy up ahead now, walking briskly, just entering the park.

"Andy! Hold it!" he yelled, running across the street, trying to watch the oncoming traffic and Andy at the same time. This is insane, he told himself. This is some kind of goddamn nightmare, and I'll wake up any minute —are my pants on?—I'll wake up laughing to beat all hell.

"Andy!" he yelled again, and this time Andy heard him, and this time Andy stopped and turned, recognizing Bud. He seemed to hesitate for a moment, and then he whirled and began running, and then he stopped and looked back at Bud once more, and then he broke into a fast trot, running deeper into the park.

A horn tooted, and Bud pulled in his backside, almost slamming into the fender of a parked car. An old man on the sidewalk selling salted pretzels started laughing insanely, and Bud glared at him heatedly and then ran to the park entrance. He could still see Andy up ahead. Andy had stopped again, several feet away from a water fountain. He was staring across the distance that separated him and Bud, staring indecisively. And then, as if he had made up his mind for the last time, he whirled and ran swiftly, turning the bend in the path, turning. Oh, Christ, I'll lose him, I'll lose him around that bend.

Bud ran past the water fountain and then headed for the bend in the path. He rounded the bend quickly, out of breath now, his throat burning. Andy was nowhere in sight.

"Andy!" he shouted. "Andy, it's me, Bud!"

A governess walked by pushing a baby carriage. She stared at Bud curiously and then hurried past with her charge.

"Andy!" he screamed, his throat hoarse.

Where, where? he thought. Where could he be? Where do you go to hide? Anywhere on either side of the path, yes, yes. Which side? Eeny, meeny, miney, max. Which side of the path? He must have got the drug and a syringe. And a spoon, yes, I have measured out my life with tablespoons. Where, which? He considered for a moment and then rushed off the left side of the path and then onto the steeply sloping grass, plowing his way into the trees.

"Andy!" he yelled again, craning his neck, twisting this way and that, climbing, searching, watching. He spotted the high rocks, and he immediately thought, *Behind the rocks,* and he climbed faster, beginning to sweat freely now, the sweat running down his chest, his undershirt sopping it up. He reached the big gray boulders and then ran around to the other side of them.

Andy was sitting on one of the rocks.

His head was bent and his arms dangled down between his knees, one hand tight around a syringe, and Bud thought, *I'm too late, he's taken it.*

"Andy," he said softly.

Andy looked up suddenly, as if someone had jabbed him in the ribs. A snarl suddenly appeared on his mouth. "Relax," he said harshly. "I didn't shoot up."

"You—"

"I didn't shoot up, bloodhound! Goddamnit, I didn't shoot up." He squeezed his eyes shut tightly, and the snarl left his mouth, a real animal snarl that suddenly vanished to be replaced by the immature lips again.

"I was going to," he said softly. He did not seem to be talking to Bud. His hands were clenched together, the syringe between them, and his head was bent, as if he were praying. The words were almost whispered. "I could taste it. I could taste the rotten stuff right in my mouth. But I didn't shoot up. I didn't."

Bud kept staring at him saying nothing.

"Don't you believe me?" Andy shouted. "Goddamnit, don't you believe me? Doesn't anybody ever believe me? Look!" His voice rose to a strident scream. "Look, you skeptical son-of-a-bitch! Look!" He lifted the syringe to Bud's face. "Here's the goddamn syringe, now do you believe me? It's empty, can you see that, can you see it, now do you believe me?"

"Andy . . ."

"Shut up!" He turned his head quickly, but not before Bud could see the tears in his eyes. "I copped on the Union Floor," he said softly, his rage spent. "The works, Bud. The H, and the spike, and the spoon. You don't need a spoon, you know. You can use a bottle cap, too. You take the cork out of it, and you cook the jive in that—if you haven't got a spoon. But a spoon is cleaner, so I grabbed one in the cafeteria, have it right here in my pocket, and I've got the stuff, too, all ready to knock the top of my skull off, and the spike . . . you see the syringe right here . . . Jesus, Jesus . . ."

He was suddenly sobbing, deep sobs that started somewhere down near the pit of his stomach and shuddered up into his throat.

"I suddenly realized what a big stupid jackass I was being. I all at once thought of the Laddy Fredericks gig, and I told myself, 'Go ahead, you dumb jerk, go ahead shoot up. Shoot up, and you shoot this audition straight to hell!' I almost threw the spike down into the dirt there. I almost threw it down like it was a snake. I would have stepped on the goddamn thing, but I borrowed the works from a guy on the Floor, and I'll have to return it. Oh, Jesus, oh, Jesus, when am I gonna learn, when the holy hell am I going to learn? I hocked your bag, Bud, forgive me for that, forgive me, please."

"That's all right," Bud said softly.

"I got ten bucks for it, and I blew the ten on this junk here in my pocket. But I'll sell it, Buddy, I'll sell it and redeem your bag. When I return the works, I'll sell it to the

guy loaned it to me. Not today. Maybe tomorrow or the
next day. I don't want to chance being left alone again, you
understand? I want to make sure. Then I'll return the
works, and I'll sell the H, and I'll redeem your bag, believe
me."

"Maybe you'd better give me the stuff," Bud said.

"No, no, I've got to sell it." He had stopped sobbing. He
reached into his back pocket for a handkerchief and then
he blew his nose noisily. "Don't worry, Bud. If I didn't
take it this time, then I've seen the light. I swear to Christ,
I could taste it. You went down for the eggs, and I put on
some Kenton, and just listening to him I began to think of
other times and, man, I could taste it, I could just *taste* the
stuff. But I didn't shoot up, Bud. I've still got it, right here
in my pocket. And here's the syringe, right in my hand, but
empty, empty. I've had it, man. I've seen the light, daddy."
He sighed and shook his head.

"You sure you don't want to return the syringe now?"

"No, he'll live without it. He wouldn't've laid it on me if
it was his only outfit, anyway. He'll wait."

"Shall we go back to the apartment, then?"

Andy nodded. He put the syringe into his pocket and
then said, "All right, let's go."

She was waiting in front of the building when the cab
pulled up. Andy looked through the window and said,
"The welcoming committee." They got out of the cab, and
he went directly to Carol and said, "Relax, I didn't shoot
up."

"I wasn't going to ask," Carol said. "Besides, I can see
you didn't."

"Is that my horn?" he asked, seeing the trumpet case on
the stoop.

"Yes. I was going to bring it over later, but I thought—"

"Gone, gone," he said. He walked up the steps quickly,
lifted the case to one knee, and opened it. "Man, look at
the mother-lover," he said. "Oh, look at it."

Bud came up onto the stoop. "Hello, Carol," he said.

"Hello, Bud."

"We had quite a chase. But he's all right."

"I'm glad. I was going to wait at the office for your call,

but I just couldn't. I begged off a few hours, and I came right here. Thank God he's all right."

"Can you use some breakfast?" he asked her.

"I think so."

"I feel as if I haven't eaten for ten years," Bud said. "There's nothing like a spring around Central Park for working up an appetite."

"And there's Arban's!" Andy said. "Christ, that old brown cover. Carol, you're an ever-loving— And what's this? Oh, gone, gone. *All* my books. Where'd you get them, Carol? My mother's place?"

"Yes. I went by last night. I thought—"

"Oh, this is great, great. Man, I can hardly wait to start blowing. Make way for the Boston Symphony!" He laughed aloud, and then he snapped the case shut and threw one arm around Carol's shoulders. "Honey, you're a doll. Did I ever tell you that? And I passed the fix by, honey, how's that for will power? I've got the jive right here in my pocket, but I didn't touch it. Now, sweetheart, is that will power, or is it? Come on, answer me? Is it, or is it?"

Carol smiled weakly. "It is," she said. Her brow wrinkled. "You still have the stuff?"

"Sure. Got to sell it so I can redeem Bud's bag."

"Give it to me," Carol said. "I'll redeem Bud's bag."

"Oh, no," Andy said. "No, no, sweetheart. I hocked it, I redeem it. Besides, this is a challenge. Right here in my pocket, you dig me? Right here where I can grab it any time I want it—but I'm not even sniffing at it. Honeydoll, that's will power. Baby, I've got it licked, I tell you."

"I'd feel happier if—"

"Now, come down, Carol, come down. You're beginning to sound like Mama Silvera. No, doll, I'm going to sell it. Now, let's go upstairs and get some food. I could eat an elephant."

He seemed quite happy. He whistled as they went up the steps, and when they came into the apartment, he said, "Somebody forgot to turn off the phonograph." He walked to the record player and lifted the arm. "Sorry, Stan," he said to the machine, and then he put the trumpet case down on the sofa and opened it, pulling out the books. He reached into his pocket for his mouthpiece, took the horn from the velvet bed, and put the mouthpiece on it. He put

the horn to his lips, puffing them out against the mouthpiece.

"Man, does this feel strange," he said.

"I'll get the eggs going," Bud said.

"I can do it," Carol said.

"You can help if you want to."

"I wonder if I should start from scratch," Andy said.
"Here, man, dig this garbage. 'Studies on Syncopation.' Tu,
tu, tu, tu, tu." He turned some pages and then stopped.
"Oh, man, look at this. Tu, tutututu, tu, tutututu, tu . . . I
wonder if I can blow it." He turned more pages. "Ah,
'Studies on the Slur,' hey, dig this, the date is here, the date
I first had the lesson, July twelfth, now how's that for something? Look here, in pencil. 'Use diaphram.' Sounds like
advice to newlyweds, doesn't it?" He laughed aloud, and
said, "Forgive me, Carol," and then he laughed again. "All
half notes. Say, I can play this standing on my head." He
began singing the notes. "Eff-ay, gee-bee, ay-cee, bee-dee,
cee-eee, dee-eff, eee-gee, effffff. Oh, simple, man, simple.
Where's all the hard stuff? This is Andy Silvera, man."

"Come on," Carol said. "Let's get those eggs." They
went into the kitchen together, and they could hear Andy
leafing through pages in the living room.

"We had a close call," Bud whispered.

"I'm sorry," Carol said. "I honestly didn't think he needed watching. I'll stay today."

"No, it's all right. You get back to work. I can keep an
eye on him. I'll be in all day, anyway. But I've got a test tomorrow. Maybe you'd better come stay with him, then."

"All right, that'll be best. I appreciate this, Bud."

"Ah, now, here's the stuff," Andy called. " 'Triple
Tonguing.' Ah, that's for me. That's what a shmaltz outfit
like Fredericks goes in for. Tu tu ku, tu tu ku, tu tu ku—
ah, that's the stuff, man. Man, I can't wait to start blowing."

"Go ahead," Bud said. "Everybody's awake by now,
anyway."

"Yeah," Andy said. "Yessir. Ah, here they are, all the
old ones I used to practice. 'Robin Adair,' and 'Loving, I
Think of Thee,' and, oh, here's a sweet one, 'Bluebells of
Scotland,' dahhh, dee-dee, ahhh, dah, ee-ah, dah-dah-dee-
dah, dahh . . . oh, man, do I remember these."

"Let's hear one of them," Bud called from the kitchen.

"Here comes the tricky stuff," Andy answered. " 'Ernani' and 'Traviata' and 'Il Crociato,' ah, and here's the one, man, here it is, right here at the end of the book, 'Fantaisie and Variations on the Carnival of Venice.' Man, you know I could play this one from top to bottom at one time? And, man, does this get crazy! Just take a look at this. He's got thirty-second notes here, and flipping up and down a full octave. You can bust your lip with this one, man! Man, I can't wait to tie into it."

"Well, the eggs are almost ready," Bud said. "It'll have to wait."

"Oh, sure, lots of time. This is real crazy, you know that? Here's 'Caprice and Variations,' that's another one I liked. This Arban gets the wildest arrangements, you know? He can really twist these tunes. Here comes Silvera, man, make way!" He started laughing again, and then he came into the kitchen with his horn hooked over his arm. He put one hand on his hip, and he tilted his nose ceilingward, and he said, "Dig this pose. 'Andy Silvera, bandleader of distinction, prefers BVDs because they fit so snug and allow his diaphragm to breathe easily.' " He laughed hilariously, and Bud laughed with him, amazed at the transformation that had come over Andy with the acquisition of his horn.

"Oh, man, I tell you I'm going to get with it again. I'm going to blow down the goddamn walls, believe me. Man, it's going to be like the old days again. Carol, I could kiss you for bringing this sweet little baby to me." He picked up the horn suddenly and kissed the bell. "Honey, why'd you want to stay away so long, huh? Honey, now don't you ever do that again, hear?" He scolded the horn with an extended forefinger, and then he began laughing again. "Right after breakfast I'm going to knock the windows out of this joint, you wait and see. The cops'll think it's a riot. Man, the cats'll come stampedin' down the avenue when I cut loose with this mother-loving ax of mine."

"Meanwhile," Bud said, "here're the eggs."

They brought the eggs and coffee to the table, and they sat down to eat, just as if it *were* old times, just as if nothing had happened to any of them during the past two

years. They were three friends sitting down to a late breakfast, and the warmth of the situation touched Bud immensely. Andy sat with the horn in his lap, and he talked
of what he was going to do with that horn, and listening to
him, there was no doubt in Bud's mind. By Christ, he
would do it this time. This time he'd break the habit, and
he'd really blow that horn, and people would sit up and
take notice when they heard the name Andy Silvera, and
that's the way it ought to have been always. They enjoyed
their breakfast, and when Carol got up to phone her office,
Bud was a little sorry it was over. She made her call, and
then kissed them both on their cheeks, and when she was
gone he and Andy turned to the task of clearing up the
dishes.

Andy would not calm down. He talked enthusiastically,
the words bubbling up out of his mouth. He talked of what
he was going to do with that horn of his, and Bud nodded
and listened, and after a while he began to lose interest.
And as abruptly as he had lost interest, Andy changed the
subject, changed it so subtly that Bud didn't realize for a
moment what was going on. And when he did realize, he
was a little disappointed because Andy was going back
again, back into the past, back on the one-tracked mind of
his, almost as if he still lived in the past, almost as if the
present were an unreal thing.

"Man," he said, "I really could blow in those days, now
admit it, couldn't I? I could blow the end, the very end,
that was me. And you guys did a lot for me, whether you
realize it or not. Oh, you probably didn't even know what
the hell you were doing, I mean *you* did but the others
didn't consciously set out to help me, I know that now.
Like I don't think the guys even knew what I was doing, or
at least what I *thought* I was doing. For me, it was a kind
of an invasion, you know? My getting into the clique, I
mean. For example, when I asked you to come along and
help me pick out a new sports jacket, why, man, I thought
I was putting something over on you. For all I know, you
may have had nothing else to do that afternoon. Or Frank
helping me buy some slotted-collar shirts. Hell, that son-of-
a-bitch just loved to shop, but did I know that? No, I
thought I was being tricky. It doesn't really make any

difference because I *did* get the clothes, one way or another, and that's what counts, I mean you guys really taught me how to dress.

"And the dancing, well, without the boys I'd have been lost. And without knowing how to dance, I wouldn't have stood a chance with Carol. For that matter, even my meeting Carol came about through the boys. Oh, not directly, I suppose. I mean, what the hell, it wasn't the boys' fault that the electricity got turned off in Club Stardust and we had to get another rehearsal hall. Mike's uncle always struck me as a jerk, anyway, but imagine a club without enough money to pay their electric bill. Jesus! But what I mean, you know, it *was* Tony's suggestion that we try some of the teen-age cellar clubs off Eastern Parkway, and if we hadn't stumbled into Club Beguine, and if Carol hadn't been there, and if I hadn't known how to dance

second chorus, i

MARCH, 1944

12

Their expedition that night, from a business viewpoint, was a dismal failure.

They worked their way from club to club, scouting either side of Carroll Street. They found only two clubs which possessed pianos, and they drew blanks at both. The president of the first club said he didn't like the idea of strangers rehearsing there in the absence of members. The second president informed them that the landlord of the house would not like a lot of noise during the daytime. As a matter of fact, the members even had to be careful about the volume of the record player at night. Tony Banner had not appreciated the president's use of the word "noise." He did not consider his band a noisemaking outfit. But he resigned himself to the fact that his idea had been a dud, and the boys settled down to enjoying an evening of dancing and prowling.

They would not have remained at Club Beguine—a cellar club which obviously took its name from the numerous plays the Artie Shaw record received that night—if Bud had not recognized a girl he knew there. The club in itself was nothing fancy to look at. You entered through a doorway at the end of the driveway, and you stepped down into a finished, furnished basement room. The finishing was confined to the blue-whitewashed walls and a canopy affair covering the ceiling pipes, plus paneling which covered the iron lolly columns holding up the first floor of the private house. The girl members of the club had sewn curtains for the tiny basement windows as an addition to the furnishing, which consisted of several wooden lawn chairs, a wooden lawn lounge, and a table upon which rested the record player. A door was at the far end of the club, and through the doorway a circular, homemade bar was visible, together with a second door to the right of which a sign hung. The sign read: *Here It Is.*

The rule of the club, as the boys knew from their previous excursions that evening, was two free dances. After that, if you decided to stay, a club member casually sauntered over and said, "Hello, fellows, will you be with us a while?" If you were going to be with them a while, you paid the club member twenty-five cents per head. If you were not going to be with them a while, the club member made sure you knew where the door was, and he smilingly told you to "drop in again sometime."

Considering its furnishing and finishing inducements, the boys would have abandoned Club Beguine instantly. Some of the other clubs they'd visited had boasted stuffed sofas and easy chairs, indirect lighting, even a juke box (into which you didn't have to dump coins) at one place. The only lure Club Beguine offered was Helen Cantor, and Bud spotted her the moment they stepped into the small room.

"I know that one," Bud said, and he headed for her instantly. Tony and Andy walked across the room and toward the toilet door. ("Here it is," Tony said, reading the sign. "Here it goes," Andy answered.) Reen went to the record player and began thumbing through the stack of records, much to the annoyance of a blond, pimply-faced club member who stood near by. Bud didn't pay any attention to the goings or comings of his friends. Bud walked swiftly toward Helen Cantor, his most charming smile on his face.

He felt somehow strange as he crossed the room. Being seventeen, and never having read the *Rubáiyát,* he nonetheless felt as if he were keeping a prearranged assignation. He knew this was sheer nonsense, but he couldn't shake the feeling that something terribly important was about to happen to him, and that this important thing had been ready to happen for a long time, awaiting only the principal players and the setting.

He knew Helen from school, and he had danced with her at a good many of the school dances, and he had liked dancing with her, and he had liked talking to her, and he wondered now why he had never asked her out, and he knew as he walked toward her that he would ask her out, and he didn't question the knowledge which had come with sudden adolescent clarity. She had not seen him yet, and he felt that this too was all a part of the plan, her not seeing him, and he felt that he already knew the exact moment when she would look up and see him, and he felt he already knew the expression that would be on her face when she did that. He studied her as he moved closer, focusing the picture that was already in his mind, wondering why the picture was there, superimposing the real picture of Helen over the vague image that nudged his consciousness: her long black hair, straight, turned into a pageboy at the nape of her neck; her green eyes, slanted slightly, faintly Oriental; her lips bright with lipstick, the contour spoiled a bit by the infinitesimal protrusion of her upper front teeth; the slender suppleness of her body— and his eyes candidly roamed over the trim suit she wore, lingering on the nylon-sleek exposure of knee where her legs were crossed. He remembered the way she danced, the pressure of her body against his, the narrowness of her waist, the way his arm completely circled that waist, the insistent nudging of her small, well-shaped breasts against his chest. He remembered these things, and they formed a strange part of his awareness.

And then she looked up.

He knew what would be on her face. He saw her lips round into a small *O* of surprise, and then lengthen into a smile. She seemed about to speak, but he was still too far from her, and so she stood perched on the ledge of articulation, her eyes holding his, drawing him to her.

She extended her hand when he came to her, as he knew she would, and he took it and squeezed it, sensing that neither of them felt this to be a handshake, knowing that she had held out her hand to him across a gulf, and that he had taken it and was now being led onto a narrow span high above treacherously swirling waters. He could not look down, and he could not look back. Helen Cantor was at the other end of that bridge, waiting.

"Hi," he said, amazed by the everyday sound of his voice. "What are you doing here?"

"I was waiting for you," Helen answered glibly, and they both started to smile, but suddenly the smiles died, as if she had said exactly what she was supposed to say, and as if they had both known she was going to say this, both somehow anticipating it and dreading it, and now that it was spoken, there was no turning back. The bridge had truly been crossed.

"You look pretty," he said. His eyes did not move from her face. He had always prided himself upon the smooth flow of his line, and he knew his opening words were too sudden and too abrupt and too badly stated to have any effect, but they seemed the right words to say now, the true words. He was surrounded with a clear, fragile, shimmering ball of sudden truth. They were alone within this crystal, and their words were unheard by anyone, and their eyes were unseen. They still held hands, as if the contact preserved the privacy and intimacy of their secret pristine glade.

"Thank you," Helen said. The pressure of her fingers tightened slightly.

"Do you belong to this club?" he asked.

"No. I just came down. With a friend."

"A girlfriend?"

"Yes," she said.

"That's good."

"Yes."

"You look pretty."

"I feel pretty. You make me feel pretty. You're staring at me."

"I know I am."

A tall boy in a brown suit sauntered over to them. "Welcome to Club Beguine," he said. He looked at them curiously. Helen stood up and smoothed her skirt, and then she went into Bud's arms, and he knew they were about to observe the convention of dancing, but he felt she would have come into his arms even if they were standing in Macy's window.

He was suddenly very happy. The room behind Helen was a dull blur. Only Helen stood out in almost painful detail, blinding almost. Helen filled his eyes and his mind, and he pulled her close to him. She leaned her body against his, and the reality of her coincided with the memory, and he smiled stupidly, his cheek against hers, and she felt his facial muscles move in the smile, and she pressed closer to him. They did not talk while they danced. When the record ended and a lindy screeched into the room, they went back to her chair, and he did not release her hand. The boy in the brown suit came around at the end of the lindy, subtly hinting that Bud should show up or shove off and he happily paid his quarter. From the corner of his eye he saw Tony and Andy emerge from the bathroom and enter the room with the record player. Tony moved easily about the room a dark wraith with a wide enameled grin and Andy clung to him like an animated shadow. He watched them holding Helen's hand all the while, waiting for Tony to break the ice. Reen was immersed in the record collection not interested in anything going on around him.

Tony stopped near two girls and began talking, introducing himself and Andy. Andy smiled and nodded acknowledgment, and Bud felt a sudden sympathy for the kid. He had so much to learn, so much to realize. One of the girls was an attractive blonde who smiled prettily and began talking to Andy enthusiastically. Bud tried to place her, but he couldn't, and he watched her for a moment, realizing that her attractiveness was a clever trap that lured one into a full appreciation of her startling beauty. He examined her dispassionately, the way he would a lovely bit of jewelry in a store window, and then he turned his full attention to Helen.

"Dance again?" he asked.

"Yes," she said.

They went onto the floor again. She was a good dancer, light on her feet, responsive to every subtle pressure of his hand and body. He held her close, and she pressed her cheek against his, and her cheek was very smooth, and he could smell the faint scent of perfume in her hair, a lilac scent, a very innocent scent.

He was consciously aware of their youth in that moment, the slender body in his arms, the music floating from the phonograph, the scent in Helen's hair, the smoothness of her cheek, the ease with which they glided over the floor. There was something powerful in their youth, and he wanted it to be springtime and not winter outside, and he wanted Helen Cantor to be the girl he had longed for, hoping she was the girl, wishing it were so, ready to accept her as such, wondering if the vague picture he carried in his mind would ever assume real flesh-and-blood shape, thinking of their youth at the same time, feeling the surge of strength that coursed through their bodies, feeling life beating there, pulsing there wildly.

He was only vaguely aware of the other dancers, vaguely surprised to see Andy on the floor with the vibrant blonde, moving quite smoothly for a beginner. The strength and power of his youth was overwhelmingly heady. He wanted to fly up there in the sky with Helen, wanted to crash the sky with wings of youth, feeling he *could* crash the sky. And, absurdly, he wished he could hear Andy playing his trumpet now, right this minute, wished the clean gold-brass would carry him and Helen up there where he wanted to be, bursting into the blackness of the sky with wings of youth. He wanted to say, "Helen, let's crash the sky," but instead he said, "Helen, let's take a walk," and he was not surprised when she answered, "All right."

He went to get Helen's coat from the cloakroom near the makeshift bar, noticing that only soft drinks were being served by a club member. When he started back toward Helen, Reen winked at him obscenely. He did not return the wink. He went for his own coat where he had draped it over the back of Helen's chair, still feeling this heady drunkenness inside him.

The stars outside were crisp and austere. The night was very cold, and she took his arm firmly and moved closer to him, and he felt that he would burst because this sudden movement was something very familiar and very intimate, and he could not banish the persistent feeling that he and

Helen had walked into the cold like this before, that she had looped her hand through his arm and then moved close to him, and that the movement had somehow built a solid front against the onslaught of winter, against the cold, against the forbidding stars—against the world.

"It's cold," she said, her breath pluming out ahead of her, her voice small and almost echoing in the hollow bowl of the sky.

"Yes."

"Do you think we ought to go back?"

"No."

They walked silently beneath the bare branches of the trees, automatically falling into step. Helen's hand clutched his biceps tightly, and her head moved to his shoulder, and they walked without speaking, and neither of them questioned the thing they knew was happening. They were seventeen, and anything that happened was right, and anything that happened was unquestioned. There was still enough of the child in them to suspend a disbelief in fairy stories, just enough of the adult to hold a healthy respect for the suspension of such disbelief. And so the magic of their meeting, and the magic of their wordless, walk, and the steady hush of the world around them, and the hollow clatter of their shoes on the pavement, and the warm intimacy of her hand on the tweed of his sleeve, and the brittle vapor that rushed out of their mouths, all went unquestioned. The adult in each of them urgently whispered that it did not happen this way—but there was youth strong within them, and the song of youth was high and keening and curiously nostalgic of an uncluttered untroubled existence, and the song of youth crooned its warm logic: It *is* happening this way.

"Do you want to go back?" he asked.

"No, it's all right."

"If you're cold, we can sit in the car."

"Do you have a car?"

He would ordinarily have lied about proprietorship. Now he said, "My father's."

"All right," she answered.

He led her to his father's car, and he held open the door for her, and then he slammed the door shut. He walked around the car hastily, as if the sound of the slam were an intrusion from a real world where magic did not exist, as if he expected her to have vanished when he entered the car. She was still there, and he sighed and then moved closer to her on the seat. He kissed her instantly. She tightened her arms around his neck, and then she pulled away from him, a faint smile on her mouth. He pulled her gently toward him again, and she turned her head and whispered, "My lipstick."

"Do you want to take it off?" he asked softly.

She stared at him curiously, her green eyes wide, as if she wanted to memorize his face. She touched his cheekbone with one hand, and then turned and reached for her purse. He watched her in the semi-darkness of the Chevvy, and there was something so sadly feminine in the gesture, something of such completely wonderful girlish surrender in it that he wanted to pull her to him and hold her close, protected in the circle of his arms, unmolested. He watched her solemnly, thinking. *She is such a girl, she is only a girl she could be only a girl, nothing else, only a girl.* She dabbed at her lips with a tissue, and he watched the motion of her hand, loving the motion of her hand, feeling closer to her in that moment because the act was an intimate one, loving the girl-business of removing lipstick, feeling more manly because of the feminine way in which she moved, loving everything so delicately female about her, the softness of her hair framing her face, the slope of her eyes, the small tilted breasts beneath the suit jacket, her delicately crossed feet.

She turned then and faced him, waiting, her head raised slightly, her eyes calmly studying his face. He wanted to touch her tenderly. Her knees brushed his, and he was conscious of the touch of nylon and he looked into her eyes, and in that moment he knew that he loved her.

He kissed her gently, and the tenderness of the kiss reached her, and she pulled back her face slowly, wonderingly, looking up at him, her eyes puzzled. He kissed her again, brushing his lips against hers, feeling her full upper lip where her teeth gently nudged it, thinking, *I love you, Helen, I love you, Helen,* loving her in that moment with a fierce, painfully sweet love.

"Bud," she said, "Buddy, Buddy, what's—"

"No," he said softly, covering her lips with his fingers.

She shook her head, and a frown clouded her brow. She moved closer in the circle of his arms, wanting to be very close to him, and the tenderness enveloped her until she wanted to kiss his hands, kiss his throat, suffocate him with her kisses, possess him with her kisses. She reached for his hand, and she moved it to her breast, wanting the tenderness to stay with them, wanting his hand close to her, the way his mouth was close to her, the way his mouth was close to her.

He did not misunderstand. He kept his hand lightly on her breast, her own hand covering it, and they sat silently in the automobile, and he wanted nothing more from her in that moment, nothing more than her proximity. If she had offered herself to him, he thought in his mind that he would refuse, now he would refuse, now was not the time for it, now was a time for a different intimacy, the intimacy of discovery, the long-awaited discovery. He felt a soothing peace spread within him, as if he had come down a long dark tunnel and found a warm, quietly pulsating brightness at the end of it. And suddenly he wanted to tell her what he thought, wanted to share it with her, and he said, "You know ..." meaning to say more, puzzled when the sentence ended as a stark declaration of fact, and somehow not surprised when she answered simply, "I know."

Andy kept his right hand in the small of her back, the way Bud had taught him, and he held his left hand extended, cupping hers, not out stiffly, but slightly bent at the elbow, so that he wouldn't seem to be drilling for oil. He saw Bud helping the girl with the dark hair into her coat, and the girl smiled up at Bud, and her buck teeth showed when she smiled. She was not really a pretty enough girl for Bud, and he was surprised that Bud would bother. Well, maybe her teeth weren't very bucked, but certainly enough so to push her upper lip out a little. Bud deserved a girl like the one he was dancing with, a really pretty girl.

". . . Andrew?" she said.

"What?" he said. "I'm sorry."

"I said is Andy short for Andrew?"

"Oh, yes," he said. "Yes, it is."

"I wondered. I know some boys named Angelo who call themselves Andy."

"No, my name is Andrew."

"Andrew is much nicer than Angelo, anyway."

She had a very soft voice, and she lifted her head when she spoke, so that her eyes met his, so that all her attention seemed to be focused upon what she was saying. Her eyes were very brown, and her skin was very fair, and her hair was a golden blond, not like the brass of a trumpet, a soft gold, maybe the way a trumpet begins to look when the acid of your hand eats at the finish. But not tarnished, not that at all, just paled sort of, a very pale sort of blond with warm alive brown eyes.

"You have a nice name," he said.

"Carol?" She laughed somewhere deep in her throat. "Do you really like it? I think it's a silly name."

"No, it's not silly at all. I mean, it's very pleasant. The sound of it. Carol."

"Carol Ciardi," she said, pulling a face. "The last name spoils it. You should put a name like Manning or Winston or Danville with it. Carol Manning." She paused and got in step with him. "What's your last name?"

"Silvera," he said.

"That's as bad as mine."

"Well, it's Italian-sounding. But it could be worse, you know. Ox's last name is Castagliano."

"Who's Ox?"

"Oh, one of the boys in the band."

"Do you play in a band?"

"Yes," he said. "Didn't you know? I thought Tony mentioned it."

"No. At least, I didn't hear him. What do you play?"

"Trumpet," he said.

"Oh, not really. Do you really?"

"Yes." He frowned. "Is that bad?"

"No, it's good. I love the trumpet. Do you really play it?"

"Sure I do."

"Are you good?"

"I'm pretty good," he said modestly.

"I mean, are you as good as, you know, the big trumpet players?"

Andy smiled. "You'll have to judge for yourself, I guess."

"Can you play 'You Made Me Love You'?"

"I guess so," he said. "If I had the music, I could play it."

"The way Harry James does?"

"Well, maybe not exactly the way he does. But I could play it."

"I love that record," she said.

"I like it, too. I like James a lot."

"I used to listen for all his new releases," she said. "And almost every week Martin Block would pick one of his records as the best. Do you remember when he did 'Music Makers'? And 'Sleepy Lagoon'?"

"Those are old ones," Andy said.

"Yes, but I mean I was a fan of his even then. Can you really play 'You Made Me Love You'?"

"Sure, if I had the music."

"Is it hard to read music?"

"Well ... gee, I don't know. I suppose in the beginning it is."

"I wish I were a man. I'd play trumpet if I were a man."

"Girls play trumpet, too, you know. Woody Herman had a fine trumpet player, a girl named Billy Rogers."

"I know, I know," she said. "But the idea of a girl playing trumpet or saxophone or—What's the thing you push up and down?"

"The trombone?"

"The trombone, the idea is sort of disgusting, isn't it? I think a girl should play piano, and that's all."

"Do you play piano?"

"Oh, no, I was just saying."

"Bud plays piano," Andy said. "He's pretty good."

"Who's Bud?"

"I don't think you met him. He was talking to the dark girl over there."

"Oh, Helen. Yes, I saw him."

The conversation suddenly lapsed, as if it were lying down to catch its breath. They circled the floor wordlessly, and he thought, She has a very good face. High cheekbones, and a straight nose, and a full mouth. They did not speak to each other until the record ended. He thanked her for the dance, but she did not release his hand.

"Let's see if we can find some James records," she said.

"All right," he answered.

They walked to the record player, and Reen looked up as they approached.

"Are you in charge of the music?" Andy asked.

"Did you have anything special in mind, sir?" Reen answered, pretending he didn't know Andy.

"Well, I don't know. We were hoping you had some James records."

"James? A trumpet player? All trumpet players stink," Reen said.

Carol looked up at him, a frown puckering her forehead.

"You don't belong to the club," she said pointedly.

"No, I don't," Reen said. "Do you?"

"Yes, I do," she said firmly.

"Congratulations," Reen answered. "Now then, sir, you said you—"

"Only club members are supposed to handle the records," Carol said. "Can't you read the sign?"

"What sign?"

Carol looked at the front of the phonograph where two slivers of transparent tape still hung. "Well, there was a sign," she said, as if she believed Reen had taken it down.

"Are you looking for trouble?" Reen asked, a sparkle in his eyes. "Are you trying to get me into a fight with your boyfriend?"

Andy caught on instantly. He took a slight step foward, balling his fists. "Now look, fella," he said, "let's watch the way we're talking."

"Your girlfriend says I can't handle the records," Reen said. "Does she know I was once a disk jockey in Kansas City?"

"I don't care if you—"

"It was me who gave Guy Lombardo his start," Reen said.

"Watch your language," Andy said. "There's a lady present."

"I'm going to get the president," Carol said.

"Now just a minute," Reen said, "just a minute. There's no need to call in Roosevelt on this. After all—"

"I didn't mean—" Carol started.

"Are you accusing me of dodging the draft?" Reen asked seriously.

"You're probably 4-F," Andy said.

"I am!" Reen bellowed. "And proud of it! My father was 4-F, and his father before him, and my great-great-great-grandfather was a shirker during the Revolutionary War. He later became a general, purely by accident. Perhaps you know his name? Arnold? Benedict Arnold?"

"It sounds familiar," Andy said, "but don't drag in your family tree. We're talking about records here."

"This is all part of the record," Reen said.

Carol was beginning to catch on. She looked at Andy suspiciously, and then her eyes narrowed.

"Your family's record doesn't interest me," Andy said. "If you're trying to cloud the issue by—"

"No one can belittle my family's issue," Reen said. "My grandmother had twelve children, all boys, all 4-effers. It's all on the record."

"Who issued the record?" Andy wanted to know, seeing the smile form on Carol's mouth.

"Bluebird," Reen said. "And later we switched to Decca."

"Can we switch to Columbia now and get some James stuff?" Andy asked.

"Why didn't you say so in the first place?" Reen answered. "Who's your belligerent friend?"

"Carol," Andy said, "I'd like you to meet Reen."

"How do you do?" Carol said. "You really had me going for a while."

"I like to bait pretty girls," Reen said.

"Why, thank you."

"Don't mention it. Has the Little One been telling you what a great trumpet player he is?"

"No, he hasn't."

"Well, he should. He makes James look sick."

"Oh, come on, Reen," Andy said.

"He's modest," Reen said matter-of-factly. "Truth is he can charm the birds out of the trees with his horn."

"Orpheus with his lute," Carol said.

"Huh?" Reen asked. "Oh, oh, yes, 'Making trees and mountaintops that freeze bow their heads when he did sing.' I thought I was the only one in the world who knew that."

Andy didn't recognize the reference. He stood by while Carol smiled up at Reen, wondering if he were going to

lose her after things had started out so well. He did not
want to lose her.

"We're still waiting for some James," he said.

" 'You Made Me Love You,' " Carol said.

"I kind of like you, too," Reen answered. He turned his
back and began thumbing through the records. " 'Swingin'
on a Star'? How about that?"

"No, thanks," Andy said.

" 'There Are Such Things'?"

"Nope."

" 'Pistol-Packin' Mama'? Ouch! Here's a James. 'Mister Five-by-Five.' "

" 'You Made Me Love You,' " Carol insisted.

"All right, all right, all right," Reen said. "You sure
you've got the damned record?"

"We've got it," Carol said.

"Ah, here it is," Reen said. "Get out there on the floor,
and I'll play it."

"You coming, Andy?" Carol asked.

"Sure," he said.

They walked to the center of the floor, waiting for the
record to begin, Carol standing in the circle of Andy's
arms. When the record started, he dipped automatically,
not even listening to the music.

"That's not . . ." Carol started.

He turned his attention to the phonograph, hearing the
honeyed tones of Bing Crosby. Reen stood at the side of
the room, his arms folded over his chest, a big crud-eating
grin on his face.

" 'Swingin' on a Star,' " Andy said.

"Oh, well," Carol sighed. "It's not really a bad song."

"No. It got the Academy Award, you know. Did you
listen to that the other night?"

"No, I didn't. I read about it in the papers, though."

"I don't think *Going My Way* should have got it, do
you?"

"Not at all. Did you see *Gaslight?*"

"That was a good picture," Andy said. "Well, she at
least got the award for it."

"She's one of my favorites," Carol said. "I go to see
anything she's in."

"Ingrid Bergman? Yeah?"

"Well, why not?"

"No, it's just that ... well, you're such different types, I mean, she's pretty in a different way than you. So I thought ..."

"My, we're full of compliments tonight, aren't we? First your friend, and now ..."

"Oh, I wasn't trying to ... Well, gee, you know you're pretty, don't you?"

"Flattery will get you nowhere, sir," Carol said, smiling.

He didn't know what to answer, so he concentrated on his dancing, listening to "Swingin' on a Star," wishing it were "You Made Me Love You." The Crosby record had a slight jump to it, and it didn't blend too well with the fox trot steps he'd learned. Some couples on the floor were lindying to it.

"Did you see *Laura?*" Carol asked.

"Yes. That was another good one."

"I think it should have won."

"It did get something," Andy said.

"It did?"

"Well, one of the stupid things. Photography, screenplay, something like that."

"Dana Andrews was very good in that," Carol said. "Better than Bing Crosby. He should have got it."

"I don't think he was even nominated."

"We should have been in charge of the awards," Carol said.

"I'd have given it to Mickey Mouse," Andy said, smiling.

"Do you go to the movies a lot?"

"Yes. Do ... do you?"

"Oh, yes."

How do you ask a girl to go to the movies with you? he wondered. What do you say?

"Maybe ... maybe we ..."

The record was coming to an end. He summoned up all his concentration and went into the final dip, holding the dip as the record played its final chord. He saw Reen at the player, and then, instantly following the first record, the golden tone of Harry James reached up for the canvas canopy of the club, and Reen smiled and winked.

" 'You Made Me Love You,' " Carol murmured.

"Reen's all right," he said out loud, wanting to think it. "He just couldn't find it before."

They did not speak at all during the record. They listened to the music, and they moved over the dance floor. She danced very well, or at least she danced very well as far as his knowledge went. She was the first girl he'd ever really danced with, and he certainly appreciated her more than he had either Frank or Reen or Bud. He held her in his arms, wanting to draw her closer to him, but afraid to. She was just a little shorter than he, and his cheek touched hers once, but he pulled it away rapidly, not wanting her to get the wrong idea. The wrong idea, of course, was the right idea because there was nothing he'd rather have done than put his cheek against hers. He kept his hand in the small of her back, and he could feel the firm flesh on either side of her spine through the thin blouse she wore. She was very well built, he thought, slender, but not with that skinny look about her, that awkward skinniness that makes a lot of girls look like slobs.

She had good hips, and nice breasts, maybe not as big as that girl with the string of pearls, but bigger than the girl Bud was with tonight. What was her name? Helen.

He could feel her breasts against him whenever he dipped, but he didn't dip too often because he didn't want her to think he was dipping just to feel her breasts. He could also feel the very slight bulge of her stomach whenever he dipped, and he hoped he wouldn't get excited, so he didn't dip at all after that. He tried the breaks Reen had taught him, and the first time he broke, his hand went too far around her back so that his fingertips could feel the sideward swell of her breast. He pulled his hand back quickly, but she hadn't seemed to notice, and he wondered if he should try it again.

He wondered what Bud would do in a situation like this, and he wondered if he should ask Bud about it, and at the same time he wondered how he could ask her to go to the movies with him. But he didn't want to start talking again because there was something very nice about just dancing with this girl, Carol, Carol Ciardi—he rolled the name on the tongue of his mind—just having her in his arms like that, as if he owned her, as if she were truly his, Carol Silvera. He felt like a good dancer with her, and he enjoyed the feeling, and he enjoyed the easy way they talked, though he certainly wished he could think of some way to ask her to the movies.

The record was running out, like the sands of time, and he felt that this might be the very last time he would ever dance with her. Suppose she left right after this record? Suppose she went home and he never saw her again, never in his whole life? Suppose the boys wanted to leave now? My God, suppose, this girl should get away?

"Carol . . ." he said.

"Yes?" She looked up at him, and he drowned in the brownness of her eyes.

"Carol . . ." *What now? How do I ask? How, how?*

"Yes, Andy?"

"Tomorrow. Tomorrow's Sunday."

"Yes?"

"I . . . are you . . . well . . . Carol . . . could you . . . would you like to go to the movies with me tomorrow? Afternoon?" He swallowed the panic in his throat.

"Tomorrow?" she asked.

"Yes," he said eagerly.

"I'm awfully sorry, Andy. I already have a date for tomorrow."

"Oh."

"But some other time, perhaps."

"Sure. Sure, some other—"

"Will you be coming down to the club again?"

"I . . . I don't know . . . it's hard to say."

"Why don't you come down again next Friday? We'll talk some more then."

"Well . . . maybe," he said, knowing he wouldn't dare come down without the boys, and not sure whether or not the boys would want to return. "We'll see."

"And Andy . . . I really do have a date for tomorrow. I'm not giving you the fast brush."

"Oh, I didn't think you—"

"I just wanted you to know."

"All right," he said.

"Try me next week."

"All right," he said.

"Is that a promise?"

"Yes. It's a promise."

Carol smiled, listening to the music that came from the phonograph. "Your friend is really Mama's little helper, isn't he? 'You Made Me Love You' again."

Andy smiled and took her into his arms.

second chorus, ii

MARCH, 1944

13

The day that Tony Banner thought he'd achieved full stature as leader of the band was coincidentally—and perhaps consequentially—the same day that Andy thought he'd achieved full stature as a member of the clique. Neither could have been more sadly mistaken.

It was preceded by the news, on the Sunday before, that Tony had booked the band for its first paying job. The fact that the booker was one of Tony's maiden aunts who'd finally managed to lure a man into marriage did not in any way detract from the joy with which the announcement was greeted. A wedding job was a wedding job, and who cared which slobs were tying the knot? The band was to be paid a total of fifteen dollars for six pieces. ("We're asking twenty," Tony had said, shrewdly businesslike, "but we'll settle for fifteen.") Of the fifteen, a five-dollar deposit was left with Tony, and Tony suggested that the total, when received, be used for the purchase of new arrangements. The band, quickly calculating that a division of the total would give them each only two-fifty, unanimously agreed to the suggestion.

Since the wedding would not come off until the Sunday after Easter, the boys had a fairly respectable amount of time in which to brush up on their music-making. They were eager to make a good first impression, but their eagerness was somewhat dimmed by the dimmed lights at Club Stardust. Knowing they could no longer rehearse there, they began avidly seeking a new rehearsal hall and were finally forced into giving up two fifths of the five-dollar deposit, a loss they suffered with pained souls. It was Tony who secured the new rehearsal hall, on the understanding

that it would be a one-shot until they could get something
better. Two dollars an afternoon was a little steep for the
boys at this stage of the game.

The rehearsal hall was actually the gymnasium belonging to St. Joseph's on Utica Avenue. The gymnasium was
a monstrously large affair, built behind the pleasant stone-
and-wood structure which was the church. It had large
windows, a highly polished floor, and bleachers and basket-
ball hoops, all of which combined to give the place exactly
the atmosphere undesirable for a rehearsal. But it did have
a stage at one end of the room, and the stage had a piano,
and even though the price was two dollars, Mike Daley (a
staunch Catholic) insisted it was for a good cause.

The rehearsal was called for Saturday, March twenty-
fifth. On Friday, March twenty-fourth, the boys had made
another sortie into Club Beguine, a sortie which had left
Andy Silvera with his head in the clouds and his feet an
appreciable distance off the ground. Carol Ciardi had
agreed, on that Friday night, to accompany Andy to the
movies the following Sunday. He could not have been
happier, and his happiness led to a sort of cockiness which
was perhaps responsible for what happened on the day of
the rehearsal.

Considering the small rehearsal fee, the boys should not
have been surprised to discover the gymnasium was un-
heated. They were, nonetheless, surprised. They were also
a bit uncomfortable, mainly because the temperature on
that March day—a March which five days before had
boasted the crash of a bus in snow and sleet through a
bridge railing in Passaic, New Jersey—inconsiderately
dipped to a very low low. They were cold. They were
goddamned good and cold. The gymnasium was a big
echoing chamber, and the wind blasted at each of the long
windows, and they felt the wind, and each time they complained about it, their voices bounced off the high walls
and jeered back at them. They tried to warm up, both
physically and musically, but their hands were cold and
their horns were cold, and Frank's bitter insistence that
Tony Banner had pulled another boner did not help the
situation any. Tony, in self-defense, suggested that the
boys take a few laps around the gymnasium, and the boys,

eager for any diversion from the cold, accepted his suggestion.

They ran around the long gymnasium grimly at first, their shoes clattering on the cold wooden floors.

"Hup-tup-tripp-fuh!" Reen bellowed, standing on the side of the room and clapping his hands over his head. "Hup-tup-tripp-fuh!"

The boys took up the chant, hup-tup-tripp-fuhing it around the room. Their voices bounced off the high ceiling, and their earlier sour mood slowly gave way to a sort of resigned joviality. Frank went to his drums and began playing a fast march beat, and the rest jogged along to the rhythm of the drums, their spirits and their body temperatures rising. By the time Andy arrived, the boys were all very warm, and they were in the process of warming up their respective instruments by marching around the room with them, blowing incessantly, tramping their feet.

Andy stood in the doorway and watched the exhibition, an amused grin on his face. Anything would have struck him funny on that day. He had still not adjusted fully to the miracle of Carol Ciardi's acceptance of his movie proposition. Last night had been an altogether fine experience. He had loved being with her, and she had somehow heightened his confidence. He had felt extremely fast and witty, and he'd actually exchanged a good five minutes of repartee with Bud, whom he considered the master of the funny comment. The confidence had slept with him, and it had awakened him, rested and much stronger. He felt he could match wits with the best of them. He felt he'd arrived, and it was unfortunate that his social arrival (for such was what he considered it) happened to coincide with his arrival for the rehearsal hall, a sub-zero rectangle of jogging, laughing, tramping musicians. He shook his head in amused amazement and walked over to the drums, where Frank excitedly kept up the march tempo.

"All we need here is a few hanging sides of beef," he said.

Frank laughed aloud, absorbed in the rhythm, watching the boys jog along to his drumbeats. Andy appreciated the laughter, and he smiled contentedly, analyzing the humor in his comment. He had not said something as dull and plodding as "This place is like a refrigerator." He had simply drawn a visual picture of a butchershop icebox, allowing Frank to draw his own conclusion from the inference. The result was excruciatingly comic, he felt, and—of course—there was also something riotously amusing about naked sides of beef. He was quite pleased with himself. Out on the floor, Ox was beginning to sound a little better. He started a Sousa march, and Tony joined in with him.

"Tony pulled a boner, all right," Frank said, smiling.

If Andy was pleased before, his pleasure soared ecstatically now. Frank had provided him with a perfect straight line. And feeling like the gagman's gagman, he immediately pounced upon it.

"Boner Banner," he said, and Frank—vastly enjoying the excitement and vigor of the marching spectacle—laughed heartily. Andy, encouraged, laughed along with him and then put down his trumpet case and took out his horn. He did not take off his coat, and there was something paralyzingly humorous about the idea of rehearsing with your coat on. Damn, if this wasn't the funniest experience he'd ever had in his whole life. Happily smiling, he rolled his mouthpiece around between his hands for a while, trying to heat it, and then he fitted it onto the horn and began blowing his long, low warm-up notes.

"My lip is stiff as a board," he said to Frank, and Frank burst out laughing, even though there was nothing whatever to laugh at. Frank kept pounding away at the snare, his eyes bright, and Andy watched him for a few moments and then tried to warm up again, amused by the awkwardness of his fingers on the valve buttons.

"Okay!" Tony yelled from the floor. "That's enough. Let's tune up now and get started." He began walking back toward the stage, spotting Andy. "Hi!" he called, waving, and Andy impishly tilted his horn a little and blew a short note which sounded something like "Hi!" drawing a laugh from Tony. Bud climbed the steps to the stage, rubbing his hands together briskly.

"Welcome to the Arctic Circle," he said, and Andy appreciated the humorous comment immeasurably. He sought in his mind for a witty comeback, but when none presented itself, he simply asked, "Are we really going to try to rehearse here?"

"Sure," Tony said. "Why not? This cold is invigorating."

"In other words, you pulled a boner," Andy said, smiling.

"Take a few laps," Tony said, smiling back. "You'll see how fast you warm up."

Andy shook his head sadly. "Boner Banner," he repeated wonderingly, and Bud exploded in a laugh, and Tony—exhilarated by his run—laughed too. The boys clambered up to the stage and crowded around the piano, taking their A from Bud and then going to their places behind the metal stands. Bud gave Andy the A, and Andy blew a corresponding B on his B-flat horn, and Bud said, "You're flat."

"Like a sewer lid," Andy replied, getting another laugh from Bud. God, he was witty today. Today he was the wittiest. And tomorrow, tomorrow he'd see Carol again. He pulled in his slide a little and blew again.

"You're still flat," Bud said.

"I'm not warmed up yet," Andy said. "This isn't going to do any good."

"You'll be okay," Tony said happily.

Bud kept striking the A, and Andy kept hitting his B until they struck some sort of compromise. The other boys kept blowing heartily, moistening their reeds, keeping their fingers active so that the cold would not attack them again.

"Okay," Tony said jovially, "let's take 'Elk's Parade' for a warm-up."

"Now there's a surprise," Andy said, and Bud and Frank laughed, and the other boys plowed through their music, putting "Elk's Parade" on top of the other sheets, ready to start playing.

"Ah-one," Tony said, "ah-two, ah-three, ah-four. Ah-one, two, three, four," and the boys began playing.

They'd have sounded bad in any case, considering the cold and considering the breaths they'd just exhausted in running around the gym. They sounded worse because the acoustics were terrible, and every note they blew ricocheted and then re-ricocheted. Andy didn't help the situation at all. There was a lot of trumpet work in "Elk's Parade" and a lot of tricky syncopation with drum and trumpet, and

Andy's lip was still stiff. He blew halfheartedly, the collar of his coat pulled high on the back of his neck, the horn huddled close to his chest. He could not help being amused. There was something terribly ludicrous about the whole situation. In his own mind he could not convince himself that they were seriously rehearsing—not bundled up this way like Eskimos. No, this was too much. This was some kind of a burlesque routine.

When they finished the number, Tony cheerily said, "Well, that was lousy," and the boys agreed, their voices scattering around the gym and charging back at them like a Mongolian horde on horseback. Even the acoustics amused Andy. He listened to the echoing voices, shivered against the cold, and said, "Why don't we give it up?"

"You should take a few laps," Tony said.

"The only lap I want right now is Carol's," Andy answered. The boys all laughed, and Andy felt again this pleasurable feeling of belonging. Simply having a girl had done that for him, simply getting a date with a girl. He could now joke with the boys on that level, too, and the knowledge that he could do that was gratifying indeed.

"No, really," Tony said. "Go ahead, we'll run through a sax chorus meanwhile."

"No, thanks," Andy said. "Thanks a lot, but no, thanks."

"Okay, suit yourself. Let's take a slow one, yes? 'It Can't Be Wrong' looks good. Number seventeen."

"Do you know what George Washington said to the Indian when he was crossing the Delaware?" Andy asked.

"What?" Bud supplied, knowing the punch line.

"*Far-may noo gatz-iddo freedo*," Andy answered, butchering the Italian.

Frank laughed idiotically, and Bud leaped in with, "Do you know what the Indian answered?"

"No, what?" Andy said.

"*Tu anche sei 'taliano?*" Bud said, laughing.

"I don't get it," Mike Daley said blankly.

"Wait till you're sixty-five," Frank said, remembering the Social Security gag, but not realizing it didn't fit here. "You'll get it then."

"Tony's used to all this cold," Andy said, ignoring Frank. "I think he was born at the North Pole." He did not remember that Reen had originated this particular gag only a week before.

"He's a real Eskimo," Bud said, still laughing.

"Mukluk Banner," Andy said, always surprised and delighted by the infinite variety of first names which sounded good with Tony's surname.

"Come on," Tony said, still cheerily, "let's rehearse."

They took the number, and Andy felt his lip loosening a bit, but he could still not take this mock rehearsal seriously. He blew with half his normal power, knowing he sounded better than Vic Andrada would have sounded, but knowing too that he wasn't playing for all he was worth. When they'd finished the tune, Tony turned and asked, "What's the matter, Andy?"

"What's the matter what?" Andy said.

"You're not blowing, boy."

"I'm blowing."

"Well, try to give it a little more, will you?" Tony said pleasantly.

"I'm freezing to death here," Andy said, "and he wants me to give it a little more."

"*We're all* freezing to death," Ox said, annoyed by all this delay.

"Except Tony," Andy said. "He's an Eskimo. Look at his complexion, there's the tip-off. Black Banner."

"Ha-ha," Tony said mirthlessly. "Come on, let's take 'I Dreamt I Dwelt.'"

"Let's take a long break," Andy said.

"Oh, come on," Tony said, "cut it out, Andy. We're trying to get something accomplished here."

"Couldn't you get a place with steam heat?"

"This is the best I could do. Come on, 'I Dreamt I Dwelt.' That's thirty-one."

"Mukluk, the Black Banner," Andy said, smiling.

"Since when are Eskimos black?" Ox asked, irritated, wanting to get on with the rehearsal.

"You're right," Andy said. "This is Swahili Banner."

"Okay, get it all out of your system," Tony said patiently, "and then maybe we can rehearse. Any other names, Little One?"

"That's all for now," Andy said.

"Andy's feeling his oats," Bud said. "He's got a date tomorrow."

"Can we rehearse now?" Tony said wearily.

"Let's rehearse," Andy said, smiling.

They took the "Harlem" number, and the sax section gave it everything they had, but Andy was still not blowing. He was blowing, of course, but he was not providing the brass spark the band needed, and in a driving number like "I Dreamt I Dwelt in Harlem," the result was disastrous. Tony called a halt before they got to the change of key.

"Hey, look, Andy," he said, "how about joining us?"

"I'm blowing," Andy said. "I'm just cold, that all."

"Then take a few laps, will you?"

"I'm not that cold."

"Then start blowing the way you know how to blow."

"I'm blowing the best I can. I know my part, anyway."

"The saxes know their parts, too," Tony said. "But this happens to be a band rehearsal."

"Oh," Andy said. "I thought it was a polar expedition."

"All right, kid around if you want to," Tony said. "We've got a job to play three weeks from now, though. I hope you know that."

"I'll make out all right," Andy said.

"You want to take 'Trumpet Blues'? You think that'll put you in the mood?"

"Take anything you like," Andy said, enjoying all the attention that had suddenly been focused on him, feeling the social equal of the boys, feeling almost a little superior to them.

"All right," Tony said. " 'Trumpet Blues.' That's twenty-seven." Ordinarily he'd have lingered on the "Harlem" number, playing it and replaying it until all the kinks were ironed out. But he seemed to sense that nothing would be accomplished that day until Andy snapped out of it, and so he'd offered "Trumpet Blues" as something of a bribe, hoping Andy would come alive during the number and continue to stay alive for the remainder of the rehearsal.

Andy did not come alive. He still regarded the entire setup as a convulsively comic fiasco. The idea of everyone's sitting around and rehearsing in overcoats and mufflers was too much for him to bear. It was all so terribly funny, and he felt so wonderfully witty, and he also, curiously, felt good-looking and cocky, but most of all he felt amused. And in keeping with the humorous slant of the occasion, he played "Trumpet Blues" as humorously as he knew how. His musical humor was a spontaneous combination of: A. Guy Lombardo; B. German brauhaus; C. Hillbilly. The result was devastatingly comic. "Trumpet Blues" was a swinging tune when it was played properly. The boys all knew Andy could play it as properly as the best. But Andy was being comical, and so he played with a sort of oom-pah lilt, interspersed with staccato rat-ta-tah passages, sounding alternately like a high-society shmaltz trumpeter, a burgher playing a tuba, and a hick struggling with a Civil War bugle. Ox was the first to break. He spit out his laughter and his mouthpiece simultaneously, his horn making a funny *ounnk* sound when he finally exploded. Mike followed suit almost instantly, collapsing in gales of uncontrolled laughter. Andy kept right on playing.

Ta-a-a-raaaah-ta-tah, ta-rah-ta . . .

"All right, all right," Tony yelled, taking his horn from his mouth. Bud and Frank stopped playing, and Andy kept up his staccato riveting for two additional bars before coming to a halt.

"What the hell are you doing, Andy?" Tony said.

"What do you mean?" Andy asked innocently, smiling.

"Look, if you feel like clowning around, sit out a few minutes, will you? Now I'm not kidding. I want to rehearse today."

"Okay," Andy said, seemingly sobered. "I'll play straight."

"I'm freezing my ass off, too," Bud said. He exhaled his breath, and a plume of vapor trailed from his mouth. "Look at that, will you?"

"Let's take 'I Dreamt I Dwelt' again," Tony said, a little annoyed now. "And for Christ's sake let's take it right this time."

"Just a second," Frank said. He reached into the pocket of his coat and pulled out a pair of fur-lined gloves which he pulled on promptly. "My hands are ready to drop off."

"You lucky bastard," Mike said. "I wish I could put on gloves."

"You just play the wrong instrument, boy," Frank said,

smiling. He picked up his sticks again and said, "Okay, let's go."

Tony called off the beat, and the band went into the number. Andy played it straight during the trumpet chorus, and it seemed like smooth sailing until the arrangement came to the sax chorus, during which Andy had a long rest. The saxes played their chorus, and when Andy came back in again, something sounded terribly wrong. He was hitting the notes sloppily, faking a lot of notes, and simply missing a good many of those he should have been playing. Tony glanced curiously over his shoulder, and then pulled his horn angrily from his mouth, standing up and whirling, glaring heatedly at Andy.

"What the hell do you think you're doing?" he shouted.

"What's the matter?" Andy asked, smiling.

Bud turned on the piano stool, wondering what was wrong. He saw what was wrong then, and he understood the sloppy playing Andy had been doing. Andy was wearing thick woolen gloves, gloves he'd apparently put on during his trumpet rest.

"Look, Andy," Tony said, "I'm through kidding around. Now take off them goddamn gloves."

"Frank has gloves on," Andy said perversely.

"Frank doesn't have to worry about fingering."

"Well, my hands are cold," Andy said. "Hell, Mukluk, we're not all Eskimos." He had expected a laugh, and he smiled in anticipation. When no laugh came, he glanced quickly at Bud, and the smile turned pasty on his mouth. Bud was sitting quite solemnly at the piano.

"And let's knock off the name-calling, too," Tony said, his anger rising.

Andy was still high on the crest of his amused feeling. "Now, now," he said, striving for a smile from Bud or a chuckle from Frank. "You worry too much, Mukluk. Honestly."

"I said knock it off!" Tony shouted.

"Hey!" Andy said, surprised by Tony's anger, wondering how much a simple bit of clowning around had gotten so out of hand. "I—"

"You going to play straight or not?" Tony roared.

"Well ..." Andy paused. The humor of the situation had somehow slipped away from everyone, but something else had replaced it. Andy weighed the something else, knowing he'd been called, and knowing he should not back down with Bud and Frank watching him. But at the same time he did not know how to handle Tony's unexpected anger.

"Take off those goddamn gloves," Tony said, "and let's cut out the kidding around. I got enough on my mind without—"

"My hands are cold," Andy said stubbornly, unwilling to give in.

"Well, my hands are cold, too! Now, look, you little crumb, are you going to—"

"Now watch that," Andy said. "Just watch that, Banner."

"Watch what? What the hell are you going to do about my watching it?"

The situation had become alarming now. He did not want a fight with Tony, but there seemed no other way out. Unless, unless he could swing things back to being funny again. If he could do that . . .

"Look, Swahili," he started, spreading his palms, smiling.

Tony dropped his horn onto the chair seat. The dropping horn made an ominous clatter, and the clatter echoed from the high-ceilinged room. Before Andy fully realized what was happening, Tony's fist was twisted in the collar of his coat. He felt himself being yanked to his feet, felt his horn slipping off his lap, and then he saw Tony's other fist cocked and ready to fire.

"Hey! What the hell—" he started, but Tony threw the fist, and it caught him on his cheek and sent him falling back into the chair, the horn falling and crashing to the floor.

"My horn!" he shouted, and he stooped to retrieve it, but Tony had his hand twisted in the collar again, and Andy's fingers scrabbled for the horn as Tony yanked him upright, and he couldn't reach or touch the glistening brass. He wondered why Bud or Frank didn't stop what was happening, wondered why they weren't moving from where they sat, and he thought suddenly of his lip, wishing Tony's fist would not damage his lip, panic smashing into his mind as he visualized a split lip. He stumbled forward, pulled by Tony, expecting the blow at any moment, tensing himself for the sharp impact of the knuckles. The blow did not come. Tony pulled him very close, almost mashing his nose against Andy's, but he did not hit him.

"Look, you bastard," he said. "I'm leader of this band, you understand? That means what I say goes. I say we're here to rehearse, and if you don't like what I say, you can get the hell out. Now is that plain enough for you?"

"It's plain enough," Andy said tightly. "Let go my coat."

"If you want to—"

"Let go my *coat!*" Andy shouted.

"If you want to rehearse with us, you—"

Andy shoved out at Tony's chest, surprising him, breaking the grip. He whirled, pulling away and rushing to where his horn lay on the stage. He lifted the horn and examined it carefully, holding it tenderly, like a mother with a new baby. Satisfied it was not damaged, he stood up, swung his trumpet case onto the seat of his chair, and unsnapped it. He did not speak until he had packed the trumpet away. He did not speak because the anger inside him made it impossible to speak without stuttering. Frank and Bud had deserted him. The thought kept pounding at his mind, and simultaneously he remembered the day Vic Andrada had quit the band, and the memory became large in his mind, taking on importance now, significance he had missed when it happened. They had let Vic go in his favor. They'd been willing to let Vic walk out, *for him!* There was still a chance. There was a chance they'd still come to his rescue, Bud and Frank, sitting there solemnly. He had to be careful. He did not want to sound the way Vic had sounded, but he wanted to brandish his weapon, and his weapon was talent.

"This is it, Swahili," he said tightly.

Tony balled his fists, ready to jump forward again. Andy wet the muscle ring, hoping he was playing this right, anticipating the apologetic interference he felt sure would come.

"I warned you—" Tony started.

"Swahili, I don't give a damn what you—"

"You'd better shut your mouth, Andy. You'd just better—"

"Blow it out, Swahili," Andy said. "You're leader of the band, huh? Well, okay, leader. Rehearse without a trumpet! Play your goddamn wedding job without a trumpet, *leader!*"

"What are you talking about?"

"What does it sound like? You made it plain, and now I'll make it plainer. I'm leaving. If you don't like the way I blow my horn, that's too goddamn bad. There are a lot of outfits who'd like it fine."

Tony paled. Placatingly, he said, "There's nothing wrong when you—"

Andy pressed his advantage. "You ever heard of Artie Parker?" He knew they'd all heard of Parker. Parker's band was not big time, but it was a well-known local outfit which played at most of the weddings and dances in the neighborhood. "Well, Parker asked me to go along with him," Andy hurled. "I told him no, but that was last week. I'm beginning to change my mind now." He waited for some reaction from Frank or Bud. Frank's mouth was compressed into a tight line. Bud seemed to be studying the situation, waiting for something, waiting for what, *what?* And now even Tony called the bluff, apparently figuring all was lost, anyway.

"Parker's welcome to you," he said flatly. "Good-by, quitter."

"Damn right he's welcome to me," Andy said, still trying. "You go get Vic Andrada, Tony. He'll do a lot for the band's sound."

"Get out of here, you little bastard," Tony said whitely.

"Strong man," Andy mocked. "Muscles Banner."

"Get out!" Tony roared. *"Get out of here!"*

"You'll bust a blood vessel," Bud said suddenly, quietly. "Relax, Tony."

Tony whirled on Bud. "I don't want him around any more. I don't want this little crumb anywhere near me."

Bud's eyes did not leave Tony's face. It was almost as if Andy were no longer in the room. Quietly, coldly, he said, "Then I guess you don't want me either, Tony."

"What?" Tony said. "What?"

"If Andy goes, I go," Bud said.

"What!" Tony blinked his eyes. "What? What?"

"Come on, Andy," Bud said. Andy swung his trumpet case up, astonished. He followed Bud off the stage. Slowly they walked to the door, a vast silence behind them. The gym was very quiet and very cold. Andy could see his own hurried breath pluming whitely from his mouth. Bud opened the door, and they stepped outside, and then Bud whirled, pulling the door shut with one hand, grasping Andy's collar with the other.

"Now listen to me, you stupid bastard," he said, his eyes blazing. "We're going back in there! We're going back in there, and you're going to apologize to Tony, and you're going to play that goddamn horn the way you know how, or I'll personally break it over your head. Have you got that?"

"But—"

"You were wrong, dead wrong, and the only reason I saved your miserable hide was because I happen to want to see this band stay together. If you'd walked out of there alone, he'd never have taken you back, never in a million years. With me gone, he's losing a friend, too—and Tony respects friendship."

"Gee, Bud, I didn't—"

"You didn't *what?* You didn't know you were behaving like a smirking little wetpants? Grow up, for Christ's sake! I'm not going to be here holding your hand forever!"

"I'm ... I'm sorry," Andy said. "I didn't realize. I was just—"

"You think I like this?" Bud hurled, his eyes blazing. "You think I like having you on my back every goddamn minute of the day? I've got my own problems, my own damn life to lead. When the hell are you gonna grow up?" He paused and then said, "Get in there. Get in there and eat dirt, and eat it a mile long and a mile wide."

Andy swallowed hard, nodding stupidly. A panic was growing inside him. He did not want to enter the gym alone, did not want to face Tony again. He wanted to turn and run from where they stood. The panic grew, mushrooming onto his face.

Bud's hand released his collar. He smiled suddenly. "All right, inside. And stop looking so goddamned pained. I'm still your friend."

The words hung between them, as brittle as the air around them. He felt the panic leaving slowly. He nodded and pulled back his shoulders. Then he opened the door, and, together, they stepped into the gym.

second chorus, iii

APRIL, 1944

14

White streamers trailed across the ceiling of the hall on East New York Avenue. A large white crepe-paper wedding bell hung from the center of the ceiling, providing the focal point from which the streamers radiated. The groom was short and squat and dark, a corporal in the Air Corps. The bride, with all due respect for Tony Banner's family on his mother's side, was tall and thin, with features strongly reminiscent of Seabiscuit's.

The band played "Here Comes the Bride" first, reading from sheets which incorporated such versatile old stand-bys as "Hatikvah," "Irish Washerwoman," "The Star-Spangled Banner," and "Happy Birthday to You." The owner of the hall, rushing about as an improvised master of ceremonies, led the wedding Party around the floor while both families beamed, exuding sympathy and joy simultaneously. The boys went into "Let Me Call You Sweetheart," and the bride danced with the groom alone until the M.C. led the best man and the maid of honor onto the floor, followed by the ushers and the bridesmaids. The best man then switched partners with the groom, and then everyone switched partners, and then all the spectators ringing the floor moved onto the floor and began dancing, and the reception started. Bud modulated from "Let Me Call You" into "Sleepy Lagoon," and the band took that all the way through and then, for lack of any other waltzes in their repertoire, played "Let Me Call You" again. When they ended the waltz set, they went into "The Man I Love," having decided upon that as their theme song. Bud and Frank played a moody, heavy introduction, and then Andy came in with a theme-songish trumpet solo, backed up by the sax section's harmony. The rest of the evening, except when a fattish lady of forty came over to the piano with some music she wanted Bud to transpose while she sang, was a breeze.

The wedding was of the type the boys later referred to as "The Genoese Brawl." None of them had ever been to Genoa, of course, but the expression served to typify the scores of Italian weddings they were to play in the weeks and months that followed. The Genoese Brawl was not to be confused with what they considered a high-class catered affair. They played several of those jobs, too, but those jobs were duck soup, and quite refined when compared to The Genoese Brawl. The Genoese Brawl was not a catered affair; it did not give the members of the wedding a meal, and whisky, and what-have-you.

It gave the members, instead, beer and sandwiches. The beer was drawn from kegs behind a bar at one end of the hall. Several members of the bride's or groom's family usually served as bartenders, drawing the beer and passing out the sandwiches. The sandwiches were kept in a large cardboard box, wrapped in waxed paper. There were usually two boxes because there were usually two different kinds of sandwiches: ham, and ham and cheese. The members of the wedding crowded the bar and shouted, "Two beers and two hams and cheese." Soda pop was also stacked in an ice-filled sink behind the bar, but no one drank soda pop except children and pregnant women.

There were a good many children at a Genoese Brawl, and almost as many pregnant women. The children spent their time running across the highly waxed floor, putting on the brakes, and then skidding for a good twelve feet. They also spent their time chasing other children in and out and around the dancing couples when they could not slide. They also spent some of their time falling, or knocking over pitchers of beer, or spitting, or stepping on the train of the bride's gown, or simply behaving as bastardly as only children who were habitués of this type of wedding knew how to behave.

The pregnant women sat at the tables around the hall and smiled Madonnalike, wondering how pretty the bride would look in six months when she'd been "caught." They occasionally smoothed their silken maternity jackets over the bulge of their maternal abdomens. They sipped at their soda pop and ate their ham and cheese sandwiches, watching their husbands dance with young and heavily rouged distant cousins from Red Bank, New Jersey.

The bride and groom sat at a long table, usually to the right or left of the bandstand. The members of the wedding filed past the table, kissing the bride and shaking hands with the groom. An envelope was usually passed during the ritual, sometimes to the groom (who instantly handed it to the bride) and sometimes directly to the bride (who instantly dropped it into a large, sacklike white silken purse she carried, pulling the drawstrings tight). The envelopes contained currency of the United States in denominations of from five to twenty-five dollars. No one dared give less than five. (A catered affair called for ten.) No one but the principals' parents ever gave more than twenty-five.

A little before the bride and groom departed for points unknown to share their first night of nuptial bliss, they went around the hall with a tray piled full of macaroons, cookies with cherries, cookies with chocolate, and just plain cookies—a tray which had been in evidence all night on the long table behind which the bride and groom sat. Someone usually accompanied the couple on their circuit of the hall, and this someone carried small white thin cardboard boxes which contained candy-covered almonds, or as the Genoese called them, "Confetti." The boxes usually carried the inscription "Wedding Bells" or "Congratulations" or, in the cases of more affluent principals, "Mr. and Mrs. Genoese." The cookies and confetti were distributed (and beware the wrath of any member who was missed during the distribution) and later carried home to those unfortunate enough to have missed the brawl.

Sometime during the evening, before the bride and groom departed (and there were always the jokes about "Hey, Harry, when the hell are you going to leave? Getting anxious, Harry?" To which Harry always shrugged stupidly and smiled a nonchalant above-such-petty-sex-habits smile), the M.C. put the couple and the entire assemblage through the primitive torture of the Grand March. The Grand March was a not-so-grand march around the hall, first two abreast, then four abreast, then eight abreast, then under-the-hands arch, then this way and that way until the floor and the party resembled a college band doing a complicated maneuver on a football field between halves. The Grand March invariably ended in stark confusion, with the M.C. rushing to the bandstand and shrieking for some dance music to untangle the knot he'd woven.

The bride and groom "sneaked" away later while everyone cheered and whistled. The band played on for an hour or more after that, depending on whether or not there was overtime. The best man paid the band with the money the groom had left him (if the groom had not already paid the band before departing), and the crowd began to thin out along about midnight or one A.M. The band played "Good Night, Ladies," and distant relatives kissed distant relatives resoundingly and longly, the kiss having to last until the next wedding. The boys packed their instruments, left, had ice-cream sodas, and went home.

Such was the pattern of The Genoese Brawl.

The pattern became quite familiar to the Tony Banner boys after their first job. With remarkable rapidity, more bookings came on the heels of, and as a result of, the first booking. And then, at almost every job they played, they were approached for a future job, until virtually all their Saturdays and Sundays were occupied with weddings, beer parties, dances, or Republican Club socials. Naturally, they dragged the girls along with them whenever they played, and neither Helen nor Carol minded very much except that their game was a patiently feminine waiting one, and there was nothing particularly exciting about a Genoese Brawl.

So when a week end popped up in which there was no booking, Helen leaped upon it with a suggestion.

"You're not playing tomorrow," she said to Bud, "so I have an idea. My parents have a place. A cottage in the Rockaways, not right on the beach, but with a private sandy walk leading down to it. I thought we might ride out there tomorrow."

This was a Friday night, and they were sitting in the back of Frank's car outside Club Beguine. She was cuddled against him, her legs curled beneath her on the seat. His hand idly toyed with the back of her neck. He felt very drowsy and very comfortable. He always felt comfortable with Helen. And proud. Secretly proud of her, bursting proud. She moved with such grace and femininity that there were times when he wanted to scoop her up no matter where they were, hold her close, kiss her, stroke her hair, trace the outline of her lips with his fingers. He loved everything about her, loved it with the deep unbending love of adolescence. But above all, and part of it all, was the sense of contentment he felt whenever he was with her.

"Do you hear me?"

"I hear you," he said.

"You're not playing tomorrow, are you?"

"Not tomorrow, and not Sunday either," he said lazily.

"Then do you think ..." She stopped. "Bud, are you listening to me?"

"I was thinking about you."

"Don't think about me when I'm talking," she scolded. "Would you like to drive out to the Rockaways tomorrow?"

"Okay," he said idly.

"That's what I call a burst of enthusiasm. Can you get your father's car?"

"I think so. Why? What's at the Rockaways?"

"My parents have a cottage. I think I can get the key. We'll pack a picnic basket. If it's too windy on the beach, we'll eat inside. Does it appeal?"

"It appeals."

"Greatly?"

"Enormously."

"That's what I love about you. You're so difficult to get along with." She paused. "I'd better tell my parents I'm going with some of the girls. They wouldn't understand."

"They never do. We sure have it rough."

"Do you love me?"

"Nope. I'm toying with you."

"I'll break your nose," she said, laughing.

He seized her roughly, pulling her to him. "How'd you happen to come my way, Helen? How'd such a wonderful bundle drop into my lap?"

She turned her head away in mock aloofness. "Your technique is barbaric," she said. "My other lovers treat me gently."

"Bah!" he snorted. "Your other lovers are milksops! I am the great Genghis Khan, ruler of the Orient! What are all these peasants compared to me?"

"You frighten me, sire," she said, her voice quavering.

"I will eat you in one swallow!" he shouted.

"Ears and all?"

"Ears especially! Mmm, you have beautiful ears," he said.

He moved his mouth toward her ear, kissed it, and she squirmed away with a small tremor.

"You give me the chills," she said.

"The better to gobble you up, my dear."

"Can you get the car?"

"Car?" he shouted, carried away. "A blazing chariot drawn by a thousand white horses!"

"I love you," she said happily.

"No wonder," he replied smugly. "Ruler of all the East."

"I adore you."

"What time, concubine?"

"Tennish?"

"On Saturday? Gad!" He paused. "Make it a quarter after tennish." He paused again. "Tennish, anyone?"

She put her hand over his face, shoved him down on the car seat, and then said, "You idiot!" and kissed him.

The beach was quiet and deserted.

The waves rolled toward the shore, slender white furrows in the distance, growing in power as they came closer, expanding, roiling, building in stature, and then rising to full height and folding up upon themselves, curling under in a green-and-white cascade of fury, and then rushing shoreward, flattened and dissipated, dissolving into white, bubbly foam, rushing onto the beach, absorbed by the sand, and then retreating leisurely, pulling the remnants of their tattered foam-robes behind them. A lone sandpiper skirted the aftermath of the breaking crests, skittering like a stiff old maid at the water's edge, pulling up her skirts with each new watery rush.

There was a strong wind blowing off the water, smelling of salt and ocean life. It caught at her hair, sent the black strands whipping about her head like an enraged gorgon. She wore a peasant blouse and skirt, over which she'd thrown a white cashmere sweater, unbuttoned. The wind lashed at her skirt, molding it against her firm legs and thighs. She tilted her head up and licked her lips, squeezing her eyes shut tightly. He stood with his arm around her, feeling the shudder of her body as the wind lunged against her. He looked down at her closed lids and the smile on her mouth, and then he focused on the eyes alone, squeezed tightly shut now, the short black lashes curled, the laugh wrinkles at the corners.

Her eyes popped open suddenly, startling in their greenness, seeming to capture a deeper green from the ocean.

"I caught you," she said, and then the eyes crinkled at the edges, crinkled in sheer pleasure, and he wanted to kiss her eyes, and he did not know why. "Look!" she said suddenly, her eyes opening, a spark of pure excitement in them. She turned partly toward him, her eyes not leaving the ocean, her fingers clutching his arm. "Buddy, look!"

He turned from her face reluctantly, scanning the ocean. He saw the fish then. It leaped out of the water in a graceful arc and then was gone.

"A dolphin," he said.

"A porpoise," she corrected. Her eyes snapped at him, and he felt the challenge in them. They sparked for an instant, daring him to pick up the gauntlet.

"A dolphin," he repeated.

"Look! Again!" The fish leaped from the water, and her eyes were a little wider as she watched, excitement in them again. "A porpoise, Buddy! Buddy, you know it's a porpoise." She turned toward him. The excitement had left her eyes. They looked at him questioningly now, almost pleading, and he forgot what question they were asking as he discovered her eyes and the expressiveness of them.

"Isn't he?" she said.

"Yes, he's a porpoise." He could not tear his gaze from her eyes.

"Buddy, he's having so much fun!" She watched the lunging fish, watched the arc of its body as it leaped from the water and then submerged again to reappear a moment later. Her head moved only slightly. Her eyes were alive in her face, darting anxiously, watching the movement of the porpoise.

She moved out of his protective embrace suddenly, ran to the water's edge and impulsively threw back her head, stretching her arms out to the sea. She leaned down and caught at the water as it pressed onto the beach, the bubbles hissing lightly as they submerged her hand.

"It's warm, Buddy!" she shrieked, and when she turned to him, her eyes were wide in childish wonder. "Let's go in!"

She was sitting almost instantly, pulling back her skirt, kicking off her shoes, rolling down her stockings. He watched her, seeing the clean line of her legs as the protective tint of the nylons disappeared to expose their warm ivory coloring. She stood, pulled up her skirt, and went into the water, and she shrieked again as the bubbles lashed her feet.

"Come in, Buddy! It's won-derful!"

He watched her, smiling, unaware of the smile. She romped girlishly at the water's edge, chasing the retreating foam, rushing back onto the sand whenever a new breaker roared its thunder and split into a crashing cascade of dissolving white and green. She laughed aloud, unaware of his presence now, losing herself in the game of chasing the bubbles and being in turn chased by their big brothers. Down the beach the sandpiper stopped its conscientious patrol, its head erect, staring at the intruder.

He felt a peaceful unity of sand and sky and water and Helen. They were alone on the beach, and her laughs fought the thunder of the waves, and she turned to him and waved limply, her eyes smiling. And then there was sudden shock in her eyes, painful almost, and she said, "Oh!" and then pressed her body toward him, and then another "Oh!" and he saw her backing into the ocean against her will, the strong undertow catching at her ankles. She struggled for balance, bent over now, the peasant blouse moving away from her body. He began running toward her, aware of the gathering power of a new breaker.

"Helen!" he shouted.

Her arms were flailing. Behind her the ocean gathered its might, building into a solid wall of green that steamrolled toward the beach. The wave broke over her, and she vanished in the green and white foam. He kicked off his shoes at the water's edge, desperately looking for a sign of her. Her head popped to the surface, and he plunged in, feeling the cold sting of the water, diving almost instantly, a shallow dive close to the surface, his arms slicing the water in a powerful crawl. She was under again, and he looked for her anxiously, and then her head appeared, and he saw her eyes first, and the eyes were a brilliant green, and the eyes were laughing. Her mouth was open, he realized, and he heard her pleased laughter above the sound of the waves, and he smiled in relief and then laughed with her. He came close to her, and she dived under again, and he went after her, catching her leg. She kicked at him, and his hand slipped, and he tried for another grip, and his fingers closed on her thigh, and his other hand captured her narrow waist. Her lips were suddenly on his, and they surfaced together, locked in the kiss, and then a new breaker caught them, and they clung to each other as it hurled them shoreward, threw them onto the sand, and then burst its glistening, foaming bubbles around them.

She was on her feet instantly, her eyes challenging him, daring him to go on with the game. He lay on the sand, sodden, exhausted, breathing heavily. He looked up at her then. Her clothes were wet through, clinging to her body, molding every line of her. His eyes moved to her face. She was still laughing, and then the laugh left her eyes and they turned knowledgeable and aware, aware of her near-nudity.

She shivered suddenly, and he felt the cold at the same moment—a sharp, knifing wind that blew in off the Atlantic.

"We'd better get inside," he said. He picked up his shoes and then the picnic basket, and she stood watching his back for only a moment, her eyes puzzled and uncertain, and then she followed him.

The cottage was small and white, green-shuttered windows carrying out the theme of ocean. They pushed open the door and stamped into the living room, trying to dislodge the caked sand from their feet. Helen was shivering now. He took off his jacket and shirt and went quickly to the stone fireplace in the center of the room.

"This is nice," he said.

Helen's teeth were chattering. She embraced herself, running her hands over her bare arms.

"You'd better change while I get a fire going," he said. She nodded and went into the bedroom. There was a wood box alongside the open mouth of the fireplace, and he dug into it, grateful for the old newspapers and heavy pieces of timber. He laid the fire carefully, and then he went to his jacket, beginning to shiver himself now, amazed by the deceptive, comparative warmth of the water, disappointed when he found his matches were wet. He went to the kitchen end of the cottage and rummaged around the stove. He found a box of wooden matches, brought them back to the fireplace, and started the fire.

"I'm freezing," he said.

From behind the closed door of the bedroom Helen called, "There's only one robe. Do you want it?"

"Do I look like a cad?"

"I can't find the sash," she said.

"I'm still freezing."

He heard her looking through the drawers in the bedroom. "Here's a pair of my brother's khakis," she said. "He's fatter than you, but any port." She came out of the bedroom wearing a white chenille robe. She held the robe closed at the front. "There's no sash or belt or anything," she said. Then, apologetically, "We hardly use the place, except in the summer." She handed him the khaki trousers and shirt, and he walked past her into the bedroom.

"A nice fire," she called.

"I used to be a Boy Scout."

"Really?"

"No."

"Wasn't the water grand?"

"No," he shouted.

"It was, too," and he could picture her eyes sparking with challenge again.

"Why don't you spread the food?" he called.

"I want to toast for a while."

"Drink one for me."

"I meant at the fire, stupid."

He came out of the bedroom. "Who's stupid?" He stood with his hands on his hips, the khakis large for him.

"You look nice," she said.

He looked at her then. Her legs were spread toward the fire, the robe exposing them where it fell open. "You do, too." She pulled the robe closed, and her eyes turned to him, and there was no embarrassment in them, only a mute question.

"Shall I get the food?" she asked softly.

"If you want."

She rose quickly, and the robe fell open, and she clutched at it and said, "Oh, goddamn this thing!"

"Take my belt," he said.

"Your pants'll fall down."

"Take it."

He pulled the belt through the loops and handed it to her. She took the belt and began wrapping it around her waist. The belt slid from her fingers, and she reached down for it, and he saw that her hand was trembling. Her hair cascaded over her face as she bent, hiding her face and her neck, and the open robe where her skin lay naked. Her fingers closed on the belt, and then she lifted her face and tossed her head back, and the hair lifted like a silken black curtain, and her breasts stood firm and erect in the opening of the robe, and he looked at her curiously, and then their eyes met, and there was nothing in them now but puzzlement and something else, something he could not identify because he had never seen it in her eyes before.

"Buddy," she said, looking up at him, not touching the robe. "I'm frightened."

He went to her and caught her gently by the shoulders, pulling her erect. He bent down and picked her up then, and she pressed her head into his shoulder, and her hair was still wet from the ocean. Her lips touched the side of his neck, and she could taste the salt on his skin, and she shivered again and said, "I'm frightened," and he answered, "No, no, don't be, darling," and he carried her to the other room.

He would never forget her eyes: alert with fear at first, the pupils almost black against a narrow rim of green. The fear gradually leaving them, the lids softly closing, opening occasionally. The green turning a softer shade now, a pale jade, the eyes seeming more Oriental as a smoke opalescence claimed them. The spark of sudden passion, with the black eyebrows swooping down like earth-bound hawks, a deeper jade, a denser green, the green of a jungle, and her fingernails raking his back, and her eyes narrowing, narrowing, waiting, apprehensive, and the sudden shocking star-shell of explosion of green stabbed with yellow, the hollow scream in the small room, the eyes filming, and then tears flooding them, covering the green, spilling down her cheeks, and then the faint shaking of her head, her arms holding him tighter, her eyes adjusting to shock and pain, her teeth clenched, her eyes clenched too, closed tightly shut in excruciating agony, her head continuing to shake and nod alternately, bearing the pain and the shock with more than patience, more than willingness, the agony fleeing for an instant as her eyes reassured him, and reassured him again, and then the sudden unclenching, her head back on the pillow now, "I love you, Bud I love you, Bud," the light film of sweat on her upper lip, her eyes brilliant, patient now, unsatisfied but content, alert and awake to every sight, darting with every sound in the room, the distant breakers on the beach.

"I'm sorry, Helen," he said.

"No, please." Her eyes were warm and wide with sudden pleading. "I wanted it this way, Bud. I wanted it."

"I love you, Helen," he said, and she pulled him close to her, his head cradled on her breasts and said, as she had said a long while before, I know."

She called her parents after they had eaten. She said the girls had decided to stay overnight, and she would be home sometime tomorrow afternoon, and would that be all right? Her father had staunchly upheld a righteous dignity in complaining about young girls who spent the night alone at a cottage on the beach, but her mother said, Yes, dear, it's all right. Are there enough blankets?

They drove back to Brooklyn late on Sunday afternoon. She sat close to him on the seat of the old Chevvy, and he looked at her face often, and her eyes were filled with deep womanly contentment.

second chorus, iv

MAY-SEPTEMBER, 1944

15

They walked home from the club together, hand in hand, idly chatting. It was a wonderful May night, with a mild breeze on the air, a canopy of stars in the near-moonless sky overhead. When they passed beneath the shade of a heavy maple, the area of sidewalk was suddenly thrown into complete darkness. Andy stopped, holding Carol's hand so that she stopped, too. He pulled her into his arms and kissed her, holding the kiss so long that she finally pulled away gasping.

"I've got to get home," she said breathlessly.

"What's the hurry?" He tightened his arms around her again, kissing her firmly. She was wearing a sweater, and he felt the warmth of her body through the wool. His fingers strayed up to her breast, and she clamped her hand onto his and pulled it away, a scolding, smiling look on her face when she looked up at him.

"Now, no," she said.

"Why not?" he asked.

"Because I say so."

She reached up to peck him on the cheek, to show him her scolding was a thing of necessity, to show him she really liked him even if he did have wandering hands. Andy pulled her close and turned the light peck into a production number.

"Andy," she said more sternly, pulling her mouth and his hands away. "Now, stop it."

"Carol—"

"Just stop it," she said severely.

"Carol," he said awkwardly, "I love you."

"Andy, Andy," she said, cupping his face tenderly. "I know, Andy, but really we can't just—"

"Carol," he said again, kissing her, his hands roaming wildly over her back, finally seeking her breasts again, cupping her breasts until she pulled away from him angrily.

"I want to go home," she said.

"All right," he answered, the excitement still raging within him, his veins gorged with blood. "All right, Carol. Carol, I'm sorry, I . . ."

She had already begun walking. He caught up with her, and they strolled in silence to her house. He could not put down the excitement. He was trembling with the fever of it.

They climbed the front steps to her house. The porch was in deep, dark shadow.

"Good night, Andy," she said, turning and taking his hand.

"I'll see you Sunday?" he asked.

"Yes."

"Carol—"

"Now kiss me good night," she said. "I have to get to sleep."

He kissed her eagerly, and his hands went to her breasts again. He could not resist trying. He wanted to hold her breasts so desperately, wanted to touch them. She did not stop him for a few minutes. He began trembling violently, and only then did she take his hands tenderly and move them away.

"Good night, Andy," she whispered.

"Good night, Carol. Carol, do you have to rush in? Can't we—"

He heard the rasp of a window opening. He glanced upward guiltily.

"Carol is that you?" a voice called.

"Yes, Louise," she answered.

"Who's with you?"

"Andy."

"Don't you think it's time you came inside?" Louise asked.

"In a minute," Carol said. She turned to Andy again. She kissed the palm of her hand and pressed the kiss to his cheek. "Good night," she whispered.

He waited on the porch until she was inside. He was still trembling. He climbed down the steps and began walking toward Eastern Parkway, wondering if he should go home, not wanting to go home because the excitement was still high inside him. Maybe the boys would go for a ride later. Maybe the ride would calm him. God, how he loved her, how warm her breasts had felt, how soft and how warm. On Eastern Parkway he caught a bus, getting off at Schenectady Avenue and walking toward the club.

They stood in the driveway outside Club Beguine, in the shadow of the tall hedges marking the property line. Even in the semidarkness he could see the wild anger in her eyes. There was almost no trace of green in her eyes now.

They seemed like two glistening black balls of fury, heatedly glowing beneath black winged brows.

"Who is she?" Helen asked. She was trying to control her voice, but she could not hide the fury.

"Somebody I knew a long time ago," Bud answered.

"How long ago?"

"When I was a kid."

"You're still a kid! How long ago?"

"Twelve, thirteen, how the hell should I know? Frank and I used to date them. Her and her twin sister. Shirley and Bernice."

"I thought her name was *Bunny!*" Helen almost spit the word.

"Well, they call themselves that. Sunny and Bunny. Look, Helen—"

"Don't look me, Mr. Donato. Get away from me."

"Well, for Pete's sake, what did I do?"

"Nothing! Oh, nothing at all! You're perfectly innocent!"

"You're raising your voice."

"It's my voice, and I'll do whatever I want with it."

She paused, banking the fires of her fury. "Why don't you go back inside to her?"

"Because I don't want to."

"It seemed like you wanted to a few minutes ago. It seemed like you wanted to plenty."

"What the hell did I do, anyway?"

"You kissed her!" Helen hurled.

"Who?"

"You! Now, look, Bud, don't try to get out of this with that baby-blue-eyed stare. I saw you, and I'm sure the whole damn club saw you, too!"

"You're crazy," he said mildly.

"Oh, Buddy, please," she said disgustedly. She paused for a long while. The driveway was very silent. "Why don't you go back in?" she asked softly.

"I don't want to. Helen, I—"

"Don't touch me!"

"Helen—"

"I said don't touch me! I'll kill you if you touch me!"

"For Pete's sake, a lousy kiss—"

"Why?"

"I don't know. I just—"

"Why? Because she's got 'tail' stamped all over her, is that why?"

"She hasn't got anything stamped all—"

"Buddy, Buddy, you know what she is, and I know what she is, so let's not kid ourselves."

"You sound catty as hell."

"I am catty as hell! Don't deny to me why you kissed her, Bud. For God's sake, if I can't even go to powder my nose without—"

"I didn't do anything," he said. "You're imagining all this." He was deeply troubled by her outburst, more troubled because everything she'd said was true. He did not know why he suddenly decided to renew a forgotten acquaintance with Bunny, or why he'd impetuously kissed her. God, right on the edge of the dance floor, right where everyone could see them. The kiss had been nothing more than that, pallid in comparison to what he'd known with Helen, and he'd felt immediately ashamed of himself even while performing the act. And then Helen had come into the room, and he'd felt her presence and looked up, and he'd seen the pain stab her eyes, the irises crumbling, and then the lids gently closing to hold back the pain. He'd have given his life not to have witnessed that look on Helen's face, or to have seen that pain in her eyes. He'd turned to her, and she'd walked past him and outside, and he'd quickly abandoned Bunny. When he found Helen in the driveway, her pain had given way to a cold, unreasoning anger. His only salvation seemed to be in denial, and now that he was on that path he could see no way of turning back. He had a vague notion that the argument was terribly important, but he didn't for a moment believe he was about to lose her.

"You're a hell of a guy, all right," she said. Her anger seemed to be dissipating. "The moment I turn my back, and then you lie about it! That's what gets me! The lying!" The anger was returning. "How can you lie like that to me? What did you see in her? For God's sake, are you blind? Can't you see she's just a painted tramp? Is that what you want?" She paused, her voice breaking, and he saw from her eyes that she was ready to cry, and he reached out his hand to her, but she turned her back on him. He stepped around her, saw her face crumble, and then she was sobbing soundlessly, trying to keep the silent tears back.

"Helen, I'm sorry. I—"

"Sorry isn't enough!" she snapped.

"Well, what do you want me to do?"

"Shut up! Just shut up and leave me alone."

"All right, I lost my head, all right? I'm sorry."

"Lost your head? Over what? For God's sake, Bud, is that all we mean to each other? That a chippie can step in and—"

"She's not a chippie, Helen. We happened to—"

"Don't defend her, or I'll crack you across the face!"

"I'm not defending her. I'm just trying to show you that it meant nothing. That it—"

"Then why'd you do it?"

"I don't know why."

"You'll have to do a little better than that."

"What the hell do you want me to do?" he asked, becoming a little angry himself. "Get down on my hands and knees?"

"Yes!"

"I apologized. I said I was sorry. I'll be damned if I'm going to—" He stopped. Her sobbing had found voice now. "Helen, look, for Christ's sake, can't we—" He pulled her to him, and she stood stiff as a board, not moving.

"Don't," she said. Her voice was bitter cold.

"Helen, can't you see how much you—"

"Don't. Bud, don't, don't, *don't!*"

She pulled away from him, cupping her face. He heard the sobs erupt into full-fledged misery. He sighed heavily.

"I . . . I'm sorry I annoy you," she said through the tears.

"You don't annoy me," he said patiently.

"I know I do," she said, crying.

"All right, you do. Listen, can't you stop that crying?"

"No," she sobbed.

"Come on, I'll take you home."

"No, I don't want you to take me home."

"Then what the hell—"

"Take your Bunny home. Take her home and finish what you started, you bastard!"

"Then how're you going to—"

"What do you care?" she said, her voice rising. "Why don't you leave me alone? Why don't you just leave me alone?" The tears came freely. She could not control them, and she did not try to control them. "Just leave me alone. Please, please, for God's sake, leave me alone."

"Helen . . ."

He heard footsteps at the end of the driveway. He peered into the darkness and saw only a figure silhouetted by the street lamp.

"Someone's coming," he whispered.

"I don't care."

"Well, can't you stop crying? For Christ's sake, someone's—"

"Bud?" the voice called. "Is that you?"

"Andy?"

"Yeah."

Helen took a tissue from her sleeve and dabbed at her face with it. Andy walked closer to them.

"Hi," he said. "Some night, isn't it?"

"Yeah," Bud said quietly.

"I'm not breaking up anything, am I?"

"No," Bud said.

"Will you take me home, Andy?" Helen said suddenly.

"Huh?" Andy glanced hastily to Bud for confirmation.

"You heard her," Bud said tightly.

"Well, gee, I don't know. I mean . . . is something wrong?"

"Nothing's wrong," Helen said. "Will you take me home?"

"Take her home, kid," Bud said. "There's someone I have to see."

He hesitated only long enough to see the pain register in Helen's eyes, hating himself for hurting her that way, but protecting his adolescent pride. He turned his back then and walked toward the far end of the driveway, turning at the corner of the house and stepping down into the club. Andy watched him go, feeling quite awkward, knowing something had happened, but not knowing quite what.

"Did you have a fight?" he asked.

"Yes," Helen said quietly. "We had a fight."

They walked to the end of the driveway and then turned left toward Rochester Avenue. She dried her eyes again, not wanting her crying to show when they reached the lighted sidewalk.

"It's a nice night," Andy said awkwardly.

"Yes," she answered. "Lovely."

"What'd you fight about?" he asked.

"Nothing."

They kept walking, stopping on Rochester Avenue, across the street from Somers Memorial Park. "Do we take a bus or what?" he asked.

"Let's walk a little," she said.

He hesitated a moment. "All right. Which way?"

She began walking without answering him, crossing Rochester Avenue and heading for the park. He walked with her, not wanting to leave her because Bud had, in essence, asked him to see her safely home. At the same time, he was not enjoying himself. He wished she were Carol, and the thought of Carol fanned the excitement that still smoldered within him.

"Your friend is a bastard," she said.

"Huh?" He had never heard a girl use that word before.

"Bud. He's a fourteen-carat bastard."

"Well, gee," Andy said. "I never thought that. You're just sore. Because you had a fight."

" 'There's someone I have to see,' " she said, quoting Bud. "That rotten bastard." She was getting angry again, just thinking about it. He had hurt her badly that night, and the hurt was beginning to fester inside. She nursed the hurt, coddled it while her anger grew. They walked into the park, passing couples hand in hand, walking beneath the spreading trees, walking on the shadow-filled concrete path that wound leisurely through the spring greenery.

"Tasteless," she said vehemently. "Completely tasteless. I wouldn't spit on someone like her."

He did not answer. He let her talk.

"What am I supposed to do? Chain him? If you can't step out of a room without someone . . . someone . . ." She clamped her mouth shut, the vision of the kiss flooding into her mind again. She could see the girl's swollen backside in the purple silk dress. Bud's arm around her, her painted face lifted for his kiss. Everyone watching. He cared a lot, he did. Making a fool of her that way. Advertising to the world that Helen Cantor was a lovesick kid who . . . "He doesn't want love," she said aloud. "I know what he wants. I know what he wants, the bastard. I wish I didn't love him so much. Is love like this, Andy? Does it always hurt so goddamned much?"

"I don't know," he said, thinking his own love was sweet and painless. Suddenly she began crying again. She hated herself for crying, and the self-hatred sought a source, and the source was Bud. She hated him viciously in that moment, loving him at the same time, the tears scalding hot on her cheeks.

"Let's sit down," she said, weary all at once. "Let's find a place to sit."

They walked, looking for a bench, not wanting to sit next to lovers. They gave it up finally and walked onto the grass, sitting in the black shadow of a big tree, far from the concrete path.

When she stopped crying, with the hatred tears still wet on her cheeks, she asked, "Is he your best friend?"

"Yes," he said.

"You picked a good friend."

"He's a good guy," Andy said. "You just misunderstood him, Hel—"

"No, I didn't misunderstand him."

"Helen, he probably—"

"I could kill him," she said tightly. "I could *kill* him." Fresh tears flowed, tears of self-sympathy washing over the hatred tears, mingling with them until she could not tell the self-sympathy from the hatred. She flung herself at Andy, burying her head in his chest, the sobs wracking her body. He tried to comfort her, but she would not be comforted. The hatred rose, and with it the self-sympathy, stronger than the hatred, choking her until she felt desperately uncertain of herself and everything around her. She sobbed against his chest, and his hand moved to her back, and he could feel the taut muscles there, and his fingers somehow tingled with the touch. She turned sideways, and he felt the electric warmth of her breast, and he pulled his hand back as if he had been burned. She was looking up at him.

"Andy?" she said desperately, her eyes wet, "does he love me?"

He did not hear what she said. He saw only her mouth, and her mouth was pleading with him, pleading for something, and he reached down and kissed her.

He pulled back suddenly, staring at her in confusion, hesitating, remembering Carol, thinking in his heart this would be unfair to Carol. She was staring up at him, surprised, and her face was a little frightened now, as if she were faced with a situation she didn't know how to handle. He kissed her again, and she drank assurance from his mouth, and he was surprised to feel the earlier excitement flare into life under his skin. He felt the excitement guiltily, thinking of Carol, thinking of the soft warmth of Carol's breasts, thinking this was unfair to Carol, but pressing against Helen anyway, losing himself in her mouth.

His excitement surprised her. When he'd kissed her, she had felt only uncanny disbelief at first. And then hatred lay gleaming like a naked skull on the desert, and she thought, *This is his best friend, his best friend, his best friend,* and when his lips had reached for hers the second time, she'd given them willingly, nurturing the woman's revenge, feeling a sweet pleasure, from knowing she was striking back at Bud.

His arms tightened around her, and she felt a sudden panic.

"Andy," she said, "don't. Bud—"

He was forcing her back onto the grass, breathing heavily now. He put his lips against hers, forced open her mouth, and thrust his tongue against her teeth. He grasped her more tightly, pinning her shoulders to the ground, and she thought desperately, *What's he doing? I'm Bud's. I'm Bud's!* and then she felt his fingers tight on her breast. She tried to free herself, but there was a wild strength in him. She turned, and his hand caught at the buttons of her blouse, and they came free, and she felt fingers catching at her breasts, felt the nipples come unbiddenly erect.

"Andy!" she said hoarsely. "Stop! Please, you're—"

She felt her skirt go up, and she kicked out at him blindly, and then his legs covered hers, holding her pinned to the ground, and she started to scream, but his mouth was over hers, and then his hand was under her skirt, and she moved her head from side to side, trying to dislodge his mouth, and she kicked, and suddenly she froze with the realization of what was happening in that instant, and she threw her hips up, trying to free herself, trying to get away from him, horror-stricken when her efforts helped him instead of hindering him. She lay still as a stone then, hearing the rasp of his breath, feeling the hardness of his body against her, and feeling completely dead within herself, dead and cold, dead white until he was finished with her body, and then she still lay dead, his stone's weight upon her, the dark secret of their tangled alliance between them, dead to the strangely cruel alliance they had forged.

Frank was the first to know.

Andy stammeringly told him the story, seeking advice, wanting to know how he could possibly explain it all to Bud. Frank was the first to know, and Frank told it all to Bud, leaving none of the details out, a curiously gleeful expression on his face as he spoke. And Bud listened while Frank skillfully twisted the knife, and he wanted to punch Frank's face, wanted to see Frank bleeding and raw, wanted to rip apart the world with his bare hands. And when Frank said, "I'm telling you this because you're my friend, Buddy," he sobered slightly, and he thought, *Yes, Frank is a friend, a true friend,* not realizing that Frank's sole motivation had been jealousy, and not realizing that even Frank didn't clearly understand his own motivation.

And when Frank left him, he sat alone in the sun porch with his father's assorted collections strewn over the bridge table, with the sunlight slashing through the windows, and he wondered what to do.

And he thought, She's to blame.

And he thought, *No, he's to blame.*

And he didn't know whom to blame because he loved them both in different ways, and the two people who'd meant most to him had seized the haft of a dagger together

and conspired to stick it between his shoulder blades. He
thought of going to Andy and hitting him and hitting him
until Andy babbled for forgiveness, until the air was clear
between them. He thought of calling Helen and concealing
his hurt and his hatred, calling her and asking her what
happened. Her number ran through his mind like mountain
lava. He went to the phone, and he picked up the receiver,
and he started to dial the number and then put the receiver
back into its cradle, and then he went into the sun porch
again, and the sun was just as hot, and the sun illuminated
an ugly, ugly day, and he wanted to cry.

He went into the living room, and he sat at the piano,
and his mother came in from the kitchen, drying her
hands on a towel, her head cocked to one side, her eyes
moist because her son was playing softly, the way she liked
him to play.

When he left the house, he didn't know where he was
going. He walked aimlessly, and he decided to see Andy,
and then he decided against it, and he decided to call Helen
and went as far as the phone booth before changing his
mind again. He went to see Reen because Reen was wise,
and Reen was kind. But Reen had received greetings from
the President of the United States, and the greetings told
Reen he would be drafted in a few weeks, and Reen had
headaches of his own, so Bud told him nothing.

*What do I say to them, what do I say to either of them,
what can I do, why did they do this to me?* he thought.
And he walked.

When he got home, his mother told him a girl named
Helen had called. He rushed to the phone, and he started
to dial, and again he didn't know what he could say to
her, and so he didn't return her call. She called six times
the next day. He did not speak to her.

At the end of May the boys gave a farewell party for
Reen, and they presented him with a sterling-silver identifi-
cation bracelet that night. The initials R.P.D. were in-
scribed on the face of the bracelet. The inscription "To the
biggest and the best, from the Boys" was on the back.
The boys drank a lot of beer and told a lot of stories and
did a lot of reminiscing, and Andy came to Bud at about
eleven o'clock, and Bud looked up from his beer and then
turned away from him.

"Bud—"

"Get the hell away from me!"

"Bud, I'm sorry. Buddy, please, I'm sorry. I'm sorry, Buddy," and Bud looked up to see him crying. He reached out tentatively and then pulled his hand back, and he felt his own face beginning to crumble, and he bit down hard on his lip, and he tightened his hand around the beer glass until he thought it would shatter.

"Cut it out," he said harshly. "The guys'll see you. Goddamnit, cut it out!"

Andy's shoulders heaved, and the tears streamed down his face, and then he extended his hand, and Bud squeezed his eyes shut, not wanting to take the hand, not wanting to, no, no, no, and then he put out his own hand and took Andy's and said very softly, "Forget it. It's done with now."

Perhaps it would have been better if, in his drunkenness that night, he had gone to the telephone and called Helen and told her that he loved her. But Andy was there, and there was Andy's need, and the stone of responsibility was heavy within Bud, and he could see no way in his adolescence of reconciling his love for Helen, and his friendship with Andy. So he had taken Andy's hand, and Andy had stopped crying, and they drank beer and ate potato chips together, all the boys, locked in arm-in-arm camaraderie. Reen said, "I've only got one thing to say to you, boys," and everyone shouted, "Speech, speech!" and Reen held up his hands until there was quiet, and then his eyes focused on Andy and Bud, and his eyes were curiously solemn, and he said, "Now, jus' remember this. A li'l hair around the balls doesn't make a man. Now jus' remember that," and everyone laughed and sang the old songs and toasted Reen and toasted Reen again, and Reen was the only one of the lot who seemed somehow sad about the whole occasion.

He left for the army the next day, and he began his training as an Infantry rifleman.

It was June, and then July, and then the summer was upon them, and one by one the boys were leaving. For Andy, this was the happiest time he'd ever known. For Andy, this was pure happiness, happiness that knew no bounds. To be with Carol and Bud, to be with his sweetheart and his best friend, this was complete happiness. If he could have chosen a time to end his life, if someone had given him the choice, he would have unhesitatingly replied, "After all this. Let the ending come after all this. Let this be the first and the only ending. Let there never be a second ending, let my life end now, after I've experienced all this, after all this happiness, now."

Bud left for the navy on September eighteenth. He kissed Carol on the cheek, and then he clasped hands with Andy. He went then to join the other boys with their overnight bags in the milling line waiting for the train.

There were tears in Andy's eyes. The tears were there because his best friend was leaving. He did not know, nor could he have known, that the end of summer was—for all practical purposes—the real end of his life.

Part 3

16

"Reen is dead, isn't he?" Andy asked.

He sat up in bed, and those were the first words he spoke, as if the knowledge had eluded him while talking yesterday and then rested on his unconscious all night long; as if his long reminiscence had touched on the truth, ignored it, stored it, and was only now reluctantly exposing it to the light of a new day.

"Yes," Bud said, "he's dead. A German bullet in the town of St. Vith."

"To the biggest and the best, from the Boys," Andy said.

"Yes," Bud answered, He had been up for half an hour already, silently washing and dressing while Andy slept. This was Tuesday morning, and his test was at nine, and he couldn't afford to be late, not after the pitiful amount of studying he'd done. He'd never been afraid of an examination in his life, but he was truly frightened this morning, knowing he was unprepared and blaming Andy for his lack of preparation.

Yesterday, while Andy had talked and talked endlessly, Bud had repeatedly asked himself, "Am I my brother's keeper?" and each time the answer had been a crashing *No!* and each time he had allowed himself to be caught in the sticky web of Andy's memory, being drawn back over a part of it. The past was dead, as dead as Reen. It had no place in the present scheme of things. Andy had no place in that scheme either, and he'd been a fool to take him in. He should have—

"I forget things sometimes," Andy said. "Like Reen."

"You'd never know it," Bud answered somewhat caustically.

"Like his being dead," Andy went on, unperturbed. "I can't get used to the idea that he's dead."

"He's been dead for a long time," Bud said.

Andy nodded. "Him and me both."

"What do you mean?"

"Nothing," Andy said. He seemed suddenly angry. "Nothing at all."

"Well, I've got to get out of here.". Bud glanced at his watch. "The exam is at nine, and I don't want to be late—even though I'll flunk the damned thing, anyway."

"You'll pass it," Andy said disinterestedly.

"Yeah," Bud said. He looked at his watch again. "Where's Carol? She said she was coming over this morning, and here it is—"

"Why's she coming over?"

"Because she wants to, I guess."

"Relieving the watch, huh?"

"She wants to see you," Bud said.

"Sure, she wants to see me. She wants to guard the prisoner, you mean."

"Look, Andy—"

"Did I say I'm blaming either of you? Well, I'm not. You probably both think I'm a lot of hot air, and maybe you're right. But I know in my heart that this time it's for good. I may be mixed up, but I'm not stupid."

"No one said you were."

"I'm not stupid, and I know this particular treadmill leads nowhere, man, nowhere. So I'm getting off it, and damned fast. I don't need Carol *or* you to watch me."

"Nobody's watching you, Andy."

"No, nobody," he said, and again there was the hurt anger in his voice. "You'd better go. You don't want to miss that exam, do you?"

"No, I sure as hell don't. Tell Carol I waited as long as I could, will you?"

"Sure. And don't worry. Nothing's going to happen."

Bud nodded. "Listen, if you want any breakfast, all the stuff is in the refrigerator—milk, eggs, butter, anything you might need. There's bread in the breadbox, and there's instant coffee and Corn Flakes in the cabinet over the stove. Just help yourself."

"The condemned man ate a hearty meal," Andy cracked.

Bud ignored him. "Carol should be here soon," he said.

"Don't worry. I won't leave my cell."

"Now look, Andy—"

"Is it all right to play some records?"

"Anything you like."

"Thanks. I appreciate all you're doing, Bud."

"Don't mention it."

"You're an honorable man," Andy said, and again there was this controlled anger in his voice. "Doing all this for old-times' sake. Real honorable."

"It had nothing to do with honor," Bud answered, beginning to get a little irritated himself.

"Maybe not. I guess you're the type who'd take in any stray dog in a storm, huh?"

"*Any* dog," Bud said nastily, finally fed up.

"I figured, man. Go take your test."

"I'll see you later," Bud said. He took a sports jacket from the closet, slipped into it, and then went to the door. "Now take it easy."

"Sure," Andy said.

Bud walked out into the hallway and then down the steps. He could not understand Andy's attitude, and his lack of understanding annoyed him fully as much as the attitude did. He had, after all, taken in what amounted to a complete stranger. He had not expected bootlicking gratitude, but he had expected civility. Andy had apparently awakened this morning with a long hair across, a distrust for everyone and everything, and a resentment toward anyone who was trying to help him.

Well, the hell with Andy.

If he wanted to be the misunderstood martyr of some misunderstood cause, that was Andy's prerogative. He seemed to hold a misbegotten concept about drugs, anyway, a concept that was hardly linked with the repentance he professed. Whenever he talked about narcotics his eyes glowed and he talked with the rapid fervor of a new father —despite his religious resolve to shed the habit. It was as if he constantly had to reassure himself that what he'd done was not really so bad at all, in spite of the fact that he recognized its badness at the same time. And so, facing this double-headed ogre of repentance and self-justification, he was forced to acknowledge aid gratefully, while simultaneously denying that he needed any aid.

Bud could understand why Andy resented anyone's watching him. If he was earnest in his desire to break the

habit, there was only one person who could help him, and
that was himself. But the people who were watching him—
and Bud had unfortunately become one of those people—
served as consciences more than jailers. They were only interested in seeing that Andy stuck to his resolve.

Or at least they *had* been interested.

Bud could not speak for Carol, but he certainly knew
that he himself no longer cared whether Andy abstained or
went right back to the needle. He had never enjoyed the
web of circumstance, feeling thwarted and frustrated in its
entangling power. Andy had gone out of his life a long
time ago, and he did not want him back in it now, and he
cursed himself for not having taken a firmer stand the moment Carol called. He had reacted weakly, and he deserved
everything he got now, but he still had himself to think
about.

He had not imagined the sneering quality in Andy's
voice whenever the impending examination was discussed.
He had felt foolish about it in the beginning, until he realized that time was passing rapidly, until he began to suspect Andy of deliberately keeping him away from his
studies.

He was certain now that he would fail the examination.
There was no doubt in his mind that he would fail it. And
the next test was tomorrow. Good God, tomorrow afternoon. If only he had more time, if only the tests were
bunched together at the beginning of next week, but no,
there was another tomorrow afternoon, and another after
that on Friday morning, and he'd be facing those with the
knowledge that he'd flunked the first one. *If* he flunked. Of
course he would flunk! He obviously could not study with
Andy around. He could tell Andy to shut the hell up, of
course, but Andy seemed to be a bottomless cup of memories that never ceased flowing. Andy persisted in going back
to the past, and—worse—he had been trapped again and
again into going back with him, a sort of helpless prisoner
enmeshed in the bowels of a persistent time machine.

Well, the time machine had certainly put the old kibosh
on the Milton exam. He discounted that as a definite loss,
fired with the knowledge that he somehow had to pass the
other exams. Once that was done he would try to wheedle a
passing grade for the course from Dr. Mason, and, know-

ing that old bitch, the task would not be a simple one. But if she were faced with the fact that only her course stood between him and graduation in three and a half, perhaps she would suffer a momentary softening of the heart, the head, and the arteries.

Sourly he contemplated the sickening apple-polishing that lay ahead of him, and the thought nauseated him.

He blamed Andy, but most of all he blamed himself. He had not been cut out for the role of thankless benefactor. He had once been that type of beatific soul who could do a good deed and then silently allow the deed to pass unpraised. But not any more. Oh, sure, Carol would pat him on the head once this was all over and tell him how wonderfully he'd behaved, but he'd long ago stopped seeking praise from anyone.

The big obstacle ahead, for the moment, was the Milton test. And maybe it wasn't a very big obstacle to Andy's way of thinking, and maybe it was a very childish thing to be worrying about, but it was nonetheless an enormous obstacle—and facing this obstacle, and realizing he could not surmount it, he felt again this surly despair, this self-condemnation for having so easily been led into the slaughterhouse of Andy's trouble.

Disgustedly he walked to the subway kiosk and boarded an uptown train.

Now that he was alone in the apartment he felt a little better.

He knew he shouldn't have snapped at Bud that way, but there were times when the all-seeing eye of Big Brother annoyed the hell out of him. Everyone seemed to be watching, every second of the day. It was like being a two-headed calf in a side show. The people came to watch you, and they watched you carefully, to see what two-headed things did. When you became an addict, you also became a two-headed thing. And maybe one of those heads understood the watching eyes, but the other head resented them immensely.

He'd also been a little sickened by Bud's behavior. All right, he was a big-shot college boy now, but don't college boys ever realize that some things in life don't jell according to the textbook? He had an examination, and that's all well and good, but he'd acted as if the examination were the Gabriel horn blowing, as if the floods and the fires were going to rain down on his goddamned head if he flunked.

That was the trouble with college boys—everything according to the book. Ants with tweed jackets and pipes.

A college boy studies Economics, and he thinks he knows the secret of a dollar. He gets sixty-five bucks a month from the government, and he studies Economics, and, man, he knows what it's all about, he knows all about getting out there and earning a buck.

Or he studies American History, and he plots a cycle, and he can interpret everything that's happening right here and now. Did a fruit get rolled and mugged up on Fiftieth and Broadway last night? Why, man, that's simple to calculate. We can draw a parallel between this and the Boston Tea Party. How many lumps, please?

He takes a course in Biology, and he knows all about sex then. He knows how the lowly snail does it, and he knows how the tsetse fly does it, but does he ever once realize there's a *vas deferens* between the dusty, dry pages of his textbook and a session in bed with a passionate wench? No, not the college boy.

The college boy lives in another world, a world in which he busily sniffs the seats of girls' bicycles—and Bud was in that world now. And it was a damn shame, because there had once been something between Bud and him, and now that something was dead and gone, and it always pained him to realize that something was dead. All the good things in his life seemed to die sooner or later, mostly sooner, and sometimes he felt that he was outliving his experiences, that he'd seen everything there was to see and done everything there was to do, and now they were all dead, and here he was a living man in a world of dead dreams, an old old man at twenty.

Twenty, was that all?

Not even old enough to vote.

Fifteen, and sixteen, and seventeen, those were the years. Those were the real years, all of them, and he and Bud had shared a good friendship then, all right, one of the best, and what's happened to it now? How do friendships become non-friendships? The College Boy and the Addict, a play in three acts discussing the rise and fall of a friendship.

"George, I'd like you to meet my non-friend Bud, who is good enough to allow me the freedom of his four walls, twelve walls if you count the kitchen and the toilet. Best little non-friend I ever had. Shake hands, non-buddy."

Oh, sure, you can joke about it. My mother always said there was no such thing as a true friend, anyway. "Never tell anyone your business," she used to say, as if she were Barbara Hutton sitting on the Woolworth fortune. Man, why are small people full of such big ideas? But Bud and I were really friends, really and truly, and you shouldn't joke about a good friendship, even though he's a college boy now, because when you joke about a good friendship that's now dead, it's the same as joking about a good man who's dead.

The apartment was very silent.

He could never stand the loneliness of silence. He never felt lonely when he was sitting in the center of a band, and he never felt lonely when he was high, either. We mustn't think about getting high, must we, now must we? No, that's all behind us, like the dead friendship between Bud and me. The friendship became a non-friendship, and now the addict is about to become a non-addict. If he could stick to it. Oh, he could stick to it, certainly he could stick to it. Was it any harder than busting double C? Well, to tell the truth, yes, it was a good deal harder, if you want to know.

There was only one real requisite for becoming a non-addict; you had to become an addict first.

What had his father called it? A dope fiend, yes. A perfect word portrait, economical and precise. The picture of a man with his eyes feverish in his head, his lips dripping saliva, his teeth glinting, holding a needle full of *(dum-de-dum-dum)*

!!**NARCOTICS**!!

That's a dope fiend.

You can use dope when you're building model airplanes, too, so, using a college boy's reasoning, we can assume that all kids who build model airplanes are dope fiends, dope.

Which reminds me a little of a tired gag I wrote back in 1492.

Morris Cohen, an intelligent little boy, says to his father upon hearing the Good Humor wagon outside, "I want an ice-cream pop."

Meyer Cohen, a man against modern development of any sort, including these newfangled ice creams on sticks, answers, "You'll get an ice-cream cone."

Whereupon: "You don't understand. I want an ice-cream pop, Pop."

Whereupon: "I understand. You'll get an ice-cream cone, Cohen."

Ah, the intricacies of the English language. Put that in your briar pipe and smoke it, Buddy-College-Boy.

You put opium in a pipe to smoke, you know. It's a very gummy thing, and you ball it between your fingers and stuff it into the bowl of a pipe, and blooie, *amigo,* there goes your skull!

Well, not quite blooie. Blooie is for the comic books.

More like shhhhhhhlooie. A sort of sliding down, or up, but sliding anyway, just sliding away from all the petty garbage and into another world, like the world my non-friend Bud inhabits. Ah, that time on opium had been the end, but it's really very dangerous stuff, opium, really very dangerous, so it's better I steered away from that junk, but still it was the end, the laziest kind of a high ever, not a slam like H, but that lazy, lazy, mother-loving . . . m-m-m, sweet.

Bud would never understand that world in a million years. No, Bud would never dig it. Nor I. Or me. Or whatever.

I don't dig it any more either. Take that sixteenth of heroin in the coat pocket of my jacket, and take the syringe and spoon in the inside pocket of that same jacket, and take a book of matches to cook the junk with—take all that, pal, and welcome to it because I'm off that kick, dad.

And I don't feel too bad this morning either. No breakfast, and maybe that's the reason. Hell, you can't throw up something you haven't had yet. But nonetheless, and even so, I feel pretty good. Which just shows to go you can't keep a good man down, even if you stick him in a prison and appoint a couple of dedicated jailers to guard him.

I need jailers like I need a hole in the head. Don't they realize I'm off it for good this time? Can't they see that I mean it this time? They must be blind if they can't see that. What do I have to do to show them?

Damnit, that's what burns my butt. Not a little knee-high fire, but that, just that. They should be able to see that I'm sincere this time. Didn't I pass a fix by yesterday? Wasn't I all set to shoot up, and didn't I say no thanks, thanks a lot, but no thanks? Didn't I have that needle all set, just, just . . . now don't start thinking about needles and fixes because that doesn't help the situation one bit. But still, it burns me up that they don't trust me. If they don't trust me, who the hell *is* going to trust me, when I can't even trust myself, when I . . .

I *can* trust myself.

I'm all alone here. Where the hell is Carol? And there's junk and the works in the closet across the room. How many steps to that outfit? Three, four, five? But I'm not making a move for it, am I? So doesn't that prove I can trust myself? What the hell else does it prove? I'm not crippled, and I can get up any time I want to and walk right over to that closet, and how long does it take to ram a needle into my arm. Now get off that kick, Dick, because that's the suicide kick. You've got the goddamn thing under control, so don't think about the closet, or the jacket, or what's in the jacket pockets. Screw that noise, boys.

Now just simmer down. That's the biggest enemy, thinking about it. When Helen was kicking the habit, she wouldn't even think about it. She wouldn't let me come near her with the stuff, and she wouldn't allow her mind to come anywhere near it either. So let's forget whatever the hell is in that closet. There I've forgotten it already, I don't even know what's in that closet, let's just forget it and think of something else.

There must be a lot of things to think about, so what shall we think about on this bright sunny morning?

Now there's a bright sunny morning, so that should give us a bright sunny idea. And there it is: a bright sunny idea. Bottle it, cork it, and paint it green. And then march with it in the Saint Patty's Day parade.

The trouble with Saint Patrick, in case anyone is interested, is that he drove the snakes out of Ireland, and all the bastards came here and became traffic cops.

Now we're doing it. Now we're beginning to think of other things. This is what the cartoonists call "snowballing."

Cops, was it? All right, cops, why not cops? Of course, the cops and I are old friends, so we mustn't speak of the cops disrespectfully. We're even better old non-friends than Buddy and me—don't you remember all the times with the cops, oh, you remember, surely you remember? Yes, I remember but we're not supposed to think about things like . . . but this wouldn't be thinking about things like that, this would be thinking about cops, like the time on the roof, don't you remember, don't you remember the time on the roof, don't you remember every single line of that dialogue? Oh, Christ, you were pretty damn sharp that day, and you hadn't even been fixed, don't you remember that day?

It was very hot up there on the roof. The sun was just a hazy ball of yellow in the sky, and it shone down on the slick tar of the roof, and it glanced off the skylight and reflected from the badges on the chests of the two cops.

The second cop was leaning over the brick wall on the edge of the roof and looking down into the courtyard. He had a very fat backside, and the blue of his uniform stretched tight over his wide, abundant buttocks. The first cop was fat, too, but not so much as the second one was. He held my elbow in one beefy paw, and then he said, "All right, cokie, what'd you do with it?"

"What'd I do with what?" I asked.

"The syringe and the package. We know you had it, pal. You dump it over the roof there?"

"I don't know what you mean by a syringe," I said. "You use a syringe for enemas, don't you?"

The second cop came back and said, "He's a wise guy, Tommy. He's one of the wise-guy type."

Tommy nodded and clenched his fists. "You just keep on being wise," he told me. "You just keep doing that. We know you're on it, son, and all we got to do is catch you. You get booked for possession then."

"Possession of what?" I asked.

"I told you," the second cop said. "He's just a wise guy."

"You high now?" Tommy asked, studying me shrewdly.

"I don't know what you mean by high."

"He don't know what we mean by high," the second cop mimicked.

"You guys come around here talking about syringes and highs, and I'm just in the dark here. Don't they teach you guys to speak any English at all?" I said.

"They speak English downtown," Tommy said. "You'll find out the first time we cop you with a package of H."

"What's H?" I asked.

"Come on, we're wasting our time," the second cop said. "He dumped the junk and the works."

"Man, you guys sure do talk foreign," I said.

Tommy shook his head sadly. "You don't know the road you're on, kid. It's a shame."

"Yeah, I bleed for him," the second cop said.

"I'm bleeding, too," I told them. "From that goddamn sun."

"Keep your nose clean, cokie," Tommy said. "Remember, we catch you with a bindle, and you'll go cold turkey behind bars."

"Don't snow me, dad," I said. "I know the law better than you do."

"What?"

"For intent to sell, I've got to be holding two or more ounces of H, M, or C. Sixteen ounces on the other junk. For a possession felony, I've got to be holding a quarter ounce or more of the big three, or two ounces or more of the other—"

"It's a misdemeanor to be holding *any* quantity of narcotics," the first cop said.

"Spitting on the sidewalk's a misdemeanor, too," I said.

"You punks think—"

"Did you find any H, dad?" I asked. "You got anything to pin on me? It's no crime to be a drug addict, you know. So why don't you go blow your whistle at traffic a little?"

"You goddamned addicts—" he started.

"What's an addict?" I asked innocently.

The second cop said, "Argh," and drew his hand like he was going to slap me across the face. Tommy grabbed him and said, "Come on, let the bastard stew in his own juice."

I did just that, man.

As soon as they were gone I cut out for the roof top across the way, and then I headed back for my pad. Helen was there that afternoon, and, oh, did her face light up the way it did because she'd been real low when she called and I'd told her to come on over. That was the day I had to swipe a jacket from Gimbel's—was it Gimbel's or Macy's? —but I got away with it clean, stashed under the old overcoat I was wearing. You'd think those stupid bastards would wonder about a guy wearing an overcoat when it was so hot outside. I ditched the coat back at the apartment, and Helen told me to hurry and get the stuff, and then I hocked the jacket and copped from Rog, real good stuff it was, too, Rog never laid a bad bindle on me ever. And if it hadn't been for the cops, we'd have both been stoned an hour earlier, but it was a good thing they chased me up on the roof at least because that way I could ditch the deck.

Which apartment was that, anyway? Man, how many pads did I fall into after I left the Jerralds band and came back to New York? Dozens, at least. First the place on the Street, and then the one on Third Avenue, and then down in the Village, and then that place one of Helen's friends got for me for the summer—that was in 1948, wasn't it?— sure, sure, and then that long string of places I lived in, when everything else was gone and when I had to duck out each month before the rent was due and even that was kicks in a way, fooling all those goddamn happy ants who worked for bread by giving you a roof, and what about the hotels, Jesus, all the one-night stands in shoddy hotels, more hotels than you can count on your fingers and toes. New York City has some of the sleaziest hotels in the world if you know where to look for them, and I knew where to look because I *had* to know where to look. What about that place on Forty-seventh—Forty-eighth was it— that night Helen and I were on the town and we latched onto that guy from Texas who talked about his oil wells and his Caddy. You had to hand it to Helen, she could look like a million bucks whenever she had to, even when she was low, except when she was real sick with it. She wasn't sick that night, though.

We'd popped off just about a half hour before, both of us at her place, and then Mr. Millionaire landed in our laps, and did Helen turn it on then, all the wattage, nine thousand volts of sparkling electricity because she wanted what Dallas had in his wallet, folded so neatly, and, man, she got it all right. When Helen wants something it's pretty damned tough to keep her from getting it. We got enough bread that night to keep us in the white stuff for two weeks. I told her she was wasting her time. I told her she should buy into one of these Park Avenue syndicates and make herself a fortune, if she could get that much from only pretending she was going all the way. She damn near scratched my eyes out that night, funny kid Helen, as if she were in a dream world, even though she knew what she was doing always. Still, it was as if she didn't want to know what she was doing, didn't want to be reminded of it. Like she was almost taking a revenge on herself or something, doing everything she had to do, and getting so goddamned hooked it wasn't funny.

And every time I'd say I wasn't hooked she'd laugh that mocking laugh of hers and tell me I was hooked clear through the bag and back again. A lot she knew about it, hell, I wasn't hooked at the time, few caps a day, well maybe half a dozen, that's hooked? I seen guys with habits as long as John Silver, when you've got a habit that long, then you're in trouble, man. Try kicking a habit like that, and you wind up in the booby hatch picking at the coverlet. Me, I just enjoyed the stuff, that's all. Some guys pick their noses, and that's a habit; me, I favored drugs—so what's so bad about either. So long as you got control there's nothing to worry about, and who can say it isn't the biggest boot alive? Who can say it doesn't knock your brains out—well, *did*, anyway, not any more now, of course, because now I'm off it, which is the only way to be, naturally. But how would you know that was the only way unless you tried the other way? And trying it was the end, trying it was really the mother-loving end, because when you want that stuff, and then when you get it and just . . .

Now how'd we get back to this again, huh? I thought we were going to steer away from this, and here we are right back to it, with a taste of it in the mouth. Now spit out that taste, spit it out. How many days has it been since I've had a fix?

How many hours, how many minutes?

Seconds?

Thanks, I haven't even had firsts yet.

That's the way! Oh, Jesus, are we sharp this morning. This morning we don't need anything to keep this trigger brain clicking. Not heroin, and not anything, why don't I just go across to that closet and dump that jive in the garbage and forget all about redeeming Buddy's bag?

Nope. Got to redeem that bag. A promise is a promise, isn't it? Who hocked the bag? We did. So who redeems it? We do.

Who do?

We do.

Man, this is the end. I've never felt this sharp since . . . since the morning I cut my razor while shaving.

Oh, dig that one! Oh, daddy-oh, beware! Beware of this cat with the razor-sharp claws.

Let's hear some Kenton, cat. This dead friend Buddy had some real hip stuff here, maybe there's hope for him yet. Even though he's worried about a Milton exam. Milton, was it? Shakespeare? What difference does it make? He's worried about his exam, man, now that's a real big worry, all right, the biggest.

In Act V, Scene III of *Omelet*, what does I-Feel-Ya say to Get-Rude?

"Get thee to a nunnery!" he shouted aloud, and then he began laughing.

Kenton, here I cometh.

He went to the record player and then fished through the Kenton album, making his selection. He put the disks in place, turned the player up full, and then lay back full length on the couch, squeezing his eyes shut.

"Tam-pee-co," the speaker blared,

"Tam-pee-co,

On the Gulf of

> *Meh-*

> > *hee-*

> > > *co . . ."*

He listened to the swinging lilt of June Christy's voice, picking out the deep tenor saxophone of Vido Musso behind her, the wild trombone of Kai Winding, hearing the intricate brass figures when the trumpet section took over, hearing the screech horn in the background, becoming a

art of the music. The record ended abruptly, and he heard
he hum of the arm swinging back, the click of the second
ecord dropping into place, the buzzing scratch as the rec-
rd began spinning and the arm captured the first groove,
nd then "Artistry Jumps" began its insinuating sadistic
ludgeoning.

There was something wild about Kenton, something like
 lightning storm unleashed, the thunder growling, but
nostly the lightning, bouncing with electric fury, illuminat-
ng the landscape of his mind. There was passion and lust
n the music, and it crashed against his soul in waves of
ound, crashed the way Dizzy Gillespie crashed, but more
olidly, the same drive, with Gillespie perhaps a little more
ubtle in his bop intricacies, Kenton more concerned with
he sheer overwhelming power of the sound bludgeon, but
ach concerned with the naked revelation of passion and
ightning. The music thudded against his ears and his body,
inking into his blood stream and into the marrow of his
ones.

He suddenly wanted his horn in his hands.

He swung his feet over the side of the couch, stood, and
walked rapidly to where his case rested near the hall closet.
He picked up the case and brought it to the couch, and his
ingers trembled on the clasps as he opened it. He lifted the
orn from its bed, and his fingers sought the valves, and he
elt the compassionate tenderness flood over him. He want-
d to play very badly now, and when he heard the sock
horus he was dismayed because he'd wanted to join in
with the shrieking trumpets. He realized abruptly that he
ould turn the record back to any groove he wanted, come
n on the change of key, or the sock, or wherever he want-
d, and play straight through to the second ending, and he
elt a gladness sweep over him again, as if he had discov-
red a basic truth about himself.

He shoved his mouthpiece onto the horn, opened the spit
valve, and blew the horn clean of moisture. His hands were
rembling, and his eyes were bright. At this moment he
wanted more than anything in the world to play with the
Kenton band. He lifted the player arm and then dropped it
n the edge of the record, and he listened while the steady
Kenton build-up began again.

He kept his horn to his mouth, flexing his lips against it,

moving the horn away for a fraction of an inch every now
and then so that he could run his tongue over the ring of
muscle.

He was very excited now, waiting for his cue as if he
were on stage someplace, listening to the slow crescendo of
the music, waiting to begin blowing. The band was gaining
steady momentum, building to the shrieking, screeching,
socking, rocking, roaring sock chorus.

Not yet.

He wet his lips again.

A few more seconds . . . a few . . .

Now!

He began blowing.

He heard a strange sound in the room, a sound like a
bleat or a moan from a wounded animal. He looked around
him curiously, not turning his head, just moving his
eyes, surprised. He kept blowing, but the sound persisted, a
curiously wailing sound, like a baby crying, like a baby who
needed his diaper changed. The sound was harsh and grating, and it clashed with the smooth, powerful, driving music Kenton was making. He could not hear himself over this
other sound, and he wanted to shout to the baby to shut up
—can't you see I'm playing, can't you see I'm playing
again after all this time? Shut up, *shut up!*

And then he knew what was making the sound.

He took the trumpet from his lips.

He felt very empty and very alone, suddenly drained of
all gladness. His eyes were wet. The Kenton band wound
up the record, the disk above it dropped down to cover it,
and he heard a new tune begin, but he could not identify
the music, nor did he try to.

He had just heard himself playing, and the memory of
the sound wrenched at his heart, filling him with a helpless
misery he had never known before. It was as if he suddenly
realized that everything was truly gone now, not only Carol, and not only his money or his clothes or his big ideas,
and not only his self-respect, because all of those things
could return if he really wanted them badly enough.

But his talent was gone, too, as if he'd never known how
to play, as if he were just a . . . just a slob picking up the
horn and putting it to his lips, not knowing how to fit his
mouth to the mouthpiece, not knowing how to breathe or

move his fingers. God, where had his armature gone? Where were his lungs? What had made that horrible sound? Oh, Jesus was that sound, that sound . . .

He threw the horn onto the couch, and then he snapped off the record player, and the room was very silent again, and he sat at the core of the silence, wetting his lips over and over.

The tears streamed down his face, and he felt himself trembling, but not with excited anticipation this time, trembling with a need for something, a need for someone to tell him everything would be all right again, he'd learn to blow again, he'd pass the audition with Laddy Fredericks, and they'd love him, all he needed was some brushing up, get the lip back in shape, shouldn't Carol be here by now, where was Bud, Helen, Helen . . .

He stared around the room helplessly, his hands dangling between his knees, the tears in his eyes clouding his vision. He was alone, all alone. There was no one to reassure him, no one to help him now, not a friend in the world, not a . . .

He stopped crying, and he brought up his head and looked toward the closed closet door.

Slowly he began to nod.

He had a friend, after all. He had a very old friend.

17

Carol came into the apartment at eleven-twenty. He opened the door for her, and he smiled vapidly, and she looked at him curiously.

"Are you all right?" she asked.

"Huh?" he said. "Oh, sure. I was napping when you knocked."

"Oh." She paused, studying his face again. "You're sure you're all right?" He looked a little groggy, but that meant nothing, of course, especially if he'd been napping.

"I'm fine, honey," he said. "Been waiting for you all morning."

"But you said you were—"

"Finally fell asleep all over again," he explained. "What took you so long?"

"I had a damned flat," she said vehemently. "Has Bud gone?"

"Yes, long time ago."

"Have you had breakfast?"

"No."

"Shall I get you something?"

"No."

"Trouble with the stomach again?"

"No. No, I feel fine."

"Then why don't you take some breakfast?"

"All right. A cup of coffee, maybe."

She was wearing a beige suit, the jacket unbuttoned over a coral sweater. She took off the jacket and hung it in the closet, and then she shoved the sleeves of the sweater to her elbows, showing her well-rounded forearms and the light golden down on them.

"You look pretty," he said.

"Thanks."

"But you always look pretty."

"Well, thanks. Where does Bud keep his coffee?"

"Cabinet over the stove. Unquote."

She went into the kitchen and found the jar of coffee. She put on some water to boil and then walked into the living room.

"This is like old times, isn't it?" Andy said.

"I suppose."

"I mean, you know. Us together, cup of coffee, stuff like that."

"Oh. Yes."

"Trouble with us, Carol, was that I never fully appreciated you."

"Let's not talk about it. Have you had any pains today?"

"Not a one."

"Good. What'd you do with that package of heroin you had yesterday?"

"Huh?"

"The heroin. The stuff you picked up when you—"

"Oh, oh, that. Still got it. Why?"

"I think you'd better give it to me."

"What for?"

"Andy, why tempt yourself? Give it to me, and I'll get rid of it."

"You planning on shooting up, Carol?" he asked, smiling.

"Oh, don't be silly. Andy——"

"I always suspected you of being a sneak addict. That's the worst kind, Carol. That's the kind——"

"Seriously, Andy. Let me get rid of it."

He chuckled. "How would *you* get rid of it? You wouldn't know where to take——"

"I'll flush it down the toilet bowl."

"Honey, you'd be flushing ten bucks out to sea. That's foolish."

"I'll give you the ten dollars," Carol said. "Where's the heroin?"

"No, keep your money. I'll be damned if I'm going to take anything else from you. *I* hocked Bud's bag, and I'll redeem it. Now, let's not have any more talk about jive. Now, do you hear me, Carol?"

"All right," she said wearily.

They sat in silence for several moments, and then she said, "Coffee should be ready. Want to come in now?"

He rose, and they went into the kitchen together, and she spooned the powdered coffee into their cups.

"Not too much for me," Andy said.

"All right."

She put the kettle back on the stove, and they sat together drinking.

"We should have got married," he said suddenly.

"Do you think so?"

"Sure I think so. I wouldn't have said so if I didn't think so."

Carol smiled weakly. "You never asked me," she said.

"Would you have married me if I'd asked? I mean, if I hadn't gone crazy with myself, would you have?"

"I suppose so."

"It could have been real nice," he said wistfully. "I think I'd have liked being married to you. I mean, like we could have had coffee together every morning like this. That would've been nice." He paused. "Don't you think so?"

"Yes, I think so."

"We used to have a lot of fun together," he said.
"Yes."

"You can't deny that, can you?"

"No, I can't deny that."

"Before Bud and the boys left for the service, and even while they were gone. You have to admit we had a lot of fun in those days, Carol."

"Yes."

"A lot of fun," he repeated, "and we made a good couple, too. We always looked good together, Carol, and that's a fact. Jesus, sometimes I wonder——" He cut himself off.

"What, Andy?"

"Oh, I don't know. I just wonder where the hell did it all go? Jesus, where the hell did it all go?"

"It'll be different," Carol said softly. "Once you're all right again, things will be different."

"Sure," he said, "sure, I know they will. Carol, do you think . . . Jesus, do you think I *can* do it? Do you think I really can kick it?"

"I *know* you can," she said.

"Oh, Jesus, wouldn't that be great? Oh, God, if I only could. If I only could do it, Carol, I'd . . . I'd give anything if I could only do it. Kick the monkey off and get back on the right road again. It's been such a damn long time since I've been on the right track. And this Fredericks gig is really something, you know that, don't you? He's got a corny outfit, but what difference does it make, so long as you're blowing steady. There's no such thing as corny, except when you're a kid and you can't be a kid all your life, can you, Carol?"

"No," she said.

"So look, look, if I can kick this, I mean really kick it, get off it for good, not even look at it any more, and if I can land the Fredericks gig, well . . . things'll be okay again, won't they? I mean, you know I can play trumpet, don't you?"

"You're a wonderful trumpet player," she said.

"Sure, so all it amounts to is staying cool, that's all, so *everybody* can know I'm good. Honey, I . . . I want that job, you know, and I'm really gonna blow when I get it— oh, Jesus, how I'm gonna blow, like . . . like I never did before. I'm gonna . . . I'm gonna practice again, every day, and I'm gonna start taking lessons again, just as soon as I land this gig, just as soon as I've kicked the habit. Jesus, Carol, I'll be free again, do you realize what that means? I won't have to be scrounging around any more, I won't be a bum—a bum, that's what I am—I'll be somebody, something, I'll stand up there and I'll knock the walls down with my horn."

He was out of breath now, and his eyes were glistening. He reached across the table and took Carol by the wrist, and his fingers tightened around the wrist, and he said, "And if I make the band, and if I . . . I'm all right again, maybe we could . . . I mean . . ."

"What, Andy?"

"Do you think you'd . . . do you think you could marry me, Carol?"

She stared at him curiously, as if she hadn't heard him. He waited for her answer, leaning across the table, his hand around her wrist.

"I know I shouldn't even ask, Jesus, not after the way I've been, not after spitting in your eye whenever you tried to help. I know I shouldn't, Carol, but I'm asking you anyway because you know you're the only one, the only girl who ever mattered a damn to me, Carol. I never should have let you go. I should have locked you up someplace, I should have killed myself before I let you go, but I'm asking you now, I'm asking you now, honey, and I'll get down on my hands and knees if you want me to, I'll kiss your feet if you want, but say yes, Carol, say you'll marry me if I straighten out, say you will, honey, please, please. Because I know now that I . . . honey, honey, tears? No, please, don't cry, please Carol, I don't want to make you cry, I don't want to make you cry ever again."

He stood and walked around the table, and he cradled her head, and she wept against his chest.

"Your shirt," she said. "I'm getting . . . your shirt all wet."

"Don't cry, Carol. Please don't."

"Andy, do . . . do you mean it? What you said?"

"Yes, oh, Jesus, yes! I've never meant anything so much in my life."

"I'd—" she swallowed hard, and then she smiled—"I'd be . . . very happy to . . . to marry you," she said.

He kissed her fleetingly, and then he went back to the other side of the table, and hé sat grinning at her, feeling somewhat guilty all at once for what had happened before she'd arrived, but feeling a new strength within him, too, and knowing that now he *would* kick the habit, kick it once and for all.

They went into the living room, and they sat quietly. The silence was not a strained one, nor did either of them make any effort to speak, as if conversational communication were no longer necessary between them. They were like a tired, contented couple in a small-town waiting room, waiting for the three A.M. train.

When the train came, neither of them heard it.

Bud shoved his key into the door lock, twisted it, and then threw the door open. He glanced briefly into the living room and then went into the kitchen and directly to the refrigerator. Carol came into the kitchen as he was pouring himself a glass of milk.

"How'd it go?" she asked.

"Lousy," he said. "I flunked."

"Bud, you didn't!"

"What choice was there? Half of it was Greek to me."

"Oh, Bud, I'm terribly sorry."

"Yeah," he said. He drained the glass and poured it full to the brim again. Andy came into the kitchen, a smile on his face.

"How's the scholar?" he asked, and he couldn't have picked a worse opening question.

"Right in his grave," Bud snapped. "Thanks a lot."

"What happened?" Andy asked.

"Just what I knew would happen. What do you think?"

"What happened, Carol?"

"He thinks he flunked."

"I *know* I flunked. Never mind any thinking. I flunked that test as sure as God made little green apples."

"Well, I'm sorry," Andy said.

"You ought to be. Why couldn't you have shut up for a little while?"

"I'm sorry. I didn't realize I was—"

"What did you think you were doing then? Did you think I could study with you rattling on about everything that's happened since the Ice Age? Did you think—"

"Bud," Carol said gently.

"No, Carol, I'm sorry, but that's the way I feel. I don't mind helping out, but goddamnit when I extend a hand I don't expect it to be chewed off at the elbow."

"I'll go," Andy said.

"Where will you go?" Bud asked. "Answer me that."

"I'll find a place."

"Yeah, you'll find a place. And then you'll be right back on the band wagon again."

"Well, I didn't want to interrupt your studying. Believe me, Bud, I wouldn't have had this happen for the world."

"That's very nice of you, but it's already happened."

"Well, what do you want me to do?" Andy asked.

"Nothing. Just shut up for the next few days so I won't flunk the whole rotten battery, that's all."

"No, I'll go."

"Oh, wipe that stupid martyred look from your face, will you? I'm getting sick of seeing you running around like Joan of Arc."

"I wasn't trying to—"

"Who the hell are you trying to kid, anyway, Andy?" Bud shouted. "You act as if everyone but yourself is to blame for your goddamn habit! Well, get that out of your head, will you? And learn to be a civilized human being. Nobody owes you anything, remember that. Anything you're getting is gravy."

"Bud, for God's sake—" Carol started.

"Let him talk," Andy said tightly.

"Sure, let him talk. Andy approves of talk. All Andy does is talk, talk, talk. Well, I'm fed up with Andy's talk. He talked me right out of a passing grade in Milton—and he may have talked me into an extra semester as well."

"Who cares whether you get out in three and a half years or not?" Andy snapped.

"I'm in a hurry," Bud answered rapidly.

"Why? Where the hell are you going in such a hurry?"

"Listen, I don't have to—"

"Never mind," Andy said. "I'm getting out. I'm not going to stick around if you feel—"

"He wants me to get down on my hands and knees and beg him to stay," Bud said. "Well, kid, you've got another guess coming. You want to go, good-by!"

"I'm going, Carol."

"Bud, couldn't we——"

"Let him go if he wants to. We can't wipe his nose for the rest of his life."

"Nobody's asking you to wipe my nose," Andy shouted. "Your own nose could use a little wiping, if you ask me. Go back to your books. Have yourself a ball. I won't bother you again, don't worry."

"We need a little 'Hearts and Flowers' for this," Bud said.

"I think you should stay here, Andy," Carol said.

"And listen to this bull? I know when I'm not wanted, all right."

"Poor little Andy," Bud said. "Nobody wants him."

"Look, Bud——"

"Look, Andy, let's get this straight between us," Bud said. "I don't care if you go or stay or drop dead, understand? I just don't care any more. When Carol called with her sob story, I figured, okay, do a turn for an old friend. Okay, I'm always ready to do a turn for an old friend. Old friend needs a place to stay; sure, bring him around. But I've worked pretty hard for the past three years, and I don't want to see all that shot to hell, understand? I may be able to squeeze my way out of one flunk, but it'll be murder if I flunk another test. If you stay here—and mind you, I'm not coaxing you because I don't give a damn one way or the other—you'd better just shut up for the remainder of the week. You'd better just pretend you're all alone in the apartment. If you feel like talking, go into the john and talk to yourself. If you want to practice, put in a mute and go up on the roof. But leave me alone. Stay or go but, either way, leave me alone."

"I'll go," Andy said.

"Fine."

"You'll stay," Carol told him.

"What for? He's made himself pretty plain, hasn't he? He wants me out. So, out I go."

"He didn't say that."

"Seems to me that's what he said."

"Why do you want to get out, Andy? So you can get some stuff?"

"I haven't even given it a thought."

"Then why do you want to get out?"

"He doesn't want me here," Andy said patiently.

"Oh, for Christ's sake, stay," Bud said. "I knew it would get down to that. Everybody bends over backward for Andrew the Great."

"Sure, Andrew the Great," Andy said mockingly.

"And here comes the self-pity routine again. Look, stay. Do me a favor and stay. Please stay, Andy, old pal. Okay? Are you happy now? Stay."

Andy did not look at Bud. "I won't make any noise or anything," he said. "I promise."

"All right."

"I'd go, but I don't know where to go. I want to break the habit, I really want to break it. Can't you understand that? Just help me do it. Just help me. Just . . . let me stay. I . . . I won't say a word, I swear it. But help me, for God's sake, help me."

Bud felt suddenly very small. He looked at Carol, and then he spread his hands and opened his mouth as if to say something, and then he shook his head and started to say something again. He closed his mouth a second time, and finally he spoke.

"I didn't mean to needle you, kid," he said. "Stay as long as you like. The place is yours. And practice whatever the hell you want to. I don't mind. I know that job is important."

"Your tests are important, too," Andy said. "Oh, Jesus, oh, Jesus, if I . . . if I . . ." He seemed ready to say more, but he just kept shaking his head, over and over again.

"I shouldn't have said what I did," Bud said. "I'm sorry."

"No, don't apologize to me. Don't do that, Bud, because you were right about everything, all of it. I'm just a headache, and I know it, and this isn't self-pity, Bud. I've been a headache to everyone who's come near me in the past— now how many years? That's why . . . why I need help. I can't do it alone, I know that. I thought I could, but now I know I can't. I . . . I need someone near me, always . . . someone to . . . so let me stay, Bud, and I swear to God I'll never be able to thank you enough. I swear to God I'll kiss your feet if you just let me stay, if you'll help me, help me."

"Sure," Bud said, unable to account for the lump in his throat. "Stay with me, Andy."

"I appreciate this," Andy said softly.

"Why . . . why don't you make some coffee, Carol? I think we could . . . could all use a cup."

Carol did not leave until five, and then Bud tried to get down to studying again, but he could not forget the way he'd behaved, and the effect his behavior seemed to be having on Andy.

Along about two Andy began to fidget. They'd been sitting at the kitchen table, and suddenly, unaccountably, he began to drum his fingers on the table top. He kept that up until he realized he was annoying both Bud and Carol, and he apologized and stopped drumming. His feet began to jiggle then. He kept his toes glued to the floor, and he bounced his knees, up and down, up and down, moving them incessantly, until you could feel the vibration of the table and the floor.

Finally, as if he could no longer sit still, even with the compensating jiggle of his feet, he rose and went into the living room, and he began pacing the floor, but pacing it with a sort of controlled fury.

"What is it?" Carol had asked, and he'd simply answered, "I feel restless."

Bud knew, of course, that a portion of his restlessness could be attributed to his abrupt withdrawal from the drug. But he'd seemed all right this morning, with none of the nervous anxiety he'd exhibited the night before, none of the vomiting, none of the varied symptoms of the addict suddenly cut from his source of supply.

His sudden restlessness, therefore, was puzzling. Bud knew very little about what was to be expected of a reforming addict, but he nonetheless imagined Andy's current behavior, after so many days of withdrawal, was strange. And, feeling guilty as hell for his earlier outburst, he blamed himself in part for Andy's fidgeting.

The fidgeting reached mammoth proportions along about three in the afternoon. Continually pacing, Andy began to scratch himself, idly at first, scratching his arm, and then his back, and then his face. Bud and Carol watched him, trying to make conversation at the same time, but

nding talk a little difficult. Andy began scratching in ear-
est then, clawing at his back, rubbing at his stomach. He
was sweating freely, and his face began to tic as if it would
all apart, the lips trembling, the eyes blinking. He wet his
ps continuously, and then he clawed at the skin on his
rms, pacing all the while, and then he said, "Jesus, oh,
esus," and he continued to claw and pace and tic and trem-
le and blink, until finally he ran into the bathroom, and
he sick ugly sound came to their ears again.

"It's very hard for him," Carol said in a whisper.

"Yes," Bud agreed.

Andy seemed to be in control of himself when he
merged from the bathroom. He looked a little pale, but
ll of his fidgeting was gone, and he sat down and joined
he conversation, and everything was all right until Carol
eft at five.

The slow build-up began again. Bud, occupied with
American Lit II, poring over the notes and trying to glean
omething from them, heard the drumming fingers first. He
ooked up and then went back to his notes, but the drum-
ning was a persistent tattoo—*br-mm, br-mm, br-mm, br-
mm, br-mm, br-mm* . . .

He looked up again, and this time he caught Andy's eye,
and Andy said, "I'm sorry," and he thrust both hands deep
nto his trouser pockets. His feet began jiggling then. And
he scratching started. And the ticcing. And the blinking.
And the harsh breathing. And the pacing. And the mut-
ering. And the yawning.

Bud looked at him curiously, and he shook his head a
little, watching his friend, wondering what was going on
nside that goddamn head of his.

And inside that goddamn head of his a lot of things were
going on simultaneously. Inside that goddamn head of his
was an overwhelming urge to bolt for the door and scare
up a fix someplace, anyplace, scare up a fix to still the clam-
or of his blood and his mind. Inside his head was the
remembrance of what the drug could do, a remembrance
that had been squashed and then tasted again this morning,
but that had been a very long time ago, and the need had
clawed his stomach to ribbons earlier today, and now it
was back again, a need he could feel and taste and sense, a
need that was as real as his trembling hands were. If he did

not get a fix soon, if he did not get a fix soon, he would
kick the windows out of the walls. He would cut off his
arm, he would pluck out his eyes, he would spit his teeth
into the washbasin. He was going crazy with the need. He
was lower than he'd ever been, sick with the need, wanting
that drug with every fiber in his body, wanting it desperately and urgently, and all he could do was pace the floor of
the apartment, and scratch the itch that was beneath his
skin, and feel his lids blink over his eyes, and feel the tic at
the corner of his mouth, and feel the roiling inside his stomach. I mustn't puke again, I have to have a fix, *I need it!*

And inside that goddamn head of his was a warring factor that threaded itself through the fabric of his need,
puncturing it with a needle as sharp as the one he desired,
a needle of self-condemnation. For if he had not touched
the drug this morning, if he had only tossed the stuff away,
smashed the works, dumped it all, forgotten it, forgotten it
forever, the worst part would have been over now. He'd
had it licked, and now he was back aboard again, and only
he knew what was spinning through his body like a hot
piece of steel, only he knew how badly he wanted, wanted,
and all because he'd weakened this morning, all because
he'd shot up when he hadn't even really wanted the stuff
—not like now, not like now when his head was ready to
swing loose at the hinges, not like now when the top of his
skull was ready to erupt, Jesus, Jesus, isn't there something,
isn't there a gun someplace, something to shoot myself
with?

What am I doing here?

What am I doing pacing here, up and down, *what the
hell am I doing?*

Why don't I get out of here? I can cop easily, bread or
no bread. I can get the bread from somebody, hock my
jacket if I have to, and then I'll find the Man, and I'll roll
into some pad where it's soft and quiet, and I'll boot that
mother-loving White God until it comes out of my ears. I'll
kick it to Boston and back, I'll kick that goddamn jive until
my eyes are bugging out of my head, until I'm so blind I
can't walk, until I'm stoned dead.

WHY AM I STAYING HERE!

Stay where you are, you simple son-of-a-bitch, his mind
pleaded. Stay where you are because where you are is safe,

but, oh, how I want it, how I want it, sweet Jesus, please, please, help me, help me get it, help me get away from it, get it, get it, get, *I need it!*

I'm not fooling, I need it. I'm not kidding, I need it bad. I'm real sick, God, I'm real sick, and I need that stuff, I need the jive, please help me, please make me, do something, something, please, please.

Easy now, easy, easy, I'm excited, but please, I'm sick, but please, I'm hungry for it, I can taste it, I want to be blind, I want to be stoned, I want to be high, high, *high, high, HIGH, GODDAMNIT, PLEASE, PLEASE DO SOMETHING FOR ME, PLEASE!*

Shake it, shake that habit, kick the monkey off your back, don't think about it, don't think about anything connected with it, oh, would I love a speedball now, even just a little cocaine mixed in with the hoss, even just a little, but-oh, would a speedball knock my brains out, oh, would a speedball gas the hell out of me, what am I gonna do, how am I gonna take it any more, what am I gonna do, have I got any left, no, all gone, but I've got the works, I've still got the works, I'll get out of here and find something someplace. A cap, cap and a half, I'll settle even for a cap, I'll settle for anything, anything, even for beat stuff, even for lemon, anything, anything at all, *CAN YOU UNDERSTAND THAT, GODDAMNIT?*

"Who's there?" Bud asked.

"Helen," the voice beyond the door answered.

Thank God, Andy thought. *Thank you, God.*

18

Bud rose and went slowly to the door. He had forgotten that Helen was coming this evening, and now, with only the wood of the door between them, he felt a curiously fluttering panic in his stomach. He reached out for the doorknob, not wanting to open the door, not wanting to see her again, not after all that had happened, knowing he definitely did not want to see her again, ashamed of himself, deeply ashamed, and not wanting this living reminder of his shame. But she was outside the door, and as inexorably as the steady creep of time, his hand found the doorknob, and twisted the doorknob, and pulled back the door, and she was standing there, unsmiling.

She had not changed much. She looked more mature, more wise perhaps, but her face was still the same, and he felt the unbidden quickening of his heart when he saw that face, when his eyes found her eyes, green and slightly tilted, Chinese eyes, wise and knowing eyes. She wore her hair short now, the pageboy gone, clipped close to her head, framing her face with a deep lustrous black. She wore a sweater and skirt, and he saw the rounded mounds of her small, perfectly formed breasts beneath the sweater, and then his eyes fled back to her face again, swallowed in the depth of her eyes, swallowed there in a sea of wisdom and knowledge and regret.

"Hello, Bud," she said softly.

"Helen," he said, "it's good to see you."

He took her hand, but she held his only briefly and then dropped it, her eyes leaping into the apartment and finding Andy. She stepped inside, and Bud closed the door behind her. She put her purse down on the butterfly chair, and Andy forced a smile and said, "Hi, Helen, I thought you'd never get here."

"How have you been?" she asked.

Her eyes did not leave his face. They searched his eyes, they spotted the tic at the corner of his mouth, they probed the blinking lids.

"Fine," he said. "Just fine."

"It's been rough, hasn't it?"

"The roughest." He smiled wanly.

"You going it cold turkey?"

"Yes."

"That's the only way. How long have you been off it?"

Andy hesitated for a moment. "Little more than a week," he said.

A cloud passed over Helen's face. "*How* long, Andy?"

"Well, maybe a little less. Maybe five days or so."

"You're lying," she said flatly.

"What?"

"I said you're lying. Has he left the apartment, Bud?"

"Why, yes. He—"

"Did you cop, Andy?"

"What?"

"I said, '*Did you cop*'?"

"I got some stuff yes, but I—"

"He didn't take it, Helen," Bud said, feeling strangely outside the conversation, feeling even outside the realm of their thought or their jargon.

"Where is it?"

"Where's what?" Andy said.

"The stuff. You said you—"

"I dumped it."

"When?"

"This morning."

"When this morning?"

"Nine, ten o'clock, I don't remember."

"Where?"

"Right here."

"Where'd you dump it?"

"Down the toilet."

"You're lying."

"I am not, Helen. Helen, I wouldn't—"

"You shot up, Andy. You shot up, and now you're plenty sick. Andy, don't lie to me because I've been through this and back again, and I know all the signs, and you don't show the signs of a man who's been cool for a week, or even for five days. You look like a man who's overdue, and, goddamnit, Andy, why'd you do it? Why'd you go back to it?"

"I didn't, Helen. I just don't feel so hot, that's all. You know how it is when you're kicking the jive. What makes you think—"

"Andy, don't lie to me. You never could lie to me, Andy, so don't start now."

"But I'm not lying, Helen. I swear to God, I haven't touched a drop since—"

"Since *when*, Andy?"

"Since—" He could not complete the sentence.

"How much did you take?"

"A cap," he lied.

"Andy."

"A cap and a half, two caps, I don't remember."

"When?"

"This morning. About nine. Maybe ten. I don't remember."

"Andy, Andy, why?"

"Y is a crooked letter," he shouted. "Don't get on my back. I got enough troubles without your climbing on my back."

"Where's the outfit?"

"In the closet. In my jacket pocket."

"Get it," she said.

He went to the closet, and Bud watched him, still feeling strange, feeling as if he were listening to an argument between a man and his wife, feeling left out of it completely, the way a little boy does when his mother and father are bickering.

Andy brought the jacket back to Helen.

"The spoon," she said, and he handed her the spoon. Helen looked at it carefully and then asked, "Where's the spike?"

He took the syringe from the jacket pocket and was handing it to her when she said, "No, hold onto it. Where'd you get it?"

"On the Union Floor. From Rog."

"He won't miss it," Helen said. "Get rid of it, Andy."

Andy stared at the syringe on the palm of his hand, puzzled, and then he asked, "*What* do you want me to do?"

"Get rid of it."

"You can get rid of it. Here, take it."

"No, I want you to get rid of it. You're the only one who can do it, Andy."

"What the hell do you want from me, anyway? I got to return the spike, don't I? What the hell are you climbing all over me for?"

"Andy, do as I say," Helen said tightly.

"No! No, I won't do as you say! Everybody wants me to do as they say. Well, I'm goddamn good and sick of doing what everybody wants me to do. Everybody can go take a flying leap at a rolling doughnut, you understand that? That includes you, and Bud, and anybody else you want to drag in! What the hell am I, a kid or something, everybody has to come around and wipe my nose for me? Well, I'm not a kid! I know what I'm doing, and if you want to get rid of that hype, you can do it yourself, you understand that?"

"Andy——"

"Shut up! Jesus, for once in your life, can't you shut up? I'm doing all I can to keep my head from busting open, and you come around screaming about a syringe—what the hell do you want me to do with the goddamn thing, anyway?"

"Destroy it," Helen said, almost spitting the words.

"What for? What harm's the hype without what to put in it? You think I've got any of the white stuff? You think I'd be sitting around with my stomach ready to split if I had any of the junk? I'd be shooting it so damn fast, it'd make your head spin. I'd be maining it like a madman, that's what I'd be doing, so what the hell are you screaming about the hype for, what do you want me to do, why the hell doesn't everyone leave me alone?"

He suddenly seized the syringe tightly, and he brought it back over his head and then whipped his arm down violently, and the syringe left his hand. It spun across the room dizzily and then collided with the plaster, bouncing off and onto the floor, miraculously still in one piece.

"Is that what you want?" he shouted. "All right, all right?"

Helen reached out for his arm, but he shook her off and lunged across the room, bringing his foot back and kicking out at the syringe. He missed the syringe, and he lost his footing and went down to the floor, landing on his back. There was shock and surprise on his face, and then his features curled into a menacing leer as he scrambled to his feet.

"Where is it?" he screamed. "Where is the mother-lover?"

"Andy, don't——"

"Where is it? *Where is it?*"

He whirled, as if searching for an elusive rat, his eyes scanning the floor. He seemed no longer to be Andy. He seemed like a strange and maniacal stranger who had come down from a mountain cave. He spotted the syringe, and his lip curled, and he raced for it and stamped at it, grazing the glass cylinder so that the syringe snapped out from under his foot, still intact, the needle glistening. He reversed his field, and he kicked out at the syringe again, missing again, kicking again and missing yet another time, out of breath now, chasing the elusive, dancing, rolling glass cylinder with its pointed needle. And then he slumped against the wall, his head bent, and he mumbled, "I can't break it, I can't break it. Helen, I can't catch up with it, I can't . . . I'm sick, Helen, I'm sick as hell, Helen, I'm sick, I'm sick, Helen, please help me, Helen, I'm sick. . . ."

She took him into the bathroom, and she stayed in there with him, and Bud could hear the soothing sound of her voice beneath the ugly sounds Andy was making. He sat outside in the living room, wondering again how he'd ever got into something like this, dismayed because he'd learned that Andy had gone back to the drug again, after all his talk, after all that. God, wouldn't he ever learn, was he a coward at heart?

He listened to the sounds coming from his bathroom, and he thought of his other tests, and he thought of Andy in that bathroom, and Helen, two strangers, two people he thought he'd never see again as long as he lived, and here they were in his apartment, disrupting his life, turning his life into a shambles. Doesn't my life count at all, is Andy the only important one around here, is Andy the only one who matters. What about me? Goddamnit, what about me?

He saw the glint of the needle lying on the floor, and he went to it and picked up the syringe, rotating it slowly in his hands. The needle was short and slender, a narrow polished arrow. He studied the pointed tip and then the graduated markings on the glass cylinder. The hypodermic seemed to own a life of its own. It sat on the palm of his hand and it seemed like an evil, throbbing thing to him, a malevolent thing which had reached out and engulfed Andy in a black, foul-smelling cloud. It was graceful and sleek, but beneath its polished good looks lay the intricate machinery of the devil, and he was tempted for a moment to do just what Andy had tried to do and failed at. He wanted to bring back his arm and throw the syringe at the wall, watch it splinter into a thousand flying fragments. He wanted to stab the needle at the plaster, stab it until the plaster chipped from the wall, until the needle was twisted and bent and useless, until all the evil life had left the syringe, until it was nothing but a broken heap of glass and steel.

"Don't blame the syringe," Helen said, and he looked up, surprised to see her back in the room. From the bathroom, he heard the sound of the water tap, and knew that Andy was washing up again.

"They should never have invented syringes," Bud said, still obsessed with the idea of it as a sentient, evil thing.

"Some junkies use eye droppers," Helen said, "Either with or without a needle. It's more difficult without a needle, and not very pretty to watch because you have to tear the skin with a safety pin or a razor blade first and then insert the glass tip of the dropper into a vein. But you don't need a syringe, Bud. Where there's a will there's a way—and there's always a will when you're a horsehead."

"I suppose," Bud said weakly. "What do you want to do with this?"

"I'll take it," she said. "I don't think it should stay in this apartment, do you?"

"No." He handed her the syringe, and she took it and went to her purse and dropped the syringe into its depths.

She turned, and he felt embarrassed watching her, and so he averted his eyes. Helen sat in the butterfly chair and sighed, as if she were very very tired.

"He'll need watching, Bud."

"Yes." Bud paused. "I can't say this is very convenient for me right now."

"It's a little inconvenient for all of us," Helen said, her voice grew suddenly sharp. "I'm sure Carol doesn't like the idea of running over here, and I don't particularly relish it either. Drug addicts are not convenient. Hardly anything in life is."

"That's not what I mean," Bud said. "I was just wondering if . . . Well, if anything would come of it."

"We won't know until it's over, will we?"

"No, I guess we won't."

"You can only fix horse races. Life—oh, what the hell—I've stopped trying to figure it out."

"Do you think he'll break it?"

"Maybe. I hope so."

"Isn't it a bad sign? That he went back to it so soon?"

"It's not good, but it doesn't mean a hell of a lot. He seems impressed by what he's done, though. He seems to know that he took a big step backward this morning. Maybe that'll help."

"Is it very hard to break?"

Helen looked at him curiously, and then she smiled maternally. "Yes, Bud, it's very hard to break," she said quietly.

Bud nodded.

"You never break it," she added.

"*You* broke it."

"Did I?"

"Well, didn't you? You don't use drugs any more."

"No, I don't."

"Well, then . . . you broke it."

"Yes, I broke it." She was silent for several moments.

"How do people get started on it, anyway?" Bud asked. "Jesus, you'd think they'd have more sense."

"You can't believe any addict when he talks about how his habit began," Helen said. "I've talked to dozens of them, and most of them lie. They'll tell you they got started on opiates because they were sick once, and a doctor prescribed morphine or one of the other opium alkaloids, and they built a tolerance and a habit and, pity the poor souls, they are now addicts. But most junkies are on heroin, and heroin is *never* used therapeutically, so what are you to believe?"

"Well, then how *do* they get started?"

"How?" Helen smiled. "We're sick."

"Oh, come on."

"Yes, believe me. And drug addiction is only one symptom of . . . well, a basic personality defect. We're like alcoholics, except their poison is liquid."

"It sounds hard to believe."

"Figure it out for yourself. What does the drug mean to a junkie? Just the kick? Just the boot? A whole lot more than that, don't you see? It's—" She shrugged— "I hate to throw psychology at you, but it's an escape mechanism. You take the drug and you wipe out all the little failures and disappointments that keep sneaking up on you. You take the drug and your ambitions stop being dreams—they become accomplishments. It's a way of escaping responsibility." She paused and eyed Bud levelly. "There are worse ways of escaping responsibility."

Bud nodded blankly.

"We're *all* of us addicts," Helen said.

"I wouldn't go that far."

"We all have fears, and hopes, and disappointments. And we all compensate for them in one way or another."

"Sure, but the normal devices—"

"That's just it," Helen said. "The addict turns to a more drastic means, but he achieves the same end. What's he trying to do, when you get right down to it? Nothing but deaden the pain of frustration. He can't compensate in the real world, so he invents his own world, and he runs into it to hide. Why is there so much addiction in slum areas? Only because the drug is more readily available there?"

"I imagine it is," Bud said.

"Hell, I can make a buy in five minutes right on Times Square," Helen said. "No, it's because so many people in those areas are trying to bridge the gap, trying to make the dream the reality."

"Andy doesn't come from a slum area," Bud reminded her.

"No, he doesn't," Helen agreed. "And neither do I. What are you asking? Our excuse?"

"Well . . ."

"How can you make a blanket observation on *all* drug addicts, when each one will have his own unique case history? The *why* and the *how*, don't you see? Sometimes they're similar, sometimes they vary. The cops concentrate on the *how*. How does a man get hooked? How does he get to know pushers? How can we stamp it out? The psychologists concentrate on the why, and the junkie himself concentrates on the same problem whenever he gives enough of a damn to question his motives at all. Why? The big *why*? Insecurity? A feeling of inferiority? Life too big? Life too small? Life too sordid? Why?"

"But if he reaches the point where he's begun to question himself, shouldn't he know the answers?"

"Sometimes," Helen said. "Usually not. He just knows that he needs something, and the Something makes him feel all right. It happens that the Something is drugs. It could have been alcohol. It could have been snuff. It could have been sweets. That's where the *how* enters. The *why* is there, and something is needed, and then the *how* offers narcotics, and the problem is solved. Stir well, heat to boiling, and you have a drug addict. Lord have mercy on his soul."

"Then if drugs weren't available—"

"But they are. In all shapes and all sizes and to fit every pocketbook. From cheap bammies you can pick up at about three for a quarter—"

"Bammies?"

"Low-grade marijuana," Helen said. "You can get the better muggles, the bombers, for about a dollar each. You can get a cap of heroin for the same price, but it'll be cut stuff. A deck of hoss might cost you a dollar, or it might cost you five. I've paid as much as five for a deck when I was real low, even though that's an incredibly high price. It depends on what the traffic will bear, you see. Once a pusher's got you hooked, he can do whatever he wants with you. A junkie likes to deal with the same pusher usually. He knows him, and he can trust him, and he's reasonably certain he won't get beat stuff from him, stuff that's cut down to practically nothing but milk sugar. The pusher sets the price, and he knows just what he can get from you. He can tell at a glance. Sometimes he'll show a burst of generosity and lay it on you practically free. Other times you'll pay through the nose. Sometimes he'll extend credit. Sometimes he'll serve as a fence for stolen goods. But the pusher is boss, and pushers aren't exactly honorable men."

"No, I wouldn't think so."

"It's a business, a multimillion-dollar business, and the men who run it happen to be vicious. You have to be vicious to put something like the speedball on the market. Do you know what a speedball is?"

"No," Bud said.

"It's a little capsule of mixed cocaine and heroin. Cocaine is an excitant, and heroin is a depressant. You put them together in one pellet and you get a speedball, and it's just that, a red-hot speedball that rips the insides out of a junkie. You're hyped up one minute, and you're ready to nod the next. When the jag starts wearing off, you begin shaking and sweating and heaving out your guts, and you can't stop until you get either a shot of C or a shot of H."

"Jesus," Bud said.

"A speedball is only one of the more uncivilized means of torture the drug bastards are selling." Something bitter had crept into Helen's voice. Her eyes were hard and bright now. "They should catch them all," she said. "They should catch them all, and they should hang them by their thumbs, and every junkie in the world should have a turn at kicking their brains out. Death should be the penalty for trading in drugs, Bud, the way it's the penalty for kidnapping. Death, because these men are kidnapping *lives,* and usually they're kidnapping young lives."

"Well, that's a little strong," Bud said.

"Is it? Is it? Look at your friend in there." She gestured toward the bathroom door. "He's going through hell to break it, and if he doesn't break it, he'll still be in hell. He's given up everything, even his talent, for heroin. He's a slave to the bastard who makes ten cents on a reefer, and a slave to the bastard up the line who buys a kilo of eighty-five-percent pure heroin in Italy for about five thousand dollars and then sells it to a wholesaler here for about fifteen thousand. And the wholesaler is another bastard who'll cut the drug all the way down, shove it into capsules or decks, and gross six hundred thousand on it. Bud, you can get a pound of M in Mexico for something like ten dollars, and by the time it's sold as reefers in New York you're realizing sixteen hundred on it. So don't ask how or why somebody gets started. It's too easy to start, believe me."

"Do you know why . . . why *you* started?"

"Yes," Helen answered. He waited for more, but she was silent now.

"Well," he said weakly, "let's hope Andy can break it, too."

"It doesn't mean breaking it for now alone, Bud," she said. "It means breaking it forever. That's not as easy as it sounds."

Andy came out of the bathroom, his face shining. He looked much better, and he seemed to feel much better, too. "What's not as easy as it sounds?" he asked.

"You look human," Helen said, smiling.

"I feel human. What were you talking about?"

"The monkey."

"Oh. That again."

"It'll always be that, Andy. You might as well face it."

"What do you mean?"

"You think this is the hardest part, don't you? The kicking it now. This isn't the hardest part at all, Andy."

Andy smiled. "Hell, it can't get much worse."

"Ah, but it can. And long after you've kicked it, or after you *think* you've kicked it. Because you'll always remember it. It's very hard to forget it, especially when things take a rough turn. You remember how easy it was to escape then. You look at what you've got, and what you've got seems almost impossible to bear. And you think of how it was when you had no real worries, nothing to plague you. And it can be a very simple thing that sets you off thinking desperately about it again. Your mother can be sick, or an aunt you loved can die, or . . . or you can have a run in your last pair of stockings, something as damn foolish as that, and all at once it'll seem like too much for you, all at once life will have closed in and you can't take it any more. You'll stare at the railroad tracks on the torn stocking, and you'll wonder how you can ever meet the situation, how you can possibly solve it, and there'll seem to be no solution whatever. And it can happen with anything that suddenly upsets you emotionally, anything that disturbs the careful balance you're trying to maintain.

"And seeing no solution, or feeling thwarted, or just feeling down in the dumps about anything at all, you'll suddenly remember what it was like to be up in the clouds. And there's your choice: down in the dumps or up in the clouds. And you begin to wonder why you shouldn't be up in the clouds? What's wrong with it? Why not? You forget all the rest of it in that moment. In that moment nothing counts but the happiness you know you can find if you go back to narcotics. The dream is better than the reality, and even the narcotics become a dream and your memory of the dream is far better than the reality of narcotics. Because the reality is really a goddamn trap, and you know that, and you realize that, but at the same time you keep thinking of it, and so you try to shove it out of your mind, and you try to find something to be happy about.

"You need help right then. You need someone to stand by you and help you see your way through this. You need

help desperately, not medical help, just the help of someone you know cares about you, just that kind of help, just
reassurance. You need reassurance desperately, but you
can't think of anyone to turn to. There's only one thing
you *can* turn to, you feel, and you try to shake the image
of the syringe from your mind, but it won't be shaken. It
sticks, and it sticks, until it blots out everything else in your
mind, and then you start your devices.

"You tell yourself you're happy. You tell yourself you
are deliriously happy. You try to behave that way. You'll
make a silly joke. You'll laugh at the joke, and whoever
you're with will think you're very strange, laughing at such
a silly joke, not knowing you're really whistling in the
dark. You'll try to maintain this buoyancy, because you
know happiness is your only salvation, and yet you know
all the while that you're really sad, and you know the happiness is a front, but you try to live up to that front because you won't admit your sadness, won't admit your utter desolation. Once you admit it, you're lost. Once you admit it, you want a solution to it, and you turn to the only
solution you know, and the solution is one that works. You
know that. You know that because you've had the solution,
and the solution works damned fine.

"You can almost taste it. The picture of the syringe is so
large in your mind that you can read the centimeter marks
on the cylinder. You can see the heroin, you can see the
spoon, you can see the stuff in the syringe, and you can
taste it. And so you try to blot it out. You try to blot out
the picture by talking about other things—anything, anything at all to kill the pain you're feeling, anything so that
you won't have to turn to the other painkiller, and all the
while wanting someone to take your hand and lead you
out, lead you to where it's safe and secure and snug. And
you try to blot out the taste by smothering it in other
tastes. You'll have a cup of coffee, and then you'll have another cup of coffee, and then another, and another. You'll
sit somewhere, and you'll talk to someone about anything
in the world, anything but what is really bothering you,
and you'll drink coffee until it's coming out of your ears,
and you'll smoke incessantly because there's something
very reassuring about a cigarette in your hand or hanging
on your lips. You want that cigarette always. You put one

out and you light another one immediately afterward. You talk, and you drink your coffee incessantly, and you smoke incessantly, and you try to ride it out, and it seems you will never ride it out. But you have to keep being happy, you have to stay happy. There's no one to help you, and so you have to help yourself. If only you can ride it out, if only you can ride it out."

She stopped. The room was very silent. Andy stared at her, a defeated, hangdog expression on his face.

"I don't want to scare you, Andy," she said. "I've ridden them out, and I hope I'll always ride them out. I wanted you to know, though, that it's a constant fight. You haven't licked it after a week, or after a month, or after a year, or maybe after ever. It's always with you."

"I guess so," Andy said.

"It's so easy to start," she said, shaking her head. "So goddamn easy. You can be on the way to being an addict after a day or after your first shot. And once you're hooked, mister, you've entered the gates of Hell, and then try to break it. Then it's not quite so easy."

"Boy, I wish I knew exactly why I started," Andy said. "I mean, what the hell, I can remember exactly how, but who knows why? I had everything a guy could want, didn't I? I had clothes, and a beautiful girl, and after the guys left for the service I began playing with a pretty decent outfit— not the big time, but a big step forward. Maybe I wasn't ready for the step, huh?" He shrugged. "Maybe I missed the guys more than I let on, maybe I still needed them, who knows? Beats the hell out of me. I didn't seem to need anything, you know? I had everything I could ever want, I suppose."

He shook his head uncomprehendingly.

"I'm sure of one thing, though, I'm going to break this goddamn habit, and I'm never going back to it."

"You'll break it," Helen said. "And you'll get on the Laddy Fredericks band. You wait and see. You're going to be all right." She stood up and looked at her watch. "I'd better get home. I'll give you a call tomorrow, to see how it's coming along."

"Don't worry about me, Helen," Andy said. "I've seen the light." He walked her to the door. "I swear to God I'll never even look at it again. If I get the urge, I'll tie myself to the kitchen sink, and I won't budge from it. I swear to God."

And he meant every word he said.

But he had sworn an oath earlier, too. He had sworn an oath two months after a party at which everyone had passed around a community needle. He had told himself, "May I drop dead in the gutter if I ever touch another drop of it." And the earlier oath had priority, and Andy Silvera had no way of knowing about that priority, or that anything he did from now on would be entirely too late because the deck was stacked and the cards were now being dealt.

Helen said her good-bys, and when she'd left, Andy cocked his head to one side and said, "Wonderful girl. Makes a lot of sense, too. Why does a guy get started? What the hell was there about me that made me start? The Artie Parker band was a good outfit. I loved Carol. What the hell could it have been? Hell, I was blowing fine in those days. Not the way I wanted to, but Jesus, I've *never* blown the way I really wanted to. So what could it have been? I guess maybe I was just too young, you know. I guess maybe somebody like you should have been around, to lend a helping hand every now and then, sort of keep the balance, do you know what I mean, Bud? But hell, you were in the navy, and I was on my own, and so I just

change of key, i

FEBRUARY-MARCH, 1945

19

The party at Buff Collier's house was starting off with a bang, or rather *had* started off with a bang some four hours before. When Andy and Carol, and the other musicians and their girls, arrived the brawl was in full swing, and they were greeted at the door like soldiers come to liberate a concentration camp.

"The music!" Buff shouted. "The music is here," and then she swayed across the room and jumped up into the arms of a tall boy with long black hair. The boy held her unsteadily, and then other healthy-looking boys and other healthy-looking teen-age girls rushed across the room and began taking coats and hats.

"How was the prom?" one of the boys asked Artie, and Artie said, "A big drag."

"Here's the piano, Artie!" someone shouted, and Artie shouted back, "Where's the juice?" and the boys in the band drifted over to where the bottles and the setups stood on a long table. Andy mixed himself a strong Scotch and soda, handing one to Carol, and then toasting themselves, and then drinking. Ox, who'd joined the Parker band along with Andy, said, "I didn't think the prom was such a drag. I thought it was fun."

"If you thought that was a good job," Andy said, "you should come along with me next week."

"Yeah? What's doing?"

"My uncle's holding one of his balls," Andy said.

"Oh, Andy," Carol scolded, unable to keep back the giggle.

"I got a card from the Banner today," Ox said, not having caught on to Andy's gag.

"What does the old Arab have to say for himself?"

"They're putting him in a band down in Miami. ComServPac or something. What does ComServPac mean?"

"That's Latin for 'To the victor belongs the spoils.' "

"Really?" Ox asked.

"Sure."

"How do you like that?" Ox said, digesting the information. "But how come Tony gets put in a band, and Bud and Frank don't? That's what I'd like to know."

"Piano players and drummers are a dime a dozen."

Ox nodded sadly. "So are sax men."

"No, it's not as bad with sax men. So they send Frank to quartermaster school, and they try to make Bud a signalman. That's life."

He waited for Ox to say, "What's life?" but Ox didn't. Ox merely kept nodding his head sadly.

Artie Parker was heading for the piano with a full fifth of Puerto Rican rum in his right hand. He uncorked the bottle, took a long swallow, and then began playing. Andy danced with Carol for a while, and when he heard a tenor sax join the piano, he picked up his trumpet case, took out his horn, and joined the session. They blew for fifteen minutes straight, blasting away at "One O'Clock Jump." He lost himself while he played, knowing he sounded good, but wanting more than he was getting, and trying desperately to get that more, and thinking of other things while he blew, not consciously thinking of the music he was making.

He'd never really tried to pin-point how he'd got involved with the Long Island set, but he supposed it was because June Tambeau was Artie's girl, and June was part of that set. Artie had met June at one of the dances they'd played, and the piano player had been whisked into the crowd, and one night June had asked Andy and Carol to come along to one of the parties, and that had been the beginning, he supposed.

He had to admit these kids knew how to have fun, a more sophisticated kind of fun than the old Tony Banner Boys had. Oh, sure, they did a lot of the same things—like going to Coney, things like that—but a lot of the other things they did were pretty damned different, and the Tony Banner Boys' fun was sort of kid stuff in comparison. Like when the Tony Banner Boys drank, well, they usually drank beer, and beer was strictly for the sparrows in this new crowd. Whenever there was a party, the liquor flowed like wine, and there was good stuff too—stuff he'd learned was good—like Canadian Club and Haig & Haig pinch, and Gordon's, and even milder stuff like Cherry Heering. And the things they did were more casual and more sophisticated, as if they didn't have to try so hard to have fun, the fun was already there and all they had to do was pick it up and enjoy it. And they all had their own cars, not beat-up old rattletraps like Frank's car, or like Bud's father's car. They drove convertibles or souped-up sedans, and one of the guys drove a red MG that positively knocked your eyes out. So the new crowd was a lot of fun, and he guessed he liked it a lot, even though he of course missed Bud. Naturally you'd miss your best friend. And this crowd all liked the way he blew that horn of his, and that suited him fine, and so he blasted away at the music, standing near the piano and listening to all the voices around him.

Artie drifted into "Summertime," and Andy picked it up and began blowing, with the tenor sax giving him a nice hunk of harmony. It was winter outside, but inside that living room the magnolias began to open and their heady aroma wafted on the air, and the sky turned velvet black, and the moon turned big and orange, and you could smell freshly cut grass, and you could see little colored kids running over the fields barefoot, and you could hear watermelons popping open, juicy and red, and you could hear the sound of voices around a lake and the lazy whisper of leaves on countless budding trees. It was winter outside Buff Collier's house, but the breeze inside was warm and sweet, captured in the bell of Andy's horn, and the kids swayed with a dreamy look in their eyes, listening to the horn, caught in its golden mist, and they weren't in suits and gowns any more, they were lounging around in tee shirts and shorts, lounging on the bank of a lake, watching a big summer sky and dreaming. And the biggest dreamer was Andy, standing there on top of the world with the clouds licking at his face, and the moon smiling, and the stars winking at him, and "Summertime" flowing from his lips and his fingers and his lungs—and his heart.

Artie modulated into a rumba, and then another slow ballad, and Andy rested, blowing a muted background for the tenor sax, and then Artie did "Smoke Rings," along which time June Tambeau discovered an unoccupied bedroom somewhere in the house. This was about two in the morning, and she yanked Artie away from the piano, and the band's bass man, a kid named Fletcher Wright, took over the piano, and the session went strong for another half hour.

Along about three some of the kids decided it would be fun to set fire to the living-room drapes, and Buff Collier thought it would be grand kicks, too. They formed a ring around the drapes, all the kids holding soda squirt bottles, and Buff herself put the torch to the heavy velvet material, and it looked as if it weren't going to catch for a minute, but then it did and the drape began burning up toward the ceiling, and everybody turned his squirt bottle on, and the fire was out as quickly as it had been ignited, with smoke pouring into the room and making everyone cough.

They opened all the windows, and since it was damned cold outside, it pretty soon got damned cold inside, and

though they were still laughing over the sport of setting
fire to drapes, they began to realize that their ears were
getting slightly frostbitten.

A girl named Alice suggested that they all go upstairs
to the master bedroom and get some blankets, so they all
started upstairs for the master bedroom and surprised a kid
named Warren Dawes and another kid named Francine
Billis (the girls all called her Bilious) in a somewhat com-
promising position. When Francine had put on her underwear again and pulled the blankets to her throat, the other
kids piled into the bedroom, and a guy and a girl hopped
into the bed Francine and Warren were sharing, and four
other kids piled into the second twin bed, and the rest of
the kids dropped to the rug-covered floor and smothered
themselves with blankets.

A boy named Tommy Baretti thought it would be fun
to set fire to the thick rug, but Buff poked her head out
from one of the blankets and shouted, "The hell you say!"
and that put an end to that.

Bilious, in her bra and panties, with Warren against her
on her right and with a boy named Simmy behind her, felt
very much in her element, and she shouted, "Why don't we
just shut up and enjoy ourselves," which everybody thought
was a damned good idea, and so everybody shut up and
began enjoying themselves, and this wasn't a very easy
thing to do, the master bedroom being as packed as it was,
nor was it a difficult thing to do, either. When the room
was silent, they realized that some of the musicians were
still downstairs playing, and one of the girls wrapped a
blanket around herself and went down to see what sport
was being offered in the living room. The other kids in
the bedroom got a little bored with this goldfish-bowl group
attitude and began drifting to other parts of the house.
(There were five bedrooms with a total of ten beds, a den
in which there were three foam-rubber sofas, a playroom
with a very thick rug on its floor, a garage with a large,
roomy-back-seat Cadillac, and a living room just over-
flowing with soft and inviting pieces of furniture.)

The musicians were in the living room, too—only three
of them now—Andy, Fletcher, and the tenor man, a boy
named Jonesy for no apparent reason other than that his
last name was Jones.

Andy had had a good many Scotches and sodas by this time, and Carol had had just as many, and Fletcher had inherited the rum bottle Artie left at the piano, and so the music was more a labor of love than it was anything else. Carol drifted over to one of the couches, kicked off her shoes, and lay down full length, and it was several moments before Andy realized she was gone, and at the same time (it was only three-thirty) he realized he was tired. He yawned, and Jonesy, the tenor man, said, "What's the matter, man? Sleepy?"

"Awm," Andy said.

"You want to crack a benny?"

"What?"

"Keep you awake, man."

"What the hell's a benny?"

Jonesy reached into his jacket pocket and pulled out a small tube. "Benzedrine inhaler."

"I haven't got a cold," Andy said.

Jonesy chuckled. "You're a card, man. Who says you need a cold?"

"That's what it's for, isn't it? Says right here, 'For relief of congested nasal pas—' "

"That's the square definition, man. Here, dig this." He reached into his jacket pocket and pulled out a pocketknife, which he unclasped. He stabbed the point of the blade into the container and then slit the container across the center, reaching in and pulling out a folded sheet of paper.

Andy saw a printed message on the sheet, and he asked, "What's that say?"

"Business about not taking this internally. It's for the birds, man. I've taken it a dozen times."

"Taken what?" Andy asked.

"The paper. Here, chew on it and then swallow it."

Andy looked at him curiously. "What are you, nuts or something?"

"Go ahead. Keep you awake. Give you a little bounce."

"Come down, man," Andy said.

"I'm serious," Jonesy said, his eyes widening. "Go on, take it."

"You want me to chew that paper? Do I look like a goat?"

"All right, *don't* chew it. Just wash it down with something, that's all. Go ahead."

Andy eyed the Benzedrine-soaked paper skeptically. "That's too big to swallow," he said.

Jonesy tore the sheet in half, and then half again, and then he wadded the torn paper into balls. "Here," he said. "Just like pills."

"I don't know," Andy said hesitantly.

"Come on, come on, for Christ's sake."

Andy shrugged, took one of the paper balls, and then washed it down with his drink.

"I don't feel anything," he said.

"You will. Here, take the rest."

Andy washed down the remaining paper pills and then waited for something to happen. "I still don't feel anything."

"Give it time. It's got to hit your blood."

"You sure I won't get sick?"

"On bennies? Get off that, man, will you?" Jonesy scoffed.

"Well, I still don't feel anything."

"You will. It'll get you."

"What am I supposed to feel?"

"Nothing much. Just hops you up, that's all."

"Hops me up how?" He was beginning to feel a little frightened now, wishing he had read the printed warning and suspecting he had swallowed something poisonous.

"Makes you jump, man," Jonesy said, laughing. "You'll see."

He began to feel it in a little while, a sort of hypertension that surged through his body, a sort of forced energy, a pseudo-drive.

"It's getting you, huh, man?" Jonesy asked.

"Yeah, I feel it now," Andy said. "What the hell is that stuff, anyway?"

"Benzedrine, I told you. Harmless. But it'll keep you awake, you can bet on that."

"Man, it really charges you up, doesn't it?"

He felt suddenly restless, as if he had a million things to do and had to get them done instantly. He rested his horn on the piano top, started to walk away, and then thought better of it. After what he'd seen done to the drapes (how the hell would Buff explain that to her folks? A careless cigarette?) he couldn't trust his horn alone. He walked quickly back to the piano, took his horn again, and then put it back into his case. For the first time in as long as he could remember, he locked the case. He looked around for Carol then, still feeling this restless pounding inside him, his head suddenly crystal clear, his entire nervous system all jazzed up.

He spotted her on the couch in the corner, and he walked to it, his steps curiously perky, his eyes bright. He turned off the light behind the couch, plunging the corner into darkness.

"Carol," he whispered.

"Mmmm?"

"Are you asleep?"

"Nom."

"Carol?"

"Mmm?"

"Carol?"

"Mmm, whuzzit?"

"Are you asleep?"

"Mmmm."

"Honey?"

"Mmm?"

"Honey, can you hear me?"

"Yezzufcuss."

"You're pretty as hell, do you know that?"

"Om."

"You're the prettiest girl here tonight."

"Nkyou."

"Carol?"

"Mmm?"

"Why don't we go upstairs?"

"Whufor?"

"You know."

"Okaysurefine."

"You'll go?"

"Huhwhere?"

"Upstairs?"

"Nuh. Stayhere."

It was very dark in the corner. He lifted the hem of her gown, pulling it up over her knees.

"Carol," he whispered hoarsely.

She was very warm beneath the gown. She stirred, and then suddenly sat bolt upright, her eyes staring wide.

"What?" she said.

He did not move his hand. He kissed her, and she returned his kiss sleepily, and only then did she become aware of what he was doing. Her own hand swooped down like a hawk, and he felt her fingernails gouge into his wrist.

"Stop!" she said.

"Carol—"

"Andy stop it this minute."

"Carol, for Pete's sake—"

"What's the matter with you, Andy? My God, what's the matter with you? All these people—"

"We can go upstairs."

"No."

"Carol—"

"I said no."

"Everybody else—"

"I don't care about everybody else. I can wait."

"Wait for what?"

"Until we're married."

"Married? Jesus, that won't be for years."

"Then it won't be for years. I still can wait."

"Jesus, Carol. Sometimes—"

"Sometimes, what?"

"Nothing."

"All right, then kiss me and shut up. And be a good boy."

He kissed her, and she guided his hand to the bodice of her gown, and then to the naked flesh of her breast, as if she and he had made a tacit agreement that this was as far as it should go, and no farther.

From upstairs, Buff Collier yelled, "Hey, is anybody awake at this damn party?"

He didn't have his brush with the cops until almost a month later. The boys were coming back from a late wedding job they'd played in the Bronx, and Artie drove his car down East New York Avenue at close to sixty miles an hour. The streets of Brooklyn were deserted at that early hour of the morning, and the boys talked very little, exhausted from a full night of music-making.

Andy was sleepy as hell. He had taken a benny during the job, but that had only charged him up for a little while, and he was wondering now if he shouldn't swallow the remaining half of the drug-soaked paper. He had learned after a while that only half of the paper was necessary to hop him up. He also had a sneaking hunch that it was illegal to break open the inhaler and use the paper. He had casually ignored all this because he couldn't possibly figure any way for anyone ever to find out what he was doing. Besides, everything seemed to be going along just dandy for him these days. He'd auditioned with a semi-big-time outfit led by a man named Jerry Black, and the Black band was leaving for a Midwestern tour at the beginning of April, and that gave him more than enough time to arrange for quitting school and getting everything in order. Carol had objected to his quitting school and taking the job, but he'd talked her out of that, and Artie had been real decent about all of it, wishing him luck and all that sort of garbage, but telling him he hoped Andy would still play with the band until it was time to leave. Andy, of course, was very happy to do that. He still had a month before leaving, and the jobs with Artie gave him spending money. And as for the Benzedrine, well, what harm did it do, provided no one ever found out about it?

So he sat in the back of the car on that March night alongside the bass drum with a cracked inhaler in his pocket and one half of the Benzedrine-soaked paper stuffed back into the inhaler, and he wondered whether he should take the other half, but he decided against it since he'd be home and asleep in a very few minutes, as soon as Artie got his goddamned gas.

Artie did not spot the green Hudson sedan that pulled out onto East New York Avenue where East Ninety-fifth Street crossed it. There were five men in that sedan. Artie had his mind on his early Sunday date with June Tambeau, and Artie wanted to gas up the car tonight so that he could sleep later tomorrow morning. Jonesy and Tack, the other occupants of the car, were oblivious to everything. They didn't even blink when Artie made a screeching turn on Utica Avenue and braked to a wild stop inside the gas station.

The green Hudson sedan crashed the red light on the corner of Utica, made a sweeping left turn, and then pulled into the gas station directly in front of Artie's car. The four doors of the sedan flew open. Three men in sports jackets piled out of the back seat, and two men in business suits spilled out of the front seat.

The five men quickly stationed themselves around Artie's car. Two stood directly in front of it. One went to the rear, another went to the right-hand side of the car, and the fifth man came to the door near the driver's seat and yelled, "Get out!"

Andy's first impression was that he was about to be held up. The five men surrounding the car were all six-footers, all mean-looking bastards. He wondered idly why they'd pull a holdup in a lighted gas station, but then he considered the fourteen dollars he had in his pocket, his payment for the night's work, and he dismissed the logic or lack of logic and concerned himself only with the possible loss.

"Get out of that car!" the man yelled again, and Artie stared at him and then, idiotically, took the key from the ignition, as if that would have prevented the theft of the car.

"Wha . . . who . . . who . . . ?" he stammered, and the man yelled, "Come on, move!"

Artie didn't move. Beside him Tack Tacconi was visibly trembling, as if he were taking a wild snare drum solo. On the back seat Jonesy sat white faced on his side of the bass drum, and Andy sat on the other side, furiously considering a way of hiding the fourteen bucks.

"You hear me?" the man shouted.

"I . . . I . . ."

"Get the hell out of that car!"

Artie, through frozen fright or stubborn obstinacy, did not move. The man clasped a hairy paw on the door handle, pried it open, and then reached inside for Artie's collar. Artie was not a heavy boy, but even if he were heavy, he'd have been no match for the giant who lifted him bodily from the car.

"Hey!" Artie shouted, and then he was being slammed up against one of the gasoline pumps, and the man said, "Let me see your license!"

"Who—"

"Police," the man said tersely. "Let me see your license."

For some strange reason, Artie didn't believe the man was a cop. He was wearing a sports jacket, wasn't he? He was driving a green car, wasn't he? No, this was just a trick. This thug just wanted Artie to hand over his wallet, that was all.

"Let . . . let me see your badge," he said bravely.

"Let me see your license," the man insisted.

"Let me see your badge," Artie insisted back, pinned to the gasoline pump, and then, apparently realizing the folly of his insistence, he moved one hand up toward his inside jacket pocket, moving to reach his wallet and his license.

The man's hand dropped from Artie's collar instantly. It moved so fast that Artie didn't know what was happening for a moment, and then it snapped into view again, and the fingers were curled around the butt of a .38 Police Special.

Artie's eyes almost popped out of his head.

"Hey," he said. "Hey, Jesus, what . . . I was only going for my license . . . I was only . . ."

"Let's have it," the man said, holding the gun at an angle so that it was pointed up at Artie's head.

Artie took out his wallet, flipped it open, and handed it to the man.

"Take out the license," the man said.

"Are . . . are you a cop?"

"What the hell do you think I am?" The man reached into one of his pockets with his free hand, flipped open a wallet, and showed Artie a quick glimpse of a silver shield.

"I'm . . . I'm sorry, officer," Artie said. "I didn't realize . . . I thought . . ."

The cop took the extended license, and sitting in the back seat Andy felt first a wave of relief, and then a wave of terror. He was carrying a cracked Benzedrine inhaler in his jacket! Suppose he was searched . . . suppose . . .

The cop examined the license and then bellowed, "All right, everybody out of the car." Tack Tacconi came out of the car first, and the cop on his side frisked him quickly and then told him to stand over near the gas pump with Artie. They put Jonesy through the same routine, and then Andy came off the back seat, and one of the cops ran his hands over Andy's pockets quickly, and he prayed the cop would not feel the inhaler, and he felt the sweat pop out on his brow.

"Whose car is this?" the first cop asked.

"M . . . mmm . . . mine," Artie said.

"You got the registration?"

"In the glove compartment."

"Check that, Fred," the first detective said, and the cop on the other side of the car climbed in and thumbed open the glove compartment. He found the registration and handed it to the first cop, and then he began tossing everything out of the glove compartment, letters, a flashlight, a couple of road maps, a tire repair kit, even a tube of June Tambeau's lipstick.

"Nothing here," he said, colossally understating the amount of garbage he'd taken from the compartment.

"Open the trunk," the first cop told Artie.

"The . . . the trunk?"

"You heard me."

Artie went back to the trunk and opened it. The cops all gathered around him like betters in a floating crap game. The first cop pointed into the trunk.

"What's that?" he asked.

"What's . . . what's what?" Artie asked.

"That," the cop said, still pointing.

"My . . . my radio, officer."

"Where'd you get it?"

"I . . . I bought it. Naturally."

"You bought it, huh?"

"Yes, sir."

The cop named Fred was in the back seat now. He put the bass drum out of the car, shoved the seat onto the floor, and then felt under the seat, probing with a flashlight.

"Whose drum is this?" he asked.

"Mine," Tack answered.

"Wh . . . what are you looking for, officers?" Artie asked politely.

"What the hell were you doing barreling down the avenue at sixty miles an hour?" the first cop asked.

"We just wanted to get home. We're musicians."

"Yeah?"

"Yes, sir."

"Better shake them down once more," the first cop said.

Standing near the rear wheel of the car, Andy felt the terror stab deep within him once again. He reached into his jacket pocket casually, his fingers tightening around the cracked inhaler. *If I just get out of this,* he vowed, *if you just get me out of this one, I'll never do it again. I swear, never again.*

He slid his hand out of his jacket, his fingers sweating. Fred was making a methodical search of Tack's pockets now, turning them inside out. The other cops were giving Jonesy and Artie the same treatment. Andy could feel his heart thudding against his rib case. He wet his lips, and he felt a sour taste in his mouth, and he hoped he wouldn't get sick. He put his hand against his trouser leg, and then he opened the fingers slowly, and he felt the inhaler slip free, and he realized it would clatter when it hit the pavement, and so he began coughing wildly, moving away from the rear wheel, covering the sound of the inhaler hitting. He did not look down at the ground. He moved away from the wheel, and Fred barked, "Where the hell you going, kid?"

Somehow he found his voice. "Just . . . just stretching my legs," he said tightly.

"Come here," Fred said.

Andy went to him, and the cop began going through his pockets methodically, finding nothing. Andy still did not look back to where he'd dropped the inhaler.

"All right," the first cop said, "where the hell were you headed, doing sixty miles an hour?"

"I didn't know we were going that fast, officer," Artie said. His father had taught him that the only way to handle a cop was to butter him up, calling him "officer" and "sir" at every turn of the conversation.

"You were going that fast," the cop said. "Where the hell were you going?"

"Just to get some gas, sir, and then home."

"Yeah?"

"Yes, sir."

"At four in the morning?"

"We're musicians, officer. We're just coming home from a wedding job in the Bronx." He paused. "An *Irish* wedding," he added shrewdly.

"Yeah?"

"Yes, sir."

"Mmmm," the cop said.

"I guess they're clean," Fred said.

"I'll give you some information," the first cop said to Artie, "and I hope you listen to it. In the first place, speed limits are in force twenty-four hours a day. I don't give a damn what time you're coming home, the speed limit applies, you understand that?"

"Yes, sir."

"And when a cop asks you for your license, you give it to him damn fast, you understand that?"

"Yes, sir. I didn't know you were an officer, sir."

"What the hell did you think I was?"

"I thought you were a holdup man, sir."

"And I thought you were the same thing, and I almost put a hole in your head when you made a sudden reach for your pocket. So don't ever do *that* again, either, you understand?"

"Yes, sir."

"Now get this goddamn car off the streets and consider yourself lucky. You seem like a nice bunch of kids, so we'll let it pass this time. We could haul you in for speeding, you know that, don't you?"

"Yes, sir, and I certainly appreciate—"

"All right, get moving."

"I'd . . . I'd like to get some gas, sir. If it's all right."

"Go ahead, get your gas."

The cops piled back into the green Hudson sedan and gunned away from the gas station. The attendant came over, his eyes wide.

"Jesus," he said, "what the hell was that?"

"Those miserable bastards," Artie said.

"Man, I was scared stiff," Tack said.

Jonesy's face was still white, and his hands were shaking. "Did you see the size of them?" he asked.

"Those miserable bastards," Artie said.

"Man, I thought they were going to . . . man, when I saw him pull that gun on you . . . oh, man . . . man, I thought I'd . . . Jesus, I thought I'd drop dead."

Artie smiled. "Those miserable bastards. Thinking we were crooks."

"You can't blame them," Tack said. "Shooting up the avenue at—"

"You want gas?" the attendant asked.

"Fill 'er up," Artie said. "How you feel, Andy?"

Andy gulped. "Okay," he said.

"Hey, dig Andy," Artie said. "Man, you look like you're ready to pass out."

"I'm just a little . . . a little shaken," Andy said.

"You'll be lucky to get out of this burg, Man, I wish I was goin' on the road."

"How about some coffee before we go home?" Tack asked. "Man, I can sure use a cup."

"Good idea. What do you say, Andy?"

"All right," Andy said.

"We can go to the White Tower on Remsen and Utica," Artie said. "Those miserable bastards."

They stood around while the attendant filled the tank, silent now, glad the episode was over. Artie paid the attendant, and they climbed back into the car. Andy hesitated a moment. He looked down to the patch of concrete near the right rear wheel. He saw the cracked inhaler nestling against the rubber of the tire. He wet his lips, staring at the inhaler.

"You coming, Andy?" Tack said.

"Yes," he said.

He opened the back door and then stopped quickly, his fingers closing around the inhaler tube. He put the tube into his pocket and then climbed into the car.

"I'm ready," he said.

20

Lying on his bed in the hotel room, Andy would hear the sounds of Michigan Avenue far below him, filtering up to and through the open window. It was still raining, but the wind was blowing from the opposite direction, and so the sharp silvery wet needles slanted away from the window and the room.

Rain in a strange town was a very depressing thing somehow. He wondered why this should be so, and then he picked up Bud's letter again and began reading from the second page.

> *. . . big-time outfit, so I guess you're really in your element now. I always knew you would amount to something, and I think you did the wise thing in grabbing the opportunity when it came along. In her letters Carol tells me she didn't think you should've quit school, but the decision was yours to make, really, and your first responsibility is to yourself, isn't it? Anyway, you've been with Black for some months now, so I guess it must appeal to you.*
>
> *The navy certainly appeals to me. I know there are a lot of guys who find it chicken, but I love it. I guess it's hard to explain, but I like them telling me when to wake up, and when to go to sleep, and when you can leave the ship, and when you have to be back aboard, and they feed you when they want to feed you, and they tell you what to wear, and that all sounds kind of lousy when you say it that way, but I like it.*
>
> *You don't have to worry about a damn thing. Do you know what I mean? All the decisions are made for you. You don't have to worry about anyone but yourself. When you think of it, you don't even have to worry about yourself. There are officers paid to do the worrying. Jesus, it's a great life. I'll tell you the truth, I'll be a little sorry when it's all over. I mean,*

when I have to come back and pick up where I left off. Not that I don't want to be back with the old crowd—hell, there was nothing like the old crowd— but, well I guess this is beginning to sound crazy, so the hell with it.

I understand they've shipped Frank to Okinawa where he . . .

Andy folded the letter and put it on the night table. He was happy that Bud was enjoying himself because he couldn't exactly say he was doing the same. It was strange, too, because he sure as hell should have been enjoying himself, but he wasn't, and that was the simple truth of it. He missed Carol, and he missed Bud. It was funny he should miss them and not his own mother and father, but he had to admit that was the way things stood.

Then, too, the band was boring him a lot lately.

There was a dull regularity to the routine of traveling with a big band. Breakfast at noon, rehearsals at two, a movie to kill the rest of the afternoon, or a few drinks in a bar; a late supper, and then onto the bandstand until two in the morning; a sandwich with the boys, and then bed. This would have been all right, he supposed, if he were enjoying the bandstand part, and he couldn't understand why he wasn't.

It was just that . . . well, hell, what was the reason now? Why the hell wasn't he really blowing the way he wanted to blow now? He had a big-time section behind him, and he had big-time arrangements, and, Jesus, Jesus, he certainly gave it everything he had, didn't he? He blew his lungs out, and his heart out, and still something eluded him, and he kept grasping for it, not even knowing what the something was, only knowing that the sound wasn't the right sound—good, yes, but not what he wanted. And because it was not what he wanted, he sought excitement, and because the excitement could never compare to this thing he wanted to achieve with his horn, he found only boredom instead.

There were ways to break the monotony, of course— the jam sessions in the all-night bistros, where musicians from every band in town congregated after hours to blow their heads off. He'd blown with Barney Bigard at one of those sessions, and Art Tatum had given him a piano background at another. He had felt excitement on those nights, blowing with the greats, and then the excitement had died—in spite of the wild applause that greeted him— because again he'd felt this empty longing, this desire to give his horn a tongue, to make his horn speak from hidden wells within him.

He had enjoyed his freedom, too, at first. No mother or father to watch him, no well-meant words about what time to get in, none of his mother's fussing over him, and none of his father's tacit disapproval of everything he did. He had enjoyed this feeling of independence immensely, until even that wore off, leaving him only a lot of empty time on his hands.

He had tried to fill that time practicing, thinking, *I will get it if I practice, I will find my horn, really find my horn.* But he did not find what he wanted, and so he spent the afternoons shopping instead, using a large part of his salary on new clothes—clothes Bud would have beamed over. He'd bought two new sports jackets and some crazy argyles in Marshall Field's, and then he'd drifted over to the college shops and gone to hell with himself there. He chose his clothes carefully, and he never bought cheap stuff, and there was excitement in his early buying sprees —until his wardrobe was stocked. He bought a few items after that, but he knew he was buying aimlessly, and the joy was lacking now, and so he stopped it.

On a day like this he supposed he should practice. Jerry had called off the rehearsal because the new arrangements weren't ready, and that gave him a long afternoon to piddle with. But the thought of another unrewarding session alone with the horn filled him with an almost physical paralysis. And so he lay on the bed, feeling a strange need within him and knowing of no way to satisfy it.

When Dick MacGregor came into the room, Andy was neither pleased nor displeased. MacGregor was on first trombone. He was a good man, a big man with a freckle-spattered face and sparkling green eyes. Andy and he shared a kidding relationship, a relationship in which Andy's exclusive line of banter centered around the fact that all you needed in order to be a trombone player was a pair of lungs and a long arm. MacGregor's arms were long and, coupled with his wide paunch and beer-barrel stature, they gave him the appearance of an extremely intelligent, jovial orangutan.

MacGregor closed the door behind him and then went to sit by the window. Andy did not move from the bed.

"You goofing?" MacGregor asked.

"Mmm," Andy said.

"Man, this rain is the eeriest," MacGregor said, peering through the window.

"How so?"

"The eeriest dreariest, man," MacGregor said, shaking his head. "Makes you want to crawl in somebody's basement and hide there."

"To each his own," Andy said.

"We could've used a rehearsal today," MacGregor said. "Hey, you dig the two broads moved in down the hall?"

"No," Andy said.

"Acrobats or something. At one of the clubs. They're built like lace-pantied tennis players. You know what I mean?"

"No," Andy said.

"Nice rippling muscles on their calves and thighs. I go for that muscular type."

"I understand there's a wrestling match tonight at—"

"Don't be wise," MacGregor said.

"Only offering a suggestion," Andy said, smiling.

MacGregor stared through the window. "Want to go down the hall and see if we can con them into a drink?"

"I'm too tired," Andy said.

"Yeah. Man, this rain sure is a drag, ain't it?"

"It sure is."

"It's blacker'n a satchel full of bowling balls out there," MacGregor said.

"Yeah," Andy said.

"Hey, are you holding?" MacGregor said suddenly.

"Am I what?"

"You got any junk?"

"What do you mean, junk?"

"Oh, come down," MacGregor said.

"I don't know what you're talking about," Andy answered.

"I got some in my room, anyway. I mean, I'm not hitting you up for a free ride."

"What the hell are you talking about?" Andy said.

"Mootah," MacGregor said.

"That explains it, all right. What's mootah?"

"Oh, come on, man, you're dusting me."

"I kid you not," Andy said. "What's mootah?"

"The kid's from Squaresville," MacGregor said to the open window. "Let it drop."

"Okay," Andy agreed. "Let it drop."

The room was silent for several moments. MacGregor kept staring through the open window at the curtain of rain outside.

"The bleariest, dreariest," MacGregor said. "Hey, you see that new movie at the State Lake?"

"No."

"You want to drift over there this afternoon?"

"Not particularly."

"Supposed to be a good show."

"Maybe later," Andy said.

"Yeah, okay." MacGregor watched the rain. "Real muscular calves and thighs. They look like stuff, too. I've got a fifth in my room. You want to give it a swing?"

"I haven't got the energy."

"Well, what the hell you gonna do, man? Sit on your butt all day long?"

"What's wrong with that?"

"Nothing. Just be careful they don't mistake you for dead and start shovelin' dirt all over you."

"I read a book about a guy who got buried alive once," Andy said. "It was called *Vendetta*. *You* ever read that one?"

"I ain't much of a reader," MacGregor said. "Is it in a pocket book yet?"

"I don't think so. I got it from the library."

"I only buy pocket books. I ain't been to the library since I was twelve."

"We used to go to the library a lot when I was back home. It was a kind of a meeting place."

"We met at the poolroom," MacGregor said.

"I mean with chicks," Andy said.

"The chicks we knew all played pool."

"Sounds like a gone crowd."

"We had our kicks. Anyway, I don't read much. Two things I read religiously are the first-trombone sheet and *Down Beat*."

"You're in a rut, man."

"Sure, but it's comfy. Listen, we going to sit around here and gas, we're gonna need a little refreshment."

"I got a jug here, if you want some."

"Who's talking about juice? Man, for a cat who blows the way you do, you sure are nowhere."

"You mean the chicks?"

"I saw one of them in the hall the other day in a leotard. One of those black things that hug—"

"I know what a leotard is."

"I wasn't sure, man, not the way you've been talking. I'll be right back."

"You going for the chicks?"

"You said you were tired, didn't you?"

"Yeah."

"So why should I go for the chicks?"

"I don't know."

"Man, you're in a fog, you know that? I wouldn't be surprised you're turned on already."

"What?"

"Cool it, man. As MacArthur once said, 'I shall return.' "

Andy watched him leave without replying. He could hear the swish of the rain outside, and beneath that the steady hum of the traffic. The ceiling bored him to tears, and he sat at the nucleus of his boredom and examined it like a man with a duplicate of a rare stamp.

When MacGregor came back into the room, he did not look up.

"You asleep?" MacGregor asked.

"No."

"Gone. Try some of this, man."

"Some of what?" He propped himself up on his elbows. MacGregor was extending a cigarette to him. "I don't smoke," Andy said.

"You're a clown, daddy," MacGregor said. "Who's asking you to smoke?"

"That's a cigarette, isn't it?"

"That's a reefer," MacGregor said.

Andy stared at the long, cylindrical tube. "Yeah?"

"Go ahead. Take it."

"What for?"

"Kill the afternoon. What the hell?"

"The afternoon's dead already," Andy said.

"This'll give it a boot in the back. Come on."

"Nah," Andy said.

"Come on, man. Hey, what's bugging you, anyway? You act like this is poison. Half the cats on this band are hip to M."

"What the hell is M?"

"Mootah, muggles, miggles, hemp, hashish, bhang, tea, pot, weed, Rosa Maria, Mary Warner, take your choice. It's all marijuana. Come on, man, it never hurt a fly."

"Yeah, but does it hurt humans?"

"You're a real clown, daddy. You want this, or nay?"

"I'll pass it this time."

"Whatever you say. You mind if I blast?"

"Do what you want to," Andy said.

"You never really lit a stick, Andy?"

"Never."

"Man, you haven't lived. Well, here's how."

Andy watched as MacGregor put the long thin cigarette to his lips. He struck a match and lit it quickly, and then he cupped his hands around it, as if he were unwilling to allow any of the smoke to escape. He took a long, sucking drag on it, air rushing into his mouth around the corners of the cigarette. He did not stop inhaling. He kept sucking repeatedly on the reefer until it was barely a half-inch long.

"There's more power when it's down to a roach," Mac-Gregor said. "You get it all concentrated down around here." He held the stub between two fingers now, his thumb and forefinger clamped on the white paper close to the burning coal. He sucked in deeply, and the cigarette burned close to his fingers, and still he sucked, until there was almost only the burning coal left in his hand. He dropped the coal into an ash tray then, and it burned out almost instantly.

Andy watched him, and he noticed no appreciable change, except that a small smile suddenly appeared on

MacGregor's mouth. His eyes were very bright, and he studied Andy with calm aloofness, as if he knew a joke and would not reveal it.

"Ah, man," he said contentedly, "that is the end, the ever-loving end."

"Yeah," Andy said blankly.

"Come on, man, try one."

"No."

"Why not?"

"I don't know."

"Oh, man, the atmosphere is rarefied up here. Oh, man, this is the unholiest. Come on, daddy, bust a joint with old Dickie-boy. Here goes, daddy, here goes now, oh, man, I'm walking on the walls. Take it." He held out the second reefer. "Take it."

"No."

"Your choice, daddy, but oh, is that rain sweet now, oh, is that rain playing our song? Oh, daddy, listen to that sweet, stinking rain, oh, listen to it, man."

"What does it feel like? I mean, smoking that?"

"Like nothing ever, man. Like everything. Like strawberry shortcake, like Rita Hayworth in a black nightgown. Oh, daddy, it's the end of the world!"

"Does it make you sick? Like ... like a benny sometimes makes you sick?"

"Benny? A benny? Oh, man, that's as bad as getting high on juice. Take the stick. Blast, daddy. Come up here with me."

Andy took the cigarette. It was a fragile thing, and he could hear the crackling of the marijuana beneath the thin paper covering.

"Does it make you sick?" Andy asked again.

"It makes you slick-sick, stick-sick, like when you're sick with wanting a girl, oh, daddy don't talk so friggin' much, just light up and join the marching camels, join the caravan, dad, here come the dancing girls in their pantaloons!"

Andy put the cigarette between his lips, and then he struck a match.

"Inhale it straight down," MacGregor said. "One continuous draw. Suck in all you can, and keep suckin, 'cause it burns like a bitch and before you know it, it's all gone. Grab it while you've got it.

He lit the cigarette and then sucked in the harsh smoke, feeling it attack his throat, feeling nothing else but the burning sensation.

"Keep at it, man! Drag! Drag!"

He kept dragging at the reefer, the smoke still harsh, smelling the sickly-sweet aroma of it as it attacked his nostrils, feeling a quickening of his pulse, which he attributed to the excitement of the situation. He sucked it down to a burning coal, the way MacGregor had done, and the last few drags were strong and potently heady, and when he dropped the coal into the ash tray, he leaned back and waited for something to happen.

He began giggling suddenly.

"What is it, dad?"

"Nothing," Andy said, giggling. "It's just . . . it don't affect me."

"It don't, huh?"

"Not at all." He was laughing uproariously, unable to control the gales of laughter. "It . . . not at all, at all, at all."

The ceiling was spinning, and he watched the spinning, and he heard the gentle hush of rain outside, and he smiled down from away up there where he was, oh, how tall he was, he smiled down at MacGregor, and he was allwise and allpowerful and allseeing, and in his majestic splendor he waved his hand limply and said, "Bring on the dancing girls, knave," and then he collapsed into laughter again, and the laughter sounded as if it were coming from someplace far, far below him, all the way down there, my God, so far down there, and he was all the way up somewhere on top of a mountain, and the air was so very sweet, and he tried to remember what it was that he had been bored about before, but he didn't feel bored any more, he felt only superior to everything around him, including MacGregor, what was that fat slob doing in his room, anyway?

"You're a fat slob, MacGregor," he said, and MacGregor began laughing.

"It's the end, ain't it?"

"It's the living end," Andy said. "Goddamn, it's the living end!"

In the beginning he knew it was wrong.

He knew damn well it was wrong, and so he steered away from MacGregor, and he tried to pretend that afternoon in his room had never happened. But he could not forget the feeling he'd had once the mootah had snapped the top of his wig. He could not forget that feeling, and there was no other way of getting that feeling because alcohol made you high, but it also made you stupid—and marijuana did not make you stupid. Marijuana made you very smart, very wise.

There was no substitute for marijuana. He went back to the Benzedrine, but, hell, that was nothing at all. All it did was give you a nervous jag, all it did was make you jumpy and hypertense. Marijuana didn't do that at all. Marijuana smoothed the ruffled feathers. Marijuana was like a big mound of breasts you just put your head on. Marijuana was floating.

But even remembering the floating he knew it was bad, and so he steered away from MacGregor, but that didn't help at all. His second stick of M came from the drummer on the band, a cat named Bash Bellew. He didn't know why he took the stick, except that it wasn't connected with MacGregor, and that somehow took the onus off it.

After that, and still knowing it was wrong, he blasted regularly. There was always one guy who was holding, and when you couldn't find that guy, the Man was always on the scene. He got so he could spot the Man instantly. A different man each time, but he always bore the unmistakable stamp of the Man, and you always knew he was around, and for half a buck, you could spin your own disk, play your own tune, leave the ants and start floating.

Fifty cents a joint, and what was half a buck to a guy pulling down a bill a week? Three joints a day, that made it a buck and a half a day, ten-fifty a week. What was ten-fifty to a guy who'd already bought all the ties and socks he needed?

And it wasn't habit-forming—that was the best part of it. The thing could be dropped tomorrow, and that would be the end of it. Dropped cold, with no aftereffects. So if it wasn't habit-forming, and if even the big medical men didn't know a hell of a lot about it, why not?

Why not, but at the same time, why?

Why indeed?

Well, why not, if it definitely is not habit-forming, and if it helps break the monotony, and if it doesn't cost too much, and if the Man is always on the scene ready to oblige, and if you could blast in your own hotel room with nobody to bother you, with no cops snooping around or even suspecting, why in hell not?

And suppose it did take two joints after a while to bring on any sort of a charge so what did that have to do with it? What the hell was a buck when you got right down to it? You got two shots of whisky for a buck and that left you a long way from being stoned, and with this buck, this buck spent on M, you were guaranteed a charge, so wasn't it worth it? And wasn't it better than mooning around over Carol, or remembering Helen's body? Wasn't this, when you really grappled with the situation, a hell of a lot better than all of that? And it didn't hurt the playing any, did it? Made it better somehow, made you sharper and cleaner, and all around better.

So why not?

Well, it's wrong, for one thing.

How is it wrong?

It's against the law.

Only if you're caught with the stuff.

You can go to jail. You can get up to ten years for . . .

If the breaks are against you, you can go to jail for almost anything. Hell, if you falsify your income tax . . .

This isn't income tax. This is fooling around with drugs.

Who said marijuana is a drug?

Well . . .

Is it habit-forming?

Well, no, not exactly.

Then why is it wrong?

Because it's a bad habit.

You just said it wasn't a habit.

It's a voluntary habit—all right? And it's bad because . . . well, what happens when you build a tolerance to it? What happens when you no longer get a boot from it? Where do you go then? What do you try next?

Man, your arguments are all wet.

No, Andy, they're not. You know that.

I know nothing. You haven't told me a goddamn thing.

It's wrong, Andy. It's wrong, and you know it is, and you can lie to me, maybe, but you sure as hell can't lie to yourself.

He knew it was wrong in the beginning, and he still knew it after the taking of a reefer had become a "voluntarily" habitual thing, like brushing his teeth. He knew it was wrong, and the knowledge plagued him, but he could see no way of escaping the boys on the band, or the Man who was always there. If a lot of them did it, if they insisted on clinging to him, clinging to him fiercely, their fingers tight and grasping, what could he do, what could he possibly do?

He could run! To Bud. Bud would know ... but Bud was away.

Run, run! To Helen then, Helen ... no, what was he thinking? Carol. Of course, Carol.

When Jerry Black told him the band was moving on to Cincinnati the following week, he handed in his notice. Jerry was stunned because he hadn't suspected anything was troubling Andy. He tried to talk him out of it, but Andy was adamant. He wanted to go home. He wanted to be back with the people he knew and needed. That was all there was to it. The band left Chicago on a Tuesday night in July, and Andy caught the midnight plane for New York at the same time.

He went to see Carol the next morning. She cried when she saw him, and she held him close, as if she never wanted him to leave the circle of her arms, and he was sure then that he'd made the right decision in leaving Jerry Black.

They went out that night, the spark of the reunion having been replaced by a warm intimacy. They talked of what they'd each done in their separation, and then Carol asked, "Why'd you leave the band, Andy?"

"Just like that," he said, not wanting to tell her about his infatuation with marijuana.

"Didn't you like the fellows?"

"They were fine."

"What then?"

"Nothing. I just decided to come home, that's all. I missed you."

"Did you get along with everyone?"

"Oh, sure."

"He didn't take any solos away from you, or anything like that?"

"No."

"Then why did you leave?"

"I told you."

"No, you didn't tell me."

"I . . . I was bored, Carol."

"Bored?"

"Yes. I . . . I just decided to come home."

"And what'll you do now?"

"Find another job, I guess."

"Playing?"

He looked at her surprised. "Why, of course, playing. What else would I do?"

"Then why didn't you stay with Black?"

"I told you. I was bored."

"What makes you think you won't be bored on another band?"

"Well, I won't know until I try it, will I?"

"You shouldn't have come home, Andy."

"That's a hell of a thing to say," he said, annoyed.

"I'm glad you're back, darling. You know that. But . . . I don't think it's good to jump from one band to another."

"Hell, musicians change their bands as often as they change their underwear."

"But you should have stuck with it, Andy. Until you were ready for a move."

"I'm ready now."

"I hope so."

"What the hell do you mean by that?"

"I just hope you're ready, Andy. You did leave a good job, didn't you? There was no reason—"

"There was a damn good reason," he snapped.

"If there was, I haven't heard it yet."

"I've told you six times already. I was bored with the band."

"Will it be any different on another band?"

"You've already asked me that. What is this, anyway, Carol? You certainly don't act very damn glad to see me."

"I am, you know that. It's just—"

"Well, you don't act it. The way you talk, I could have

stayed in Chicago for the rest of my life, and you wouldn't have given a good goddamn."

"I'm sorry I gave you that impression."

"I'm sorry, too. Believe me."

They fell into a heavy silence.

"There was a good reason for leaving," he said.

"Yes, I'm sure," she answered, still not believing him.

"Come on, let's go home. We'll make a fresh start tomorrow."

"All right. If you say so."

"Well, we're certainly not getting anyplace tonight, are we?"

"It doesn't seem so."

"I don't know what the hell's wrong with you, Carol."

"Nothing."

"Then why've you been giving me the business?"

"Because it was your idea to leave school, and I said no, and now you've left what turned out to be a good job, that's why. Now please take me home because I don't feel like arguing any more."

"Sure."

"Sure," she repeated.

"You'll feel better in the morning," he said.

"I certainly hope so. And maybe you'll see what a fool you've been in the morning."

"I doubt it."

They went home in a sullen, uncommunicative mood. On her doorstep he said, "I'll call you tomorrow, Carol."

"Yes," she answered.

"Good night."

"Good night."

She went into the house without kissing him, and he stood on the front step for a long time, annoyed with her lack of understanding, and annoyed with his own temper.

He looked at his watch. It was only eleven-fifteen. What the hell kind of time was that to be coming home? Jesus, why couldn't she understand? Couldn't anyone ever understand him?

He walked down to Eastern Parkway and stopped in a candy store. He went to the phone booth on impulse, looked up a number, and then dialed it rapidly.

"Hello?" the voice said.

"Helen?"

"Yes."

"This is Andy."

"Who?"

"Andy Silvera. You know, Andy . . ."

"Oh. Oh, yes." There was a long pause. "What is it, Andy?"

"How are you?"

"Fine. Is . . . is anything the matter? It's . . . it's not Bud, is it? Nothing's happened to—"

"No, no, he's fine." He heard her catch her breath on the other end of the line.

"Well, how have you been, Andy? I understand you were on the road?"

"Yes. Helen . . ."

"Yes?"

"You sound like you were sleeping."

"I was. My parents are away for a few weeks. In Rockaway. I've been getting to bed early."

"Have you?" he asked, his voice thickening.

"Yes. I have." There was another long silence. "Well," she said, "it was nice of you to call, Andy."

"Helen, listen, Helen, I was wondering . . . can I come over?"

"What?"

"I want to come over."

"Why?"

"I . . . I need somebody to talk to. Helen, I . . . look, about that time . . ."

"Let's not bring it up, Andy."

"Can I come over?"

Helen hesitated. "Now?"

"Yes."

"I'm not even dressed."

"Helen, I . . . I need someone. To . . . to talk to. I need you."

He waited anxiously, hating himself for what he was doing, but hating Carol at the same time, and hating the homecoming she'd given him, and the petty questions, and her lack of understanding, hating all of it, and waiting breathlessly for Helen's reply. He heard her sigh heavily.

"All right," she said. "I'll look for you."

21

They dropped the first atomic bomb on August sixth.

Sixty per cent of Hiroshima was obliterated by the blast. Five major industrial plants disappeared completely, and only 2.8 square miles of the city's total 6.9 square miles remained intact to leer at a puzzled, battered, awe-stricken Oriental population. On August eighth Russia declared war on Japan, and the United States dropped a second atomic bomb on an important shipping and industrial city called Nagasaki, a city which had only been part of an American song before the fiery blast. President Truman warned the Japanese people that the atomic bomb would lead to their utter obliteration unless they surrendered unconditionally —and the world read the headlines and leaned forward expectantly for news from the men in the East.

The Japanese government offered to surrender under an interpretation of the Potsdam surrender ultimatum on August tenth, and then the surrender offer worked its way through the official channels, and on August eleventh President Truman spoke for the Allies, explaining the terms under which the emperor would be allowed to remain on the throne.

The world waited.

On August twelfth, an erroneous news broadcast flashed into millions of American homes, announcing that Japan had accepted the surrender terms. The news flash was killed two minutes after it went over the wire, but it touched off wild celebrations which reluctantly petered out during the next two days of expectant waiting.

Japan surrendered unconditionally on August fourteenth.

Helen went into the streets that night. Everyone was in the streets, it seemed, singing and shouting and reeling and rioting. There was wild jubilation in the air, an excitement that throbbed in her body. She was kissed a hundred times, a thousand times. There were strange hands briefly touching her, strange bottles being put to her lips, and beneath all the reckless release of tension there was a wild triumphant singing in her blood, an ecstasy born of the knowledge that it was all over.

The block parties began the next night, all over Brooklyn, banners hung, bands hired, beer kegs rolled into the streets, dancing, and singing, and cheering, and shouting, and all of it fun, all of it a complete sort of happiness she had never really known before, a release of fear, and a release of anxiety, a victorious, happy, surging feeling of delight.

She went from party to party, and she didn't know how or why she ended up at this particular shindig, and she suspected she was not entirely sober when she got there, but that didn't matter because all of Brooklyn was drunk that night—the whole city was drunk, the whole world was drunk.

She wasn't sure she was seeing clearly at first, wasn't sure because that looked like Bud and Tony, but Tony was somewhere in Florida, wasn't he? And Bud . . .

She was dancing with someone when she saw the two boys, and she blinked her eyes over her partner's shoulder—she couldn't even remember his name now, someone unimportant, one of the long line of unremembered people she'd danced with and kissed with and drunk with in those few wild days of celebration—and then she said, "Oh, look!" and she broke away from the boy and started running over to where she thought she'd seen Bud and Tony standing.

She was running over to Bud, she knew, wanting the end of the war to symbolize the end of what was standing between them, but when she realized she was doing that, she faltered for a moment and then, carried on by her momentum, rushed over to both of them and swung Tony around and said "Tony! For God's sake!"

They both looked very handsome in their dress blues, Tony with a lyre and two red stripes on his sleeve, and Bud with two crossed flags and only one red stripe on his. Tony lifted her into his arms and shouted, "Helen! Honey, what are you doing here? I was beginning to think there wasn't a friendly face left in Brooklyn!"

"You look won-derful!" she shouted, and she glanced sidewise at Bud, and he smiled and very softly said, "Hello, Helen."

"Haven't you got a kiss for the victors?" Tony asked, and Helen kissed him soundly and happily, and when he released her she looked questioningly at Bud, wanting to say, "Bud, what happened to us? Can't we forget all this? Couldn't we . . ."

But he stood there solemnly embarrassed, a pained smile on his face, as if her kissing Tony had somehow pierced the blue of his uniform and lodged in his breast like a sharp, narrow shaft.

"Have you been drinking?" Tony asked suspiciously.

"Damn right I've been drinking," she said, feeling the liquor again now that Tony had reminded her of it.

"I've smuggled in a jug," Tony said, "but don't let any of these sloppy beer drinkers see it."

He reached under his jumper and sneaked out a pint of cheap whisky, which he uncapped and passed to Helen.

"No glass," he said. "I hope you're not proud."

"Not at all," she said, and she tilted the bottle and drank from it freely. She passed the bottle back to Tony, and he handed it to Bud.

"Buddy?"

"Thanks," Bud said. He drank from the bottle, and then Tony took a long draw from it. Someone on the flag-decorated bandstand was making a speech about "the brave boys who defended our homeland in her hour of need and who would now return to . . ." and someone standing over near the beer key yelled, "Come on, let's have some music!" The man on the bandstand terminated his speech abruptly, and a piano player, a sax man, and a drummer went back onto the bandstand and began playing "Beer Barrel Polka," and everyone rushed into the street and began dancing. There were pennants and banners stretched across the street from building to building. "Welcome Home, Boys" and "V-J Day!" and "Victory," and, for no apparent reason now, "Slap the Jap!" There were a lot of servicemen, and a lot of young undraftable kids in sports jackets, and some kids in tee shirts and dungarees, and old women in housedresses, smiling, and old men in undershirts, smiling, and pretty girls in summery dresses, the flush of excitement and alcohol on their faces, their bodies taut with spring-coil energy.

"Are you on leave, Tony?" Helen asked, and he replied, "Sent most of us off the minute they heard them whistles blasting in the bay. I caught a plane out from the army base."

"What about you, Bud?" she asked.

"We kept just a skeleton crew on the ship. We're still up in Boston, you know."

"I'd heard you went overseas."

"No. We were supposed to, but someone got the bright idea of changing our ship to a picket ship. We've been in drydock ever since our second shakedown."

"Is that good or bad?" she asked.

"It's a honeymoon. Boston's a good town."

"Do you come in often?"

"Once in a while," he said, and she thought she detected a sudden wariness in his voice.

"Hey, how about dancing, Helen?" Tony asked, and without waiting for her reply he scooped her into his arms and went polka-ing off with her. She watched Bud over Tony's shoulder. He was looking around now, sizing up the girls in their thin frocks. Tony collided with someone on the floor, and she was rammed up hard against him, and she felt the bulge of the whisky pint tucked into the waistband of his trousers. She pulled away, and they went into the polka again, Tony swinging his arm wildly as if he were flagging a train. The polka ended and the band went into a fox trot, and Tony pulled her close to him and she could smell the whisky on his breath, and she wondered idly if she smelled the same way. And then, curiously, she recalled the nights she'd spent with Andy. The first night he'd called her, and the thin desperation in his voice that night. And the talking they'd done, and then the other nights before he left with another band, the whisky they'd consumed on those nights, the things they'd done, and she wondered why she had, except that he seemed to need someone so badly, and all the while she watched Bud.

He was still looking around, taking his time in picking a partner, looking somehow restless in the midst of all the obvious joviality. He did not move from where he stood near the curb. He kept his arms folded across his chest, his fists clenched, his white hat cocked over one eye. He did not turn his head. Only his eyes moved, and they moved quickly, restlessly, and he seemed dissatisfied with what those eyes saw. He looked up at the bandstand, as if making some mental calculation, and then he gave a small nervous shrug and started out into the street which served as the dance floor.

She wondered where he was going for a moment, and then she realized he was coming toward her and Tony, and she realized at the same instant that she'd been hoping he would do just that. She wanted very much to talk to him, to be able at last to clear the air, to expose her heart and tell him about what had happened, exactly as it had happened, so that things would be just the way they were that time at Rockaway, before Andy and before Bud had been taken away from her by the navy. She could feel the hammering of her heart beneath the clinging silk of her dress, and she was sure Tony could feel her heart drumming, too, and then she saw the embarrassed smile form on Bud's face, and then his hand reached out, and he clapped Tony on the shoulder, and Tony looked up, absorbed and then surprised.

"How about sharing the wealth, mate?" Bud asked.

Tony backed away and bowed from the waist, and then swept his arm across his knees like a cavalier. He reached for the bottle under his jumper and moved off the dance floor to the sidewalk.

They did not speak to each other for several moments. She moved into his arms, and they kept a respectable distance between them because their bodies were strangers now. And, oddly, she did not want to be close to him. Not yet. There was a transparent film hanging between them, and they would have to tear through that first, rip it away, and, until then, until then, they would still be strangers to each other, going through the motions of polite society, making inane remarks about the weather. The big trouble was still between them, and it would not vanish until they sought it out and exposed it to the light, and then there would be time, then there would be all the time in the world.

"Real cornball, isn't it?" Bud said.

"What?"

"The band."

"Well," she said, smiling, "nothing could ever compare to the Tony Banner Boys."

"You can say that again," he said.

They swung around the floor awkwardly, the habit of dancing together having grown rusty. "You've grown up, Helen," he said.

"Have I?"

"Yes. You look damned good. When's the last time I saw you?"

"I don't know. Last spring, was it?" She knew the date exactly. She could reel off the date and the hour and the minute exactly if she wanted to. "Long ago."

"You've changed."

"Is that a compliment?"

"You're prettier now."

"Thank you."

"You always were the prettiest girl around, anyway. For my money. Helen, you look damned good. Listen, do we . . . do we have to stay here?"

"What?"

"I've got my father's car. Can we take a ride?"

She heard his voice, and she heard his suggestion, and the words came to her in a rushing roar, as if he were standing somewhere far off on a crag overlooking the sea, and the sound of his voice was mixed with the thunder of the rushing waves. And then she realized the thunder was only the roar of her blood, and she felt suddenly so elated that she wanted to scream aloud because he was asking her just what she'd wanted him to ask her, and she knew that now they would talk, at last they would talk it all out, and get all the festering poison out of their systems, and be the way they were again.

"Yes," she said. "I would like to take a ride."

He seemed surprised. She watched his face, and she loved the surprise that spread over it, and she squeezed his hand, but only very slightly because things weren't really all solved yet, and because the familiarity of squeezing his hand, even this small familiarity was strange to her, and because she felt that so much talking had to be done before they would really know each other again, before their eyes and their hands and their bodies could become familiar again.

They left the block party without telling Tony where they were going. She noticed that there was a quickness to his step, and she marveled at the way he walked, a real sailor's roll having replaced his earlier loping gait. And the quickness of his step found a responding note in the steady drumming of her heart, and she told her heart, *Be still, be still, this is only the beginning, we've so much to learn.*

They rounded the corner, and she saw his father's old Chevvy, and she thought again of how long it had been, how long since she'd been inside this car, since she'd known the intimacy of its upholstery, the intricacy of the window mechanism on the right-hand door—hit the door first and then turn the handle very very slowly—how long since she had used the glove compartment as a personal storage locker for her lipstick and her tissues and her purse. And seeing the car, she felt that she was finally coming home, and she realized how silly she was being because the car was really just a beat-up old rattletrap, but it belonged to her now, and she wanted to be sitting in it again, alongside Bud, and they would talk, and they would clear this all up, and she would explain what had happened and how . . .

"Recognize it?" he asked.

"Yes. Oh, yes," she said.

The car was parked beneath an old tree heavy with leaves. Very little light filtered down through the thick foliage. There was only a mottled lacelike tracing of pale silver on the roof of the car. He opened the door for her, and she climbed in, feeling comfortable at once in the car, leaning over from habit to open the door for him on the other side. He hesitated outside the car for a moment, taking off his hat and flipping it onto the back seat. There was something strangely impatient about the gesture, and a momentary frown puckered her brow, and then he bent, and the frown vanished, and he was inside the car beside her, and she heard the door slam, shutting out the night.

He reached for her instantly.

His fingers caught at her shoulders, and then he pulled her toward him, and she felt herself shaking her head, and then his mouth came down on hers, and the kiss was cruel, a grinding kiss that hurt her mouth. Her lips were not ready for his kiss. Her mind and her body were not ready for this yet.

She pulled back from him, shocked, her eyes wide.

"Bud—" she started, wanting to talk. Couldn't he see that there was so much to say, so much time to span with words before . . .

"What's the matter?" he asked. "Do you want to take off your lipstick?"

The words were familiar to her, very familiar, and their familiarity was as jarring as his kiss had been. She couldn't answer him for a moment. She sat staring at him, speechless when there was so much to say, her hands folded in her lap, her body stiff.

"Come on," he said.

"No, I—" She shook her head—"no."

"What's the matter?"

She was suddenly cold all over. She began shivering, and she hoped her teeth would not rattle. He moved toward her again.

"Helen?"

"What?" she asked dully.

"What's the matter?"

"I don't know."

"Aren't you glad to see me?"

"Yes. Yes, Buddy, you know that. Buddy, can't we . . . ?"

His arms were around her again. She saw his face above her, and then the face blurred, and she turned away, avoiding his kiss, and he drew back, surprised again.

"You want to go somewhere else?" he asked.

"No."

"Then what is it?"

"Bud, this isn't . . . isn't what I want." The words would not move out of her throat. She swallowed. "I wanted us to . . . to . . ." How could she explain to him? Couldn't he see, didn't he know? Didn't he know that this was all wrong, that this would solve nothing?

"Helen," he said, "my ship won't be in drydock long. After that, God knows where the navy'll send us. Just because the war is over doesn't mean they're going to let us all out tomorrow, you know. Hell, it might be another year yet. So . . ."

She turned her face away from him and then began shaking her head, and he changed his tack instantly, and she recognized the falseness of his new approach, and her ears were dead to it even before it gained full momentum.

"I've thought about you a lot, Helen."

"Really?" she said, the pain in her heart and in her mind, almost unable to bear his words because she knew they were false and she wanted them so desperately to be true.

"All the time. Aboard ship, in strange towns. I've always thought about you, and . . . and what we had together, and what a jackass I was. Helen, I was just a kid then. I know better now. I know the things that matter now."

For a moment she believed him. She looked up, and her eyes were bright with the effort of believing, and her experience with Andy rushed up into the throat, burned there, begged to be told, and she said, "Really, Bud?"

"Sure, honey," he said smoothly, pressing his advantage. "Come on, Helen. Come on." He slid over on the seat, and he pulled her toward him roughly.

Her eyes lost their luster. "Bud," she said slowly, "sometimes I wonder if you'll ever grow up."

"What?"

"Bud, will you do me a favor?"

"Anything."

"Go back to your ship, whenever you have to go back, and forget about meeting me here tonight, will you? Will you do me that one little favor? Pretend—"

"I don't want to pre—"

"Pretend it was all over just when we thought it was all over, last spring outside Club Beguine. Do you remember that night, Bud? Bud, forget we ever knew each other, forget our paths ever crossed, can you do that for me? Just forget you ever knew anyone named Hel—"

"I don't ever want to forget you."

"Bud, Bud—"

"Why do you want me to do that?"

"Just do it, please."

"Are you drunk, Helen?"

"No, I'm not drunk."

"Then why don't we take a little ride and—"

"I don't want a little ride, Bud. That's not what I want."

"Then what do you want? Name it, Helen, and I'll get it for you."

"Oh, Bud, please," she said impatiently.

"What have I done wrong?" he said plaintively, as if he couldn't understand why his careful approach had failed.

"Go back to your ship, Bud."

"All right, I will. But what about the meantime?"

"There is no meantime."

"Why not?"

"Bud, for God's sake, stop it! Stop it before I start bawling all over your pretty blue jumper. Please!"

"What?"

"Oh, nothing! Goddammit, you're the stupidest male I've ever met."

"What did I—"

"Bud, Bud, Bud, please shut up, please. Please."

"I thought this was going to be a happy reunion," he said. "So many months since we've seen each other, and instead—"

"You thought—"

"Instead you treat me like dirt. Well, I guess I know when I'm not welcome."

"I guess you do," she said tiredly.

"I'm not saying I understand you, Helen. Mind you, I'm not saying that. I thought—"

"I know what you thought."

"Well—"

"You thought all you had to do was crook your little finger. And then all the hurt, and all the misunderstanding, and everything, everything would just disappear. We'd kiss and make up, just like the song says. Well, Bud, the song is wrong. You can't do it that way. It's no good that way. Bud, can't you see that we have to—"

"Helen, you just don't understand me," he said.

"I understand you fine, Bud." She paused for a long time. "Do what I asked you to, will you? Forget all about it."

"I don't want to forget all about it."

"Then write to me. When you get back to your ship,

write to me. I'll be waiting for you to grow up. I want to be around when you grow up."

"I'll be nineteen next month," he said defensively.

"A man," she said.

"Look—"

"Write to me."

"Sure," he said dully. "A lot of hell good writing to you is gonna do."

"It might do a lot of good," she answered. "Come on, Tony is getting lonely."

She stepped out of the car, not waiting for him, not looking back. She heard his door slam viciously. She stopped then, not knowing why she was stopping. He came up to her, and she stood before him, looking up at him. She reached up and touched his cheek gently, and her eyes were sadly puzzled, and she said, "It's such a shame, Bud," and he didn't know what she meant.

Tony was half crocked when they reached him. He handed the near-empty pint to Bud, and Bud tilted it to his mouth savagely, drinking until Helen took the bottle away from him. She put it to her own mouth and almost drained it in a single swallow.

"This is a good night to get drunk," she said. "Let's have some beer, too. What do you navy boys call it, Tony? A boilermaker, isn't it?"

"Boilermakersh!" Tony bellowed.

He staggered over to the beer keg with Helen, and they drew two glasses and then poured the remainder of the whisky into the beer. Bud watched them for a while and then asked the piano player if he could sit in, and the piano man—anxious to dance with a brunette who'd been ogling him all night—hastily relinquished the stool.

Helen and Tony came to the bandstand in the middle of the set.

Bud looked down from the piano, and Tony said, "We leavin', mate."

Bud's face did not change. His eyes shifted from Tony's to Helen's, but his face did not change. She watched him carefully, wanting him to say something, wanting him to say the words that would make everything all right, wanting him to tell her he understood now.

"Good night," he said.

"I'm takin' Helen home," Tony said. "You wanna come along?"

"No," Bud said. "I'll stick around here."

"Bud?" Helen said.

"Yeah?"

"C'mon, Helen," Tony said. "Le'sh go."

"Bud, write to me."

"Sure," he answered, and then he turned back to the keyboard.

22

This was Wednesday.

This was three days since Andy had invaded Bud's apartment, one day since he'd taken any drugs. One day since yesterday morning, and yesterday morning he'd been left alone with a deck of heroin and a syringe. One day, and more than two months since he'd attended that party at which he'd "blown out his brains."

He had stuck to his promise. He had sworn avidly before Helen and Bud, and he had not touched another drop, and he had not even sought the drug, and Bud could see the toll he was paying for his abstinence.

It had not been easy to live with Andy Silvera. Andy Silvera was a sick man, sick with the physical torment of withdrawal, sick with the memory of the drug still etched on his mind. Bud had not managed any studying the night before. It was impossible to study with Andy around. But this was Wednesday, and Wednesday carried a test, and the test was at 2 P.M. this afternoon.

This was Wednesday, and the walls of the apartment had closed in the night before, like the spiked walls in a neighborhood movie serial, wedging Andy and Bud closer together, biting at them. It was not easy to cater to an invalid —yes, damnit, *an invalid*—when you had your own worries, and Bud was seriously worried about his tests now. He had flunked one, flunked it in heroic proportions, and the next one hung over his head like a hatchet ready to descend. Sometime during the long night he had hit upon a plan. He would go to the school library this morning and cram for the afternoon test. It would be quiet there, and perhaps he could stuff enough knowledge into his head to rate a passing grade. The library opened at nine, and he would be there when the doors swung wide. But first he had to wash and dress and catch a quick breakfast. He began doing these things, starting with his shoes and socks while Andy kept up a running monologue, while the hatchet swayed dizzyingly above him. The hatchet owned a very keen blade. The hatchet was in the hands of Andy Silvera.

"Why can't I play some records, Bud?"

"It's too early in the morning," Bud said.

"Why do you have to shout at me?"

"I wasn't shouting. Andy, for Christ's sake, go back to bed, will you? I'm taking a test today, and I've got studying to do, and I'm trying to organize some sort of study plan in my mind. So just, please, please, stop the babbling."

"Why can't I play the records?"

"Jesus, if you mention those records one more time . . . Look, Andy, go back to sleep. You can sleep all morning. I won't be here. You can sleep then or play records or practice your horn, or whatever you want. But just relax now, will you? What the hell's wrong with you, anyway?"

"I'm all right."

"Then try to calm down."

"Sure, calm down. I can't calm down. I feel lousy, if you want to know. I feel as if I want to . . . to bang my head against the wall or something. It wasn't like this last time. Last time it was bad, but not like this. I . . . I feel all . . . all . . ." He paused and shook his head. "My eyes are burning."

"Lay down then. Go to sleep. I've got to dress. Andy, I can't flunk this exam!"

"I want to listen to some records."

"How can you—"

"Don't argue with me. I'll kill you, you bastard! I swear to God, I'll kill you if you argue with me."

"Now just a minute. Let's just—"

"I'm sorry. Sorry. I shouldn't have said that. This headache, this—"

"Take an aspirin."

"I took four already."

"There's some empirin-codeine in the medicine chest. You can—"

"That's what I took. But I still have the headache. Why should I have a headache like this? I didn't have a headache last time. Why should I have a headache now?"

"Have you been vomiting?"

"Yes. I got up twice last night."

"Maybe your stomach's empty. Maybe you should eat."

"I'm not hungry."

"How do you know? Why don't you try? Take some coffee or something."

"All right, a little coffee maybe."

"If you put it up now, maybe I can have a fast cup before I go."

"All right, some coffee."

"And look, can we knock off the chatter until I get out of this place? I'm trying to think, Andy, believe me. I'm not making a big thing out of nothing. I've got to tackle this or I'll fall flat on my—"

"Oh, who the hell cares whether or not you flunk!"

"It doesn't matter what you—"

"I shouldn't have said that either. I should care. I should care whether or not you flunk. Jesus, my head is splitting. Where's the coffee?"

"In the kitchen cabinet."

"I'll make some coffee. Maybe that'll help. Did you say you wanted some?"

"If you can deliver it fast."

"All right, I'll make some coffee."

Bud buckled his belt and went into the bathroom. He turned on the tap, and Andy followed him, standing in the doorway.

"Is this apartment damp or something?" he asked.

"Damp?" Bud said. "What do you mean?"

"Damp, damp! Jesus, do I have to spell out everything? What does damp mean if not damp? Moist, wet, clammy, damp! How else can you say damp? Don't you know what damp means?"

"I know what damp means," Bud said, wearily picking up a bar of soap.

"Well, is it or isn't it?"

"No, it isn't. Why?"

"I've got this aching in my bones. I feel pain all over."

Bud began soaping his face. "That's the drug." He spat into the sink. "That's leaving the drug."

"Then why didn't I feel this way last time?"

"I don't know. I thought you were going to make some coffee."

"I am. Where is it?"

"I told you. In the kitchen cabi—"

"I'm going to take another one of those pills. All right?"

"Sure."

Bud threw open the cabinet with a soapy hand. He reached for the empirin-codeine bottle and handed it to Andy.

"I've got to knock this headache out some way. It's banging my head apart. *Gong, gong,* inside my head, like a goddamn crew of riveters. I've got to beat this headache."

He shook two of the tablets onto the palm of his hand. "I need a glass of water."

"Jee-sus Christ!" Bud exploded.

"What's the matter?"

"Nothing! Nothing at all! I'm trying to wash so I can get out of this place! Goddamnit, can't you go into the kitchen? There're a hundred glasses there. You can take any damn one you like! You can use twelve of them if you want to."

"All right, don't get excited."

"You're enough to—"

"Just don't get excited. It's not my fault I've got a headache."

Andy left and went into the kitchen. Bud rinsed his face. He heard the water tap going in the kitchen, and then Andy's voice calling, "Where's the coffee?"

"In the cabinet," Bud said patiently. He shook the water from his hands and took a towel from the rack. There was a peculiar odor to the towel. He sniffed it it, recognized the smell of vomit and quickly threw the towel into the hamper. He took a fresh one from the shelf, squeezed his eyes shut tightly and began drying his face. When he took the towel from his eyes, Andy was standing in the doorway again.

"I'll use this pot. All right?"

"Use any damn pot you like," Bud said.

"If I'm bothering you, I'm sorry. I'm awfully sorry, but you haven't got the headache I've got, and your joints don't ache all over. Someday you ought to try this, if you think it's any fun."

"I didn't say it was fun," Bud answered, taking his toothbrush from the rack.

"I can read it all over that haughty smug face of yours," Andy said. "What the hell have you got to be so proud of, anyway? You're sucking money out of the government, and you think——"

"Listen, this is still my house. If you don't like it, you can damn well leave!"

"You think I'm crazy about this dump? I've slept in better flophouses in the worst cities in America! What the hell do you think you've got here, a palace?"

"Nobody said——"

"You make me sick. You think you're a big shot, don't you. Just because you took in a friend, just because you're allowing me the extreme pleasure of sharing this dump with you. Well, get off that kick, Dick. Stop patting yourself on the back for something any goddamn human being would do!"

"Sure," Bud said. "I see everybody scrambling to take you in. I see the mad rush in the street outside. There's a real riot scene down there, everybody dying to lend Andy a helping hand."

"No, not everybody," Andy said.

"Not *anybody*, if you want to know the truth!" Bud snapped. "Not a living soul but Bud Sucker Donato!"

"It kills you to be doing this, doesn't it?" Andy said. "It just tears the living guts out of you. When's the last time you helped anybody but yourself, Big Heart? When's the last time you gave a thought to anything but that own miserable hide of ours?"

"Look, Andy, cut it out. I don't have to take this kind of crap from anybody, least of all you!"

"Why least of all me? What am I, some kind of cockroach that crawled out of the closet? Look at me, you bastard! Put down the toothbrush and look at me!"

Bud turned wearily.

"What am I, some kind of germ or something? Just because I'm an addict? What makes you any better than me? I'm a human being, too! You son-of-a-bitch, you *owe* me this apartment!"

Bud's eyes opened wide. "I owe you this apartment? I owe it to you! Jesus Christ, that takes the——" He stopped suddenly. "Are you still harping on that three hundred you lent me? Is that what gives you the idea? I paid you back, pal, in spades."

"I wasn't even thinking of the loot. You've got a real

high-type mind, College Boy. You're concerned with a hell of a lot, all right. You're concerned with Bud Donato, and that's all, and everybody else be damned, everybody else can go to hell."

"And you can lead the parade," Bud said heatedly.

"Sure, and you'll be waiting there to greet us. And you won't give a thought as to why you're there. You'll think you're there, man, because you flunked a Milton exam. You won't even suspect the real reason."

"And what *is* the real reason, mastermind?"

"Because you don't know why you owe me this apartment. You don't know why, and brother I bleed for you."

"All right, I owe you the apartment. Go make the coffee. I want to brush my teeth."

"Sure, brush your teeth. And brush the taste out of your mouth while you're at it. You must be one hell of a guy to live with, all right. How'd you manage it all these years? I can barely stand it, and I've only been here three days."

"You can leave whenever you like."

"Sure. You'd just love that, wouldn't you? That would make things simple again, wouldn't it? You'd have nothing to worry about then. You wouldn't have to settle up with anybody, not even with yourself. You'd tell yourself you offered your hand, and it was bitten. But I'm not leaving, Bud. I'm staying right here. I'm staying because you *owe* me a place to stay."

"All right, all right, we're all human beings, and I owe you—"

"No, we're *special* human beings, you bastard! Somewhere back there we touched hands, and we touched minds, and we crossed lives. And maybe you can write that off the way you'd write off a bad debt, but you can't do it if you've got something in *here*." He thumped his chest suddenly. "You owe something to every goddamn human being on earth, but you owe more to those you singled out."

Bud put down the toothbrush and stared at Andy, startled by his sudden passion.

"That's what," Andy said, trembling. "That's what."

"Sure," Bud said. "Go make the coffee."

"In one ear and out the other. Mustn't let common sense filter in among all those notes for calculus, must we? Keep it all clear and clean for the important things in life, the college courses. Forget all about what you owe *people!* Hell, everybody else has forgotten it, why be any different?"

"Look, Andy—"

"You make me sick. Just shut up and leave me alone, will you? I'll be out of here as soon as I land that job, and then you can—"

"Amen," Bud said.

"Don't vilify it, crumb," Andy said, and he went back into the kitchen.

Bud began brushing his teeth. He could still smell the vomit in the bathroom, and the vomit made him feel suddenly ill, that and what Andy had said. What the hell had he meant? *Touched hands, touched minds, crossed lives.* Everybody crosses his life with someone else's. That was nonsense, pure nonsense. Then why does it upset me? Well, it shouldn't upset you. You're doing all you can, aren't you? You've given the rotten bum an apartment, haven't you? Are you supposed to hold his hand for him now? What does he want you to do, hold him over the bowl when he vomits, the way Helen . . .

Yes, Helen did that.

Yes.

But who wants the smell of vomit on his hands? Who wants the smell of it in his house? Who wants Andy here, and *what* do I owe him, what the hell do I owe him? We walked out of each other's lives, we left it all behind a long time ago, I'm not responsible for him any more, I never was responsible for him, you don't *have* to be responsible for anyone else, why should you be, who the hell says you have to be?

What are you supposed to do, what the hell are you supposed to do? Throw everything over for somebody else? Forget you yourself exist, is that what he's asking me to do? Who's coming today? Who'll be with him while I'm gone? Helen, Carol? No. He'll . . . he'll be alone. But he won't go back to it, he won't, and what do I care, why should I give a damn, these tests are important, I'll get out of school next year, and if not that, what? The semester afterwards. But what if Andy flunks out? There's no semester afterwards for him, there's the same semester, year in and year out, if he flunks out, he won't flunk out, *hands touched, minds touched, lives crossed.* Why don't people touch each other? Except shaking hands. You shake hands, and you say, *I am touching you, we are friends.* You only touch friends. If you accidentally touch a stranger in the subway, she calls a cop if she's a woman, and he punches you in the nose if he's a man. Hands do not touch enough, and eyes do not meet enough, Jesus, but what am I supposed to do? Jesus, why did he have to come here, why did he have to pick on me? Because we were friends, and our hands touched, sure, put it in poetry, Andy, put it in powdery language and it sounds good as hell, but who's going to take those tests for me? Who's going to see everything he worked for shot to hell?

He walked out of the bathroom. He began putting on his shirt, and he looked at his watch. He still had a little time. It seemed like such a long morning all at once. He walked into the kitchen. Andy was standing near the stove watching the heating water. "Andy," he said.

"Yes?"

"You . . . you should practice your horn a little. You . . . you haven't picked it up since you got here." That was not what he wanted to say. He didn't know what he wanted to say.

"I don't feel like practicing," Andy said. "I feel . . . lazy. And my eyes burn. How can I read music if my eyes burn?"

"Well, you know, if you keep making excuses—"

"All right," Andy said wearily, "I'm making excuses. I tell you my eyes burn. All right, that's an excuse. This headache is an excuse, too. My whole life is an excuse. I'll bet I have a fever. You want to bet I've got a fever? Have you got a thermometer?"

"In the bathroom," Bud said gently.

"I'll bet I've got a fever. Goddamnit, you think I'm clowning around, but you never tried dropping heroin, did you? Well, this is the worst it'll ever get. Where'd you say that thermometer was?"

"In the bathroom."

"How much do you want to bet I've got a fever?"

"I don't want to bet."

"You're chickenhearted, you bastard. I'll get the thermometer. I'll show you."

He went out into the bathroom and rummaged around in the medicine chest. When he came back into the kitchen, he was shaking down a thermometer.

"Don't you ever have any steam in this dump?"

"Steam? In May?"

"I'm chilly."

"I thought you had a fever."

"I'll bet I have, but I feel chilly, too. Maybe the coffee'll warm me up." He went over to the stove, still shaking down the thermometer. "Won't it ever boil? Jesus."

He put the thermometer into his mouth. He paced nervously, clinching and unclenching his hands.

"You'd better sit down," Bud said. "If you haven't got a fever, you'll raise one that way."

Andy ignored him. He continued to pace, and then he mumbled around the thermometer, "Y'iming this?"

"You've got two minutes to go."

"Eesus."

"This quiet is wonderful," Bud said, smiling. Andy didn't answer him.

" 'R mush longer?"

"You can take it out now," Bud said.

Andy took the thermometer from his mouth and studied the numbers on it. "There, what'd I tell you?" he shouted triumphantly. "A hundred point five. Is that a fever, or isn't it?"

"Shall we get a doctor?"

"No, this is cold turkey, friend, that's what it is. There ain't a doctor in the world can help me. Dammit, why don't they give you any steam?"

"Maybe the coffee'll help you. I think we can pour it now."

"My back hurts," Andy said. "Listen, aren't you chilly? Do we have to have that window open?"

"No, not if you don't want it."

Andy went to the window and closed it. Bud began shoveling coffee into the cups. "I've still got the chills," Andy said. "They should give you steam when it's cold outside."

"It's not cold outside. It's a lovely day."

"Then why the hell am I shaking all over?"

"Maybe you've got malaria," Bud said, smiling.

"Ha-ha, very funny," Andy said. "Jesus, I'm itchy." He scratched his arm violently, and then he studied the area and held his arm out to Bud. "Look at this, will you? A bump! Right under the skin. Jesus!" He opened the throat of his shirt and looked down at his chest. "I've got the damn things all over me! Goddamnit, I've itched before, but this is the worst yet."

"Come on, take your coffee." Bud sat at the table and looked at his watch again.

"Even my back aches from this headache, would you believe it? I can feel it right through here, and all through my body, pound, pound, pound. If I get through this, I'll never look at another ounce of heroin as long as I live. This is murder, pure unadulterated murder. Why should I have it so bad, huh? It was only a sixteenth I shot up, and now it's like I'm going cold turkey from scratch. Is that fair? I put in a week off the stuff, didn't I? So I shoot a little, and now there's hell to pay, my arms and legs aching as if I've got rheumatism, and my back, and my damn eyes burning me, and this rotten headache. Is that fair, should a guy have to suffer this much for a lousy sixteenth? I'd rather have syphilis, I swear to God."

"Maybe you've got a little cold," Bud said.

"I always have a cold. Addicts always have colds, didn't you know that? But this isn't a cold, man. This is cold *turkey*, that's what this is, and a son-of-a-bitch it is, too, This shouldn't happen to your worst enemy. This shouldn't happen to *me*, that's for sure."

He sat at the table, picked up his cup, and took a sip. "Oh, you lousy son—"

"What's the matter?" Bud said.

"It's too hot. I can't swallow it. I can't—"

"Maybe you've got a sore throat."

"My throat does feel sore," Andy said, "but, oh, Jesus, is this hot!"

"Then don't drink it," Bud said.

"I'll vomit if I drink it, anyway," Andy answered. "What's happening to me? Why should I have this hell? Isn't it enough that I've seen the light? What is this? My punishment? Can't a man go off the junk without losing his mind? Oh, my head, my ever-loving head, it's going to bust right in two. Do you think my fever has gone up?"

"I don't know."

"How will this day ever end? How will this goddamn day ever pass?"

"It'll pass," Bud said.

"I'm going out of my mind." He scratched himself again, digging at his flesh. "Don't sit there and watch me."

"I wasn't watching you."

"I'm going to take another of those pills," Andy said. He put down his cup and walked into the bathroom. Bud heard the cabinet door open, and then the water running, and then the water being turned off suddenly. He glanced at his watch. It was time to go. He went into the living room and took a jacket from the closet. Andy was coming out of the bathroom, his eyes wide.

"My . . . my skin," he said. "Look at my skin."

"What's the matter with it?"

"Can't you see it?"

"It looks fine to me." He shrugged into the jacket.

"It's . . . it's yellow," Andy said. "Like . . . like I've been taking opium. *Jesus, my skin is turning yellow!*"

Bud looked at him carefully. "It is a little yellow."

"Jesus, I haven't taken opium in . . . Jesus, does H do it, too? I . . . I don't feel so good, Bud. I . . . I'd better lay down. Jesus, my skin is turning yellow. Oh, my God, my skin is turning yellow."

"Rest a while," Bud said. "Come on." He took Andy to the made-up sofa, waited until he was comfortable, and then started for the door. "I'll see you later," he said.

Andy nodded. "Oh, my back," he said. "Oh, Jesus, this is murder!"

And then, despairingly, he said, "I wish I was dead."

23

Andy watched the door close.

He was alone.

It was very good to be alone. The idea of being alone

excited him. There was no one to watch him now, no one to snap at him and yell at him, no one to see. He was alone, and that was how he wanted to be, and yet the apartment was deathly still and ominously bleak, and he dreaded his aloneness while relishing it. *Alone,* he thought. *Alone.* He rubbed his fists into his eyes.

His eyes burned very badly now. His body ached as if someone had spread him on a medieval torture rack. He could feel the aching, and the burning of his eyes, and the headache, and the itching, and the words "cold turkey" rushed through his mind over and over again until he could almost see the plucked turkey hanging in a butchershop, stripped of everything but its flesh, naked to the world.

He was naked to the world.

He had thrown it all away, all of it, and now he was naked to the world, trying to wipe the slate clean, and it seemed in his aloneness that he would never wipe it clean, never in a million years, never in a million light-years. He was alone and naked, and he was sick. And he knew why he was sick.

He was sick because he'd taken a shot, and now there was nothing else to take. He was sick, and he was very low. He was so low he had to reach up to tie his shoelaces. There was a real monkey on his back, and, gee, ain't that a jazzy way of saying it, real gone, a little organ grinder's monkey in a sharp red jacket perched on his back. How clever, how George, these hopheads sure know how to put things, hey!

But it's not a monkey, kid, it's not a cute little organ grinder's monkey at all. There's no tambourine involved here, kid, and you don't feed this monkey with pennies left over from an ice-cream soda, kid, because he's not a monkey at all.

He's a gorilla.

I don't know if you know very much about gorillas, kid. Gorillas aren't very friendly animals, not my gorilla. I tell you the truth, I don't know anything about the African variety of gorilla, I only know the New York variety, the kind who is on my back. He's not friendly at all. He gets angry as hell for no good reason, and he's liable to rip you all to pieces with his sharp teeth and sharp claws if you don't feed him.

And it costs a lot of money to feed this gorilla of mine.

He's got a special-type diet, and there are men trained to prepare his food, and they'll give you all the food you want —provided you have the money. You *have* to have the money because this gorilla, he's pretty attached to you, you know. He's right there on your back, and he's very heavy, not like an organ grinder's monkey at all. He's so heavy that sometimes you think you'll fall flat on your face from carrying him, flat to the sidewalk, and he'll still be on your back, smelling of gorilla sweat, smothering you with his jungle breath. He never gets off your back. He sits there with his sharp little fangs, and he looks almost human, this gorilla of mine, but he's not human at all, he's the most inhuman beast there is.

And he gets so hungry, so very goddamned hungry, and when he begins to bellow for his food, dad, you've got to go out and get the loot. It doesn't matter how you get it. You can hock everything but your shoes, and you can hock those, too, the gorilla doesn't care. He hears those fellows out in the kitchen banging their dishes, and he knows they're mixing up his lunch, and he's so goddamned hungry that his stomach is aching. If you've got nothing to hock, he doesn't care about that either, because this gorilla, you understand, he doesn't think like everyday human beings do. He's not a person, you know, he's just a jungle beast, so he doesn't know about hocking things, and he doesn't care, so long as he eats. So if you've got nothing to hock, you steal. If you have a gorilla, I can guarantee that you will steal. You will steal, and you will mug, and you will roll, and you will mingle with the scum of the earth, you will do anything to feed that gorilla because he is the boss and not you.

He is giving the orders. And he only wants to eat.

I wish I had known all about gorillas a long time ago. I wish I had known because then I wouldn't ever have wanted one for a pet. Of course, gorillas have little brothers, and the little brothers could be called monkeys, and maybe that's what you had in mind, kid, the little monkeys called reefers. They are cute as hell, kid, I'll admit that. These little reefer monkeys are just so adorable you could squeeze them to death. And they don't hurt you, do they? No, not much. So go ahead. Have one.

And kid, you are meeting the gorilla family. Kid, you are having a grand-scale introduction. You are on the way to mainlining it. Kid, you are getting hooked, kid, because you are not chicken and because you are not afraid of cute little monkeys. And once you're hooked, your worries are over. You're just not a person any more.

When you're hooked, you're dead.

It takes a lot of guts to make yourself dead, kid, more guts than you think, more guts than you were thinking of when you grabbed that cute little bammie. When you are dead, there is nothing but heroin. There's a big H written across the sky, and that's all there is. H, and it doesn't stand for heroin, it stands for Hell.

There's nothing brave about being in Hell. There's nothing brave about it at all. And you won't think you're being brave, you won't think of anything, you will only think of H. And all the advantages of being alive will simply disappear because there's nothing to your death but H. You will eat it, and drink it, and sleep it, and think it. And nothing else. You will not want a girl, or car, or clothes, or movies, or beaches, or talk, or music, or anything but H. That is it. You will slowly and surely and without doubt sink into the gutter with your gorilla on your back.

There is *shit* in the gutter, my friend.

And the man who feeds your gorilla will drag you face first through the shit, and if you like the taste of human excrement, then being dead is for you. Being dead is wanting, wanting, wanting.

You will wake up wanting heroin and go to bed wanting it, if you go to bed. You will always and ever want it, and there will be no other thought in your mind but heroin. There will be a single purpose to your life, and your every waking minute is devoted to that purpose, and that doesn't leave time for anything else, not even thinking about anything else, it does not leave time for anything but H, there aren't enough hours in a day, you are married to H, you are married to death, you are married to the fat bastards who are eating steaks in fancy restaurants on the nickels and dimes and pennies you scraped up for them, the loot you dug up to feed your gorilla.

You are a sucker, my friend.

So come on. Get brave!

He lay on the bed and stared up at the ceiling. He needed something.

No, he thought, I don't!

I'm through being a sucker, I'm through with it all, but, Jesus, I need something. He rose abruptly and went to the record player. The hell with Buddy-boy, he thought. The hell with him and his goddamn orders, I'm playing these records, and if he doesn't like it, he can stuff it. He put the Kenton album on the turntable and then turned the volume up full. The music slammed into the apartment and he felt suddenly better. He listened to the moody brass of "Concerto to End All Concertos," and he found himself moving his lips with the horns, tonguing with them, going through the motions. I can think better now, he thought. I can think better with all this sound around me, you have to have music around you, music makes a nice high wall, and you can add to the wall when you're blowing. A big fat wall, especially when it's loud, and Christ it is loud this morning, blast away, Stan!

He walked to the window, the sound all around him. He touched the pane of glass and felt the vibration of sound, and then he closed his eyes and tried to read the sound with the tips of his fingers, like a blind man. The music was very loud, and within the music, like a bleak hollow core, he felt lonely and deserted.

I'll never break it, he thought. I'm kidding myself. I'll never break it, and I know it. I died a long time ago, and now I'm just going through the motions. I died a long while back, and I slammed my own coffin lid shut the day I hocked my horn, and you don't come back from the dead.

He looked down at the street, feeling more misery than he had ever known. There seemed nothing left, nothing whatever. He was alone in a vast directionless land, and he was lost, and there was nothing left for him anywhere, because now that he knew he wanted to break the habit, he knew with equal conviction that he would never break it. And knowing this, he stared down at the street, thinking, I am dead, I am a dead man.

He saw the people below him, moving on the sidewalk, and the new thought popped into his mind.

Why not?

If I am already dead, then why not, why not?

It must be nice to be *really* dead.

The apartment reverberated with sound now, and he wondered about the stillness of death, was it really as still as they pretended it was, could anything really be that still, so quiet that there was no sound whatever, not the sound of breathing, not the sound of a pin dropping, not the sound of a feather shifting, an empty soundless space of white, soft white.

They put you in the ground, he thought.

Of course, they put you in the ground, and there's the rub. There are dead people on your right and on your left, and sometimes even above you, but if death is quiet and peaceful and non-feeling, then what difference does it make where they bury you or with whom? And even if there are people you don't like, there are people you don't like in life as well, so what difference does it make if only you can lay down and rest, and get rid of all the aches and pains, and the burning eyes, and the vomiting—and the wanting.

And you can kick the habit then, all right.

You can kick it because death is the Big Fix, the fix you never come down from. Christ, but dead men are lucky. They can have a platter of hoss right in front of them and a mile-high syringe, but they won't be tempted, they'll be only content. God, what is it like to be content? Can you be content that way? If you are dead, really dead, not the death of drug addiction, but really, really dead, does everything else stop? Is there just a hush, and a softness, and a restful peace you have never known before?

Oh, God, it must be terrific!

Oh, God, if I could only . . .

A knock sounded on the door. The knock annoyed him, and he frowned, and then he shouted over the noise of the record player, "Who is it?"

He heard a muffled answer from the other side of the door, but the voice made no sense.

"What do you want?" he shouted, becoming angrier. He crossed the room and went to the door, and then he shouted, "Who is it?" at the wood.

"Mr. Donato?"

"He's not here," Andy said. "Go away!"

"I want to talk to him," the voice insisted.

"Just a minute, just a minute," he said impatiently. He unlocked the door then and opened it.

A frumpy woman was standing outside the door. She wore a faded housedress and old house slippers. Her hair hung loosely on her forehead, as if it had been placed on her head haphazardly, like an old brown felt hat. She looked Andy over from head to toe and said, "Where's Mr. Donato?"

"He's not here," Andy said. "What do you want?"

"Who are you?" the woman asked.

"I'm his friend. What do you want?"

"I'm the landlady here," the woman said. "What are you doing in Mr. Donato's apartment?"

"I came to burglarize it," Andy snapped, and when he saw the woman's mouth pop open, he quickly added, "I told you I'm a friend of his. I'm staying with him for a few days."

"Are you the one what's playing the records?" she asked.

"Yes," he said, "I am."

"Don't you have no sense? Person can't hardly hear herself think. Turn it off."

"What for?"

"Or turn it down, either one. I got tenants who are still asleep."

"It's time they were up," Andy said. He stared at her for several seconds, becoming very angry now, resenting her intrusion and her petty tyranny. "I like it loud."

"Now look here, young man," the landlady shouted over the roar of the record player. "I've never had no trouble with Mr. Donato, and I don't expect none from his friends. Now go in there and turn it down."

"Maybe you didn't understand me," Andy said tightly. "I said I like it loud."

"Well! Of all the—!" The landlady put her hands on her wide hips. Her face turned red, and she stared at Andy silently for several moments. Andy stared back coldly.

"Turn it down!" she said finally, spacing the words with cold even precision.

"Go to hell, you fat bitch!" Andy said, and he began to close the door in her face.

The landlady shoved the door back with a heavy arm.

Her brows shot down like angry falcons. Her eyes blazed. "I'll turn it down myself, snotnose!" she shouted, and she started into the room. Andy took her arm and swung her around.

"Stay out of here," he said. "Keep your nose out of here."

"Let go of me!" the landlady screamed.

Andy shoved her back through the open doorway. "Go back downstairs and hit the bottle, you hag," he said, and then he slammed the door.

"I'm calling the police!" she shouted. "You wait and see! I'm calling the police!"

"Call them!" he yelled at the closed door. He locked it and thought, Go ahead, call them. You rotten fat water sack! What are you trying to do, take even the records from me? Haven't you stripped enough from me already? What more do you want? Can't I even listen to music? Are you denying me that, too? What more do you want from me? What more?

Oh, Jesus, what's the use?

What's the use of even trying, why don't I just . . . Why don't I . . .

Yes, but . . .

He made up his mind in the flash of an instant.

It was almost as if he had been debating it all his life, and now he made up his mind, and he knew just what he was going to do, and he felt suddenly glad because in the directionless waste there had been presented a direction, a goal, and he hurried now to fulfill that goal.

He went into the bathroom, again as if the means had been decided a long, long time ago. He went directly to the medicine chest and opened it. He found Bud's razor, and he opened it and removed the single-edge blade, and he stood with the blade in his fingers for a long time, staring at its sharp cutting edge.

He looked up into the mirror over the sink then, staring at his reflection.

Yellow skin, yellow skin. Look at it. Jesus, look at it.

He shook his head and then he held out his wrist. The skin on his arm was a pale yellow, everything turning yellow, it didn't pay, it didn't pay.

He didn't want to get blood all over the floor.

He at least owed that to Bud. So where? Over the toilet bowl? Over the sink?

He threw back the shower curtain. Yes. Yes, that was the ticket. Turn on the shower, not too hot, not too cold, put the wrist under it, and then slash it. The water washes the blood down the drain, and everything is clean that way, and you don't even realize you're bleeding.

Quickly he turned on the cold-water faucet, and then he adjusted the hot water so that he got a lukewarm mixture.

Well, he thought, this is it.

Well.

He sat on the floor beside the tub. His mind was peculiarly blank. He put his left wrist under the water. The water was just right, perfect.

He looked at the sharp cutting edge of the razor blade in his right hand.

Slowly he put his right hand into the stream of water and brought the blade down toward the veins on his left wrist.

He should not have left Andy alone in the apartment.

Walking to the subway kiosk, he knew that. He knew that, and he almost turned and went back, but he didn't. There was studying to do.

Yes, studying.

Yes, studying, and the studying is important. I have to pass that test this afternoon. If I don't pass that test this aft — Stop rationalizing.

I'm not rationalizing. Nothing's going to happen to Andy. He's too shot to move. He went out and got some heroin on Monday, and he took it yesterday, and he feels lousy, and he's sworn to St. Peter and all the angels that he won't touch it again, and besides Helen chewed him out good, and besides Helen has the syringe. What difference does that make? He can go out and get another one, the same place he got the last one.

But he won't.

He simply won't, and there's no sense torturing yourself with what he'll do or what he won't do, because he isn't going to do anything. He's going to lay on that bed and look up at that ceiling, and in a little while he'll fall asleep.

And he looked shot enough to sleep through the whole day, if not the whole week, provided he doesn't have to vomit, in which case he'll go right back to bed afterward anyway.

So don't worry about Andy. You don't have to worry about Andy.

Andy can take care of himself.

Sure.

Oh, sure.

Andy can certainly take care of himself, all right—that should be obvious to anyone who has a pair of eyes. Andy has been taking care of himself for a good long time now, and Andy has done one fine job of it. Andy has descended to one level above the crawling reptiles. So it's obvious he can take care of himself.

He took care of himself fine yesterday.

He cut out of that apartment on Monday. He cut out and rounded up a bagful of heroin, and yesterday he took care of himself fine. All you have to do is leave Andy alone for a half hour, and he takes care of himself. On Monday he got the stuff and on Tuesday he shot it up. What's he going to do for an encore, poor bastard?

He's going to sleep.

Yes, that's what we keep telling ourselves in these parts, mister. That's what we keep trying to believe—that Andy is going to sleep like an innocent babe on a Daumier breast, but we can't rightly believe it, because the truth is we don't know what the hell Andy will do next.

And we don't care.

Well, that may sound a little callous. We do care, actually.

We just don't care very much.

There's a difference, you know. But *don't* we care very much? And if we don't care, why are we worrying about him? We aren't ten minutes from the apartment, and he's all we can think about, because we don't care what that poor tortured son-of-a-bitch is going to do next, and we *do* care, we do care what he does, we do!

I have to study, oh, God, I have to study, I can't worry about him.

He'll be all right.

He'll . . . be all right.

Bud slipped a dollar bill under the grilled window of the change booth and waited for his change. He pocketed all but a dime, inserted it in the slot, shoved through the turnstile, and went down to the platform.

The downtown express trains flashed by, loaded to the gunnels, carrying the workers crammed in like rolled anchovies. The uptown platform was not very crowded, but, as usual, the uptown train was a long time coming. He stood on the platform and watched the noisy express trains rumble past, and he tried not to think of Andy alone in the apartment. The platform was dim, a subterranean mole's hole stretching the length of Manhattan. He paced the platform impatiently, momentarily distracted when a pretty blonde in a tight silk dress descended the steps and walked to the gum machine. She put in her penny and then stooped over to pick up the gum that clattered into the receiving slot, and he watched the way the silk tightened across her firm buttocks, and then he turned away from her and thought about Andy again.

Nothing would happen, he was sure of that.

You had to place some trust in the guy or he'd begin to feel like a vegetable. You had to assume he now knew what he was doing and what he shouldn't be doing, and you had to express some faith or you'd defeat him from go. You had to assume he'd simply lie on that couch until he fell asleep. *I wish I was dead.*

What?

Hadn't he said that? Wasn't that what Andy had said? As I was leaving the apartment?

I wish I was dead.

A faulty use of grammar, lacking the subjunctive, I wish I *were* dead, were, was, the thought is the same, and the thought is suicidal.

Let's not leap to conclusions, my friend. Lots of people say I wish I were dead, but hardly anyone means it. I've said it many times myself, I wish I were dead, and I certainly didn't mean anything of the sort.

And Andy wasn't feeling so hot, the headache and all, so naturally that was the thing for him to say. A most natural thing to say. The same thing you or I or that blonde, Jesus, but she's stacked, would say under similar circumstances, not meaning a word of it, just an expression, just an old cliché, just a peculiar American colloquialism, nothing to it, hell, meant nothing at all.

But what is he going through right now, and does he feel it's worth while, and might he really contemplate suicide, and contemplating it, might he not actually attempt suicide, alone in the apartment, alone, Jesus, he's all alone and he said, *I wish I was dead.*

He heard the distant thunder of the approaching uptown train. The blonde walked close to the edge of the platform. At the other end of the station the red light turned green, and then the train came into view, its front lights piercing the blackness of the tunnel, The station rumbled as the train bore down on it. A newspaper lying on the platform flapped wildly and then was swept up against the trash basket. The blonde's tight skirt pressed against her thighs and her legs as the train swept into the station, drowning all sound with its roar. The doors slid open.

He hesitated on the platform.

The blonde had already entered the train. She sat and crossed her legs and then took a copy of *Baby and Child Care* from her purse.

The door was closing.

He reached out and caught at the rubber guard on the door. The door resisted him for a moment. He shoved it back and then slid into the car. The conductor pressed his button, and the train lurched out of the station.

He sat down and spotted John Front almost instantly. He turned sideways on the seat, trying to hide, but Front had already seen him, and there was nothing to do but sit it through. Front rose from his seat and staggered up the length of the lurching train, wearing his usual loud sports jacket, his usual wide enameled grin.

"Donato! Hey there, Donato!" he said, and he staggered up the aisle and plopped his ample buttocks into the seat alongside Bud.

"Hello, Front," Bud said.

"You got a test this morning?"

"No, this afternoon. I wanted to do some studying at the library."

"Best place in the world for it, fellow," Front said. "I've got a lulu at nine. History of the English Language. You ever take that course?"

"Yes," Bud said.

"You have that four-eyed bitch for it?"

"Altman?"

"That's the number," Front said. "I think I'll strangle her when the course is done with."

"Do that," Bud said.

"You think I won't? I could strangle her with my bare hands." Front clucked in sympathy with his own homicidal drives. "Grimm's Law," he said. "Pee on Grimm. He should have stuck to fairy tales."

"His brother Wilhelm twisted his arm," Bud said.

"Say, you're a regular font of knowledge, aren't you? What does b become?"

"What?"

"B. What does it become. P?"

"I don't remember."

He did not want to listen to Front. He had tried to shake the guilt of having left Andy alone in the apartment, and he could not do that, and now Front had come along, and he did not want to listen to him. He wanted to go back to the apartment. At the same time he realized his need for studying. He had to study. He had to get some quiet where he could study. The test was at two, and he had to cram until just about that time, a pattern in complete antithesis to his usual study habits, but any port in a storm. He had to study and he couldn't be worrying about Andy, but at the same time he felt this overwhelming urge to get back to the apartment. *I wish I was dead*, Andy had said. *Thanatopsis*. Stop relating everything to college-boy courses, stupid, if Andy kills himself it will have nothing whatever to do with a college education or a lack of same.

" . . . she can barely speak English herself. That's what gets me. She comes around with this Southern drawl, and she tries to explain the history of our language. Sometimes I think she was a contemporary of Grimm's. She's grim enough to be his sister. Hey, you get that, Donato?"

The train was pulling into another station. He wanted to get up, wanted to get out on the platform and then mount the steps and cross over to the downtown side. He wanted to do that, and he saw the faces of the people waiting on the platform as the train pulled in, and he heard the sound of Front's voice, and then the train shuddered to a stop, and the doors slipped open, and the people were getting aboard, and Front was saying, "D becomes th or some damn thing, so how the hell am I supposed to get it straight in my head when all her pronunciations sound like some sort of Southern molasses? I tell you, Donato—"

Bud rose suddenly. "See you, Front," he said, and he rushed for the doors.

"Hey!" Front shouted, and then the doors closed behind Bud, and Bud could no longer hear his fellow student's voice.

Up the steps and cross over, he thought.

Take too long. Should I grab a cab? Jesus, cab'll get caught in traffic. Why am I doing this anyway? Never mind why! Just do it. Hurry, hurry!

The phone. Call Andy. No, he won't answer. If he doesn't answer, I'll go crazy, not knowing what's going on. He may simply be sleeping, and if the phone rings it'll wake him. How about Carol? She works on the West Side. She can get there faster. What's her number? Where does she work? Think. What was the number Louise gave me? What was the name of the outfit? Come on, College Boy, apply your study methods to something practical. Think, think!

Benson. Benson something.

That was Carol's office. Benson what?

He spotted the phone booth, ran to it, and then began thumbing through the Manhattan directory. Benson, Benson, Benson and, Benson and . . . Benson and Parke! He traced his finger across the page, got the number, rushed into the booth, deposited a nickel, and dialed it.

"Benson and Parke, good morning."

"Miss Ciardi, please," he said.

"One moment." He waited, thinking, I've been through this before, this is *déjá vu.* I'm living through it all over again. This is what Hell is—living through endless phone calls and being channeled through hundreds of extensions—"*I don't know*"—and waiting for operators to look things up—"*That's extension fifty-one, sir*"—and then the ringing, and then . . .

"Bookkeeping."

"Miss Ciardi, please."

"This is Miss Ciardi."

"Carol?" He was confused for a moment. For a moment he didn't remember why he had called her, or what he wanted to say. "Carol, is that you?"

"Yes. Who—"

"This is Bud. Carol, I left him alone in the apartment. I know I shouldn't—"

"Buddy, why, why? Oh, Buddy, for God's sake, why'd you do that?"

"I'm going back there now, Carol. But it might take a while. Can you get over there?"

"I just got into the office," she said, almost to herself. Then, more strongly, "Yes, I'll go. Bud, you shouldn't have left him. You know that, don't you?"

"Yes, I know. Get over there, will you?"

"Yes, I'll leave right now."

"Good. I'll see you."

He hung up and glanced at his watch. He could hear a train approaching on the uptown side. He ran for the steps and then over the tracks descending on the other side just as the train pulled into the station.

24

The record player was going full blast when Bud arrived, and Carol was waiting in the hallway. She rushed to him as he mounted the steps.

"What's the matter?" he asked. "What happened?"

"I don't know. The door is locked, Bud. I knocked, and I shouted, but he's got the music up so loud . . . Bud, I thought I'd go out of my mind waiting for you. What do you suppose . . . do you think . . ."

"I don't know," he said. He took out his key hastily, and unlocked the door. The music assaulted the open doorway. "Andy?" he called.

There was no answer.

"Look in the kitchen," Bud said. "I'll take the bathroom." He crossed the living room, snapped off the machine, and then walked to the bathroom door. He tried the knob. The door was locked.

"Andy?"

In the sudden silence of the apartment he could hear the shower running behind the closed door. Why, sure, he thought. Hell, he's just taking a shower, that's all. Sure.

"Andy? This is Bud. Open up, will you?"

From beyond the closed door, all Bud heard was the steady drumming of the shower.

"Andy!"

"Go away," Andy said.

"Andy, what are you doing in there?"

"Go away."

"Andy, for Pete's sake . . ."

"Leave me alone," Andy said. His voice was very low, barely audible.

"You going to open this door, or do I break it in?" Bud asked.

Andy didn't answer.

"Andy?" Bud waited. "Andy, I'm going to break it in."

Carol was in the living room now. She stood beside Bud, her hand to her mouth.

"Okay, Andy," Bud said. "Okay." He backed off a few paces and then lurched forward, throwing his shoulder against the door. The door did not budge.

"Andy, goddamn it, open this door!"

He threw his shoulder at it again, and then he backed off, lifted his foot, and rammed the flat of his shoe against the lock. The lock snapped, and Bud stumbled forward, carried by the momentum of his push. He pulled himself up short against the sink, and then he saw Andy sitting on the floor near the tub, his hand under the shower.

"Andy, what the hell . . ."

Carol was behind him now. She looked over his shoulder, saw Andy, and then almost instantly saw the razor blade in his right hand. She opened her mouth and screamed, a piercing, penetrating scream that filled the small room with echoes.

"Oh, God," Bud said. He reached into the tub and turned off the shower.

"Go away," Andy said. "Leave me alone."

The razor blade in Andy's right hand was stained with blood. And now that the water had been turned off, Bud could see a thin, narrow red streak across Andy's left wrist.

"Is he . . . is he all right?" Carol asked. She kept the knuckles of her hand pressed tightly against her teeth. She was not crying. Her eyes were brimming, ready to let loose, but she staunchly held back the tears.

Bud looked at Andy's wrist. It didn't seem to be bleeding very heavily. He looked at the narrow line more closely.

"You won't die from that," Bud said. "You're lucky you're even bleeding." He felt suddenly let down. Even in suicide Andy had failed.

Andy looked up. His eyes seemed yellow now, too, the white stained against the deep brown pupils.

"Come on," Bud said, "let's tape that up." Disgustedly, he went to the medicine chest. "He barely got through the skin, Carol. He couldn't have borne down very hard."

Andy was crying. The tears began suddenly, and he made no effort to control them. "Can't even kill myself right," he said. "Have to foul up even that. Buddy, my head hurts. Buddy, I can hardly see my head hurts so much. And my eyes are burning, why'd I have to foul up, why should I have so much pain in my body?"

"Take it easy," Bud said. "We're going to get you a doctor. As soon as I tape up your wrist we're calling a doctor."

"No!" Andy said sharply. "No doctor! I don't want a doctor around here telling me what to do and what not to do. You call a doctor, and I'll kill you."

"Give me your wrist," Bud said calmly. He wadded the absorbent pad in place and then began taping the wrist.

"Bud, no doctor, please. I don't want a doctor. They don't understand, you follow me? Doctors, I mean. They don't know what's inside a man, they don't understand. No doctor."

"Andy," Bud said, "you need help."

"Call Helen then. Call her. She's been through this. She knows. Call her. Please."

"What's her number?" Carol asked.

She listened while he gave it to her, and then she went to the phone.

"Helen'll know what to do," Andy said. "Am I very hot? Bud, feel my head. Am I very hot?"

Bud put his palm on Andy's forehead. "You're hot," he said. "Do you want to take your temperature?"

"No, no. Must be all this excitement. Jesus, it looked like such a good idea. I mean, I really *wanted* to, do you know what I mean? I could just picture being dead, Jesus, it must be great, it must be great just to lay there and not have a goddamn—"

"Don't talk like that," Bud said sharply.

"I'm alive, ain't I? I goofed, didn't I? I slashed the blade across my wrist, and all I drew was a little blood. It seemed funny to me because I thought, Jesus, you should bleed more, you know? But I guess I was scared. I guess I didn't really slash away because I was scared death would . . . well, I don't know what I was really scared of, except, suppose . . . suppose it wasn't what I . . . well, how could you know, Bud? So when I drew that razor across my wrist, I guess I didn't push very hard. I didn't feel anything, would you believe it? I just saw the blood come out behind the razor and then the water was washing it away, and I thought, Good, you're going to die, and all the while I knew I wasn't really going to die, but the idea of dying was a good one, and so I tried to tell myself, Yes, you *are* going to die, all the while knowing differently, and all the while afraid that I *would* die because death, too . . . it might be . . . I don't know . . . I . . . oh, hell, there's nothing I can do right."

"You're shaking the habit," Bud said. "You're doing that right."

"Am I? Am I doing it right? I shot up yesterday, didn't I? That's some way to shake it, all right. And what happens when it gets rougher, like Helen said it would get? What do I do then? Slash my wrists whenever it gets rough? The funny part was I didn't even feel like taking a shot this morning. I was just laying here, and all of a sudden there didn't seem to be anything left for me, and I thought how great it would be to be dead, really dead. Why did I have to miss? Why couldn't I have done it the right way?"

"Shut up, Andy," Bud said.

Into the phone Carol said, "May I speak to Helen Cantor, please?"

"Have you got her?" Andy said.

"I'm waiting."

"She'll know what to do. You don't mind, do you, Carol? That I want her to come over?"

"No."

"It's just . . . she's been through this, you know? She'll know how to handle it. She knows the tricks."

"I don't mind," Carol said. She waited. The boys were silent. "Hello?" she said at last. "Helen? This is Carol . . . No, everything's all right . . . that is, well he tried to . . . he cut his wrist . . . No, he's all right . . . He wants you to come over . . . He doesn't feel well . . . Do you think you can? . . . Yes . . . well, yes . . . all right, fine . . . We'll be waiting for you." She paused. "Helen? . . . thank you." She hung up.

"Is she coming?"

"Yes. She said she'd take a cab. She should be here in a few minutes."

"A wonderful girl," Andy said. "A rock. Solid as a rock. Jesus, a wonderful girl, Helen."

"Lay down," Bud said. "Get some rest. God, you're burning up."

She was wearing green, a green woolen dress that picked up the color of her eyes. She looked very cool and very efficient when she walked into the apartment, and Bud couldn't help contrasting her calm demeanor with the way he and Carol looked. There was despair on Carol's face, a sadness she could not hide. She was struggling valiantly to keep from crying, and the struggle put a pained look on her face, and the pain robbed her of her beauty. Her blonde hair hung limply, even her clothes seemed to have grown suddenly stale. Her shoulders were hunched, and she kept her arms folded tightly across her chest, as if she were huddling against the cold.

He looked at Carol, and then he looked at Helen and the contrast was so vivid that he felt a sudden uplifting of his own spirits. Helen *was* a rock. Andy was right. In Helen there was strength. You could count on Helen, you could always count on Helen. He had not, until seeing her, realized how much the suicide attempt had shaken him. It had been a pitifully weak attempt, an attempt that magnified Andy's own weakness. It had drawn only a little blood, but it had still been a harrowing experience, and he trembled now as he thought of what could have been, and he was extremely grateful for Helen's presence.

She walked to the sofa where Andy lay stretched out.

"How's the patient?" she asked.

"Hello, Helen," he said.

"You goofed, huh, dad?"

Andy smiled weakly. "I goofed."

"I'm kind of glad you did. It wouldn't be the same around here without you."

"Thanks."

"No more of that, huh?"

"No, Helen."

"Is that a promise?"

"Yes."

"Good." She put her hand on his forehead, and her face clouded momentarily. "You're—" She didn't complete the sentence. She turned to Bud. "Have you called a doctor?"

"No. No, we didn't know what to do. We . . . we thought we'd wait until you got here."

"We'd better get one," she said.

"No, Helen," Andy pleaded. "No doctor."

"You lay back and relax, Buster," she said. "Do you use anyone in particular, Bud?"

"No, I've never . . . I mean, I haven't got a family doctor."

"I'll call the nearest one. Where's your phone book?"

"On the end table. Underneath. Where the phone—"

"I see it."

"Helen, I *don't need* a doctor!"

"I don't see why . . ."

Helen went to the end table and took the Classified from where it rested on the lower shelf. She was opening the book when the knocks sounded on the door.

"Who is it?" Bud asked.

"Police," the voice answered. "Open up."

"Wha—" Bud looked to Helen.

"Answer it," she said.

"But wha—"

"You won't know until you answer it. There's nothing illegal going on here. Go ahead, answer it."

"All . . . all right," Bud said.

He felt very weak and tired. He pulled back his shoulders and went to the door. Police. What could the police . . . He opened the door. Mrs. Heald, his landlady, was standing there with two patrolmen. Mrs. Heald looked very angry. The patrolmen looked indifferent.

"I see you're back," Mrs. Heald said heatedly.

"Yes. Yes, I am," Bud said, puzzled.

"Is your friend gone?"

"My—" He stopped. Did she know about the suicide attempt? Was that why the police were here? God, would they . . . why was all this happening to him? Why did trouble follow trouble? Couldn't he have a clear stretch of hours without trouble? "My friend," he stammered, and his mind went blank, and he was suddenly incapable of cohesive thought. He stared at Mrs. Heald's seamed and angry face, stared at the imperturbable faces of the patrolmen.

"I don't hear any record player," one of the patrolmen said.

"It was going full blast!" Mrs. Heald shouted. "You should be ashamed of yourself, Mr. Donato. And the way he talked to me. The young snotnose! I'm old enough to be his mother. Shouting at me, and pushing me out of the apartment! It's a wonder I didn't fall down and break my neck. What kind of friends do you have, anyway? What's going on in this room, anyway?" She stared into the room, seeing Carol, and seeing Helen at the telephone. Bud could hear Helen's voice. She had located a doctor. She was giving the address now. Her voice was calm and level.

Helen is a rock, he thought, Helen is a rock, and he could think of nothing to say to Mrs. Heald or the patrolmen.

"Who are you?" Mrs. Heald shouted, pointing her finger at Carol.

Carol turned, frightened. "I'm . . . I . . ."

"What's going on here, Mr. Donato?" Mrs. Heald screamed. "I run a clean house. I don't like these goings-on. I don't like it one bit. I want your friend arrested. I want him arrested this minute!"

"Now, calm down, lady," one of the patrolmen said. "The record player ain't going now."

"It *was* going, and I'm not going to lose my tenants because of a . . . a bunch of bums. Now you arrest him, do you hear me? Where is he, Mr. Donato? Where have you hidden him?"

"We . . . we haven't hidden him anywhere, Mrs. Heald," Bud said. "If he was playing records, well, well gee, I'm sorry, but you see I wasn't here when it happened, so I don't know—"

"And what are these girls doing here at this hour of the morning? I don't like this, Mr. Donato!" Her voice was high and shrill now. "I don't like it, do you hear me?"

"Yes, of course, but—"

"Disturbing the peace! That's what your friend was doing! And that's against the law. I want him arrested! I want him—"

"I wish you'd keep your voice down," Helen said, coming to the door.

Mrs. Heald's eyes flared. "What! What! You young snip, I'd like to tell you—"

"Officers," Helen said gently, "I've just finished calling the doctor. There's a very sick person here, and all this shouting isn't going to help him."

"Well, miss," one of the patrolmen said, "we got this complaint about the record player, so—"

"And long enough it took you to get here!" Mrs. Heald screamed. "God forbid somebody was getting murdered! God forbid we really needed a policeman!"

"He won't play the records any more, officers," Helen said. "I promise you. We're waiting for the doctor now. Do you think—" She smiled pleasantly.

"Come on, Sam," one of the patrolmen said, "the guy's a sick man."

"Aren't you going to arrest him?" Mrs. Heald shouted.

"He's sick, lady! For Pete's sake, the records ain't going now, are they?"

"What difference does that make? They *were* going! Are you just . . . just . . ."

"Come on, Sam."

The patrolmen walked away from the open door. Mrs. Heald stared into the room, fuming. She looked at Bud and said, with great dignity, "I think you had best look for another place to stay, Mr. Donato." She turned on her heel then and started down the steps.

"Mrs. Heald!" Bud called. He turned back into the room. Helen was standing beside him, her face impassive. "I . . . I've got to talk to her," Bud said. "Jesus, I can't get kicked out of here. I'll . . . I'll be right back."

Helen smiled briefly. Carol seemed struck dumb. She huddled on one side of the room, her face white. Bud ran out of the room, and Helen closed the door.

"Mustn't lose the apartment, must we?" she said quietly. "I'll bet Mrs. Heald thought our young Bud was running a brothel here."

Carol nodded. She was beginning to tremble now.

"Get a hold of yourself," Helen said sharply.

"I'm sorry. I . . . he . . . almost killed himself."

"Hardly," Helen said, a cutting edge to her voice. "For God's sake, stop it! It's bad enough Andy's a mess. Stop it."

"Yes, yes, I must. I know I must. If only I could be . . . be . . . but he tried to kill himself . . . he almost killed himself. Helen, I . . . I love him so much . . . if he . . ." She shook her head again, and she began trembling violently, and Helen went to her and put her arm around her shoulders and said gently, "He'll be all right, Carol. Please try to get hold of yourself."

"Yes," Carol nodded. "Yes, I will. Yes."

They were both silent for several moments. Carol sat in the butterfly chair. Helen sat on the sofa. She rose once to arrange the blanket around Andy, and then she sat again.

"Do you think he'll be here soon?" Carol asked.

"He said he'd come right over."

"Good." Carol's eyes blinked. "I want to thank you for all you're doing." She paused. "Are you in love with him?"

"What?" Helen said.

"Andy. Do you . . . love him?"

"Why . . ." Helen was staring at Carol, a surprised expression on her face. "Why, no."

"It doesn't matter. I just wondered. Your coming here and . . . and helping. I wondered why you would bother unless you . . . loved him."

"No, I don't love him."

"Did you and he . . ." Carol lowered her eyes. "Forgive me, I have no right asking."

"It won't make you any happier to know, will it?"

"I don't know."

"Andy needed someone, Carol. He needed someone very badly. I think he always will. It's very hard to turn your back when someone needs you."

"Yes."

"He'll be all right. Don't worry."

"Do you really think so?"

Helen hesitated. "Yes, I do," she said.

"I hope so. I wish I . . . I wish I could do more for him. I feel so helpless just sitting here and watching him and not being able to do anything." She shook her head, and they were silent for several moments. Then, uncomfortably, she said, "I know about what happened. I mean long ago. With you and Andy."

"Do you?"

"Yes. Oh, he didn't tell me. Andy didn't. And Bud didn't, either. Do you know Frank?"

"Yes."

"Yes, of course you do. Frank told me in one of his letters. During the war. He told me casually, as if he thought I already knew about it. I think, though, I think he knew I *didn't* know. I think he just wanted to tell me. I don't know. I never liked him much after that. I don't think he's a nice person."

"No, he isn't."

"It must have been terrible for you. You must have hated Andy very much. For . . . for what he did to you."

"No. Only for what he took away from me."

"Bud, you mean. Yes. You should have gotten together again. In all my letters to Bud, I always mentioned you. I always said he should call you. I always thought you should be together."

"We did get together again," Helen said quietly.

"Oh? I didn't know that." She paused. "Then why—"

"There's no percentage in hatred, Carol," Helen said suddenly. "I hated him so viciously I—" She stopped, shaking her head.

"Andy, do you mean?"

"No. Not Andy."

"I . . . I don't understand."

"Well, let's forget it." She sighed heavily.

"Andy's asked me to marry him," Carol said. She smiled weakly, the first smile Helen had seen on her face since she'd come into the apartment.

"Good. Did you accept?"

"Oh, yes." The smile broadened. "Yes, I did."

"I'm very happy for you. He's a wonderful guy, Carol, but . . . just stick with him. He needs someone by his side, that's all." She paused. "Most of us do."

"I think he'll be all right. I mean, once the doctor comes. I don't think this is anything serious, do you?"

"I don't know."

"Probably all the excitement. He's been through a lot in the past few days. Well, you must know. You've been through it, too."

"Yes," Helen said. She looked at Andy. His mouth was open, his eyes closed. He was breathing heavily. "Yes." A frown passed over her brow as she watched Andy. She reached out and touched his forehead.

"Is he still very hot?" Carol asked.

"Yes, he is."

Carol shook her head. "I wish the doctor would hurry."

The door opened and Bud came into the apartment. He smiled weakly.

"All squared away with your landlady?" Helen asked.

"Yeah," he said. He felt embarrassed over having crawled to his landlady, felt even more embarrassed now that it was all over. "Yep, we got it all settled. Seems Andy was playing the records pretty early. You can't blame her, I guess. I mean, she does have other tenants."

"Yes."

"And she's really not a bad person."

Helen smiled pleasantly. "She seemed like a bitch to me," she said.

"Well, well, I suppose. But you can't blame her for wanting to keep an orderly house. Hell, things haven't been exactly . . . well, quiet around here, have they?"

"Far from it," Helen said.

"Yeah, so you can't blame her. I explained it all to her."

"Did you tell her your friend was a drug addict?"

"Why, no. No, I didn't." Bud frowned. "I didn't think it was any of her business."

"It isn't."

"Then why'd you ask if I told her?"

"I thought you might have."

"No, I didn't."

"All right."

He was suddenly miffed. There was something exasperating about Helen's calmness. There was such a thing as carrying this rock idea too damned far. It was all well and good to be cool and detached, but not if it made everyone around you feel awkward. He looked at Helen and coolly asked, "When's the doctor coming?"

"Soon."

"Did he say when?"

"As soon as he could, he said. He'll be here."

"You're pretty damn calm about all of this, aren't you?" Helen returned his stare. "Someone has to be," she said.

"Sure, and it might as well be you. You're a rock."

"What?"

"Nothing."

He turned away from her and went to the window, wondering why he was so annoyed.

"He'll be here soon, Bud," Carol said.

"Well, let's hope so."

Go ahead, he thought, sit there like a rock. Helen Cantor, the Rock of Gibraltar. You weren't such a steadfast rock when we . . .

Let's not think about that.

"You should have asked him *when* he was coming," he said.

"I did," Helen answered. "He said he'd be here as soon as possible."

"You should have told him it was an emergency."

"I told him Andy seemed very sick."

"You should have made it stronger!"

"What's eating *you?*" Helen said sharply.

"Nothing," he snapped back.

"Then don't take out your own guilt feelings on me!"

"Guilt feelings! What the hell are you talking about?"

"Figure it out for yourself."

"Because I left him alone, you mean? He didn't kill himself, did he?"

"No, he didn't."

"All right, then leave me alone. You think I have nothing to worry about but Andy? I've got a test at two o'clock, and I haven't even cracked a book for it!"

"Why don't you go into the bathroom and study now?" Helen asked.

"How the hell can I study when we're sitting here waiting for the doctor?"

"That's your problem," Helen said coldly.

"Yes, and Andy's problem is *his* problem. And I don't mind telling you I didn't ask to be dragged into it, and I'm not happy about being dragged into it."

"Poor little Buddy," Helen said mockingly. "Everybody comes to him with their problems."

"What do you mean by that?"

"Buddy, dear Buddy," Helen said, "everything in life is a problem. Every damn waking minute of it. When you get rid of one, there's another one right around the corner. Don't you think it's time you recognized that?"

"I recognized it a long time ago. And my problem right now is a test at two P.M. And there's another one right around the corner on Friday."

"Very big problems," Helen agreed. "Practically insurmountable."

"Don't get sarcastic."

"I was sympathizing."

"You've got a peculiar brand of sympathy."

"Bud, I was only trying to tell you—"

"Helen, can't you see I'm—"

They stopped talking simultaneously. They stared at each other across the length of the room. He wanted to explain to her that he hadn't meant to sound the way he sounded, but he couldn't find the right words. He stared at her, and she still seemed very calm and very composed, and he admired her strength, and he envied her strength, and he was somewhat embarrassed by it.

He thought back to the way she had handled the policemen at the door, the way she had stepped into the apartment and created order out of despondent chaos. He thought of her cool efficiency and his own fumbling awkwardness, and he wondered how someone as levelheaded as Helen could possibly have turned to drugs.

And he knew why.

He knew why, and he turned from her because he could not bear looking at her face.

He knew why, and he told himself it wasn't so, he had had nothing to do with it, hadn't she labeled it herself yesterday—a personality defect, hadn't she said so? But he could see no defect in her now. She seemed superior to everyone in the room now, superior to any situation. And if she was so strong now, why did she once turn to heroin?

He could not blame himself. That was stupid. Besides, he had done everything that had been asked of him, handled it the way it should have been handled—how else could anyone handle it?—and yet he knew he had not done everything possible, but he shouldn't even have been asked, more should not have been asked of him.

And yet she had become an addict. True, she had broken the habit and that took strength, so how could someone as strong as Helen have turned to drugs, and again he knew the answer.

No, his mind screamed, *no!*

Problems, sure, problems, and there are enough of your own without having to worry about everyone else's. What do you owe people? Didn't I see it through, didn't I do what I should have done, wasn't I honorable? Then why ask more of me, Helen, why ask more?

Helen, couldn't we have left it the way it was? Why did Andy have to come back, and why did he drag you along with him, and why are you both in my life again? I thought you were out of my life, I thought I had escaped it, *touched hands, touched minds, crossed lives.*

Helen, I loved you, you know that, don't you? Helen, I loved you with every fiber in my body, but I just couldn't . . . I had other things to worry . . . I had . . .

I know, I know, I know.

You needed me, but people are always needing, and how much of yourself can you give, and when do you stop giving, and where does it end? Doesn't it ever end? Are you always face to face with it? *Where's the goddamn doctor?* Do you turn around and find life staring at you always? It can't be that way. How could you stand it if it were always that way, how could you stand it?

When do you rest? When do you find peace and contentment? Is that why Andy tried to take his own life? Jesus, what a hell of a juvenile thing to try, but he wanted peace, I guess, he didn't want to . . . to face it . . . face *what?*

... you don't know what you're talking about any more,
you don't know.

Helen, try to understand. Sit there in your big superior
strength and understand that I was free—free from that
night the navy let me go, free from that moment on, and I
wanted to stay that way, I had to stay that way, so understand, understand, please understand.

sock chorus, i

JULY, 1946

25

It was very hot, even for July, and the rotating fan overhead only rearranged the thick blue smoke in the place.
The smoke hovered like early morning mist over a meadow,
swirling up where the fan pulled it reluctantly into its vortex. There was noise in the place, too, thicker than the
smoke, buzzing over the tables like hungry flies around a
felled horse.

Every now and then a high shrill laugh pierced the
smoke and the hovering hum, a laugh that bubbled from
the lips of a redhead at a table near the bandstand. The
redhead was sitting with a Negro, and the Negro kept
leaning over the table with a perpetual small smile on his
face, talking in hushed whispers, as if he were confiding
state secrets. The redhead would listen carefully, her lips
moving ever so slightly as she watched his lips, like an
actress anticipating her cue. And then the cue would come,
and her laugh would burst into the smoke-filled room like
a skyrocket, dripping its incandescent shrillness from the
ceiling, and the Negro just kept leaning over the table and
smiling his small smile and telling his state secrets.

Bud was sweltering in his blues. He was sweltering, and
he also felt a little stupid. He kept cursing his mother for
having given away all his clothes while he was gone, and he
tried to listen to what Andy was saying, and all the while
the redhead kept erupting into the room with that infuri-
atingly high laugh of hers.

". . . started by a guy named Dizzy Gillespie, Bud,"
Andy said. "You should see him. He wears a little beard

here under his lip, a sort of a goatee, a little triangular thing. We call it a 'Dizzy kick' in the trade. He wears a red beret, too. Those are his trade-marks—the kick and the beret. When all this first started, I bought a beret, too, but you can't keep your hair combed too well if you wear one, do you know what I mean?"

"Yes," Bud said. "These navy hats are the same."

"Carol didn't like it, either. She said it looked silly and affected. She digs bop, though. Bop really sends her."

"I'm anxious to hear some of it," Bud said.

"Oh, you will, man, that's what we're here for." He glanced at the bandstand. "The—" Bud heard the red-head's laugh starting again, and Andy shifted his eyes ever so slightly in the direction of her table, and he tilted his head a little, as if he were straining to hear what the Negro was saying. The laugh ended abruptly, and Andy, liberated, said, "The combo should be back any minute. I think you'll like this, Bud. You have to get used to it, just like anything else, but you'll like it. All it is, really, is playing around with chords. Well, you'll see. Did you do much playing in the navy?"

"A little," Bud said. "There was another piano player on my ship, and we scared up a piano whenever we could. We played some nice boogie together. We were the hottest thing in Sasebo and Yokosu—"

"Yeah, well, boogie's dead and gone now, you know that, don't you? If you play boogie now, the crowd throws stones at you."

"No, I didn't know that," Bud said.

Andy nodded. "It's a damn shame I missed you on V-J Day. That was after I quit Jerry Black, wasn't it?"

"Yes."

"I was with a guy named Marv Lipton then—he changed it from Marv Lipschitz—a nowhere outfit, but at least I got to see D.C., and that was a wild town then, man. So tell me, how does it feel to be home for good?"

"You want the truth?"

"Sure."

"Lousy."

Andy burst out laughing, and then he glanced quickly at the table with the redhead and the Negro, and Bud got the feeling he was laughing for their benefit, as if to show them he was having a good time, too.

"It can't be as bad as that," Andy said, bringing his eyes back to Bud's face. He had learned a trick with his eyes, Bud noticed, a way of squinching them up in wry amusement, so that it gave the peculiar expression of his eyes smiling while his mouth did not. His mouth had not changed at all. It was still a remarkably immature mouth, a weak mouth, even though the rest of his face had lengthened into angular maturity. And, of course, the muscle ring was still there, stronger now than it had ever been. He was wearing his hair long, and from what Bud had noticed when he'd turned his head, he sported a D.A. in the back.

"Are you listening to me?" Andy asked suddenly.

"Yes, of course."

"Oh, I thought you were studying me," he said. "Have I changed much?"

"Not very," Bud told him.

"Haven't I grown up?" he asked, and he did his eye trick again, the edges of his eyes crinkling while his mouth remained expressionless, the warm amber-flecked brown glowing with secret amusement.

"I don't know," Bud said. "Have you?"

"I've done a lot of things since the last time I saw you," Andy said, and now there was trickery in his eyes, only the glow now, and the glow was not an amused one. It burned with an inner light, an almost eerie light. "A hell of a lot of things. And there's a hell of a lot more to do yet."

"I guess so," Bud said.

"What don't you like about being home?" Andy asked.

"Everything. My mother gave away all my clothes, and it's hot as hell in these blues, and I feel as if I don't know anybody any more, not even you, and I'm scared I'll curse at the dinner table."

"I know that joke," Andy said. "It's a good one." He laughed that too-loud laugh again, and this time he glanced unmistakably at the redhead and Bud felt a momentary prick of irritation.

"You'll get used to the changes," Andy said and the

redhead burst into laughter, and Bud suddenly realized that Andy and the redhead were bellowing out mating calls, and it annoyed the hell out of him because they were supposed to be old pals out on the town in a great big glorious reunion, and here he was making birdcalls at a strange redhead. If Andy'd wanted to go hunting, that would have been fine with Bud, and he'd certainly have gone along with him. But it had been Andy's suggestion to come to this place on Fifty-second Street where they could "talk and listen to bop. You'll like bop, Buddy."

He had not listened to any bop so far, and the talk had consisted of the kind of inane drivel you pass back and forth with a stranger on a chow line. He didn't mind polite casual conversation but he had really hoped to get down to brass tacks with Andy, had really hoped his friend would set him straight on what had happened since last summer, and here he was carrying on with the redhead.

"I hope I get used to it," he said patiently. "So far it's been one hell of a big disappointment." His eyes met Andy's pointedly.

"The changes, you mean," Andy said abstractedly, and then he swung his chair around so that he could get a better look at the redhead, and Bud turned his head and saw that she had one elbow propped up on the table and that she was leaning over, and that she was wearing a very low-cut Shantung dress, and that she was really not a bad looker at all—none of which facts exonerated Andy so far as he was concerned. "Well," Andy said, "tomorrow we'll go on a picnic or something, huh? With Carol, and maybe she can get a girl for you."

"Thanks," Bud said. "Tomorrow I'm going shopping."

"Say, tomorrow's Saturday, isn't it?" Andy said. "Well, I couldn't go, anyway. I've got a fitting for band jackets. With the new band I'm on—Jam Jerralds. You ever hear of him?"

"No," Bud said.

"Well, he's got a B band, but things are beginning to get a little tighter in the field, now that the war's over. He's no small time, you understand—used to play with Tommy Dorsey and Claude Thornhill—but he's not big time, either, like he doesn't play the Paramount. He cuts a lot of disks, though, and there's extra loot in that. And even though he plays trumpet, he gives his trumpet men solos, too, so it sounds like a good deal. We'll be leaving week after next, you know. Hey, here come the boys now!"

Bud turned and saw the musicians climbing onto the bandstand—three colored fellows who waved out at the crowd. One of the musicians stopped to talk to the man with the redhead, and Andy watched him and said, "I know that guy. I met him at a session in Harlem. He blows a wild tenor sax. He really blows up a storm."

The piano player and the drummer made themselves comfortable, and a fourth musician came from behind the drape near the bandstand, climbed up to his chair, and picked up his trumpet. The tenor man called off the beat, and then the piano and drums got to work on something very soft with a lot of high treble and cymbal work. It took Bud several moments to realize they were fooling around with "How High the Moon," and then he listened more carefully, hearing the intricate variations the piano man was lacing around the basic chords.

"Can you hear how cool it is?" Andy asked, and Bud nodded and listened, absorbed, following the progression now and marveling at it. The tenor man put his horn to his lips and came in, blowing very easily, effortlessly performing the same slight-of-ear with the chords. It was fascinating to listen to, and Bud lost himself in it and he wouldn't have noticed the redhead walking past their table if Andy hadn't suddenly swung around in his chair. He looked up then and watched the girl walk across to the Ladies' Room. She wasn't wearing a girdle, and the Shantung hugged her body, and Andy glued his eyes to her and didn't turn away until the door to the john closed behind her.

"How's Carol?" Bud asked pointedly.

"She's great. Did you dig that redhead? Mmmm, man. Edible."

"Are you still going together?"

"Why, sure," Andy said, surprised. "Hell, we're gonna get married one of these days. What makes you ask?" Bud shrugged noncommittally, and Andy apparently caught on then because he said, "The redhead, you mean? Daddy, you're dead when you stop looking."

"Sure," Bud said.

"Oh, man, Carol and me are like that." He held out two fingers and pressed them together. "Just like that. But there's a lot to do, man, you know? Hell, I'm a young kid."

"I know."

"Buddy," he said seriously, "we're only young once, and when that's gone, what's left? You take a look at my old man and you'll see what I mean. Some things you can only do when you're young. And, dad, I'm going to do them all."

"Go ahead," Bud said. "Do them."

"Oh, I will, don't worry." Andy paused. "When are *you* going to find someone like Carol?"

Bud smiled foolishly. "I'm still looking."

"You think you'll ever find what you want?"

"There's always another streetcar," Bud said, shrugging.

"Sure, but only if you're going someplace."

"Huh?"

"I mean, what the hell, there must be *some* girl."

"Not yet," Bud said.

"What about Helen?"

"What about her?"

"Nice kid."

"If you like nice kids."

"Seriously, Bud."

"No," Bud said.

"Why not?"

"What do you mean, why not? Does there have to be a reason? It's just no, that's all. Helen and I were through long before I went into the navy. You know, you and Carol make me laugh. Just because a guy hangs around with a girl for a while, you think he's—"

"Is it because she's Jewish?"

"What?"

"You heard me."

"Oh, for Christ's sake!"

"I just asked."

"Well, don't."

"Then what is it with Helen?"

"Jesus, I don't know what you want me to say!"

"Is it because of . . . her and me?"

"Partly, I guess."

"Man, you know the percentage of women who are pure when they get married?"

"No," Bud said.

"Well, it's damn slim. You ever write to Helen?"

"No."

"When'd you see her last?"

"When I was in on V-J Day."

"And you never called her again?"

"I went overseas. Even if I had wanted to call her, I couldn't have. And, besides, I didn't want to."

"Why not?"

"Look, can we drop this? If you don't mind, I'd like to drop it."

"All right, all right," Andy said placatingly. "Hey, you mind if I sit in with these guys?"

"No, go right ahead."

"You want to try your hand?"

"At bop? You're kidding, Andy."

"Got to learn it if you expect to pick up where you left off."

"I don't expect to," Bud said.

"What do you mean?"

"Just that I'm not planning on being a musician. The piano is a lot of fun but . . . well, I'm going to college."

"Man," Andy said, "the only thing to be is a musician."

"Well, I don't feel that way. Frank doesn't either. We're both enrolling at City College next week."

"All the way up there?"

"It's a good engineering school. Frank wants engineering. Besides, I may take my own apartment."

"*Tony's* continuing with his music," Andy said defensively.

"Yes, I know."

"Have you seen him yet?"

"I stopped by this afternoon. He's still got his Florida tan."

"He's nowhere, you know that, don't you? As a musician, I mean. No ideas. He's the corniest bastard in the world."

"Well," Bud said noncommittally.

"I think he's registered at Julliard. How they ever took a crumb like him is beyond me."

"I thought you liked Tony."

"Who said I didn't? What's that got to do with the way he blows his horn. Tony thinks all there is to being a musician is knowing how to read music. Man, you've got to achieve, you've got to express. If you don't express with your music, you might as well be dead."

"He's not so bad."

"He's the world's worst," Andy said. "I'm gonna sit in."

"Go ahead."

Andy shoved back his chair and walked past the redhead's table and then to the bandstand. The tenor man's face lit up when he saw Andy. He stepped down from the stand and took his hand and shook it heartily, and Andy clapped him on the shoulder and said something, and they both laughed. Then Andy gestured toward the trumpet chair, and the tenor man nodded his head happily, and the trumpet man came down and shook hands with Andy. He handed Andy his horn, and Andy took the holstered mouthpiece from his jacket pocket, unsnapped the holster and then fitted the mouthpiece to the horn. The trumpet man wandered off toward the bar, and Andy clambered up to his chair, and the tenor man called off the beat, and they went into "Body and Soul."

Andy's playing had changed considerably, in keeping with the new style. The old forcefulness of his horn was gone now, replaced by a quietly intricate playfulness, a tour de force of his chord knowledge. The same grasping quality was there, though, a restless searching feeling, as if he were groping for the answer to life through his music. It was a peculiar sound to listen to, a lonely sound somehow, and yet a sound that demanded empathy, a sound you wanted to help, a sound that forced you to identify with it, as if Andy's struggle were your own struggle and the struggle transcended the mere medium of music. Bud listened to it, admiring as always Andy's artistry and feeling this peculiar mounting, reaching sensation within himself, so that he wished he could help Andy somehow, wished he could get up there with him and help him push the notes through the horn, help him battle his way out of the maze and climb up above the obfuscating clouds to where everything was very clean and very blue, up there to where you could breathe deeply and wash out your lungs. But you couldn't get there. You fought with it, and you willed it, but it was always out of your grasp, you were chained to earth, and there was always this despairing disappointment when Andy stopped blowing, this feeling of almost, almost having touched it, and yet within this disappointment there was a compensating factor of almost-achievement, just a little way to go now, just a little farther and you would be there, if only you could stick with it, if only you could blow away the mist and find what you were looking for, this knowledge that here was promise and it was . . .

Better to have . . .

Even . . . even a promise . . . because most have . . .

Nothing at all.

His music drained you. It left you washed out and tired, but it also left you happy in a strangely sad way.

The boys played through a set, and then Andy came back to the table with the tenor man.

"Bud," he said, "like you to meet Eddie Cann, one of the best tenor men in the business. Eddie, meet my boy, Bud."

Eddie extended his hand and Bud took it. "Pleased to know you, man," Eddie said.

"Same here," Bud answered.

"My boy won't approve of this," Andy said, "but who's the carrottop at the next table, Eddie?"

Eddie glanced over his shoulder. His eyes were very white in his brown face, and a sheen of sweat clung to his forehead. He grinned broadly and then said, "Iris, man. You dig her?"

"I dig her," Andy said.

"She a real music-lover," Eddie said. "What I mean, a *real* one."

"I'm hip," Andy said. "How about an intro?"

"Gone, man. Come on over."

"Come on, Bud," Andy said.

"I want to get home," Bud said.

"What for?"

"I've got a lot of clothes to buy tomorrow."

"My boy's up for readjustment exercises on the morrow," Andy said to Eddie. "Look, Bud, stick around a while longer."

"No, I've got to go."

"You don't mind, do you? I mean, my sticking around like this. That chick has eyes that are the biggest, you know that, don't you?"

"I kind of figured."

"Yeah, well .. anyway, you're home for good now, so what's the rush?"

"No rush at all. Have a good time." He lifted his jumper and pulled his wallet from where it was jackknifed over his waistband. He put a ten and a five on the table and said, "That ought to cover it."

"Oh, come down, man," Andy said. "This is on me."

"No, let me take it," Bud said. "I'm flushed with mustering-out pay."

"Suit yourself," Andy said airily. "You sure you're not sore?"

"Nothing to be sore about."

Their eyes met. "Look, man," Andy said, "stick around, huh?"

"No," Bud said, "you don't need me—" he paused— "any more," he added softly.

"What?" Andy said.

"Come on, dad," Eddie Cann said, "let's meet Iris."

Bud watched while Andy went over to the next table. Eddie introduced him to the redhead, and he sat down beside her, and the redhead gave him her undivided attention, leaning over the table. Bud took a cigarette from his jumper pocket, lit it hastily, and then started out of the club.

He was angry, but in a strange way he was relieved too. A great weight had been lifted from his shoulders, and he could not have described what that weight was if he'd tried.

He only knew that the air outside the club smelled very clean and very sweet—the way oxygen must smell at high altitudes, high above the earth, where everything was unpolluted, where birds flew in complete and absolute abandon.

26

In October, with the leaves a molten red and gold, with the air crisp and biting, with the weather ideal for a freshman enjoying his first semester of college, a Hunter College House Plan invited a City College fraternity to a gathering at Roosevelt House.

Bud and Frank were pledging in the City College fraternity, and so they went to the gathering.

Bud had never held a very high opinion of anyone who went to an all-anything school, and he appreciated even less the girls who inhabited a convent like Hunter College. He was surprised, therefore, to find himself having a good time. Some of the boys from his frat had smuggled in a fifth of Old Grand-dad, which they'd discreetly poured into the punch bowl, and he and Frank had visited the bowl often. Some of the House Plan girls had lugged along their boyfriends, a few of whom were Hunter College Veterans —why would anyone want to go to an all-girls' school, ask a silly question you get a silly answer. Most of the boys, though, belonged to Bud's frat, and so he felt right at home. He danced with several of the House Plan girls, and he kept hitting the spiked punch bowl, and he was enveloped in a warm rosy glow of comparative comfort when Frank came up to him at about ten o'clock.

"Guess who's here?" he said.

"The Maharaja of Mee-aho," Bud said.

"No, come on, get serious."

"Who?"

"Give a guess."

"Julius Caesar."

"Very funny."

"Who, then?"

"Guess."

"Jesus Christ!"

"Are you expleting or guessing?"

"Frank, why don't you drop dead?"

"Helen Cantor," Frank said.

"What?"

"Helen. She's here. Talked with her a few minutes ago. She goes to Hunter now, how do you like that?"

"Are you kidding me?"

"Hell, no. Don't tell me you're interested! I thought you were all wrapped up making Carol comfortable while friend Andy is on the road."

"Lay off that Carol routine, will you? We're friends, period."

"I'm only an observer," Frank said, winking.

"Well, you're crazy. For Christ's sake—"

"Crazy like a fox. Anyway, Helen's here."

"Good for Helen."

"I thought you might be interested. She looks very collegiate. She's wearing a little button marked *hostess*. She looks too clean to suit me. I guess Andy didn't teach her very much that night, eh, Buddy?"

"Knock it off," Bud said.

"What's the matter, pal? You still sensitive."

"No, I'm not still sensitive. Helen and I ... oh, what's the use explaining anything to you?"

"You know what's wrong with you?"

"No, tell me. What's wrong with me?"

"You take your friend's girl on platonic dates, you eat yogurt, and you bay at the moon."

"Frank," Bud said seriously, "you are really very witty this evening. You are so witty, I can hardly stand you. It's a wonder you can even stand yourself."

"I think I'm pretty damn sharp," Frank said. "You going over to say hello?"

"Maybe."

"She looks too clean," Frank said sadly.

"Well, that's life."

Frank didn't pick up the opening. "Yeah," he said dully. "I'm gonna dance." He walked away from Bud and over to a brunette in a fuzzy pink sweater. Bud watched him for several moments, and then he turned and walked over to the punch bowl. A girl was standing with her back to him, near the cups. He reached for a cup, and the girl turned, and he did not recognize her for a moment, and then he did, and his eyes went wide with surprise, even though Frank had told him she was there.

There was a sudden joy on her face, and then the joy retreated, as if it had been carefully and calculatedly pulled back. They stood a foot apart from each other, and neither spoke, and then Helen shook her head in bewilderment and said, "Bud, what are you doing he . . . I . . ." She shook her head again, and then she gave a short confused laugh, and Bud said, "Hello, Helen."

"I . . . forgive me . . . I didn't expect to see you here. How are you, Bud?"

"Fine, thanks. And you?"

"Fine." She paused and studied his face. "You didn't write."

"No. I was busy."

"Growing up?"

Bud shrugged, and then smiled noncommittally. "Do you belong to this House Plan?"

"I'm Recording Secretary."

"Well, bully for you."

"Indeed." He was smiling, and she realized that she was smiling, too, and she wondered why there wasn't more tension between them, and she searched his face again. He seemed so very much at ease—no, that wasn't the word she wanted, not simply at ease with her, or with his surroundings, at *peace*, yes, yes, he seemed to be at peace with himself—and on impulse, and because she somehow sensed a change which she could not as yet describe, she tentatively asked, "Are you still busy?"

"What?"

"I mean . . . right now."

"Not at all," he said.

"Well, I'm supposed to be a hostess. Come on, I'll introduce you around."

She took his hand unconsciously, and only after his fingers closed on hers did she realize what she'd done. And yet she felt no embarrassment, no uneasiness. The taking of his hand had been the most natural thing in the world for her to do, it seemed. And recognizing the validity of her intuitive gesture, she purposely submerged any conscious doubts, and she found herself thinking she would take this as it came, expecting nothing, and therefore avoiding any disappointment that might result from great expectations. They walked together to where a knot of boys and girls were standing near the record player.

"Here's Helen now," one of the girls said. "Helen'll know. Helen, what was the theme of Freshman Sing last year?"

"Comic Books," Helen said instantly.

"There, you see?" the girl said.

"I still think it was the Gold Rush," a bespectacled boy said.

"Oh, what do you know about Sing, anyway?" the girl answered.

"Kids, this is Bud Donato," Helen said. "Bud, meet, left to right, Gladys Aronowitz, Marcia Steele, Dave Annunziato ..." The boy with the spectacles extended his hand, and Bud took it.

Helen gestured to a tall thin boy with a crew cut and brown eyes.

"Rick Dadier, Bud."

Bud took his hand. "Nice knowing you, Rick."

"Same here," the boy said. He dismissed Bud almost instantly. "Helen, have you seen Anne? I've been— Never mind, never mind, there she is. Excuse me, will you, Bud? Nice meeting you." He left the circle and headed over toward where a pretty blonde was chatting with what appeared to be a faculty adviser.

"Whatever the theme was," Annunziato said, "it was lousy."

"You're prejudiced," Gladys said. "You expect freshmen to be lousy, and so your stereotyped picture prejudices your entire outlook. If you—"

"Would you like to dance, Bud?" Helen asked, seeing his discomfort.

"Yes," he said eagerly.

They went onto the floor together, listening to the music, and then—surprisingly—flowing into it instantly, the way they always had done, as if their training were able to survive the longest separation. She thought back to the last time she'd seen him, at the block party, and the awkward stumblings they'd experienced that night, and she felt again this sense of everything's going perfectly, and she was frightened for a moment that it was going too perfectly, that something would happen to spoil it, that this change she sensed in him was not a real change at all.

"Since you are Recording Secretary," Bud said, "I surmise you are now going to Hunter."

"Yes. And since you are here, I likewise surmise you are going to City."

"Yes."

"Round one," Helen said. "Draw."

"How do you like it? School, I mean?"

"Very much. I've turned into a regular bookworm."

"Have you?"

"Yes. You wouldn't recognize me, Bud."

"You look the same to me."

"Oh, well, I didn't expect it would show."

"How have you been, Helen?"

"Fine, Bud. Are you glad to be home? That's a stupid question, isn't it?"

"Well, it's fairly stupid yes," he said, smiling.

"That's what I love about you. Your frankness." She had used the word "love," and the word had not pained her, and it seemed not to disturb him, but it caused them both to fall into a momentary silence. And then, as if the word generated his next question, he asked, "Are you married, engaged, pregnant?"

"None, thank you."

"Well, that's good." He seemed genuinely pleased. He seemed, in fact, almost relieved.

"Is it?"

"Well, sure. Maybe we can . . . get together sometime."

"Maybe," Helen said. She did not press it further. She kept expecting the bubble to explode. "Who spiked the punch bowl? One of your boys?"

"Yes."

"We can use more spiked punch bowls at Hunter. The only spiked things at Hunter are the shoes on the girls' feet."

"Well, you've got men now."

"Oh, yes."

"Maybe I'll transfer."

"You'd be in your element. Something like twenty to one, I'd imagine."

"You still dance very well," he said.

"I thank you, sir." She paused. "We didn't dance well together at all the last time we ..." She hesitated, wondering if she should touch upon so hazardous a subject. Again her intuition took over, and she threw caution to the winds. "I meant, at the block party."

"Oh, yes. Did you have a good time with Tony that night?"

"He took me straight home," she said.

"Oh, I see."

"I wanted to be with you."

"That doesn't make much sense."

"It did, at the time. Things are a little different now."

"How do you mean?"

She looked up into his face. "You seem changed, Bud."

"I'm not, really."

"Well, you seem so. Besides, maybe it isn't right to question a person's motives so thoroughly."

"Which means?"

"Which means ... perhaps I should have behaved differently the last time we were together."

"Which further means?"

"How should I know? Why don't you pay attention?"

He laughed and squeezed her closer, and she laughed with him, reflecting that this was the first honest laugh she'd had in as long as she could remember.

"I should have written to you, Helen."

"I know you should have."

"Isn't it funny?"

"What, Bud?"

"I feel as if I'd seen you only yesterday and not— It's more than a year, isn't it?"

"That's our fate, Buddy. We meet every year, on schedule. We exchange a few words, and then both go off to our separately revolving worlds, bitter and disillusioned."

"You sound like an English major."

"I'm not. Psych."

"Not kidding?"

"Certainly. Do you know something?"

"What's that?"

"Half the Psych majors at Hunter are afraid they're neurotic or psychotic. That's why they take the major.

It's cheaper than a psychiatrist. What's your major?"

"I don't know yet. I'm just drifting with the tide."

"Well, the tide seems to agree with you. You're looking well." She smiled. "And I'm glad to see you're beginning to dress sensibly."

"What was wrong with the way I dressed?"

"Nothing. But those pegged pants, really, Bud!"

"Andy still pegs his slightly. Says it gives the pants leg a better look."

"How *is* Andy?"

"He's on the road again. Fine, the last time I heard. Headed for Sioux City, I think. Had you seen him recently?"

"Not for a long time. He's a nice boy. A little confused, but nice."

"Confused?"

"Yes, well ... I mean, I don't think he knows what he wants exactly."

"Does anyone?"

"I suppose not," Helen said. "But everyone's not as talented as Andy is. There's a difference."

"The trouble with Psych majors—" Bud started.

"Yes, and I promise I won't discuss basic feelings of insecurity at all tonight, all right? And please forgive my babbling, but this is the annual meeting of the Cantor-Donato Society for the Prevention—"

"Don't, Helen."

"I'm sorry," she said softly.

"I'm enjoying myself. Let's not spoil it."

"I don't want to spoil it, Bud."

"Neither do I."

She looked up at him, convinced now that her intuition had been correct, glad now that she'd followed it, surprised when her thoughts found voice.

"I do believe you have grown up, Bud."

"Oh, sure," he said, smiling. "Almost old enough to vote. Big college man, my own apartment, saving for a car, got a—"

"Did you move out of your folks' place?"

"Few weeks ago. Would you like to—" He cut himself short. "Never mind."

"What were you going to say?"

"I was going to ask you if you'd like to see the place. But I realized how it would sound. That's the worst part about having your own apartment. Everyone thinks you should have etchings to go with it."

"And you, of course, have no etchings."

"Of course not."

"I'd like to see it, anyway," Helen said.

"You would?" he asked, surprised.

"Yes. Understand, of course—"

"I understand," he assured her.

"Let me make my farewells and get my coat." She paused. "Bud, if I'm throwing myself at you, please stop me."

"You're not."

"You're sure?"

"I'm sure, Helen."

"All right, I'll be with you in a moment."

It had been very cold outside, and the radiator in Bud's apartment was sizzling and inviting when he opened the door and snapped on the light.

"Come in," he said. "This is it."

Helen stood in the doorway and examined the room. "It's not what I expected," she said. "It's not a reflection of your personality."

"I know. It's a furnished room, a reflection of my landlady's personality. Someday you've got to meet my landlady."

"She won't mind, will she? My being here, I mean."

"She probably will, but the hell with her. Take off your coat."

"I wouldn't want you to get into trouble with your landlady. Not with apartments as difficult to find as—"

"My landlady will have no cause for worry," Bud said, smiling.

Helen took off her coat and looked around. "It's very nice, Bud. And I'm beginning to see touches of your personailty already."

"Like for instance?"

"Like the school pennants over the table, for instance. Princeton? Why Princeton?"

"Wish fulfillment," Bud said.

"And the pipe rack on the table. I didn't know you smoked a pipe."

"I don't. I keep them there for atmosphere."

"And the record player, and the album of Woody Herman stuff next to it. And isn't that a James album I see on the floor there near the chair?"

"Yes," he said.

"And, of course, the Petty-girl calendar. This wouldn't be your apartment without a Petty-girl calendar."

"A friend of mine left that here," he said. He went to the closet and hung their coats away. "So," he said, "what can I get you? I've got rye, and I've got some sherry, take your choice."

"The sherry sounds safe," Helen said.

"Sherry it is, then. Put on some records, why don't you?"

He went into the kitchen and she called, "How does this work?"

"Turn the gizmo to ten-inch, switch the other gizmo to seventy-eight r.p.m., and then just pile the records on and throw the switch."

"Will you trust my choice?"

"Certainly."

"I'm picking all ballads."

"Fine."

He came back into the living room and handed her the glass of wine. "Forgive the kitchen tumbler. I haven't any stemware."

"It's the thought that counts," Helen said, smiling. "Shall we toast?"

"If you like."

"I never let an opportunity to toast go by. It's like getting a free wish on a star, and you get the drink in addition to it. What shall we toast?"

"You name it."

"No, the man should make the toast."

"To us?" he asked.

"Well, it's somewhat clichéd, but I suppose it'll suffice. To us. And to . . . well, to us."

They clinked glasses together and sipped at the sherry.

"It's good," Helen said.

"It should be chilled."

"Should it? I don't know much about wines."

"Neither do I. But I like it chilled."

"You're not a connoisseur?"

"Nope, 'fraid not."

"You've developed honesty. Did you always have that?"

"I don't know."

"Answer me something honestly."

"Shoot."

"Why'd you ask me up here?"

"I wanted you to see where I lived."

"All right."

"Do you believe me?"

"Yes," Helen said. "This is very good wine."

"Ninety-eight cents for the bottle."

"It's still good. Music is good for wine, too. This is very nice, Bud."

"Yes," he said.

"Tell me all about you," she said. "My God, it's been such a long time."

"There's not much to tell."

"There must be."

"No, Helen, really."

"Why didn't you write to me, Bud?"

"I didn't want to."

"Why not?"

"I was angry. I didn't think you'd treated me fairly."

"Maybe I didn't."

"I got just what I deserved," Bud said, "only I didn't realize it at the time. I thought ... well, I figured your rejecting me was a slap in the face, even though ... well, I can't say I was being very sincere about anything that night. And then your going home with Tony, that added insult to injury. Do you understand?"

"Yes," she said, and she did understand, and all her fears seemed to be gone now, and she wondered what it would have been like if she'd approached their last meeting with the same trustfulness, and she knew instantly it would have been impossible. This Bud was not the Bud of a year ago, not the impatient sailor she'd met on V-J Day. And it was Bud himself who somehow generated this warm trust within her now, and she knew with firm conviction that everything would be all right between them this time. This time nothing could possibly happen to them.

They were silent for a long time, listening to the music. The quiet voice of a singer came from the speaker, whispering at them.

"More wine?" Bud asked.

"No, I've got to be going soon."

"I'll be seeing you again, won't I, Helen?"

"Are you chasing me out already?"

"No, no, I didn't mean—"

"Do you want to see me again?"

"Yes."

"I mean, not next year?"

"Not next year."

"Well, fine."

"I'll be busy for the next week or so. I'm in charge of decorations for the Fall Ball, and we've got meetings almost every damn week end arguing about one thing or another. They're really excuses for get-togethers, I suppose, but anyway I'm all tied up until the— Say, would you like to go with me?"

"Where?"

"The Fall Ball. It's not as pretentious as it sounds. It's just a dance in the gym. It's on the eighth, that's a Saturday night."

"I'll consult my calendar," Helen said.

"All right, and I'll give you a ring and—"

"I was kidding, Bud. I'd like very much to go."

"Well, fine, fine. Then . . . then that's settled."

"Yes."

A new record dropped into place.

"*Skylark,*" the voice sang,

　　　　　"*Have you seen a valley green with spring . . .*"

"Oh, I love this," Helen said.

"*Where my heart can go*

　　　　　　　a-journey

　　　　　　　　　　ing . . ."

"Reminds me of Andy," Bud said.

"Does it? Why should it do that?"

"I don't know."

They listened to the record, absorbed.

"And in your lonely flight,
Haven't you heard
the music
of the night . . ."

"I really must be going, Bud," Helen said.

"Sure," he answered. He went to the closet, taking out their coats and folding his own coat over the arm of the chair. He held Helen's coat for her, and she slipped into it quickly and then turned.

"Bud . . ." She was standing very close to him, and she lifted her face and her eyes and very softly said, "This was very nice."

"I enjoyed it," he told her.

"I almost . . I almost don't want to go."

She looked at him curiously, as if she wanted him to say something further, as if she were testing him somehow, wanting him to make the suggestion, wanting him to say, "Well, honey, you don't really have to go, you know."

"It's late," he said, and then he began putting on his coat.

She smiled briefly, a smile kindled by happiness. "Yes, it is late."

They went to the door, and he opened it and took a last look around the apartment through force of habit. He flicked out the light switch then, and she took his hand. The light at the end of the hallway illuminated the doorframe in a pale golden rectangle. They stood in the doorframe, her hand in his.

"Bud?" she said, her voice very small.

"Yes?"

"Let's not go yet." He almost could not hear her.

"What?" he asked uncertainly.

"I . . . I don't want to go yet." She spoke the words with great effort, as if they were torn from her despite her wishes. She squeezed his hand gently and led him into the apartment, and then she closed the door, and the soft golden rectangle was gone, and there was only the darkness, and she close to him in the darkness, and then she lifted her face to his and kissed him. They were very bulky in their overcoats, moving with the grace of dinosaurs.

"Bud, Bud," she whispered, and her mouth found his again, and he pulled her closer to him, feeling the warm moistness of her lips.

"Helen, I didn't want—"

"I know, I know, but I love you so much, Buddy, so very, very much. Please kiss me, darling."

He kissed her again, and his hands went beneath her coat and onto the warm silk of her dress and the swelling fullness of her breasts. She kissed him again, putting all of her love for him into her kisses, and then they broke apart and walked to the modern sofa. She took off her coat, and she could hear him taking off his coat in the darkness, and she waited for him on the sofa.

He clicked on the record player again, and the record resumed where it had left off, and she could hear him moving toward her, and she waited for him expectantly, knowing she had waited for this moment for a very long time. He sat beside her, and she leaned back into his arms, and his hands found her breasts again, and his hands on her felt very natural and very good. He kissed the side of her neck, the music flooding the apartment.

"Bud, about Andy ... I ... what I'm trying to tell you ... I don't want you to think—"

"I'm not thinking anything, Helen. Except what a fool I've been. Helen, I think I love you. Helen, I love you, Helen."

And he felt again the way he'd felt that night long ago in Club Beguine, when she'd been in his arms, when the sky was a challenge to their youth, when the strength of youth had rushed through his body. He felt this same surge of emotion now, an emotion almost too painfully sweet to bear, a feeling of wanting to hold her where she was forever, of wanting to protect her, and love her, love her ...

His fingers were gentle on the buttons at the neck of her dress, hesitant fingers, surprisingly tender, boyish. He unbuttoned her dress to her waist, and his hands lingered on the nylon net of her brassière for just an instant, and then she helped him with the zipper on the side of her dress, arching her back toward him.

The record player was very loud in the stillness of the room.

"Skylark," it sang,
*"I don't know if you can
   find these things,
        but my heart is riding
            on your wings . . ."*

He did not see her for the next few weeks. He was very busy, as he knew he would be, with the Fall Ball, and his time was really not his own. They called each other frequently, though, spending hours on the telephone, getting to know each other again, looking forward to November eighth, when they would see each other again.

She called on November sixth.

She said, "Bud, this is Helen." Her voice sounded curiously distant.

"Oh, hi. I was just thin—"

"I don't know how to tell you this, Bud. I wish I didn't have—"

"What is it, Helen?"

He heard her catch her breath.

"I'm pregnant."

sock chorus, iii

NOVEMBER-DECEMBER, 1946

27

The Fall Ball was in full swing inside. They could hear the music sifting through the banks of windows and passing through the russet leaves on the trees around them. They sat in a darkened corner of the stone steps in front of the building, and they heard the laughter and music inside, and they spoke in hushed whispers. Helen's hands were thrust deep into the slash pockets of her coat, and her collar was high on her neck. The stubs of six half-smoked cigarettes rested at her feet. She kept staring at the ground, listening to Bud, but not looking at him.

"Are you sure?" he asked.

"Yes," she said. "I'm sure."

"Well"—he paused—"what are we going to do?"

"I don't know. Did you mean what you said?"

"About what?"

"That you loved me?"

"Yes. You know that, Helen."

"Do you still love me?"

"Yes."

"What do you want to do?"

"I don't know."

"Do you want to marry me?"

"I want to marry you, Helen. Yes, I want to. But not now, and not . . . not this way. Unless you want to. I'll do whatever you want."

"What . . . what else can we do?"

"You can take some pills."

"Oh."

"Well, you can."

"I know. What good will pills do?"

"We can go skiing and sledding and things like that. We can try to . . . to do away with it."

"Stop calling it 'it.' You make it sound like some monster or something."

"What do you want me to call it? Buddy, Jr.? Helen, be sensible."

"I'm trying to be sensible. You're not helping very much."

"What do you want me to do?"

"Is marriage out of the question?"

"I'm a Freshman, Helen, and I haven't got a pot to . . ." He paused. "If you want me to marry you, I will." He paused again. "It's just . . . I . . . I haven't anything to give you."

"You can give me love," she said.

"You can't eat love."

"I can work. After the baby comes, I can work."

"I . . . I don't think that's the solution, Helen. Please try to understand me, honey. I . . . I just don't think something like this would work. We'd always be . . . be wondering if we'd have got married if . . . if we weren't forced into it. I . . . I don't like the thought of being forced into it."

"You don't want to marry me, is that it?"

"I didn't say . . ."

She looked up at his face and into his eyes. "I wouldn't

force you into anything, Buddy. You know that."

"This isn't the right way, can you see that, Helen? This is starting with two strikes against us."

"Yes, I can see that," Helen said. "Will you get the pills for me?"

"Yes," he said.

"Do you know where to get them?"

He swallowed. "No, I don't."

"Do they exist, these pills of yours?"

"Why, sure they do."

"I've heard of pills to bring you on if you're late—but there isn't anything to bring you on if you're pregnant. You know I'm pregnant, don't you, Bud? I hate to use that word because it has such an ugly sound, but I am pregnant, there's no question about that, the doctor told me—"

"I know you're pregnant, Helen. What are we talking about if not the fact that you're pregnant?"

"You can speak a little more quietly. I don't want your whole faculty to know about it."

"No one can hear us."

They were silent for a long time. The music seeped out onto the campus, mingled with the rush of the wind and the rustling leaves. A campus lamppost captured their shadows and hurled them onto the steps.

"Will you try to get the pills for me?" she asked.

"Yes. I'll see what I can do."

"Suppose the pills don't work?"

"Well, we can do other things. Strenuous things. It shouldn't be too difficult to—"

"And if these ... strenuous things don't work? What then?"

"Well ..."

"Are we discounting the possibility of having the baby?"

He waited several moments before answering. "I ... I don't think marriage would be a good idea."

"I didn't mean marriage. I meant having it and making some arrangement for its adoption. That's done, you know. It wouldn't—"

"It sounds ... awfully involved, Helen ... I don't think we should get so . . so involved."

"I see." She paused. "I just wanted to know where I stood, Bud."

"You understand . . ."

"I understand completely. Do you want me to have an abortion?"

"There won't be any need for that. The pills will work."

"You're sure they'll work," she said flatly. "You know for certain that they'll work."

"No, I don't know for certain. But I—"

"Do you know anyone who would do an abortion?"

"No, I don't."

"Are you washing your hands of this, Bud?"

He seemed honestly surprised. "Of course not. I'm going to get the pills for you, Helen. Now don't worry."

"Yes, but what happens after that? Buddy, I'm scared. I'm scared stiff."

He put his arm around her. "There's nothing to be afraid of, Helen. Now don't start getting rattled."

"I can't help it. I am rattled. I don't want to be pregnant. Not if you don't want it. Not if . . . Buddy, I'm scared."

"Look, we've got time yet. I'll try to get the pills. After that . . . well, we'll see."

"And you do love me?"

"Yes," he said. "I do love you."

"Have you got a cigarette?"

He took a package from his pocket, lit one for her, and then put it to her lips. "You shouldn't smoke in your condition," he said, trying to make his voice light.

"Don't joke about it, Bud. God, don't joke about it."

"I'm sorry." He was quiet for several moments. "I can't understand how it happened, can you?"

"No."

"If it weren't a fact, I'd swear—"

"It is your baby. You know that, don't you?"

"I never once thought it wasn't."

"Well, if you did think so, it's not so."

"I never thought otherwise, Helen."

"Well, in case you did, I want you to know. I don't want you to have any doubt on that score."

"It isn't fair," Bud said, shaking his head.

"No, it certainly isn't fair." She paused. "I wonder how many other people have said those same words about this very same thing. It isn't fair. It shouldn't happen to me." She sucked in on the cigarette and released a long plume of smoke. "But it has happened, hasn't it?"

"It would seem so," Bud said.

"And first we're going to try the pills, is that right?"

"Yes."

"And if they don't work, we'll ... we'll jump around and things."

"Yes."

"And then ... ?"

"Then we'll see."

"I'll have to have an abortion," Helen said. "I just know I will, and that's what scares me. I was even scared when I had my tonsils taken out. Bud, an abortion is a major operation!"

"It's not such a difficult thing."

"How do you know?"

"Well, I don't know really, but I've heard stories. It's like ... like having a cyst removed. Something like that."

"They'll have to cut me, won't they?"

"I don't know."

"Buddy, Buddy, I'm scared. Hold me. Please hold me."

Miltie Abrahms had a mother who was a nurse. Miltie was a boy in Bud's frat, a nice enough guy except that he was a Speech and Dramatics major, and sometimes he got a little too dramatic about things. He was a very thin boy who fancied himself to be another John Carradine, which he was not. He wore his hair long, combed into a high crown at the front of his head. He owned a widow's peak of which he was uncommonly proud, and which Bud suspected he tweezed to keep from looking fuzzy. He also owned pale gray eyes, and those eyes stared across the cafeteria table at Bud now, cold and emotionless.

"Yes," Miltie said, "my mother is a nurse. Why do you ask?"

"A friend of mine needs help," Bud said, hoping Miltie would not see through the "friend" routine.

"Yeah? What kind of help?" The gray eyes did not

leave Bud's face. There was a flicker of interest behind them now.

"He's . . . ah . . . he's been going with a girl."

"He knock her up?" Miltie asked.

"He . . . he thinks so. He asked me if I could help him, and so I thought of you. Because your mother is a nurse, you know."

"What does your . . . friend . . . want? An abortionist?"

"Well, no, no. I don't think he wants that. Do you know anyone? I mean, would your mother know anyone?"

"No," Miltie said flatly.

Bud tried a smile. "My friend doesn't want that, anyway. He . . . ah . . . he . . . just wants some pills."

"What kind of pills?"

"Pills to . . . to . . . you know."

"Who's this 'friend' of yours?" Miltie asked.

"You don't know him."

Miltie smiled. "Lots of people have 'friends' who get caught. Thank God it's not you, eh, Bud?"

Bud's smile broadened falsely. "You can say that again, pal. So . . . can you get them for me? For my friend?"

"Sure," Miltie said. "Anything for a friend. Or a friend's friend, eh?"

"Thanks, Miltie," Bud said. "I appreciate it."

One pill every three hours, Miltie told him, until the bottle is finished. The bottle should be finished in two days. If anything was going to happen, it would happen by the end of that time. Miltie also added that these pills were no damn good if the girl was really and truly pregnant. They'd only help her if she were naturally late.

Bud didn't tell this to Helen. He gave her the instructions, but in his heart—despite what the doctor had said—he still believed there might possibly have been some mistake. He offered the pills to her, and she seized them eagerly as a cure-all. He did not consider the hope Helen would put in them or the torment failure would bring to her.

Responsibility had suddenly reached down for him again and clenched him tight in a hairy, oil-smelling fist. He did not want responsibility, and his first urge was a panic-stricken need to run! He did not run. He recognized the responsibility, and though his feet urged him to get the hell away as soon as possible, his mind forced him to hold his ground. He loved Helen. His mind kept repeating it over and over again, he loved Helen, he loved Helen. But this was not like love, this was not pleasant, this was not romantic, this was cold, bare facts, this was facing a pregnant woman and being expected to have all the answers, and having none of them, none of them at all. And when she looked at him and asked, "What do we do now?" with her heart in her eyes, what could he tell her? What could he say? Could he say, "Helen, we can't get married because it's no good"? Could he say that? He had already said that, and he had seen the pain in her eyes, but didn't she know he was right, and didn't she know it couldn't be good that way? And didn't she know he loved her?

But what were the boundaries of his love, and where did love end and responsibility begin, and why should responsibility be forced upon him, he was too young for responsibility, he wanted to go to sleep someplace and wake up when it was all over, he wanted to forget he was a part of it, forget all of it, but how could he leave her, leave her in a ditch, so wide, so wide, would they ever cross it, should he marry her?

He was face to face with responsibility, and responsibility would not budge an inch.

The failure of the pills was inevitable. When it came, even though he expected it, he was disappointed. Helen was frantic. What do we do now? she asked. And he gave his ineffectual answers.

They went bowling, and they went horseback riding, and they prayed for snow so that they could ski or sleigh, but no snow came. It was a dry, bitter-cold November, and snow was for lovers, and they had ceased being lovers and became only plotters. They took long walks, and they went swimming at the St. George, but at the end of November, Helen was still pregnant.

They had another long talk, this time in Prospect Park, sitting on a bench, huddled against the cold November wind.

Helen puffed incessantly on her cigarette. Her face was worried. She had gained a little weight in the past month, and she had already begun to experience morning sickness. There were dark circles under her eyes, and the eyes above those circles were dull and lusterless.

"Everybody can tell," she said. "They just look at me, and they can tell."

"No," he answered. "You don't show at all, Helen."

"I know I do. Buddy, Buddy, what a mess!"

"I know." He put his arm around her, and she rested her head on his shoulder and sighed heavily.

"I spoke to my aunt," she said.

"About . . ."

"Yes."

"You shouldn't have done that."

"No, it's all right. She's more than an aunt, Buddy, always has been. And I could never have gone to my mother with something like this. If she ever found out, it would kill her. I had to . . had to go to my aunt, Bud, and . . . my aunt knows someone. She knows someone."

He felt a sudden gladdening of his heart. He turned to look down at her. "Someone to . . . to help us?"

"Yes."

The fist of responsibility loosened its grip slightly. "Who?" he asked.

"She wouldn't tell me. But she's going to arrange it. We'll . . . we'll need money, Bud."

"How much?" he asked quickly.

"Three hundred," she said.

"I'll get it."

"Are you sure you want me to . . . to do this?"

"I can't see any other way, can you, Helen?"

She hesitated for a long time, and then she sighed. "No, I guess not."

"You can use my apartment," he said.

"No. My aunt's place will be all right. She prefers it that way. This person . . . this person who will do it, he knows my aunt. He might not . . might not go to a strange apartment."

"I'll be there with you, Helen," he said, feeling a sense of lightness now that the responsibility had released its grip, feeling almost happy, feeling as if he had cheated responsibility.

"You don't have to, Bud. I think she'd rather you didn't. This is . . . illegal, you know."

"Yes. But I'll come."

"No. It's . . . it's going to be a mess. I wish you wouldn't. Just call me afterward, Bud. At my home. Just call me and let me know you're there."

"Are you frightened?"

"Yes."

"Don't be."

"I am."

"Don't be, Helen."

"Buddy . . ."

"What?"

"I . . . I wish there were another way. Buddy, when I think of this, I get cold sweat all over me. Even now, just talking about it, I'm beginning to shiver."

"Helen, please, don't get excited. Try to relax, try to—"

"I'm sorry, Buddy, but I am excited. I'm not looking forward to this, you know. I can't be calm about the whole thing. Am I supposed to be calm about it? Buddy, Buddy . . ."

"Helen, please don't cry."

"I'm . . . I'm sorry."

He held her close, letting her cry it out, and then he asked, "When is it going to be, Helen?"

"Next . . . next month."

"Why so late?"

"He can't do it before then." She paused. "He's . . . he's busy."

"I'll have the money by then. Don't worry."

"I know you will. I wasn't worrying about that." She shook her head, and then she bit her lip, holding herself in, not wanting to cry again. He held her in his arms, protecting her from the wind.

He could not ask his parents for the money, and he didn't know just who he could ask until he thought of Andy, who was on the road.

His wire read:

NEED THREE HUNDRED DOLLARS URGENTLY. CAN YOU SEND?

BUD.

He waited all that day, and the return wire came late that night.

MONEY ON WAY. ARE YOU IN JAIL, DAD?
ANDY

He never told Andy why he needed the money. He paid it back to him the next time—and the last time—he saw him. He paid so soon because of an unexpected dividend on his GI insurance, but he never told Andy why he needed the money, and Andy never asked.

He gave the money to Helen, and then they sat back to wait. They saw a lot of each other now, and he tried to comfort her whenever they were out together. He could not completely understand his new role, but he felt something like a bystander, watching the drama with no concern whatever, feeling the responsibility all gone now, and knowing it had been replaced by a tremendous feeling of relief. And with the relief came a deep anticipation, as if he were waiting for something, knowing he was waiting for the day of the abortion, and yet sensing this something else he was waiting for, wanting it to happen soon so that he could ... what, what?

He told himself he didn't know.

He told himself he was happy with the way things had worked out, and he told himself he still loved Helen, and yet he could not shake this feeling of waiting.

It happened on a December night.

He called her afterward, and she began crying on the phone, saying only, "It's all over, all over, Bud. It's all over."

"Are you all right?" he asked.

"Yes," she said, and with that word the last fingers of responsibility released their tenuous grip. He felt free. He felt free, and his freedom was a happy thing—but there was a faint shading of sadness in it. He did not question the sadness. He knew only that his brush with responsibility had been all too close, and now everything was all right, and now he could go back to being himself again, without having to worry about things, without having to take care of anyone. Why did everyone come to him to be taken care of, why, why?

He did not call Helen again.

He told himself he was being a coward. He told himself the unpleasantness was all over with now, now it would be the way it had been before, now it would be Bud and Helen, in love, enjoying themselves, happy, but he could remember the icy-cold fingers of responsibility, and so he called himself a coward, and he let it go at that, feeling ashamed of himself, but gradually putting the shame to rout in the days that followed. He had seen her through it. He had been with her until it was all over. He had not deserted until he'd known she was all right.

And now he was free.

He didn't see her again until two days before Christmas. He was wrapping presents when the knock sounded on his door, and he shouted, "Just a minute."

He went to the door and threw it wide, surprised when he saw Helen standing there smiling.

"Helen," he said.

"Yes, Helen," she answered thickly, and he realized she was drunk. "You going to ask me in?"

"Yes, of course. Come in, come in. Gee, this is a surprise." He watched her carefully, and the surprise was not in her coming but within himself because he found he wanted to clasp her into his arms, hold her close.

"Sure, big surprise," she said. She staggered into the room and flopped down into the butterfly chair, stretching her legs out in front of her. "Just love surprises, don't you?"

"How are you, Helen?" he said. "I've—"

"I'm fine. I told you that, didn't I? When you called me? When was that, Bud? Long time ago, wasn't it? When you called, and I said I was all right, and you ran for the hills?"

"Helen—"

"Oh, it took me a while to figure it out, Buddy. A close call, wasn't it? You almost became a man, didn't you? But you got out of it, all right. Honorably, to be sure. Honorable to the end, the very end. Saw Helen to her door step, and walked on the outside all the way, and once you found out her skirts hadn't been muddied, you headed

for the hills. And Helen sat by the telephone. And at first
Helen was too damn sick to think about anything, even
you, even her lover who almost became a man. And then,
when Helen was feeling a little better, she almost picked
up the phone to call, and then she realized it was a little
strange, your not calling in all that time, and then she
put two and two together."

"I should have called, Helen."

"Yes, yes, you should have. What are you doing, wrap-
.ping Christmas presents?"

"Yes, I was."

"You going to offer me a drink?"

"What would you like?"

"Anything you've got. Any damn thing you've got."

"Sherry?"

"Ah, sherry. Ah, yes, sherry. It started with sherry,
didn't it? Well, it started with sherry, so let it end with
sherry."

"It doesn't have to—"

"I came to give you your present, Buddy. Thought you'd
like to know all the details. You paid for it, didn't you,
Buddy, so you deserve the details. Where's the sherry?"

"I'll get it," he said. He went into the kitchen and poured
a glassful, his hand trembling. He did not know why his
hand was trembling. He left the bottle on the table and
brought the glass back to her.

"Thank you," she said. "Here's a toast to the Perennial
Youth, Bud Donato." She chuckled ... "I used to think
there was only one of you, only Andy, but now I know
better. The lame leading the halt. Here's to Buddy-boy,
may he live a child always, and may he drop dead a child.
May he never assume the responsibilities of manhood.
Cheers, Buddy-boy."

"Drink hearty," he said.

"Choke, you mean," she answered. She drained the
glass. "Good sherry." She put down the glass and eyed
him soberly, steadily. "You want to hear all about it?"

"The only thing that counts is that you're all right,
Helen," he said honestly.

"Ah, nobly spoken. You are the noblest Roman of them
all, Bud. And I'm fine, just fine. Still hemorrhaging a lit-

tle, but Helen's going to be all right, all right. Helen was all wrong about a lot of things, but she's going to be all right now. You glad to hear that, Bud?"

"I'm always glad—"

"We used my aunt's apartment, Bud, just the way we planned. She handled everything. Got the man, gave him your money—three hundred dollars, can you believe it? Costs so much to do away with just a little embryo. Nice lady, my aunt. Got this man to do it, and he was supposed to come over at six o'clock that Friday night. I told you that, remember? You have any more sherry?"

"Helen, I don't think you should have any more."

"Now, now, don't talk like a man with responsibilities, Buddy darling. Don't talk like anything but Peter Pan." Her eyes sparked. "Get me some more sherry! It's the least you can give me!"

"All right," he said. He went into the kitchen and came back with the bottle. He poured for her, and she held the drink without tasting it.

"Supposed to come at six, but six rolled around and he wasn't there, and then it was seven, and seven-thirty, and he still hadn't come, and I began to get a little nervous. My aunt told me to calm down, said he was a reliable man, said there was nothing to worry about, so we waited. He came at eight. He was a small man, a tense little man, not the kind of man you'd choose to deliver your baby, but he wasn't there to deliver a baby, was he? He was there to kill one.

"I was cold with sweat when he came in. Wet all over, shaking, scared stiff. My aunt kept telling me everything would be all right, but I couldn't stop shaking or sweating. He unpacked his instruments, and then I lay down on the kitchen table, Bud, the kitchen table—and he went to work. He didn't use any anesthetic. He couldn't, you see, because if anything went wrong he didn't want any evidence of an operation. It—" she swallowed the wine hastily —"it hurt like hell. I don't think anything can hurt more than he hurt me, but I couldn't scream because we were committing murder in that apartment, so I just bit down on the back of my hand until it started to bleed, and he sawed away at my insides. I . . . caught a glimpse of what he took out of me, not a good look but enough of a look to know that it was something human, and then he took it away and disposed of it because what we did was illegal and he had to get rid of the evidence. I wanted to scream again when it was all over. I wanted to scream, but with relief this time, even though I could still feel the pain. I felt so relieved, so, so relieved—and at the same time I felt like a murderess. Do you know what it feels like to think you've killed someone, Bud? Do you have any compassion for what he took out of me? Your baby? Your baby?"

"Helen . . ."

"I went home afterward. My parents were out, and the apartment was very quiet, and I could feel my blood, as quiet as the apartment, my quiet, secret, guilty blood, and I waited for your call. And when you called, I cried on the phone, and I told you it was all over, but I thought only the hardship for us was over, Bud, the hardship all behind us. I didn't think it was really all over, not all of it, not you and me. I thought we could grow from the pain, and grow from what we'd learned, and then you asked me if I was all right, and I said I was, and we talked a little more, and then I went to bed.

"My parents knew I was sick over the week end, but they didn't know how sick. I was very sick, Buddy, too sick to think of you, and when I did think of you, I knew we were through, I knew you'd had the chance to grow up and you'd thrown it out the window. I'm still hemorrhaging, you know, but I'm going to be all right now. No postoperative care involved here, you know. You pay the man, and he kills your baby, and that's the end of it. He leaves the murder on your conscience. You happy, Bud? This is your Christmas present. All the details you paid for. All your cast bread coming back on the wat—"

"Helen, I'm sorry I—"

She got to her feet unsteadily and went toward the door.

"It takes more than 'I'm sorry,' Bud, so much more. So don't say anything. Stay there in your shell and be a little boy for the rest of your life. Helen took care of it for you, didn't she? Sure, she did."

"Helen . . ."

She stopped at the doorway, her hand on the knob.

"Helen took care of it, and now Helen doesn't give a damn about anything any more, Bud, because Helen's done the worst, Helen's done murder. But don't let that bother you. Don't let anything bother you."

She opened the door.

"Not even that I hate you like hell. Not even that I hate you, Bud. Don't let anything bother you at all."

She went out of the apartment.

"Merry Christmas," she said dully, and then the door closed.

sock chorus, iv

JANUARY, 1947

28

Andy came home shortly after New Year's.

He told Carol and Bud that he'd quit the Jerralds band in Sioux City, that he could no longer abide the eccentric, arbitrary rule of the leader, and they accepted his story as gospel. He certainly seemed earnest in his search for another job. He went down to the Union Floor every day, and every day there was a harried, expectant look on his face—and they didn't know what the look meant.

When Bud got his dividend check, he called Carol and asked if Andy would be there that night. She told him yes, and he said he was coming out to Brooklyn with a surprise. He put three one-hundred-dollar bills into an envelope, sealed it, and then headed for Carol's house.

They were sitting in the living room when he got there. Andy was staring at his shoes. Carol sat stiffly in her chair, her face cold.

"Hi," Bud said. He went directly to Andy, and he handed him the envelope. "Here's something I owe you," he said.

Andy took the envelope, stared at Bud for an instant, and then said, "Thanks."

"Boy, I had a hell of a time getting here. The lines were all tied up between Fourteenth Street and—" he stopped and looked at Carol curiously. "Is anything wrong?"

"Yes," she said.

"What . . . well . . . what is it?"

"Ask him," she said.

"She's crazy," Andy said.

"What's the matter?"

"She's crazy," Andy said. "She greets me with a crazy story, and then she gets angry. Don't listen to her."

"What kind of a crazy story?" Bud asked.

"The real reason he's home," Carol said. "Ask him the real reason."

"You left the band, didn't you?"

"Sure, I left the band."

"He didn't leave the band," Carol snapped. "I ran into Ox today. He says everyone in the music business knows about it. He told me all about it. All about why Andy left Sioux City."

"What are you talking about?" Bud asked, puzzled.

"She doesn't know *what* she's talking about," Andy said. "That's the whole trouble."

"What is it, Carol?"

"He was kicked off the band."

"What!"

"I was not. Ox is crazy. What the hell does Ox know about what happened in Sioux City?"

"You were kicked off. Tell him why, Andy. Tell him why Jerralds fired you."

"He *didn't* fire me!"

"He fired you and a tenor man named Rog Kiner. Don't lie, Andy. He fired you because you're a dope addict!"

"Oh, for Christ's sake," Andy said.

The room was suddenly dead silent.

Bud blinked. "What? What did you say, Carol?"

"I said he's a dope addict. He's been taking heroin. He's been taking it for a long time now, ever since he met up with this Rog Kiner. He's an addict, an addict, can you understand me?"

"No, I—"

"An addict!" Carol screamed. "Bud, for Christ's sake, can't you understand? He's a drug addict."

Bud glanced hastily toward the kitchen.

"No one's home," Carol said. "Don't worry."

"Is it true?" Bud asked Andy.

"No."

"Then where'd Ox get it?"

"How the hell should I know?"

"Is he talking about marijuana? I know you were fooling around with—"

"Heroin," Carol said. "Andy, Andy, what's the matter with you? Don't you know it's poison?"

"No, I don't know it's poison. Look, what the hell is everybody so hysterical about? Do I look any different? Have I changed any?"

"You are taking drugs?"

"Yes, yes, I am," Andy said impatiently.

"What for?"

"What the hell kind of stupid question is that? Why shouldn't I, if I've got it under control?"

"Have you?"

"Of course I have. You listen to what Carol says, and you'll go crazy.

"But Ox—"

"Look at me. Do I look like an addict? Do I look like someone who's hooked?"

"I don't know what an addict looks like," Bud admitted.

"Then how the hell can you talk about it intelligently?"

"Andy, look, we're trying to help you. For Christ's sake, don't—"

"If you want to help, you'll mind your own business. You don't know anything at all about this, and yet you're tryint to tell me what to do. Well, I don't need your advice or your help. I'll get along fine, thanks. And that goes for you too, Carol."

"Andy, how can you do this?" Carol said. "Don't you know you're ruining yourself?"

"Heroin is out of your league, Carol," Andy snapped. "Forget about it."

"Why are you doing it, Andy?"

"Because I like it, okay? That's why. Any other questions?"

"You don't need it, Andy. You've got a big talent, and a—"

"A big talent! Hah! Jesus Christ, you don't know anything, do you? Look . . . look, will you leave me alone?

Will you please just leave me alone? You don't know anything about this."

"I know it stinks," Bud put in.

"You know nothing. Zero."

"Why don't you drop it?"

"What for?"

"Because it's no good, and you know it's no good."

"I can drop it any time I want to."

"Then why don't you?"

"I don't want to."

"Why not?"

"I like it. I like it fine. If it's not hurting me, I don't
see what business it is of yours."

"It's hurting Carol."

"Carol hurts too damn easily. I didn't think she'd turn
out to be such a goddamned pollyanna, that's for sure."

"If you love her, Andy—"

"Of course I love her! What the hell does that have to
do with it? If she loves me, she'd take me the way I am,
heroin or no."

"You're throwing your life away, Andy. Can't you
see . . . ?"

"It's my life," Andy snapped. "What's so special about
my life, anyway, that heroin's going to hurt it?"

"Andy—"

"Shut up! Jesus Christ, can't the both of you shut up?"
He rose suddenly. "I'm getting out of here. If I stay here
another minute—"

Carol stood up. "Andy, where are you—"

"What the hell do you care? Out of here, that's for
sure. There's about as much understanding here as—Oh,
the hell with it."

"Hold it, Andy," Bud said firmly. "It's not going to help
if you—"

"Friend," Andy said, "friend, you don't know . . ." He
stopped and shook his head. "Thanks for the envelope. I
can use it."

"Andy, look . . .

"You don't understand, do you? Not at all." He shook
his head sourly. "Jesus, let me out of here before I bust!"
He walked to the door, and he slammed out of the house,

and Bud stared at the closed door, not realizing he wouldn't see Andy again for close to two and a half years.

She stood alongside him in the dimly lit hallway. The door was somewhere down in the bowels of a tenement, and she could smell the rank basement odor, and she was a little frightened, but he did not seem scared at all, and so she stood close to him in the darkness while he knocked on the door. She could hear her own labored breathing, the sound of Andy's fist against the wood. There was no other sound in the hallway, no sound from beyond the closed door. The door opened a crack, and she saw an eye, and then a deep voice said, "Oh, Andy."

There was no life to the voice. It was the voice of a dead man, and she felt a shudder start at the base of her spine, and then Andy's fingers closed on her arm, and he was leading her into the apartment.

There was no music in the apartment. The apartment was slovenly furnished and very badly lighted. She stood alongside Andy, and her eyes grew slowly accustomed to the darkness, and she could make out the dim shapes sitting around the room. There seemed to be no life in anyone. A girl looked up at her and then turned her head away.

"Come on, Helen," Andy said.

"What's the matter with them?" she whispered.

"Huh?" Andy said. "Nothing. Come on."

She looked at the people again. They seemed to own no spines. They seemed to have been dropped into their seats. They sprawled in their chairs loosely, disjointedly. They seemed to be listening for something. Their eyes were half closed, their faces pale in the darkness. She walked through the room, and they did not stir, except for the girl who looked up again at Helen as she passed. The girl was a thin blonde. She wore a dirty skirt and an old pink sweater. Her hair was stringy, and it hung limp on either side of a young face that looked old. Her legs were crossed, and she sat leaned over onto one side of the easy chair, her head at a curious angle. She wore mocassins and no stockings. Her arms, even in the darkness, showed the scar tissue of her habit.

Andy was walking into a small room with a sink. She followed him there. The counter alongside the sink was covered with bottle tops. The cork lining had been removed from the caps, and the insides were coated with a thin layer of what looked like chalk dust. Several of the caps were overturned, and she saw that the metal was burned and black. The twisted, curled ends of matches lay strewn over the counter top.

"What's the matter?" Andy asked.

"I . . . didn't expect this. You said a shooting party. I thought . . ."

"What?"

"I don't know."

"A twenty-piece orchestra with violins? Everybody in formal wear? For Christ's sake, Helen!" His voice was suddenly harsh.

"Don't get angry with me," she said. "I just didn't know."

"All right, so now you know." He paused. "Do you want to leave?"

"No."

"You can leave if you want to, you know. Nobody's forcing you to stick around." His eyes blinked. "I'm staying."

"I said I'd come with you, didn't I?"

"Well, you're here now. If you want to chicken out, go ahead."

"I'm not—"

"I thought you wanted—"

"Andy, please . . ."

"Look, do whatever the hell you want to. I came here for—"

"All those people," she said quietly. "Are they . . . addicts?"

"I never asked them."

"They don't look . . healthy."

"They're as healthy as you are."

"They look dirty," Helen said.

"Look, are you going to start— Look, you had a snort, did you like it or didn't you?"

"I don't know," Helen said softly.

"If you don't know, then what the hell are you doing

here? Helen, look honey, you'll like this. This is the only way. I mean, look, baby, snorting is for the sparrows, you know?"

"Yes," she said in a small voice.

"Look, these people . . . they're okay. Look, don't let the neighborhood throw you. They're okay, Helen. They're . . . well, they're my kind of people. Our kind of people."

"Yes."

"So . . . so you can't expect, you know, real plush surroundings. Like . . . like if the cops busted in here, they'd find enough stuff to . . . well, look, Helen, holding's against the law, so you got to . . . well, look, it's good to be with your own, you know? You'll see. But let's get started, huh? Jesus, let's get started."

"Yes."

"You all right?"

"Yes. But . . . they look so dirty."

"Jesus!"

"Dirty," she said again, and then a strange look passed over her face. She sighed heavily. "Let's . . . do what we have to."

"Well, gee, don't say it like that. Hell, this is a lot of kicks. Jesus, you don't have to say it like that." He paused. "Hell, you're not punishing yourself or anything, baby." He chuckled loudly.

"No," she said.

"Okay, okay. So, come on, let's see a little smile. Come on, come on, live it up a little."

She smiled weakly.

"There. There, now that's a hell of a lot better." He picked up two bottle caps from the sink. "Come on," he said.

They went into the other room. The skinny blonde had moved. She was sitting up in the chair now. The room was more crowded than Helen had originally thought. There was a sickly-sweet aroma to the room, a nauseatingly sweet smell mixed with the stink of body sweat. She looked for a window, spotted one high up on the basement wall. A candle burned in the neck of a beer bottle, and she realized abruptly that this was the only source of light. Someone struck a match, and she saw the angular bones of a grayish masculine face, and then a cigarette flared

into life, and then the match died, and there was only the
flickering light of the candle again, and the blonde in the
light lifting her skirt.

No one looked at the blonde. Her legs were very thin,
pipestem legs with bony knees, covered with thick blonde
fuzz, sickly white in the pale glow of the candle. Helen
stared at her and then blinked.

The inner soft fleshy white of her thigh was stained
with the same blurred pattern of puncture marks that had
been on the girl's arms. Only here they seemed more de-
structive. Here, the flesh seemed more vulnerable. Here,
the needle had attacked a secret flesh, a private flesh, and
Helen stared, wanting to turn away, but fascinated and
incapable of turning. The girl had something in her hand.
It took Helen several moments in the dim light to realize
what it was. A safety pin.

The girl moved with the awkward precision of a robot.
She brought the pin down against the white flesh, and then
she began poking at it, tearing at the flesh. Helen stared. A
blue area of puffed skin capped the upper part of the scar
tissue like a tarnished crown. The girl poked at the bruised
area, piercing the skin, ripping it, and then quickly, she
dropped the safety pin and picked up an eye dropper.

Helen felt suddenly ill. She turned away, her stomach
churning. She could not watch. She wanted to run out of
this basement room, wanted to get away from these people
but something inside her urged her to stay. She had to
stay. She had to stay. She had to do . . . she had to do . . .

"Can't see my friggin' hand in front of my face," someone mumbled.

A light snapped on. The blonde blinked her eyes against
it. Her face was pitted. The eye dropper lay on an orange
crate beside her chair now, a blackened bottle cap beside
it. The girl was beginning to doze. In the light Helen
looked at her exposed thigh, and again she felt her stomach
churning.

A man came over to Andy. She looked at the man's
arms. His shirt sleeves were rolled up, and she saw the
scar tissue, and then she saw a series of festering scabs and
sores.

"They picked up Alverra, you hear?" the man said.

"Yeah," Andy said.

The man shrugged and went into the kitchen. Sitting on one of the chairs, another man began humming "Blues in the Night" off key.

She followed him, and she sat. He was loading a syringe. She saw the milky white fluid ooze out of the bottle cap and into the glass cylinder. He depressed the plunger, forcing any air bubbles out of the syringe, and then he looked down at her. He took a piece of twine from his jacket pocket and wrapped it around her arm, and she watched as the vein bulged, blue against the white of her skin.

"You ready?" he said.

She squeezed her eyes shut tightly. This was what she wanted. This. Andy had what she wanted. Andy had offered what she wanted. This. These were her people.

She did not answer. She nodded, and then someone flicked off the light again, and she heard the whisper of shoe soles against the floor, and then the creak of wood as the person sat again. The vein slid with rubbery resistance beneath the needle. Andy clasped her arm more tightly, and then the needle pierced her flesh, and she felt only a slight pain, and then the needle was gone.

It hit her hard and fast.

She was beginning to float. She felt clean and strong and pure. She felt marvelously free. She didn't care about anything, anything!

It only took sixteen seconds for the drug to pass through her heart and her lungs and then roar into her blood stream. And in sixteen seconds she had stopped hating herself.

Andy did not remember much afterward.

He very rarely remembered much afterward.

Everything seemed blurred together in a haze of half-remembrance. But there was music, a faint music, there was always music, queer and weird, but a perfect music, half understood and half harmonious, but cacophonous too, but music, always music, all music, always the clear hard bite of brass, music he wished he could make himself.

And there was a ceiling somewhere very far off, and there were walls which slanted to touch the tiny square of ceiling so very far off. And there was a vast field of white.

He walked across the field, and he left no footprints.

There was sound everywhere in the field, but it was a soundless sound, a music he alone could hear. There were no trees in the field, no bushes, no growth of any kind. The sky was a pale blue, cloudless, a wash of color against the field of white.

He could touch the sky.

He was enormous against the white field and the pale blue sky, and he could reach up and touch the blue, and the God Father smiled at him when he reached the sky, so close to Heaven was he, and he could hear his own breathing, echoing and re-echoing to become a part of the music, the way someone breathes when he is sucking in ether, and he could feel the warmth of the music all around him, a trumpet blowing soft and lazy, warm, moist, and he knew he was in another land, and this other land was good, and he did not want to go back because this was good, this was good.

He found the lunch pail, and he opened it, and there was a trumpet inside the lunch pail, and he touched the trumpet and the trumpet felt vibrantly alive to his touch. The field of white was wet now, and he walked through it with his rubbers on, and his feet did not get wet, but the white was scalding hot, whitely hot, scalding in its intensity, and he was suddenly frightened, and he ran with his trumpet clutched to his chest, the lunch pail clattering soundlessly to the hot field of white, the rubbers, slipping from his feet so that the white burned the soles of his feet, and he thought in panic. *I'm in Hell, in Hell, in Hell, in Hell, in*, and he was no longer afraid, and then he was nodding, and then he was asleep, and there was only a very tiny insignificant red dot of blood among the puncture marks on his arm to show that a needle had entered his flesh at all.

Part 5

SECOND
ENDING

29

"Helen?" Bud said. He turned from the windows, and he walked to her, and she looked up from where she sat on the corner of the couch.

"Yes?"

"That . . . that Christmas . . . that time . . ."

"Yes?"

"I wanted you to know . . ." This was very difficult. He could barely look at her, and yet he felt he should put it into words, felt things would be better if he could put it into words. "I wanted you to know I'm sorry, truly sorry."

She stared at him for a long time. "All right," she said.

"And Helen . . ."

"Bud, I said it then. I don't want to say it again now."

"What?"

"It takes a hell of a lot more than 'I'm sorry.' "

"I know, Helen, and I realize . . ."

The knock sounded on the door. Bud glanced at his watch. It was eleven o'clock. Helen opened the door, and the doctor entered. They took him to the couch where Andy had lain quietly through the morning. They stood by anxiously while he examined Andy. He was very thorough, a young man with a pale blond mustache, a meticulous young man. He packed his instruments with loving care when he was through.

"Your phone?" he asked.

"Over there," Helen said. "What is it?"

"I'm calling an ambulance," the doctor said. "Your friend is in a coma."

The rain began at noon.

A slow steady rain that pressed against the windows in the hospital corridor. The corridor was very white and antiseptic. It smelled of ether, and it smelled of clean starched linen, and it smelled of sickness. There was a room at the end of the corridor, and there was a lettered

sign on the door of the room, and the sign read: QUIET.
NO ENTRANCE, and Andy Silvera was in that room. There
was a basket of soiled linen outside the door of the room,
and a wheel chair was against the wall farther up the corridor, and in the middle of the corridor was a desk, and a
white-starched nurse sat at the desk. And sitting on the
bench opposite the desk were Mr. and Mrs. Silvera and
Carol. And standing to the right of the desk under the huge
hanging light were Bud and Helen.

Mr. Silvera was a tall, cadaverous-looking man, an
accountant whose eyes were weak and magnified by thick
lenses. Mrs. Silvera was a small woman with pitch-black
hair and deep brown eyes, eyes her son had inherited.
They sat side by side on the bench, wearing their pain like
a black cloak. A clock on the wall above the desk ticked
loudly.

When the doctor came, he consulted a chart and then
said, "What is this? A convention?" Mr. and Mrs. Silvera
flinched under the blow of his words.

"We're his parents," Mr. Silvera said.

"And we're his friends," Carol added defiantly.

The doctor glanced coldly at Helen and Bud, shrugged,
and then said, "He was taking drugs, did you know that?"

"Yes," Carol said.

"Which may explain how he contracted the disease," the
doctor went on. "In the past few years we've learned that it
can be transmitted by the use of contaminated syringes or
needles, or by the administration of convalescent human
serum. Even tattooing has come to be regarded as a
dangerous means of transmission. If he was an addict, and
there doesn't seem to be much doubt of that, he may have
come into contact with a syringe that had been used by
someone with the disease. It's not at all unlikely." The doctor stroked his jaw. The doctor was a young man used to
crowded wards and sudden death. He looked at Andy's
parents. "Your son is now in a coma. The coma was
undoubtedly preceded by various symptoms—nausea, vomiting, right upper quadrant pain or distress, headache,
perhaps diarrhea. And, oh—" the doctor thought, scanning
his voluminous medical knowledge— ". . . acute chills,
fever, anorexia, joint and back pain, urticaria, burning of
the eyes"—he stopped, sighed—"and, of course, the jaun-

dice. It's not a rare disease. It is becoming more and more common among drug addicts. The amazing thing is that he didn't seek medical aid sooner. When the symptoms presented themselves, he should have—"

"What does he have?" Carol asked.

"Acute hepatitis. Probably homologous serum hepatitis, although we can't differentiate for sure between virus IH and the virus SH without a knowledge of the incubation period, which we do not have."

Incubation, Bud thought, and he remembered the party Andy had described, where a community needle had been passed. Had it been then? How many parties like that had there been? When had he been infected? How long ago?

"Is it . . . is it very serious?" Mrs. Silvera asked.

"I shall be quite frank with you," the doctor said. "Until recently, our experience with acute hepatitis has not included recovery after coma. However, we have been using certain drugs with notable success, and we are trying them on your son."

"What drugs?" Carol asked.

The doctor sighed impatiently, knowing the names of the drugs would mean nothing to Carol, annoyed because he had to transmit the information to her. "We have so far given him two hundred and fifty milligrams of cortisone intramuscularly, and intravenous glucose with five hundred milligrams of terramycin and forty milligrams of vitamin K."

"What are his chances?" Helen asked, and Bud realized she had been unusually silent since they came to the hospital, and he searched her face and found only intense concentration on it, and again he admired her strength and her courage.

"His chances right now?" The doctor shrugged. "Fifty-fifty."

"May we see him?" Carol asked.

"We want to keep him absolutely silent. We don't want—"

"Please," Carol said.

"His parents, perhaps." He hesitated, studying Carol's face, and then added reluctantly, "And you, of course."

"We'll wait for you," Bud said.

"The priest has been here?" Mrs. Silvera asked.

"Yes, we thought it best to . . ." The doctor hesitated again. He seemed very nervous all at once. "Would you come this way, please? He won't recognize you, you realize. He's in a coma. But if you want to look at him . . ." The doctor shrugged, incomprehendingly, and then his eyes blinked and his voice softened, and he said, "Please, this way."

They went down the hall to the door marked QUIET. NO ENTRANCE. Bud and Helen waited by the desk while Carol and Andy's parents entered the room.

"He's going to die," Helen said. "I know it."

"He's got a fifty-fifty chance," Bud said.

"If he takes it."

"What?"

"If he takes the chance. He may not want it."

Bud shook his head. "Such a kid. Why should he have to—"

"Such a kid, yes," she said. She stood as stiff as a post, her shoulders back, her head high. Her eyes were bright and staring, and her mouth was a tight line across her face.

Carol was coming down the hallway again. He heard the tap of her heels, and he turned as she approached.

She was not crying. Her face was a deadly white, and there was shock in her eyes, as if someone had punched her with a heavy fist. Her body was trembling, but there was no sobbing, no crying, and he put his arm around her awkwardly, trying to comfort her, and she kept staring blankly ahead of her, and then she began shaking her head.

She said, "Why should I feel responsible for him?" but she was not asking Bud the question, and her voice was curiously cold and dead.

"You shouldn't!" Bud snapped. "We . . . we can't. Carol, he's not going to die . . . he's . . ."

"Aren't we all responsible for each other?" she said, still not looking at him. "If we aren't, shouldn't we be?"

"I want to leave," Helen said suddenly. "I want a cup of coffee. I don't want to be here when he . . ." She shook her head, and then she reached out and touched Carol's hand, and she turned and started down the corridor toward the elevator.

"Helen," Bud said, "wait." She stopped, looking back at

him. "Carol," he said, "I've got to go now. I'll be back a little later. Will you be all right?"

"Yes," she said dully.

"You don't mind, do you?"

She looked up at him curiously, her eyes still blank. "No," she said. "I don't mind at all."

He squeezed her hand, smiled briefly, and then went down the corridor after Helen. "I'll buy you a cup of coffee," he said. "I've got to get uptown in a little while."

"All right," Helen answered.

"What's the matter?"

"Nothing."

"You sounded— Are you all right?"

"Yes."

They took the elevator down to the main floor, and then they walked out of the hospital together. There was a small restaurant on the opposite corner, and they went to it and took a table in the corner. Bud took off his coat and then helped Helen with hers. It wasn't quite one o'clock yet, but every light in the place was on in defense against the rain.

They sat, and Helen was very quiet, and he watched her and wondered what her silence meant, and he said, "Helen, what I was trying to say before—"

"Don't, Bud," she said.

"All right, but I . . . I wanted you to know . . . I wanted to apologize."

"You've already apologized," she said. "Have you got a cigarette?"

"Yes, sure," he answered. He took the package from his pocket, shook one loose, and then lit it for her, putting the pack on the table.

"He'll die," she said. "The poor son-of-a-bitch will die, and all of us will ask why." Her voice was very low. She squeezed her eyes shut and sucked in on the cigarette. One hand was on the table, clenched tightly, the knuckles white. "I mustn't . . . I mustn't," she said, and she shook her head.

"Mustn't what?"

"Nothing." She smiled suddenly, and the smile was so unexpected that he blinked his eyes. "This is good weather for dying, anyway, isn't it?" she said, still smiling. "I al-

ways say if you're going to die—and there's no reason to
believe we all aren't, is there?—then you might as well pick
a nice gloomy day for it. Of course, most of us don't have
a choice."

"Helen, what—"

"Can't we have some coffee? I think this place is staffed
with dead men. Waiter!"

The counterman came over to the table. "What'll it be?"
he asked.

"Two coffees," Bud said. "And a ham on rye. You eating anything, Helen?"

"No."

"That's it," Bud said, and the counterman walked away.
Bud looked at his watch. "I hope he makes it fast."

"Big test this afternoon, huh?" Helen said.

"Yes. Well, it wouldn't be so important if I hadn't
flunked the last one, but . . . well, you know, I've got a lot
of catching up to do now."

"Yes, of course. You have to catch up. I knew a man
once who spent all of his life catching up. He got out of
bed late one morning, you see, and so he lost a half hour,
and he spent the rest of his life trying to catch up. He finally died trying to catch a train." Helen laughed suddenly, a
curious laugh, and Bud stared at her because he didn't
think she'd said anything so very funny.

"My cigarette's out," she said. "Why can't cigarettes stay
lighted?"

He reached for a matchbook, and she said, "No, I have
some. Women carry all sorts of junk in their purses, didn't
you know? Knew a woman who carried the *Encyclopedia
Britannica* in her purse, believe it or not, on the head of a
pin. A pinhead, naturally." She laughed again and opened
her purse, and he saw that her hands were trembling, and
he stared at her hands fumbling inside the purse, and he
saw the book of matches she reached for, and alongside the
matches something else, and he stared at the something
else, not knowing what it was for an instant, and then realizing it was the syringe she had taken from Andy yesterday.

She took out the matches, and she snapped the purse
shut, blotting out sight of the syringe, and he watched her

hands shaking as she struck the match and held it to the cigarette, and he tried to remember all of the things she had said yesterday, and he couldn't remember, except some of them, and they hadn't seemed very important then, but they seemed important now as he watched her sucking in on the cigarette.

. . . you'll smoke incessantly because there's something very reassuring about a cigarette in your hand or hanging on your lips. You want that cigarette always. You put one out, and you light another one immediately afterwa—

"Ah," Helen said cheerfully, "here comes the coffee now. I can use a cup of coffee, all right. I'm part Brazilian, you know, and down in Brazil we take baths in the stuff. Of course, you sometimes get a coffee bean stuck in your navel that way, but it's the spirit of South Americanism that counts, you know, especially when you're doing a Samba in the bathtub."

"Helen . . ."

"Thank you, my good man," Helen said to the counterman, and she squashed out her cigarette in the ash tray and then picked up the coffee cup instantly. "Eat your sandwich, Bud," she said. "You've got a big test this afternoon, haven't you? You need your strength. God give me strength, God said, and there was no one to give him any strength because he himself was God."

"Helen, are you all right?"

"Me? I'm fine. I haven't felt so good in a month of Blue Mondays. This is perfect dying weather, so when I get home I think I'll dye some of my undies. I've always wanted red undies, but I could never muster up the courage to wear them. Why, suppose your skirts should blow up on a windy day? People seeing those red undies would automatically assume you were a Communist, and the one thing I absolutely fear is people calling me a Communist. Eat your sandwich. You haven't got much time."

No, I haven't got much time, he thought.

I haven't got much time at all, and if I run into a fouled-up transit situation, I'm liable to be late to begin with. I haven't got much time—*you try to blot out the taste by smothering it in other tastes. You'll have a cup of coffee, and then you'll have another cup of coffee, and then anoth-*

er—but there's the test, what time is it? Jesus, one-fifteen already, what am I supposed to do, she's got a syringe in her purse, what am I supposed to do?

"Where are you going now?" he asked. "From here?"

"Oh, I don't know. To the Union Floor, maybe. Give Rog back his syringe. Damn decent of him to lend it to Andy. Never realized a pusher had a decent bone in his miserable body, but it just goes to show you can have people pegged all wrong, doesn't it? Listen, do you mind if I have another cigarette? I'll smoke you out of house and home, but some days you're a natural mooch, isn't that so? What do *you* smoke? I smoke O.P.'s And can we get some more coffee?"

"Another coffee!" Bud shouted at the counterman.

You'll make a silly joke. You'll laugh at the joke, and whoever you're with will think you're very strange, laughing at a silly joke, not knowing you're really whistling in the dark, and she's headed for the Union Floor, and I have a test to take . . .

"Helen, he'll be all right," Bud said desperately.

"He'll die," she said, her eyes narrowing. "Buddy, he's going to die and do you know something? There's not a goddamn soul except the five people who were at the hospital who'll give a good goddamn. Twenty years old, and he's going to die."

Aren't we all responsible for each other? If we aren't, shouldn't we be?

"The doctor said fifty-fifty. Andy wants to live. He wouldn't have fouled up his suicide attempt otherwise. Helen, he'll live."

"No," she said flatly. She squashed out her cigarette. The counterman brought another cup of coffee, and she picked up the cup at once. "You'd better get going. Your test is at two, didn't you say?"

"Yes."

"Then go ahead."

"All right," he said. He went to the coat rack and took his coat from it. He came back to the table. "Helen . . ."

"Leave me another cigarette, will you?" she asked.

You need help right then . . . just the help of someone who cares about you . . . just reassurance . . . someone to take your hand and lead you out . . .

"Helen . . ."

"If you're going, you'd better get started. Go ahead, Bud."

"I'm . . . I'm not sure . . ."

"You are going, aren't you?"

"Yes, I . . ." *no,* he thought, *no!* "Helen, look . . . I . . . can we . . . well, suppose we go to a movie or something . . . I mean, for the afternoon . . . and then . . . would you . . . would you like some dinner? Tonight, that is . . . and . . . and maybe we could . . . could spend the rest of the day together . . . until . . . the rest . . . do you think so?"

"You have an exam," she said, looking up into his face.

He leaned onto the table, fumbling for words, his eyes clear. "Yes, I . . . I know I do . . . I have one, I know . . . but . . . I thought we could spend the day together, Helen . . . I figured . . ."

"Why?" she asked.

"I don't know," he said.

"Because you think I need help? I don't need any help, Bud. I've been through this before, and I've always got out of it. I don't need any help, thanks."

"I know, Helen. I just thought . . . well . . ." He shrugged. He seemed about to go. He started away from the table, and then he turned back, and she was surprised to find him crying. He sat opposite her, and he reached across the table, and he took her hand, and he said, "Helen, you've been through it, and you'll get out of it, but I want to be sure. I want to be sure, darling, can you understand that? And I've never been through it, never really, and this time I don't want to turn my back, Helen. I can't turn my back for the rest of my life, so let me help you, let me take you home with me, Helen, let me take you home, please."

She stared up at him, searching his face and his eyes and his mouth, looking for a sign of weakness, and then looking only for strength, looking only for the knowledge that he was strong enough at last, that he was telling himself the truth at last, and seeing that, and smiling, curiously at peace, and finally saying, "I think I've been waiting half my life for you to take me home, Bud."

coda

Lying in the darkness of the room lying with the pain in his body and the harsh breathing and the hot skin and the darkness all around him he knew that death was coming and the shadows hovered over the bed and he wanted his horn in his hands and he wanted to be young again if only he could be young again if only he could be back again when he was young an old man now a man who had seen it all and done it all but none of it like when he'd been young all of it a bust all of it nowhere nowhere the horn if he could only lift his horn to his lips now he would find it he would find the music he would find the music of death was coming death was coming he knew that death was coming he wanted his horn so badly he wanted his horn so that he could blow his horn could blow away death liss-en to that goddamn wind blow blow that horn blow that Gabriel horn if only he could do that before it came if only he could blast the sky apart with his horn find his youth again find what he had lost somewhere along the way where had he lost it where had he lost the magic and the surprise Helen help me please Helen help me please help me find my Carol my horn help me find my horn help me find my life help me find everything I need I need I need before I die because death too death too will be a will be a disappointment